"From the first sentence, the voice of the narrator, Bethany, rings true and never falters. I loved the rich cast of characters, each with his or her own history, each distinct and colorful but never a caricature. Sherri Emmons has created a large extended family and put me down right in the middle of its messes and miseries. By the end of the book, I cared for every aunt and cousin, mother and sister, even the most troubled and dangerous. *Prayers and Lies* is the story of a family that knows how to love and forgive and get on with life."
—Drusilla Campbell, author of *The Good Sister*

"*Prayers and Lies* is a sweet, revealing tale of family, friendship, long-held secrets and includes the all-important ingredients of forgiveness and love."
—Kris Radish, author of *The Shortest Distance Between Two Women*

"When I was reading *Prayers and Lies,* the voice was so genuine, so sincere, I felt like Bethany was standing right before me, barefoot, earnestly telling me her story, alternately laughing, crying, wondering, confused, and scared. I was on the edge of my seat, listening, every scene coming into full, bright, Technicolor detail as one prayer was heard, one lie was shattered, one family's raw, haunting life laid bare. I loved it."
—Cathy Lamb, author of *The First Day of the Rest of My Life*

"Prepare to stay up all night reading! Sherri Wood Emmons perfectly captures the devastating impact of family secrets in her beautifully written—and ultimately hopeful—debut novel. With its evocative setting and realistically crafted characters, *Prayers and Lies* is a must read for fans of rich family drama."
—Diane Chamberlain, author of *The Lies We Told*

Books by Sherri Wood Emmons

PRAYERS AND LIES

THE SOMETIMES DAUGHTER

Published by Kensington Publishing Corp.

The Sometimes Daughter

SHERRI WOOD EMMONS

KENSINGTON BOOKS
www.kensingtonbooks.com

KENSINGTON BOOKS are published by

Kensington Publishing Corp.
119 West 40th Street
New York, NY 10018

All Kensington titles, imprints, and distributed lines are available at special quantity discounts for bulk purchases for sales promotion, premiums, fund-raising, educational, or institutional use.

Special book excerpts or customized printings can also be created to fit specific needs. For details, write or phone the office of the Kensington Special Sales Manager: Attn. Special Sales Department. Kensington Publishing Corp., 119 West 40th Street, New York, NY 10018. Phone: 1-800-221-2647.

Kensington and the K logo Reg. U.S. Pat. & TM Off.

ISBN-13: 978-0-7582-5325-5
ISBN-10: 0-7582-5325-7

First Kensington Trade Paperback Printing: February 2012
10 9 8 7 6 5 4 3

Printed in the United States of America

In loving memory of Lambrini Stergiopol,
my second mother, who took me to the L. S. Ayres Tea Room
and told me I could be a writer.

ACKNOWLEDGMENTS

What I have discovered is that one of the best parts of writing a book is getting to thank the people who have helped along the way. And so . . .

To my fabulous editor, John Scognamiglio; my publicist, Vida Engstrand; and the other great people at Kensington Books—thank you for making it all possible.

To my wonderful agent, Judy Heiblum, and the other good folks at Sterling Lord Literistic—thank you for working so hard on my behalf.

To Patricia Case, Verity Jones, and Marti Steussy—thank you for reading the manuscript and for your helpful critiques and comments. The book is better for your efforts.

To Shirley Aschen, who created and maintains my beautiful Web site, thank you.

To my amazing circle of friends—Tina Burton, Mitra Akhavan Spicklemire, Resa Robertson, Rhonda Hooks Tyner, Maureen McCrae, JoAnn Kriebel, Elizabeth Winningham, and Kaye Edwards—thank you for keeping me sane and always being there. Special thanks to Mitra, for schooling me on Persian Bahá'í culture, and to JoAnn for sharing recipes from the L. S. Ayres Tea Room.

To Mary Crenshaw, for researching those amazing Snow Princesses, thank you.

To all the readers who wrote kind reviews of my first book, blogged about it, left messages on my Web site, and e-mailed me, thank you.

To the funny, kind, and amazing women at the Mother House of the Sisters of Lorreto, in Nerinx, Kentucky, and to the wonderful people at the Chrysalis Retreat Center in Lynchburg, Virginia—thank you for your gracious hospitality while I worked on this book.

To my parents, Thomas and Peggy Wood, who have always been there for me, even when I was trying hard to push them away, thank you.

To my children, Zachary and Kathryn Spicklemire and Stephen Emmons, who make my life so much more fun and interesting, thank you.

And to my husband, Chris Emmons, who makes me happy and loves me even though, thank you.

I love you all.

PART 1

LIFE WITH MAMA

$$\approx 1 \approx$$

I was born at Woodstock.

At two minutes past three on the morning of Monday, August 18, 1969, I made my squalling appearance in a tent pitched on a muddy field at Max Yasgur's farm in rural Bethel, New York.

My mother, blissfully stoned, put me to her breast and nursed me while Crosby, Stills, and Nash opened their now-famous set with "Suite: Judy Blue Eyes."

And so she named me Sweet Judy Blue Eyes, even though my father told her my dark blue eyes would probably turn to brown, like his. Most babies are born with blue eyes, he said, but usually they turn brown after a few days. She would not be swayed. Sweet Judy Blue Eyes Webster is the name on my birth certificate. Mother: Cassie Skylark Webster. She changed her name from Cassandra Elaine when she married my dad. Father: Kirk Alan Webster. He did not change his name, despite my mother's pleading.

I have a grainy Polaroid photo to record the event of my birth. My mother's blond hair hangs limp around her pale face; her green eyes are heavy-lidded and tired. She looks terrible. I guess that's what three days with no baths and then birthing a baby will do to a woman. My father, wearing a ridiculous dashiki and sporting a scraggly beard, sits beside her on the ground, his arms wrapped around her tiny figure. I am wrapped in a Vietcong flag. My fleetingly blue eyes stare suspiciously at the camera.

A few hours later, Mama took me to the pond to baptize me. My father trailed behind her, fairly certain that dunking a newborn in a cow pond was not a good idea but unable to stop the force of nature that was his wife.

Hundreds of people cheered as my parents waded into the muddy water, then submerged me briefly in the shocking cold. Their yells drowned out my screams. My mother cried, then passed out.

My earliest memories of Mama are in our little apartment on Whittier Place in Indianapolis. Daddy worked at a guitar shop and took college classes at night, so mostly it was just Mama and me.

Our attic apartment was sparsely furnished with threadbare furniture—a faded blue futon, ratty wicker love seat, Formica table, and three red-vinyl chairs. The only new item was a stereo, which constantly blared the music Mama loved—the Beatles, Bob Dylan, Arlo Guthrie, Janis Joplin, and of course, Crosby, Stills, and Nash. She twirled me around the living room, dipping and spinning till she fell to the couch, dizzy and laughing. The music of Woodstock filled my days and my nights; the sweet smell of pot was the incense of my nursery.

Mama had lots of friends, who variously lived with us for periods of time. I never wanted for a lap to sit in or a willing playmate. Sometimes we took our games outside, confusing the neighbors with our elaborate entertainments. Mama always made the rules, and she changed them at a whim. Sometimes we played at charades, other times we simply ran for the joy of running, whooping and leaping down the quiet side street, some adult or another stopping to swoop me up as I toddled along behind.

In the summers, Mama set up an inflatable pool in the front yard and let me splash about naked . . . until one of the neighbors said she'd call the police if Mama didn't put some clothes on me.

That night, Mama and her friend Derrick made spaghetti for dinner, sitting me in the bathtub naked to eat mine, so she could wash me afterward. I was three years old.

Lifting me from the tub, Mama swayed slightly, her bloodshot eyes sparkling bright.

"Come on then, my Sweet Judy Blue Eyes," she whispered as she wrapped me in a towel. "Let's go have a moonlight swim."

Running naked from the house to the wading pool, carrying me on his shoulders, Derrick laughed as he dropped me into the pool, then plopped down beside me, his black skin shining in the moonlight. Mama, equally naked, joined us, carrying two cans of beer. Derrick lay back and rested his head on the edge of the little pool, Mama lay with her head on his chest, and I rested my head on her stomach. We lay in silence, watching the stars blink in the dark sky.

"Always remember, my sweet baby girl, rules were made to be broken."

Ten minutes later, the police arrived.

I screamed as they hustled us back into the house, screamed as the officers watched Mama and Derrick get dressed, screamed as they handcuffed my mother and pushed her head down as they shoved her into the police car. I screamed as our neighbor from downstairs held me on the porch while we watched the police car pull away, Mama's wide eyes staring at me from the back window. I screamed until Daddy came home from his class and retrieved me from the neighbor's apartment, returning me to our own home, still strewn with the dirty dishes from supper.

Daddy drove me to his parents' house, where I spent the night crying, despite my grandmother's hugs and shushing.

The next morning, Mama arrived, laughing and unrepentant, to collect me. Grandma glared at her as she scooped me into her arms and danced me around the room. My world was safe again. Mama was home.

That night, no music wafted into my room from Mama's stereo. Instead, I lay awake listening to the unfamiliar sounds of my parents' angry voices.

"For God's sake, Cassie!" My father's voice shook. "What were you thinking?"

"I was thinking it would be nice to let our Sweet Judy Blue Eyes play in the water and look at the stars."

Mama's voice was lower, but it had the tinny, sharp tone it sometimes took when she'd had a bad trip . . . or a run-in with our next-door neighbor.

"You can't just traipse around naked in public," Daddy yelled.

"Why not? Why the hell can't I traipse naked in public? That's the way God made me! Being naked is the natural way to be."

"Maybe in Borneo, Cassie, but not in Indianapolis! Not with a baby . . . and not with another man!"

"God . . . poor Derrick." Mama sighed. "I can't believe you couldn't bail him out. He's probably still sitting in that cell."

"Look, it was all I could do to get the money for you. I couldn't very well ask my parents to bail out your lover, too!"

"Not my lover, my friend. Derrick is my friend."

"Yeah, right," Daddy huffed. "The friend you're screwing!"

"Look, Kirk, I'm your wife. That doesn't mean you own me. When we got married, we both agreed . . ."

"We agreed when we were eighteen years old, Cassie. We were kids. We didn't have a baby. When are you going to grow up?"

"Never!"

Mama's voice grew louder.

"Not if it means worrying about what the old bag next door thinks. I am never going to grow up, if that's what you mean."

"Cassie!" Daddy was shouting now. "You have to grow up sometime. You can't just keep smoking pot and drinking every day, and sleeping with whoever you want. You're a mother now."

"Hush," Mama hissed. "You're going to wake Sweet Judy."

"Judy?" Daddy laughed. "That child sleeps through the damned music you blare every damned night! She'd sleep through a hurricane."

But Daddy was wrong. I wasn't sleeping.

"Look, I'm sorry you had to come bail me out. I'm sorry you had to borrow money from your parents. I'm sorry you don't like the way I take care of the baby." Mama's voice sounded tired.

"But mostly I'm sorry for you," she said. "What's happened to you, Kirk? You used to be so much fun. Now you're just . . . God . . . you're getting to be just like your father!"

With that, the angry voices stopped, the front door slammed, and the music began. Soon, I drifted off to the strains of Paul McCartney singing about a blackbird learning to fly.

❧ 2 ❧

Just before I turned four, Daddy graduated from college. The picture Grandpa took that day shows Daddy in a black robe, smiling broadly. His hair is cut short and the scraggly beard is gone.

Mama stands beside him, holding me. She is wearing a skimpy top and a brightly patterned skirt she'd made for the occasion. I'm wearing a dress made from the same fabric. I am smiling at the camera, too. Mama is looking off toward something else.

"You need to put Judy in preschool," Grandma said as we sat in her backyard eating grilled hamburgers after the ceremony. "She's almost four. She needs to be around children her own age."

Mama just laughed, waving a fly away from my sandwich.

"My Sweet Judy is just fine," she pronounced airily. "She's better off at home, with me."

"I don't know, Cassie," Daddy said. "Maybe she should be in preschool."

"I am *not* turning my daughter over to the thought police. She's too young."

Mama squirted ketchup onto my burger and smiled down at me.

"In fact," she continued, "I might just keep my Sweet Judy Blue Eyes at home . . . maybe I'll homeschool her, you know?"

Daddy laughed, but Grandma did not look pleased.

"Cassandra," she began.

"My name is Cassie, Anne." Mama frowned at her mother-in-law.

"Whatever." Grandma sighed. "You can't keep the child at home forever. She needs to go to school."

"Why?" Mama demanded, raising a can of Budweiser to her lips. She drank deeply, then wiped the back of her hand across her mouth. "So they can turn her out at eighteen thinking like a damned robot?"

"Come on, Cassie," Daddy began.

"No, Kirk. I'm serious. They take in these innocent children and beat all the creativity and free will out of them, so they can mold them into sheep . . . sheep who won't question authority, sheep who will follow their generals into war. That is *not* going to happen to Sweet Judy."

"You have to send the child to school," Grandma said firmly. "The state says so. Besides"—she smiled at Daddy—"the school system didn't do so badly by Kirk."

"Oh, Kirk." Mama spat. "There's my prime example! Look at how . . . conventional he's gotten!"

Daddy laughed, but his eyes looked sad and tired.

"Come on, honey," he said. "A college degree doesn't make me conventional. It makes me educated. And with a law degree I can do a lot more to help people than I could without one."

"You've sold out." Mama rose, lifting me from the picnic bench. "You've sold out to the man."

With that devastating pronouncement, she carried me the four blocks to our little apartment, where she turned on the stereo and lit a joint.

I didn't know who *the man* was, although Mama spoke about him often. *The man* held people down. *The man* squashed people's rights. *The man* sent people to war. I imagined *the man* must be like an overseer. Mama had told me all about slavery—how men with dark skin like Derrick had been slaves. And not just grown-up men; women and children, too, had worked for the man. And if they tried to run away, the overseer hunted them down and beat them.

Mama told me all about it one evening, after we'd had a bad experience at the park. Mama had been pushing my stroller and Derrick was singing a Bob Marley song, and then someone threw a beer bottle from a passing car. The bottle crashed on the sidewalk at Mama's feet, and a man yelled from the car, "Nigger lover!"

So that's why Mama told me about slavery and racism.

Now, I couldn't imagine why Daddy would sell anything to *the man*.

"Don't you worry, sweetie," Mama said, plopping down onto the floor beside me. "I'll always be here. I won't ever sell out."

Later, when Daddy came home, Mama kissed him on the mouth, her arms draped around his neck.

"I'm sorry, baby," she said, smiling up into his brown eyes. "Your mom just sets me off, you know?"

"She means well."

"I know." Mama sighed. "But she worries at me all the time about Sweet Judy. I shouldn't take her to demonstrations. I shouldn't let her stay up so late. I shouldn't tell her about the war and racism. No"—she waved her hands in the air—"according to Anne, I should treat Judy like a china doll and protect her from everything that's going on in the world."

Daddy smiled and sat down on the couch to remove his shoes. I crawled into his lap and he hugged me tight.

"But you know, Cassie, I think Mom's right about preschool. I think Judy would like being with other kids."

"Why?" Mama demanded. "So she can learn to be a *good little girl?* Learn how not to run or laugh too loud or ask questions?"

"No," Daddy said. "So she can make some friends."

"She has friends," Mama said, sitting beside him on the couch. "She has Amy and Rhonda and Derrick."

"Honey," Daddy said, shaking his head. "I mean friends her own age, not grown-ups who act like children."

"Well, she has me," Mama said firmly.

"And she'll always have you, Cassie. But don't you think she might want to play with other children?"

Mama sat quietly for a minute, then smiled at Daddy and said, "Well then, let's ask her."

She leaned down to look straight into my face.

"Do you want to go to preschool, Sweet Judy Blue Eyes?" She watched me carefully.

I sank deeper into Daddy's lap.

All afternoon I'd been thinking about it. I loved playing with Mama and her friends. I loved the charades and the races and the elaborate cardboard playhouses they made.

But sometimes when I watched the other kids heading off for school in the morning, I wondered what it would be like to go with them, to have someone small like me to play with.

I looked up into Mama's beautiful, hopeful face.

"No, Mama," I said firmly. "I want to stay here with you."

And so I did not begin preschool that fall. Instead, I watched from our attic window as the other neighborhood kids left for school with their backpacks, laughing and shoving at each other.

Some kids wore the same clothes every day, the boys in dark blue pants and white shirts, the girls in blue checked jumpers with white blouses. Those children went to Catholic school.

"That's even worse than public school," Mama explained, when I asked her why they were all dressed alike. "They are going to have their poor spirits squashed."

But when they came home from school, laughing and running down the street, they didn't look squashed to me. They looked happy.

Mama loved to bake. She made bread and chocolate chip cookies and soft, chewy brownies. Often when Daddy came home from work, she had a plate of home-baked goodies waiting. He would eat dinner with us, then drive back downtown to his night classes at law school

One afternoon, just as Mama took a pan of brownies from the oven, the front door swung open and Rhonda arrived, carrying a huge bouquet of daisies.

"Aren't they gorgeous?" She grinned.

I liked Rhonda. She was small and thin and freckled, and she read stories in the nicest voice.

She joined Mama in the kitchen while I watched cartoons on the television. Shortly after that, Derrick arrived.

"Hey." He grinned at me. "Who brought my favorite girls those daisies?"

He joined the women in the kitchen, and soon after, the smell of pot filled the apartment.

When Derrick and Mama headed into the bedroom for a nap, Rhonda joined me on the floor in front of the small television. She sat a plate of brownies on the floor.

"Can I have one?"

I loved Mama's brownies.

"Sure, sweetie," she said, not looking at me. She seemed transfixed by the television.

The warm chocolate was wonderful, slightly gooey in the center and crisped at the edges. I chewed each bite slowly, savoring the dark fudge taste.

"Rhonda?" My voice sounded like it was coming from very far away.

"Hmmm?"

"I don't feel good."

Rhonda tore her gaze from the television to look at me.

"What's wrong, baby?" I saw her mouth form the words, but my ears were filled with a high-pitched buzzing. At the edges of my vision, a dark circle was closing in.

"Cassie!" Rhonda's voice pierced the buzzing in my head. "Something's wrong with Sweet Judy!"

The last thing I saw before the dark circle covered my eyes completely was my mother's pale face staring down at me, her green eyes wide. Above her stood Derrick, his dark skin glistening with sweat.

I awoke to the drip of Mama's tears on my face. I lay with my head in her lap. Her hands stroked my damp hair.

"Oh, baby, oh, my Sweet Judy Blue Eyes . . . are you okay?"

I turned my head and threw up in her lap.

Derrick laughed then. "She's all right," he said. "Let her get it out of her system."

Mama carried me into the bathroom and put me in the tub. Then she undressed and got into the bath with me.

"I'm so sorry, my Sweet Judy," she crooned, splashing warm water over my body. "I'm so sorry, sweet baby."

After the bath, she put me to bed. My ears still rang with a soft buzzing and the afternoon sun came through the window too brightly. As I drifted off to sleep, I heard Mama yelling at Rhonda.

"What were you thinking, giving her those brownies? I told you I had a second batch in the oven for her. Jesus fucking Christ, Rhonda, you gave my baby pot brownies!"

I awoke shortly before Daddy got home. Mama was sitting on my bed, watching me.

"Hi, sweetie." She smiled. "Do you feel better now?"

I nodded. "Yes, Mama."

"That's good, honey. That's so good. Why don't you get up, and we'll set the table for dinner. And, Judy . . . baby? Let's not tell Daddy that you got sick today, okay? Daddy gets so sad when you're sick."

I nodded again. Daddy had not seemed particularly sad when I had the flu two months before. But maybe I hadn't noticed it.

After dinner, Mama brought out a plate of brownies.

"Sweet Judy Blue Eyes." She smiled at me. "Do you want a brownie? I baked this batch just for you."

"No, Mama."

"What? Is Judy turning down a brownie?" Daddy laughed. "Well, I guess we'd better keep an eye out for flying pigs tonight."

3

One afternoon in winter, Mama and I were in the kitchen kneading bread dough. Mama always gave me a piece of dough to knead and shape into my own loaf.

Mama was singing as she pounded the dough, and I sang along: "Inch by inch, row by row, gonna make this garden grow."

When the phone rang, Mama wiped the flour from her hands and answered, "Blessings to you, friend. This is Cassie Skylark."

I watched as the smile drained from her face. Her voice became sharp and fearful.

"When?"

"Is he okay?"

"What hospital?"

When she hung up the phone, Mama's hands were shaking.

She stood for a long moment in silence, then lifted me from the chair I was standing on by the counter.

"Come on, Sweet Judy. We're going to have a bath."

"But, Mama, what about the bread?"

"The bread will have to wait."

She filled the bathtub, climbed in with me, and began washing my hair.

"Ouch! Mama, you're pulling too hard."

"Sorry, sweetie."

"Why are we taking a bath?"

"Because, my Sweet Judy, when your daddy gets home from work, you and I are going to take the car and drive down to Bloomington to see your grandma and grandpa."

"Why are they in Bloomington?"

My grandparents lived just a few blocks from us. We saw them every week.

"No, sweetie." Mama smiled as she poured warm water over my head. "Not your Grandma Anne and Grandpa Earl. We're going to see *my* parents . . . your Grandma Pat and Grandpa John."

I had never heard of Grandma Pat and Grandpa John before.

"Why?" I asked.

"Because your Grandpa John is sick, and we need to go see him."

She toweled me dry and chose a dress for me to wear, then braided my hair into a long coil down my back.

When Daddy arrived, we were dressed and ready to go.

"My sister called," Mama said as Daddy walked in the door.

"Karen? What did she want?"

"My dad had a stroke."

"Is he all right?"

"I don't know, Kirk. He's in the hospital. I need to use the car. I have to go see him."

"I have class tonight."

"Can't you take the bus?"

Daddy looked at her for a minute, then pulled her into a tight hug.

"Yes, honey, of course I can take the bus . . . or I'll borrow Dad's car. Are you going to stay the night?"

"I don't know," Mama said. "Maybe."

"Well, call me when you get there, okay?"

They kissed, then Mama picked up the suitcase she'd packed and we left for Bloomington.

The hospital was big and smelled of Lysol. We rode the elevator to the third floor, and I followed Mama down a long hallway to a room where several people sat in silent clusters.

"Hi, Mom." Mama's voice echoed in the quiet room.

A tall, slender woman rose from a couch. She looked blankly at Mama.

"Cassandra," she said, finally. "I wasn't expecting you."

She didn't move toward us, didn't smile.

Finally, Mama walked to her and wrapped her arms around the woman's neck. The woman let Mama hold her briefly, then took a slight step back, away from her.

"Karen called me," Mama said. "How's Dad?"

"He's going to be fine," the woman said. "It was a small stroke, and there doesn't seem to be any paralysis. There was no need for you to come."

"Oh." Mama's shoulders slumped slightly. "I guess . . . I thought you might want to meet your granddaughter."

She turned to me and held out her hand.

"Mom, this is my Sweet Judy Blue Eyes."

She pulled me toward the woman.

I stared at the woman in silence. She didn't look like a grandmother . . . at least not like my grandmother.

Grandma Anne was soft and round. She wore housedresses and fuzzy slippers and curlers in her gray hair.

The woman standing before me was thin and well dressed . . . like the ladies who worked at the bank. She wore a dark gray skirt and a cream-colored sweater and very high-heeled sling-back shoes. A single strand of pearls circled her slender throat. Her dark blond hair was cut short around her face.

She knelt before me, staring into my eyes.

"Her eyes aren't blue," she said after a long silence.

Mama sighed.

"Hello, Judy." The woman smiled at me, but the smile didn't reach her eyes. "I'm your Grandma Pat."

She hugged me briefly, her arms light around my shoulders. Then she stood, one hand smoothing her skirt, the other touching the pearls at her throat. I watched her, wondering how she could maneuver in such high heels.

"So then"—she turned back toward Mama—"there really was no need for you to come, Cassandra."

"Can I see Dad?" Mama asked.

"No." The woman shook her head. "I don't think that's a good idea. You'll just upset him."

"But, Mom, I brought Sweet Judy just to meet him."

"You've had four years to bring your child, Cassandra. It's a bit late now, don't you think?"

Mama stood in silence, but I could see she was shaking. After a long minute of awful silence, she straightened her shoulders, took my hand, and pulled me back toward the hallway.

I looked back as we walked away down the hall. The woman stood watching us for a moment, then returned to the couch and picked up a magazine.

We sat in the car for a few minutes before Mama finally started the motor.

"Mama?"

"Yes, baby."

"Why doesn't she like us?"

Mama sighed and reached out to stroke my hair.

"Because she's a mean woman," she said softly. "I'm sorry I brought you here, sweetie. I'd forgotten what a mean woman she is."

Mama bought me dinner at Burger Chef and drove in silence as I ate a lukewarm hamburger and French fries.

By the time we got home, it was dark and I was only half awake. Mama carried me from the car, up the three flights of steps to our apartment, and laid me in the bed she shared with Daddy, not even bothering to undress me.

A few minutes later, the familiar sweet smell of pot filled the room. Then the sound of Paul McCartney came crooning, "Yesterday, all my troubles seemed so far away. Now it looks as though they're here to stay. Oh, I believe in yesterday."

Soon after, I felt Mama curl herself around me in the bed, the way she did sometimes when Daddy was away late at class. Just before I drifted into a troubled sleep, I felt her tears hot on the back of my neck.

4

On my fifth birthday, Mama threw an elaborate party. Streamers draped from every window and light fixture in the apartment, cardboard cutout circus animals marched across the walls, and balloons covered the floor. Rhonda and Amy helped Mama build a huge cardboard castle on the front lawn, using appliance boxes they'd found behind the hardware store. Painted neon pink with bright green trim, the castle stood a good five feet tall. A bright purple sock flew in lieu of a flag. It was perfect.

Grandma Anne and Grandpa Earl joined us for the festivities, and even they liked the castle. Daddy grilled hot dogs and laughed as he watched Mama dance with me on the lawn. Mama had no sense of rhythm, but that never deterred her from dancing. I guess it would have embarrassed me had I been older, but I didn't know better then. By the time I did, Mama would be long gone.

After lunch, Amy and I sat in the castle, looking through the spyglass she had given me for my birthday. Rhonda slept on the lawn in her bikini, her body shiny with baby oil. Grandma and Grandpa had gone home, and Mama and Daddy sat on the front steps of the house, drinking beer. Mama's head rested on Daddy's shoulder, her hand rested in his lap. Life was good.

"Hey, where's the birthday girl?"

I poked my head out of the castle to see Derrick on the sidewalk, grinning broadly. In his arms was a big wrapped box.

"I'm here," I called, running to hug him. Derrick hadn't been around for a while.

"Happy birthday, munchkin!" He kissed my hair and set the box in front of me. Then he sat down on the grass to watch me pull away the wrappings.

"Mama! Look! Look what Derrick brought me!"

A perfect pink bicycle emerged from the box, just big enough for a five-year-old girl. The bike sported a white basket in front and two training wheels behind. It even had a bell.

I danced from foot to foot as Derrick pulled the bike free from the wrapping paper.

"Derrick," Mama called. "How in the world did you get that?"

She ran across the lawn to see the beautiful bike. Daddy stood on the steps, shading his eyes with a hand, frowning.

"Ask me no questions, I'll tell you no lies." Derrick laughed, watching as Mama scooped me up to perch me on the bicycle seat.

"Kirk," she said, turning toward my father. "Come see the bike!"

Daddy turned abruptly and walked into the house. The screen door slammed behind him.

"Come on, Sweet Judy." Amy was pulling the bicycle forward. "Let's see you ride this thing."

I watched Mama stand a moment, looking from me and the bicycle to the screen door. She smiled at me and said, "Go ahead, honey, show Amy how you can ride." Then she turned and walked into the house.

Derrick and Amy cheered as I wobbled the bike down the sidewalk, showing me how to apply the brakes and steer. Rhonda watched from the lawn. I waited for Mama to reappear. But she didn't.

Finally, I climbed off the bike and ran toward the house. Amy followed.

"Wait up, Sweet Judy," she called. "Wait for me."

But I only ran faster.

At the top of the stairs, our apartment door was closed. Behind the door, I could hear Mama yelling.

"For God's sake, Kirk, it's just a bike! It's not like he bought her a car! Why can't you be reasonable?"

Amy pounded up the stairs behind me, calling ahead, "Judy, wait for me. Just wait for me."

Behind the door, the yelling stopped. I stood with my hands on the doorsill, my heart pounding hard.

The door opened, and Mama smiled down at me.

"It's okay, sweetie," she crooned, hugging me tight. "It's all right."

Daddy brushed by us, knocking Mama off balance, then pounded down the stairs past Amy. A moment later, we heard the car start and the wheels screech out of the driveway. I looked out the window and saw Derrick still standing on the front lawn, watching Daddy's car drive away.

"Come on, Judy." Amy held her hand out to me. "Let's go ride that bike."

I shook my head and clung tight to Mama.

"It's okay, Amy," she said. "Come on in. Let's have a drink."

We sat at the kitchen table. Mama poured grape juice for me and vodka tonics for herself and Amy.

"I don't need the bike, Mama," I whispered.

She brushed the back of her hand across her eyes.

"Don't be silly, Sweet Judy," she said firmly. "That's your bicycle. It's your birthday bicycle. And nobody is going to take it away from you."

Rhonda came in then, pulling a T-shirt over her bikini. "Derrick left," she announced. "What's with Kirk?"

Mama sent me to my room then, to look at books. I lay on the bed and listened to Mama and Amy and Rhonda talking in the front room.

"Why does he have to be such a pig?" Mama said. "It's not like I asked Derrick to buy it."

"Men!" Rhonda spat the word out like it tasted bad in her mouth. "Bourgeoisie, capitalist, domineering, patriarchal bastards!"

"Amen!" Mama's voice sounded slurry.

"Well," Amy spoke softly. I had to strain to hear her. "You can't really blame Kirk. Sweet Judy is *his* daughter. He wanted to get her a bike. And it's got to hurt that he can't, but Derrick can."

"Why can't he just be glad she got a bike?" Mama said. "God! I even told Derrick not to come! Why can't they *ever* just do what we tell them to do?"

"Is there a man in the world smart enough to do what a woman tells him?" Rhonda's voice shook with laughter. "They're just not that smart."

They erupted into giggles. I heard their glasses clink together.

"Who wants another drink?"

Daddy came home long after Rhonda and Amy had gone. Mama and I had cake and ice cream for dinner, and she let me sleep in her bed. I didn't hear him come home, but he was there in the morning, sleeping on my left with Mama on my right.

Life was good again.

Over Mama's protests, I started kindergarten that fall. Trembling, I held Daddy's hand tight as we climbed the stone steps to Indianapolis Public School Number 57, a big brick building just a few blocks from our house. Daddy had insisted that he would take me on my first day. Mama would pick me up at the end of the morning.

Standing in the doorway to the classroom, my heart pounded so hard I wondered if everyone could hear it. The room was full of children. Kids sat on the shiny wood floor working puzzles, or at tables pounding clay. A small group of girls clustered in one corner that had been decorated as a kitchen, complete with a wooden stove and refrigerator. I had never seen so many children.

I'd been to concerts with Mama and to demonstrations. I'd been to parties and cookouts and even a pig roast. But I had never seen so many children.

"Come on." Daddy pulled me forward into the room. "It's going to be fun."

A woman with white hair and an ample belly approached, stretching out her hand to me.

"Hello," she said, as I shrank away. "What's your name?"

"This is Judy," Daddy said, pushing me toward her. "Judy Webster."

"Ah, yes." The woman looked up at Daddy. "Just Judy, then?"

"Yes, please." Daddy smiled at her, shrugging. "It was the sixties, you know. And my wife . . ."

"No explanations." She laughed. "Last year I had a Skybird and a Rainbow. Sweet Judy is fine.

"My name"—she knelt in front of me—"is Mrs. Landon. I'm going to be your teacher."

She smiled.

I clung to Daddy's leg, trying desperately to disappear behind him.

"She hasn't been to preschool," Daddy said, trying hard to disentangle himself from my clutch.

"That's fine," Mrs. Landon said. "We'll be fine. Good-bye now."

She nodded firmly at my father, who hesitated for just a second, then nodded back.

"I'll see you tonight, honey. Mama will pick you up after class."

With that, he was gone. I was alone in a sea of children.

"Now, Judy." Mrs. Landon took my hand and pulled me toward the girls in the kitchen corner. "This is Carol and Susan and Lee Ann. It's their first day of school, too. Girls, this is Judy."

With that, she turned and left me alone, facing the three girls. They stared at me. I stared at them. Finally, one of them asked, "Do you like Barbies?"

I nodded mutely. I had seen Barbie dolls on the television, although I'd never actually held one. Mama said they were fascist and paternalistic, designed to turn women into objects. But I thought it better not to mention what Mama thought of Barbie just then. For the first time in my life, I told a lie.

"Sure," I said. "I like Barbies."

And that was how I got my first friends.

Carol, Susan, and Lee Ann had a multitude of Barbies at their houses. But since they couldn't bring them to school, I was spared the humiliation of admitting that I didn't have a single one.

By the end of the morning, I was feeling comfortable enough to relax. Carol, Susan, and Lee Ann simply added me to their tribe, including me in their kitchen game, saving a seat for me at story time.

"Excuse me? I'm here for my daughter."

Mama's voice was anxious and loud. Every head in the classroom turned toward the door.

Mrs. Landon walked toward her, smiling. "It's five more minutes till the bell," she said, her voice smooth and firm. "Why don't you have a seat here, and you can wait."

Mama stood still, and for one awful moment I thought she was going to argue. I could see the entire scene play out in my head. *Please, Mama*, I pleaded silently. *Please just sit down.*

And she did sit down, waving to me and smiling brightly at Mrs. Landon and Carol, Susan, and Lee Ann.

When the bell rang, some of the children lined up to board the school bus. Others waited in the room for mothers or siblings to walk them home. Mama took my hand and we fairly danced our way home. She wanted every detail, every nuance. What was my favorite part of the day? Were the other girls nice? Did the teacher try to squelch me? Did I want to go back tomorrow?

"Because, you know," she said as she pulled the house key from her purse, "you don't have to go, if you don't want to. I can teach you at home."

"It's okay, Mama," I said, climbing the stairs to our apartment. "I like it at school."

She smiled as she unlocked the apartment door, but her eyes didn't smile. So I knew I had answered wrong.

So a new part of my life began—the lying part. At school, I lied to my friends about what I did at home. At home, I lied to Mama about what I did at school.

The lying at school came easily and at once. I knew somehow that I shouldn't mention dancing naked in the rain, or Mama's psychedelic punch, or Derrick. Nobody had to tell me. I just knew.

The lying at home I learned gradually, by making mistakes.

At dinner after my first week, Daddy asked me what I had learned that day. I recited the Pledge of Allegiance. Mama exploded into a tirade about American imperialism and the fascist indoctrination of children in public schools.

A few days later, I mentioned that Lee Ann's daddy had been to Vietnam. I guess I thought that might please Mama, since she talked about Vietnam so often. Mama stared at me, aghast. Then she told me to go to my room, and then I heard her yelling at Daddy about sending me to school with warmongers and racists.

When Carol told me that her parents were sad because people were being mean to Richard Nixon, who was the president, Mama looked as if she might cry. More yelling after I went to bed that night about the warmongers and fascists.

By Veterans Day, when Lee Ann's daddy came to talk to our

class about being a soldier, I had learned to withhold such news with Mama.

In December, Mrs. Landon told us we were going to be part of the school Christmas program. My class was to sing "The Twelve Days of Christmas," and some kids were chosen to hold up cardboard props. I was given the five golden rings. Susan got the partridge in the pear tree, but Lee Ann told me the golden rings were even better, because we sang that part longer.

I could hardly wait to tell Mama as we walked home from school.

"A Christmas program?" she said. "How can a public school put on a Christmas program? That's obscene!"

She was walking faster now, pulling me along by the hand.

"I cannot believe that in 1974 a public school would put on a Christmas program! Haven't they ever heard of the separation of church and state? No, of course not! This is Indiana . . . goddamned redneck Indiana. What else should we expect?"

I kept my head down and my mouth shut and let her drag me along toward home. When we got there, I ran to my room and closed the door. But I couldn't block out the noise as she banged around the apartment.

"Damned rednecks . . . unbelievable, just fucking unbelievable. I can't stand this place!"

By the time Daddy got home, she had calmed down enough to put dinner on the table.

"Tell your daddy what your school is doing." She glared at me as if it were my fault the school had decided on a Christmas program.

I hung my head, afraid to speak.

"They're putting on a Christmas pageant!"

Mama waited for her words to sink in, waited for Daddy to explode in anger at the sheer injustice of it.

Instead, he looked to me and said, "That sounds like fun. Don't you think it will be fun, Judy?"

Mama stared at him in silence. I kept my head down and concentrated on my plate, pushing lentils and rice around with my fork.

"Judy?" Daddy's voice was soft. "Are you excited about the program?"

"Of course she's not excited!" Mama snapped. "And of course she is *not* participating! I told her how wrong it is. What are they thinking, celebrating a Christian holiday in a public school? What about the Jewish kids? And the Buddhists? What about anyone who isn't a Christian?"

Daddy looked at her for a long minute, and then he laughed.

"I sincerely doubt there are any Buddhists at School 57."

"That's not the point and you know it! It's the principle, Kirk. What about . . ."

"For God's sake, Cassie, it's a Christmas pageant. It's not a fascist plot to overthrow democracy. Honestly, honey, you need to put it in perspective."

Mama glared at him.

"Now, Judy, what are you doing in the program?"

"I'm holding the five golden rings," I whispered, glancing from him to Mama.

"That's terrific, honey! The five golden rings . . . that's a big part! I'm proud of you." Daddy beamed. I smiled at him and then looked at Mama, afraid she'd seen me.

She was watching Daddy, her eyes wide, her mouth set in a thin line.

Finally, she looked at me and her lips smiled. "So, you want to be in the program, Sweet Judy?"

I knew the answer she wanted. I knew I could make her happy if I said no, I did not want to be in the program. I knew if I only said that, her eyes would smile and everything would be all right.

Then I thought of those five cardboard rings painted gold. I thought about standing at the front of the class, holding those rings aloft. I remembered what Lee Ann had said about the rings being even better than the partridge in the pear tree.

"Yes, Mama," I whispered. "I want to be in the program."

"Oh," she said. "Well . . . that's fine, then. That's . . . fine."

She picked up her fork and began eating. Daddy patted my arm and smiled, then began talking about a case his class in law school was discussing, about a man who was being prosecuted for burning an American flag. He looked at Mama now and then, but even that case didn't draw her interest. She ate in silence.

That night there was no yelling, only Daddy pleading.

"Cassie, honey, it's a kindergarten play. She's five years old and it's Christmas. Let her enjoy it. Don't make such a big deal about it."

No response.

"She's not rejecting *you,* Cass. She just wants to be like the other kids. Can't you understand that?"

The front door slammed, and I heard Daddy sigh.

6

"Please, Mama? Please, can I go?"

"I've already said no," she said, her voice cross. She didn't look up from the tarot cards on the table before her.

"But why?"

"Because I said so, that's why!"

I stared at her a long moment, then turned on my heel and stomped into my room, slamming the door behind me. I threw myself onto the bed and began sobbing, big, gulping sobs. Why was she being so mean? Why couldn't I go to Lee Ann's birthday party? Every girl in our class was going . . . everyone but me.

I stared sadly at the invitation. What would I tell Lee Ann? What would they think of me at school?

Mama turned on the stereo in the living room and began singing along with Mick Jagger about not getting any satisfaction. I harrumphed and turned my back to the door.

When Daddy came home and called me to dinner, I emerged from my room with the invitation clutched tight in my hand. Before Mama could say a word, I put the invitation in Daddy's hand and said, "Lee Ann is having a birthday party on Saturday. Can I go?"

Daddy looked at the invitation and smiled, but before he could say a word, Mama snatched the card away.

"You go to your room, young lady!"

She grabbed my shoulder and pulled me toward the bedroom.

"Cassie! What are you doing?" Daddy stared at her, his eyes wide. Mama hardly ever yelled at me, and she had never grabbed me like that before.

"You stay out of this." She glared at him. "I have already told Judy she is *not* going to that party."

She let go of my shoulder when we reached my room and stood still a moment, just staring at me, an expression on her face I'd never seen there before.

"And you, missy . . . you can just stay in your room until you're ready to apologize."

She slammed my bedroom door behind her, leaving me shaking, red marks on my shoulder where she'd grabbed me.

"What the hell is wrong with you?" Daddy's voice was angry.

"Nothing is wrong with me!" Mama spat at him. "I told Judy she couldn't go to that party, and then she turns around and asks you. That's what's wrong."

I heard pans slamming in the kitchen, then Daddy's voice, much quieter than before.

"Okay, look," he said, "I get why you're mad. She shouldn't have asked me after you said no. But, Cassie, there's no reason to go ballistic. She's only five. She just wants to go to a party."

Mama said nothing. I heard the chairs scraping on the floor and a spoon against the serving bowl. She had made fried rice, and it smelled heavenly. My stomach growled.

"Honey?" Daddy's voice was soft, cajoling. "Why can't she go to the party?"

Mama sighed loudly. "Because, Kirk, it's on Saturday. We're going downtown on Saturday for the protest. Don't you remember?"

Daddy laughed. "Oh, Cassie, for Christ's sake," he said. "Let her go to the birthday party. It will be a lot more fun for her than a protest."

Mama said nothing.

"Honestly, honey, it's time she started doing things with friends her own age. She's five years old. She's supposed to go to birthday parties and be in school plays. You can't keep her all to yourself forever."

"But who'll go with me on Saturday?" Mama's voice was sad. "Will you come?"

"I can't this week. I have a mock trial. Maybe Rhonda or Amy will go. And if not, you can go by yourself. You're a big girl."

Daddy's voice was teasing now.

"Kirk?"

"Hmmm?"

"I don't want her to go to that house."

"Why?"

"Lee Ann's father was in Vietnam! He's probably a baby killer or a rapist or . . ."

"Okay, now you're just being ridiculous. He was a soldier. Now he's an insurance salesman. He seems like a good guy."

She sighed again.

"She used to like going with me."

"She still likes going with you, Cassie. Look, she's not rejecting you, okay? She just wants to go to a birthday party."

I sat by the bedroom door, listening intently, willing Mama to let me go.

"Oh, all right," she said finally. "Judy," she called.

"Yes, Mama?"

"Come out and eat your supper."

Lee Ann's party was glorious. We played pin the tail on the donkey and made fancy paper hats and ate cake and ice cream. We pushed dolls up and down the block in her stroller. We dressed Barbie dolls and brushed their hair.

At four o'clock, Daddy arrived to take me home. Mama was still at the protest, so Daddy warmed leftovers for dinner. When it began to grow dark, Mama still wasn't home. Daddy paced the apartment, lifting the curtain to look out the window now and then.

He called Rhonda, then Amy. Neither of them had gone to the protest or knew where Mama was.

"I'd go downtown to look for her," he said into the phone, "but she has the car. And I have Judy."

At nine, Daddy told me it was time for bed.

"Mama's not here," I whined. "Where's Mama?"

"Mama will be home soon," he said. "But now it's time for bed."

I put on my pajamas and came back to the living room.

"Who will tuck me in?" I asked.

"I will." He smiled. "I can tuck you in sometimes, can't I?"

We settled on the bed and he had just begun reading *The Story About Ping* when we heard footsteps on the stairs.

"Thank God." Daddy sighed. "There's your mama."

I ran into the living room as the front door swung open, and there, indeed, was Mama. Her hair was mussed and her cheeks flushed. Her eyes were bright and glassy.

Behind her stood a tall, thin man with a full beard and a long ponytail. He grinned at me.

"Cassie, where have you been?" Daddy sounded cross.

Mama giggled and waved her hand in the air.

"You must be Kirk," said the man with the ponytail. "I'm Glen." He extended his hand to my father, who shook it briefly.

"Cassie and I have been talking politics," the man said. "And she invited me to crash here for a few days. Hope that's cool with you."

Daddy stood still, staring at the man. Finally, he turned to Mama. "Cassie, can I talk to you in the kitchen?"

"Oh, Kirk." Mama sighed. "Don't get bent out of shape. Glen's in town for the protest. He helped organize it. God, it was amazing! I learned so much today. You need to listen to Glen. He knows so much about the war."

"I'm sure he does," Daddy said softly. "But I would really like to talk to you in the kitchen."

He took Mama's arm and guided her toward the kitchen. "Have a seat." He nodded to Glen. "We'll just be a minute. And Judy"— he turned to look at me—"you go on to bed now. I'll finish your story tomorrow."

He and Mama disappeared into the kitchen, and I stood still in the living room, staring at the strange man.

He dropped the duffel bag he'd carried on his shoulder and settled himself on the futon.

"How old are you?" he asked.

"Five."

"Well, you're a lucky kid. You're lucky to be alive in a time like this, when so many people are working to make the world a better place for you. And you're lucky to have such a cool mom."

I didn't reply. I simply watched him as he sprawled across the futon. He seemed completely at home.

After several minutes, my parents returned, Mama smiling, Daddy looking grim.

"I told you to go to bed," Daddy said firmly, glaring at me. "Scoot!"

In my room, I sat by the closed door, listening intently.

"Look, you can stay a couple days," Daddy said. "You can sleep on the futon."

"Thanks, man," Glen drawled.

"But if you stay here, you will stay here clean. No dope. We have a kid."

"No problem."

"I mean it." Daddy's voice rose. "I don't care if you smoke a little pot, but I won't have you bringing this shit into my house!"

"God, Kirk! Lighten up. It's just a little acid. It's not like I'm doing heroin." Mama's voice was sharp.

"I've told you before I don't like it, Cassie. I think it's dangerous."

Mama sighed, then said, "All right, no acid in the house."

"But"—her voice trailed as she walked into the kitchen—"we do have some wine."

The next morning when I woke up, Glen was sitting in my chair at the kitchen table. Mama sat beside him. They were looking at a big map.

"This is where we're going to build the bake house," Glen said.

"We've already got a great kitchen, but if we're going to sell bread, we need more ovens."

"Are we making bread, Mama?" I loved kneading dough.

"Oh, hey, Sweet Judy. Good morning. No, we're not making bread today. Glen is showing me where he lives on a big farm in Kentucky. A whole bunch of people live there all together, and they grow their own vegetables and all work together, and everyone helps everyone. Doesn't that sound great?"

"Look, kiddo." Glen pointed to a building on the map. "That's our school. The kids can walk there in the morning and come home for lunch. And they learn by doing, instead of just memorizing shit. It's a great place for kids." He was smiling at Mama now.

"Can I have Fruit Loops?" I asked.

Mama poured my cereal and set the bowl at Daddy's place.

"Where's Daddy?"

"He had to work today." Mama frowned. "He's always at work or school," she said to Glen. "He's hardly ever at home."

"Sold out," Glen said grimly.

Mama nodded.

"That's what's so groovy about the farm," Glen said. "We work hard, but we're all together. Even the kids help. You've got to come."

"I want to," Mama said. "I just have to convince Kirk. He's gotten so weird. He wants everything to be all safe and normal. God, he used to be so much fun."

"Well, if he won't come, maybe you and Judy can come on your own. Just to check it out."

"Maybe," Mama said. "Maybe we'll just come for a visit."

"You can come with me when I go." Glen reached across the table and covered Mama's hand with his own. "It'll be fun."

"Maybe," she said again, smiling.

Mama and I did bake bread that day. Glen left mid-morning to meet up with some of the other protest organizers. So we made freeform loaves—my favorite kind.

By the time Daddy came home from work, the apartment smelled of fresh-baked bread.

"That smells great," he said, pulling Mama to him and kissing her mouth. "How'd you know I've been thinking about bread all day?"

"I guess I just know how you think." Mama laughed.

"Don't!" she said abruptly, as Daddy reached for a loaf.

"Why not?"

"Those are for dinner," she said.

"There's plenty for dinner and then some," he said, tearing a hunk from the loaf. "It's best while it's still warm."

"Damn it, Kirk! I worked all day on those and you've ruined one of them."

"What's wrong with you?" Daddy asked, smiling at her.

"I just . . . damn it! You didn't even ask, you just took it. Like it's just your God-given right to exploit my labor."

Daddy looked at her in silence, chewing a bite of bread.

Then he walked to the refrigerator and pulled out a gallon of milk, poured himself a glass, and left. I followed him down the stairs to the front porch and sat beside him on the steps.

"Why is Mama mad?"

"I'm not sure, sweetie. I think maybe she feels like we don't appreciate her. Or maybe she's just cranky today."

"Daddy, are we going to go live on Glen's farm?"

"No, baby. We are definitely *not* going to live on Glen's farm."

"Okay." I felt the tension in my shoulders relax. "I don't want to live in Kentucky. I like my school."

"Well, don't worry about it. We're not going anywhere."

Four days later, Mama and I were sitting on a Greyhound bus with Glen, heading south on I-65.

Daddy had left for school that morning before I was awake, so I didn't get to say good-bye. Mama left him a note on the kitchen table, right next to a batch of brownies she'd baked before we left.

I cried when she told me we were leaving. I told her I didn't want to go live on Glen's farm. I didn't want to leave my school. I didn't want to leave Daddy.

"You'll love it when we get there," she said, stroking my hair. "If you don't love it, then we'll just come back."

I buried my face in her lap. For the first time ever, I didn't believe my mother. I didn't believe she would bring me back if I didn't love the farm.

We rode on the bus for three hours. When we got off the bus, a friend of Glen's was waiting in his VW van to drive us to the farm. That took another hour. By the time we pulled up in front of the big, shabby-looking farmhouse, I felt as if we might be in another country altogether.

"Come on, Sweet Judy. Come see our new house!"

Mama pulled me from the van and picked me up. "Isn't it beautiful?" She was smiling all over.

I stared dully at the house, the barns, the endless fields stretching in all directions across gently rolling hills.

"You're going to love it here. I promise. There's so much to do. And there are animals, Judy! Look, in that barn there are horses. And over there are some chickens. Do you want to see the chickens?"

"Hey, babe." Glen was pulling bags from the back of the van. "Which of these are yours, and which are Judy's?"

He was sorting our luggage into two piles. Mama pointed out her bags, and then mine. When she was done, Glen began carrying Mama's bags into the big house. Mine still sat on the ground by the van.

Another man appeared and began gathering my bags. But instead of taking them into the farmhouse, he walked across the road to a long, low building lined with windows.

"That's the children's dormitory," Mama said, watching me anxiously. She chewed her lip, then said, "You'll like it there. You'll be with all the other kids, just like at school."

I nodded, not yet comprehending what was happening.

Glen reappeared and took Mama's hand. "Come on," he said, "I'll show you around."

I trailed behind them as Glen pointed out the dining hall, several small cottages, a large pond, and the horse pasture. When we came to the schoolhouse, he stopped and grinned at me.

"This is your new school, kiddo. What do you think?"

We walked inside. It did not look like my classroom at School 57. The large room was mostly empty. No desks stood in rows. No dolls lay in cradles. No kitchen corner, no blocks. Just a big room with some beanbag chairs, a chalkboard, and a huge globe.

"How many kids are here?" Mama asked.

"About fifteen," Glen said. "It varies. People come and go, you know."

A large bell clanging startled me.

"Dinner," Glen said. "Come on, let's eat."

We walked to the dining hall, where people were already standing in line, plates in hand.

Glen introduced Mama to several people. They smiled, hugged her, shook her hand. Everyone seemed friendly. We filled our plates with brown rice, squash, and bread, then sat at a long table to eat. The noise was deafening. People talked and laughed, children ran around the table, a dog barked at the door. My ears hurt from it all.

"What's your name?"

A girl stood across the table, staring at me.

"Judy," I said.

"What?"

"Judy," I said more loudly.

"I'm Liberty," she said, smiling. "Are you gonna live here?"

I looked up at Mama, and she smiled. "Yes, Liberty. We are going to live here. I've heard so many nice things about this place."

"It's okay." Liberty shrugged. "You want to see the pigs?" she asked.

I did not want to see the pigs. I did not want to leave Mama's side. But Mama was pushing me to go. "You'll like the pigs," she said. "And you have a new friend!"

I looked at Liberty. She was about my age, maybe a little older. She wore a dirty T-shirt and shorts. She smiled, and I saw she was missing a front tooth. She seemed nice enough, but she wasn't Lee Ann or Susan or Carol.

Sighing, I followed her out of the dining hall and down a dirt road.

"How long have you lived here?" I asked.

"I don't know," she said. "A long time. Before, we lived in Louisville. But my dad wanted to live here."

"Do you like it?"

"It's okay," she repeated. "School is fun. We do lots of cool things. But, we work a lot. I don't like that part."

"What do you do?"

"We work in the garden, mostly. I pull weeds and pick stuff. Sometimes I feed the chickens. We help in the kitchen, too. And other stuff."

It sounded like a lot of work.

"It's okay," she said yet again. "But I miss my old house."

I nodded. I had not yet been gone a whole day, and already I was homesick.

Liberty climbed onto a fence and grabbed a big stick.

"Watch," she said. "They like this."

She leaned over the fence and several huge pigs walked toward her. She used the stick to scratch their backs and they snorted and grunted and pushed at each other to get closer to the stick. After a few minutes, she gave the stick to me. "You do it."

So I scratched the pigs and wondered how secure the fence was. The pigs were very big.

A bell clanged again, and Liberty sighed. "Meeting," she said. "Let's go."

I followed her back to the dining hall, where the plates had been cleared from the tables.

"Okay." A man was talking loudly. "First, let's say thanks to the folks who made our meal tonight."

Everyone clapped.

"And now, I have a couple introductions."

He smiled at Mama. "This," he said, pointing toward her, "is Cassie Skylark. She's from Indianapolis. She came down with Glen."

Everyone clapped again.

"And this"—the man pointed at me now—"is Sweet Judy Blue Eyes, Cassie's daughter. You should know that Sweet Judy was born . . . at Woodstock!"

Everyone clapped loudly. I shrank into Mama's lap, wishing they would look at anything besides me.

"Cassie's going to be working in the kitchen," the man said.

"She's going to help us set up the bake house. I understand she makes some mean bread."

Everyone smiled.

"Now, let's have our rap session. Who wants to talk?"

Several people wanted to talk, as it happened. One complained about someone who wasn't doing her fair share of work in the laundry. Another reported on the progress made in building a new latrine. The meeting lasted a long time. By the time everyone had finished talking, I was half asleep, my head in Mama's lap. It had been a very long day.

"Hey, kiddo." Glen was grinning at me. "Looks like you're ready to hit the sack."

He lifted me from Mama's lap.

"Come on, I'll show you your new digs."

Glen carried me to the long, low building, Mama trailing behind.

Inside were two rows of bunk beds.

"This one is yours."

Glen sat me down on a lower bunk near the back wall.

"See, Sweet Judy?" Mama's voice was anxious. "You get to sleep in here with all the other kids. Won't that be fun?"

I simply stared at her.

"Where's your bed?"

"Oh." Mama knelt in front of me. "I'll be sleeping in the other house, right over there." She pointed toward the door.

"Why can't I sleep with you?"

Mama looked up at Glen. He shook his head.

"Let's just give this a try for a couple nights, okay? I think you'll like it when you get used to it."

Mama's eyes were too bright, her smile too stiff.

Other children began coming into the dormitory. Some climbed into bunk beds. Others gathered toothbrushes and headed for the sinks. Liberty arrived and plopped down on my bed beside me.

"I'm right over there," she said, pointing at a bed across the aisle. "So we can talk, if you want."

"Okay, then." Glen stood and took Mama's hand. "Let's let

Judy settle in." He began walking toward the door. "Good night, kiddo."

Mama pulled her hand from his and bent to hug me. "It's gonna be all right, baby girl. I promise you're going to like it here."

She kissed my forehead.

"Okay, kids. Ten minutes till lights out!" A woman's voice rang through the room.

She stood by the doorway, smiling at Mama.

"She'll be fine, Cassie. It's hard on them at first, but they adjust pretty quick. And I'll be right here if she needs anything." The woman gestured to a curtained corner where a bigger bed stood.

Mama nodded, kissed me again, and turned away. Tears welled in my eyes as I clutched at her blouse. I'd only ever spent one night away from Mama, the time she'd been arrested for swimming naked.

"Mama, wait!"

"I'll see you in the morning, baby. Sleep tight."

Mama walked out of the building and the door closed behind her.

"Hi, Sweet Judy." The woman stood by my bed. "My name is Mandy. I'm the dorm mother. So if you need anything, you just let me know, okay? Do you have your toothbrush? Good, there are the sinks. Go brush your teeth. The toilet is out that door," she pointed to a door at the back of the room. "I'll go with you the first time, so you'll know where everything is."

She smiled at me.

"You'll like it here," she said. "Everyone likes it here."

I nodded at her, but I didn't think I would like it one bit.

I cried myself to sleep, wondering where Mama was and where Daddy was. And why Daddy had not come with us. And why he let Mama take me away.

7

L ife on the farm was a lot of work. We rose early to feed the chickens and weed the garden before breakfast. I always sat with Mama at meals, edging as close to her as I could, trying hard to block out the cacophony of noise in the dining hall. After breakfast, I went to school. Most days, our teacher was a plump young woman named Caroline. She read to us, helped us with math problems, and told us about places around the world, pointing them out on the globe as she talked. Sometimes Glen taught us about the war in Vietnam, and how the United States was killing innocent children and babies there. I thought a lot about Lee Ann's father then. He didn't seem like someone who would kill babies.

After lunch, we had playtime. Liberty and I climbed trees and built forts and scratched the pigs. Then more lessons before dinner. And always, after dinner were the rap sessions. These went on sometimes long into the night, and I would fall asleep stretched out on the bench with my head in Mama's lap.

Mama loved the farm. She worked hard in the garden and in the bake house. Both of us got sunburned, then peeled and burned again. Mama spent a lot of time with Glen.

Every night, after Mandy turned out the lights, I lay in bed and cried, thinking about Daddy and my grandparents and my school in Indianapolis. Sometimes, Liberty heard me cry. Then she would crawl into bed with me and hold my hand until we both fell asleep.

One morning, after we'd been at the farm for a few weeks, Liberty and I were pulling weeds in the garden when we heard shouting. We peeked around the edge of the barn and saw a police car in front of the main house, doors opened, lights flashing. A policeman stood between Glen and another man, whose back was turned to me.

As we watched, Mama emerged from the house and ran to stand beside Glen. She was shouting, too.

And then I saw who the man was, shouting at Glen and Mama. It was my father.

I ran past Liberty, down the dirt road toward the house. "Daddy!"

He turned, and a huge grin spread across his face. He ran toward me and pulled me into his arms, holding me so tight I felt squished.

"Judy, oh, thank God! Oh, I missed you."

"Sweet Judy!" Mama's voice cracked. "Come here! You come here right now!"

"Now, ma'am." The policeman's voice was low but firm. "Your husband has a writ of custody. You took the child unlawfully, and he is taking her home. If you want to fight for custody, you'll have to file a claim in a court of law."

"Kirk!" Mama screamed at Daddy. "Kirk, don't take her! You can't take her away from me!"

Daddy didn't reply. He gave Mama a long, cold stare, then carried me to the police car, put me in the backseat, and climbed in beside me. Outside, Glen was holding Mama tight, so she couldn't get free.

The policeman climbed into the front seat of the car, closed the door, and started the engine. As we drove away from the farm, I could hear Mama screaming for me. "Sweet Judy! Noooo! Come back."

I leaned into Daddy's chest and cried.

∽≈ 8 ≈∾

Daddy and I moved out of our little attic apartment and into Grandma and Grandpa's house on Ohmer Avenue. It was directly across from the Missions Building, an old, vine-covered brick building that housed the denominational offices of the Disciples of Christ. Lots of my friends' parents worked at the Missions Building. It seemed like half the kids in my class were ministers' kids, PKs we called them. Daddy worked full-time at the guitar store and still took classes for law school at night, so Grandma took care of me most of the time.

When I returned to School 57, my friends all asked where I had been. And for once, I didn't lie. I told them about the farm and Liberty and Glen and Mama.

"Your mama is crazy," Carol said.

I nodded mutely. I wasn't sure if Mama was crazy, but it seemed best to agree.

"It's okay," Lee Ann said, taking my hand. "We still like you."

And so another phase of life began—life without Mama. I missed her so much sometimes it took my breath away. Grandma loved me and fussed over me and fed me and read me stories. But she didn't make brownies like Mama's. And she didn't get in the bathtub with me. And she didn't read the stories using funny voices like Mama did. And every night I slept alone in my bed in the room Grandma had decorated for me with ballerinas and butterflies.

One day in May, I sat at the table in Grandma's kitchen, coloring with crayons while she cooked dinner. The doorbell rang and Grandma walked into the living room, wiping her hands on a dishtowel. She opened the door and I heard Mama's voice.

"Anne, where is she? Where's my Sweet Judy?"

I ran to the living room, where Grandma stood blocking the doorway, her sturdy frame between Mama and me.

"Mama!" I ran to her, but Grandma put her hand out to stop me. Holding me tight by the arm, she never looked away from Mama's face.

"Cassandra," she said firmly, "you can't be here. You can't see Judy without a court order."

"Please, Anne!" Tears streamed down Mama's face, her beautiful green eyes never leaving mine. "I have to see her. I *have* to! Please."

"I can't let you in," Grandma said, her voice quavering. I tore my eyes from Mama's to look up at Grandma. I was surprised to see tears on her cheeks.

"She's mine," Mama said softly. "She's my baby. I have to see her. Please, Anne, just for a minute."

Grandma stepped back from the doorway and Mama rushed in, dropping to her knees and pulling me into a tight hug.

"Oh, baby! Oh, my Sweet Judy. I have missed you. Oh, God, I've missed you so much."

I heard the door close behind us and the deadbolt latch. Over Mama's head, I watched as Grandma moved cautiously toward the telephone, her eyes never leaving Mama.

"You're hugging too tight," I said, squirming.

Mama smiled then and plopped onto the floor, pulling me into her lap.

"I'm sorry, baby. I've just missed you so much. Are you okay? Did you miss me, too?"

I curled into her lap and nodded. "I missed you, Mama. I missed you so much. Why didn't you come back?"

"I'm here now, baby. And I promise I won't ever leave you again."

Grandma's voice was wavering on the phone. "Kirk, you need to come home. Cassie's here."

Mama looked up at her with pleading eyes. "Anne, please. I need Judy with me. You can't keep her away from me. You can't."

Grandma moved in front of the door again, standing between Mama and escape.

"You can't take her, Cassie," she said, her voice firm again. "You can see her here, but you can't leave with her. I won't let you."

We sat like that for a while, Mama and me on the floor. Grandma never left her post by the door.

"How are you, baby? Are you okay? Is school okay? Are you sad without me?"

I didn't answer the barrage of questions, just clung to her, smelling her skin, feeling her tears drip onto my face.

"I'm so sorry," Mama crooned again and again. "Oh, Sweet Judy, I'm so sorry I let them take you away from me. But I'll fix it. I promise I'll fix it. I won't let them keep you from me. I promise."

I heard tires crunching on the gravel driveway. A minute later, Daddy's key was in the lock. He nearly shoved Grandma over as he burst into the room.

"What the hell do you think you're doing?" His voice was angry, his face grim.

"I had to see her," Mama said, holding me more tightly. "You can't keep her away from me, Kirk. She's my daughter."

Daddy stood staring down at her, his fists clenched, his eyes wide. He took several deep breaths.

"Okay," he said finally. "So you can visit with her here, for a little while. And then we'll talk. . . . Not now," he said, as Mama started to say something. "Not here. First you visit, then we'll talk in private."

He dropped into the chair by the door and nodded at Grandma, who walked back into the kitchen.

Mama held me in her lap and talked about the farm.

"Everyone misses you," she said, stroking my hair. "Liberty

misses you a lot. She wants you to come back. And I want you back, baby. I've missed you so much. Don't you want to come back to the farm with me?"

I dropped my head, not wanting to see her tears. I knew what she wanted. She wanted me to say yes, that I would go back to the farm. My heart beat fast inside my chest. I felt like I couldn't breathe. Finally, I shook my head.

"I don't want to go to the farm," I whispered. "I want you to come home and live with us."

"Oh, baby," Mama said. "I can't do that. This place, it was killing me."

"Stop, Cassie," Daddy said. "Don't do this to her."

"Damn it, Kirk!"

Her voice, loud and sharp, startled me. I pulled away from her, staring from her to Daddy and back again.

Immediately, she was shushing me, reaching for me. "I'm sorry, Judy. I didn't mean to yell. It's okay."

But it wasn't okay. Nothing was okay. I crawled to Daddy and held on to his leg.

"I don't want to go to the farm," I repeated. "I want you to come home!"

Mama sat in silence for a long minute, not even wiping away the tears that dripped from her chin. She stared at me sadly. I wavered, clinging to Daddy's leg. I knew I could make her happy again. It would be so simple. But then I looked up at Daddy and saw he was crying, too. There was no way I could make them both happy. Daddy reached down to pull me into his lap as I began to sob, heaving so hard I shook all over.

"I think you'd better go," he said softly over my head.

Mama rose and reached out to stroke my forehead. "It's okay, baby. I promise you, Mama will make it okay."

She looked at Daddy, her mouth set in a straight, tight line.

"This isn't over," she hissed. "I'm her mother. She belongs with me."

She kissed the top of my head. "I'll be back, Sweet Judy. Don't you worry, I'll be back."

Then she left, slamming the door behind her.

I sat in Daddy's lap and cried for a long time, his arms tight around me.

"Daddy?" I finally sputtered.

"Yes, sweetie?"

"I don't want to go to the farm."

"Don't worry, Judy. I won't let that happen."

"Daddy?"

"Yes?"

"Make her come home, okay?"

"I'm sorry, baby. I can't do that. I can't make her come back if she doesn't want to."

I cried until my stomach hurt while Daddy held me and patted my back. After a while, Grandpa came home. He kissed my head and disappeared into the kitchen. Then Grandma appeared in the doorway. "Come on, now," she said, smiling at me. "It's time for dinner. I made spaghetti."

A few days later, sitting on the playground with Susan, Carol, and Lee Ann, I saw Mama, standing just outside the fence, watching me. When she saw I was looking at her, she motioned me to come over. I sat still.

"What's wrong?" Susan asked. "You look sick."

"My mama is here," I whispered.

My friends looked over at Mama, who smiled brightly and waved. Then she walked around the fence and onto the playground.

She came straight to where we four sat on the ground, stopping in front of me.

"Hello, girls. I'm Sweet Judy's mama." She smiled down at them. Her eyes were glassy bright.

Carol, Susan, and Lee Ann simply stared at her. Lee Ann reached over to take my hand.

"Come on, Sweet Judy." Mama reached her hand out to me. "I'm taking you home now."

"It's not three o'clock," I said, holding tight to Lee Ann.

"I know, honey. But Grandma asked me to come get you early. We're taking you out for ice cream."

She reached down to take my shoulder.

"Mrs. Landon!" Carol was shouting. "Mrs. Landon, come here!"

"Hush," Mama spat at her, pulling me up. "Just hush now. This has nothing to do with you."

She held tight to my arm as Mrs. Landon walked swiftly toward us, panting slightly.

"Hello," she said, smiling sweetly. "I'm taking Judy home now."

"I'm sorry, Mrs. Webster," Mrs. Landon said, frowning. "I can't let you do that."

"The hell you can't!" Mama's voice was sharp. "I'm her mother and I'm taking her home."

"Girls," Mrs. Landon said, reaching for my hand. "You take Judy inside now. I need to speak with Mrs. Webster."

Carol, Susan, and Lee Ann rose. Lee Ann reached for my hand again and held it tightly. She pulled at me, but Mama held firm onto my shoulder.

"Please, Mrs. Webster. You can't do this. Let go of her."

By now, all the kids on the playground were watching us. Another teacher walked toward us, motioning for kids to move away.

"You can't keep her from me," Mama was yelling now. "She's my daughter. I am taking her home *now!*"

From inside the school, the principal came running. He was a big man, balding and paunchy. "What's going on here?" he demanded.

"I am taking my daughter home right now!" Mama repeated, staring from him to Mrs. Landon.

"I can't let you do that," the principal said firmly. He reached for her arm, the one clutching my shoulder.

"Don't you dare!" Mama shrieked. "Don't you touch me, you fascist pig!"

The principal took Mama firmly by the arm and pulled her away from me. When her grasp on my shoulder released, Lee Ann pulled me toward the school building, past the other kids who stood staring.

"No!" I heard Mama screaming. "You can't take her. She's my daughter. She's mine!"

Mrs. Landon was behind us now, hurrying us back into the

school building. We walked to the classroom, where she closed and locked the door behind us.

"Are you all right, Judy?" She knelt beside me and pulled me into a hug. "Are you all right?"

I shook so hard I thought I might fall over. Leaning into my teacher's embrace, I let myself cry. Carol and Susan and Lee Ann simply stared.

"She *is* crazy," Carol whispered. And this time I knew she was right.

After a little while, Daddy arrived. He spoke for a few minutes with Mrs. Landon and the principal, then took my hand and led me to the car.

"I'm sorry, sweetie." His voice sounded sad.

"Is she crazy, Daddy?"

"What?"

"Is Mama crazy?"

He stroked my hair and tilted my chin up so I had to look him in the eyes.

"No, honey, your mama's not crazy. But she is . . . sick. I think she's taking some medicine that makes her sick. That's why she's acting this way."

"But why does medicine make her sick? Why does she take it?"

Daddy sighed deeply. "It's complicated, honey. She feels like she has to take it, I guess."

He started the car's engine and pulled out of the parking lot.

"But I promise you, I will take care of you," he said, glancing toward me. "I will keep you safe, Judy. I promise."

Over the next few weeks, I caught glimpses of her sometimes, standing across the street from Grandma's house or following behind us as we walked to school. Once I saw her across from the school playground. I bent my head and pretended not to see her.

I didn't know then about the courtroom battles that were happening. Mama tried to convince a judge she was a good mother. Daddy and my grandparents argued she wasn't. Mama's friend Amy told the judge that I'd be better off with Daddy. Even Mama's parents testified that Mama was unfit. I learned all about it later. I wondered then how Mama must have felt, hearing her husband and friend and parents talk about her like that.

In the end, the judge said I should live with Daddy. He said Mama could have supervised visitation once a week. And so, once a week, Daddy drove me to a big building downtown, where we rode the elevator to the fourth floor and walked down a long hallway to a room filled with toys. There, Mama sat waiting. An older man with glasses sat silently by the door, paging through a magazine.

Mama and I played with blocks and colored pictures. Sometimes she read to me. She asked lots of questions. She sang to me. And every week, she cried when it was time to go.

"What does your grandma cook for your dinner?" she asked as we colored in a book.

"Lots of things," I said, concentrating on the red crayon in my hand. "Last night we had Hamburger Helper."

Mama made a strangled noise. I looked up, and her face was grim. "She's poisoning you," she spat. "Feeding you crap like that."

The man in the corner turned a page and cleared his throat. Mama glared in his direction.

"Don't you worry, Sweet Judy. When we get this all straightened out, I'll cook you lentils and rice . . . or stir-fry. Would you like that?" She looked anxiously into my face. Mama always seemed anxious in the little room.

"I wish you would make bread," I said.

"Next week, I'll bring you some bread. And I'll bring some granola for you, too. You can take that back to Grandma's to have for breakfast."

She hugged me too tightly. "It's just for a little while, baby. Just till we get it all straightened out. Then we'll go back to the farm."

The man in the corner cleared his throat again, glancing at us over the top of his magazine.

"I don't want to go to the farm," I said softly.

"Oh, baby, sure you do." She stroked my hair. "Only next time, you can sleep in the house with me, just like we used to do. Would you like that?"

I scribbled hard with the red crayon, making a mess of my picture.

"And you can see Liberty again and play in the tree house."

I shook my head, refusing to look at her.

"You'll love it, baby. I promise you will."

"No!" My voice was loud in the small room. Mama sat back, startled.

"No! I won't love it. I want you to come home, Mama. When are you coming home?"

The man in the corner put the magazine on a table and leaned forward, watching us.

"Oh, Sweet Judy, I can't come back," Mama said, her eyes sparkling wet. "Your daddy won't let me."

"I think that's all for today," the man in the corner said sharply, rising from his chair. "Come along, Judy. It's time to go home now. You'll see your mother next week."

"It's not time," Mama yelled. "I've still got ten minutes. No!" She screamed as the man reached for my hand. "No! You are not taking her yet. She's mine!" She slapped the man squarely across the face.

Deftly and silently, the man took her wrist. "Ma'am, you're upsetting your child now. Don't do this," he said softly.

I sat on the floor, shrinking into a corner, watching as Mama struggled against the man, crying and repeating, "She's mine. She's mine." Then with her free hand, she dragged her fingernails down his cheek, leaving long red welts.

At that, the man pulled her arm behind her back and held her tightly against him. She was shrieking now. "No! You can't do this. I still have ten minutes. Take your hands off me, you Nazi!"

The door to the room swung open and Daddy appeared, followed by another man in a policeman's uniform. Daddy picked me up from where I crouched on the floor and carried me out of the room, down the long hallway, and into the elevator, shushing me softly while I cried. As the elevator doors closed, I could hear Mama still screaming.

After that, I didn't see Mama for a long time.

PART 2

LIFE WITH DADDY

❧ 9 ❧

In the spring of 1978, Daddy and I moved out of Grandma and Grandpa's house and into our own house on University Avenue. Daddy had graduated from law school and was working as a public defender. The house was just a block from Grandma's, and I still walked to her house every day after school and stayed until Daddy got home from work.

I liked the new house. It was two stories, with a big front porch and lots of trees in the yard. Daddy had hung a swing from one of the trees, and in the summer we were going to build a tree house out back.

Lee Ann's family lived just up the block, and we played records on her record player, drew chalk pictures on the sidewalk, and sometimes rode our bikes to the fountain at Audubon Circle. Some nights I slept at Lee Ann's house. Her mother made spaghetti and meatballs or tuna noodle casserole. Some nights Lee Ann slept at my house, and Daddy ordered pizza or brought home Chinese food.

Irvington was a tightly knit community, like a small town surrounded by the city of Indianapolis. Tree-lined streets curved past Victorian houses and post-war bungalows. There were lots of churches and just one bar, a dingy-looking place on Washington

Street next to the ten-cent store. People tended not to lock their doors during the day, even when they weren't home. I could ride my bike to the grocery or the movie theater, the park or the library.

I was happy in our new house and happy that we had stayed in Irvington, close to Grandma and Grandpa. Some of my friends had moved away after the city of Indianapolis desegregated its public schools. Our lily white grade school was now home to black kids, too. Some kids were afraid of the newcomers, but I remembered Derrick and the birthday bike, so I wasn't afraid. Daddy said it was about time the schools were integrated. Sometimes he argued about it with Carol's father, before Carol's family moved out of town. Lee Ann's dad thought integration was a good thing, too. He had served in the army in Vietnam with lots of black soldiers. So Lee Ann and I tried to be nice to the new kids. One new girl in our class, Vernita Combs, was especially nice. She was small and quiet, wore glasses, and loved to read. She quickly came to fill the hole left in our group after Carol left.

My friendship with Vernita cost me some grief with other kids, of course. But I didn't care much. Lee Ann, Susan, Vernita, and I formed a world unto ourselves. Vernita was the only other kid I knew whose parents were divorced. She lived with her mother and two older brothers in an apartment in the projects—that's what the kids called the apartment complex where she lived. Vernita said her family's apartment was nice, but lots of the others weren't. Her mother worked in a bakery, and her oldest brother had an after-school job. They were saving money to buy a house someday.

I had not seen Mama since the final disastrous visit with the social worker, but I got letters from her and sometimes phone calls. At first the letters upset me, because I missed her so much. In that first year after she left, sometimes I missed her so much I thought I might just die of sadness. Some nights Grandma had to lie in my bed with her arms around me while I cried myself to sleep. Other nights Daddy sat on the bed strumming his guitar and singing softly the songs that Mama used to sing.

After the first year it got better. I still missed Mama, but the pain wasn't so sharp and new. Mostly, that is. Some days were still hard, even now, especially on holidays or at school pageants when all the other kids had their mothers with them. One time I saw Lee Ann and her mom sitting on the porch swing at their house. Mrs. Dawson was brushing Lee Ann's hair and they were both smiling, and it hurt so much I felt like I'd had the wind knocked out of me. Then Mrs. Dawson saw me standing there, watching them. She smiled and patted the seat beside her. When I sat down, she put an arm around me and one around Lee Ann, and for a minute I almost felt like I was hers.

Mama had left the farm in Kentucky and moved to California with a man named Noah. She seemed happy, painting pictures with words of her new life in a big house with lots of other people.

And, as it turned out, Mama was thinking a lot about race relations, too. She had joined a church in San Francisco, which surprised Daddy. Mama had never been interested in church when she lived with us. But this church was different, she explained. White people and black people all lived and worked together to build a better world. And, she explained, the pastor had helped her to quit using drugs. Daddy seemed happy about that.

"Someday I want you to come out here," Mama had written in March. "I want you to meet my new friends. I know you would love them. There are lots of kids. And we are doing amazing things— feeding hungry people and getting kids off the street."

Daddy shook his head and smiled when I read him Mama's letter. "At least she's off the drugs," he said. "I hope to God she's finally happy."

I hoped so, too.

That summer was glorious. Lee Ann, Susan, and I practically lived outside, riding bikes, climbing trees, playing kickball and kick the can with other kids in the neighborhood. Vernita wasn't part of the fun. She lived too far away to come over and play. I talked to her on the phone sometimes. In August, Vernita's older brother drove her to our house for my ninth birthday party. Mama sent me a beautiful skirt with all the colors of the rainbow and a funny card. Daddy bought me a record player of my own.

Mama's letters came regularly now. She wrote of weekend bus trips to Los Angeles, where her church had another temple—that's what she called it, Peoples Temple. She wrote of the church's leader, calling him Father and sometimes Dad. And then she began writing about a trip she had planned to a country in South America called Guyana. The church had built a farm there, and Mama was going to visit in the fall.

Daddy's brow furrowed when I told him about the farm in Guyana. "Oh Lord," he said, wringing his hands. "What has she gotten into now?"

He seemed relieved when he read in Mama's letter that the church was affiliated with the Disciples of Christ. We knew lots of people who were Disciples, and they weren't crazy or anything.

That fall, I started the fourth grade at School 57. I felt very grown up, moving to the older kids' wing of the building. Sometimes after school, Lee Ann or Susan came to my grandparents' house with me and we sat in Grandma's kitchen, eating pretzels, drinking Cokes, and telling Grandma about school.

Some days we rode our bikes to the drug store for ice cream, other days we rode to the park. One day we stopped at the railroad tracks to stare at bloodstains on the ground. A girl had run in front of the train the spring before and been killed.

"What do you think it's like to die?" Lee Ann wondered.

"Well, if you're a Christian you go to Heaven," Susan said.

"What if you're not a Christian?" I asked.

"Then you go to hell." She said it with such certainty, I believed her.

"Do you think that girl was a Christian?" I stared at the dark stain on the sidewalk.

"I know her family goes to church, so I'm sure she's in Heaven."

"Are we Christian?" I asked Daddy that night at dinner. His fork stopped midway to his mouth and he looked at me for a long minute before answering.

"Well, I was raised a Christian. So, I guess that makes me a Christian."

"What about me?"

"Well, if I'm a Christian that makes you a Christian, too."

I nodded, hoping he was right.

"Why do you ask?"

"Susan says if you're not a Christian, you go to hell when you die."

Daddy ran his hand through his hair before answering. "I'll tell you what I think, Judy. I think if you try your best to be a good person, then that's enough for God. I don't think God cares if a person is a Christian or a Jew or a Buddhist, as long as you try to do the right thing."

"But what if you're nothing?"

"What?"

"Like, what if you're not a Christian or a Jew or a Buddhist or anything?"

Daddy smiled. "I still think as long as you're trying to be a good person, you're okay."

"Okay."

"And, Judy, don't ever say that you're nothing, honey. Because you are the opposite of nothing. You, Sweet Judy, are everything."

10

Daddy and I were sitting on the front porch one evening in October. I was eating ice cream while he strummed his guitar. The fall breeze was warm, the leaves on the trees a symphony of reds, yellows, and golds.

Inside, the phone rang. I ran to answer it.

"Judy? Is that my Sweet Judy?"

"Mama!" I cried out, excited to hear her voice. I hadn't spoken to her since June.

Outside, Daddy stopped playing the guitar.

"How are you, baby?"

"I'm okay. How are you?"

"I'm better than okay. I'm great."

She sounded happy.

"How come you didn't call on my birthday?" I asked.

"Oh, honey, I'm sorry. I've been working so much the last few months, sometimes I don't know if I'm coming or going. Honestly, I meant to call. I just didn't get a chance to."

"Oh," I said. I felt a familiar knot forming in my stomach.

"Did you have a birthday party?" she asked.

"Yes."

"Was it fun?"

"It was okay."

In reality, the party had been wonderful. The whole day had been wonderful. Until I went to bed and realized Mama hadn't called to wish me a happy birthday.

"Did you get the skirt I sent?"

"Yes, Mama. It's pretty, thank you."

"I have one just like it, so when you wear it you can think of me, okay?"

"Okay."

She asked me about school and my friends, and told me what she'd done that day. Then, abruptly, she asked, "Is your daddy there? I need to talk to him."

I called Daddy in from the porch and sat down as he picked up the phone.

"Hey, Cassie. What's up?"

He listened for a minute, his brow creasing. Then he motioned me to go outside.

I sat on the porch by the screen door, listening.

"Absolutely not! There is no way, Cassie. No way."

Silence. Then, "I mean it. No. You are not taking her out of the country. Don't even think about it."

Another pause, then Daddy said, "Seriously, you can't take her. And, Cassie, I don't think you should be going, either. It sounds crazy."

A long pause, and then Daddy yelled into the phone, "God damn it, Cassie! I said no, and that's final. I have custody, and I will *not* let you take Judy to some godforsaken commune in Guyana."

He slammed the receiver down and stood still a moment. I could see his fists clenching from where I sat on the porch. Finally, he shook his shoulders and turned to see me watching him.

He sat down beside me on the porch step and drew me into his arms. "I'm sorry, honey. I shouldn't have yelled."

I leaned against him for a minute, and then put my hand on his cheek.

"Daddy? Don't let her take me, okay? I don't want to go away again."

I began to shake then, like I was freezing, even though it was warm outside. What if Mama came and took me away? Would Daddy be able to find me again? Or would I be gone forever?

I began crying then, my head buried in his chest. What would I do without Daddy? Without Grandma and Lee Ann? Would Mama know how to take care of me, now that I was nine? Would she help me with my homework, like Daddy? Would she make me mint cocoa like Grandma? Would she leave me again?

Daddy wrapped his arms around me tight while I cried.

"I don't want to go," I said, over and over again. "Don't let her take me away."

"I'm so sorry, baby," he crooned. "I'm sorry she took you before. I'm sorry I didn't stop her. I just didn't know she would do it. I really didn't think she would do it."

He lifted my chin to look straight in my eyes. "I promise you, Judy. I *promise* you that I will not let her take you again. I messed up last time. I won't do that again."

We sat on the porch like that for a long time. When it was time for bed, Daddy sat in the rocking chair in my room, playing his guitar until I fell asleep.

She was there on the porch, her arms opened wide, beautiful just like before. She smiled as she pulled me into a hug that was too tight. I struggled to breathe, to scream, but I couldn't make a noise. I jerked my head back to stare into her face, but now she didn't look like Mama at all. She had Mama's hair, but her eyes were huge and black, and her mouth a violent slash of red as she grinned at me.

"Away," she yelled, laughing hysterically. "Away we go."

I tried to scream again, to call for Daddy. But no sound came from my throat as Mama carried me down the sidewalk, away from home.

I woke to find Daddy still sitting in the rocking chair, the guitar on the floor beside him. His head rested in his hands. I thought at first he was sleeping, but then I heard low sobs. I climbed out of bed and into his lap and cried with him for a while. Then he carried me into his room and lay me on the bed, curled around me, and I fell asleep again.

The next day Daddy walked to school with me, left me at my classroom door, and went to talk to the principal.

"What's going on?" Susan asked. Daddy usually let me walk to school with her and Lee Ann.

"Mama called last night. She wants to take me away with her."

Susan took my hand and held it tightly. "Don't worry," she said, "your daddy won't let her do that again."

For the next few weeks, Daddy walked me to school every morning, and Grandma walked me home every afternoon. I did not go to recess with the rest of my class. Instead, I sat in the library under the watchful eye of Miss McInerny, the librarian. I did not go to the park or ride my bike with Lee Ann and Susan. I sat in Grandma's house, watching TV or reading. And outside my classroom, a security guard stood each day, scanning the hallway with his eyes.

The other kids in my class looked at me differently now. I'd become a freak . . . again. The girl with the crazy mom. The one whose parents were divorced. The one who'd been kidnapped and taken to a commune. For a year after Mama left, kids pointed at me, whispered behind my back. It seemed like no one else in the world had a mother who'd left. No one else made Mother's Day gifts for their grandma instead of their mom. No one else lived with their grandparents.

When we moved into our new house, I felt like I had turned a corner. I still didn't have a mother, but I did live in a house with my dad. I invited friends over sometimes for dinner and even for overnights, just like other girls in my class. I was normal, inconspicuous even. Now I was the oddball, again. All the normalcy I'd worked so hard to build was crumbling around me.

Susan and Lee Ann stuck up for me, of course. And after I told her about Mama, Vernita became my fiercest defender. One day in the lunchroom, a boy from another class started tiptoeing behind me with his hands raised, as if to snatch me. Other kids were laughing, and I fought the tears that were stinging my eyes. In a flash,

Vernita was out of her chair and in front of the boy. Before I could even see what was happening, she had punched him squarely in the stomach.

Teachers came running, and Vernita, the boy, and I were all called to the principal's office. In the end, Vernita had to write *I will not use my fists to solve my problems* a hundred times. But the boy got paddled.

≈ 11 ≈

On the Sunday afternoon before Thanksgiving, Lee Ann and I sat in my bedroom, cutting out turkeys and pumpkins from construction paper to make place settings. The sun was setting outside on a gray and cold day. When the phone rang, I ran out to the hallway to answer it, picking it up just as Daddy picked up the receiver downstairs.

"Kirk?" It was Grandpa. "That church Cassie joined, the one that moved to Guyana, is it Peoples Temple?"

"Yeah, I think that's it," Daddy answered. "Why?"

"I just heard on the news that some people in that church shot a congressman yesterday who went down there to check on them."

"What? Are you sure?"

"It was on the news just now. A congressman from California went down there with some reporters, and they shot him."

"Oh my God!"

"Is Cassie down there?"

"I don't know, Dad. I know she wanted to go. Oh, God."

"Daddy?" My voice caught in my throat. "Is Mama okay?"

"Hang up the phone, Judy. I'm sure your mother is okay. Come on downstairs and let's find out what's going on."

I ran downstairs, Lee Ann trailing behind me.

"What's going on?" she asked, pulling at my arm.

Daddy stood in front of the television set, dialing from one channel to the next until he found a news broadcast. A reporter sitting at a desk was talking about Peoples Temple and a U.S. congressman named Leo Ryan.

"The footage you are about to see is graphic," he warned solemnly. Then the scene cut away to an airstrip in a jungle. A cameraman was recording a group of men in a truck firing guns at some other people, who were running and screaming. Then, suddenly, the picture went to black fuzz.

"Daddy?" I whispered.

"Oh, baby." He flipped off the set and pulled me into his lap, cradling me there.

"Is Mama okay? Did those people shoot her?"

"No, baby," he crooned. "She wasn't shot. She wasn't there. I'm sure she's okay."

Behind him, Lee Ann stood staring, her eyes wide.

"How do you know?" I asked.

"I just know," he said. "If your mama was dead, I would know." He sounded sure.

"Why were those people shooting?"

"I don't know, baby. But don't you worry. It's going to be okay. Do you hear me?" He pulled back to look straight into my eyes. "It's going to be okay."

We walked Lee Ann home and stayed a few minutes while Daddy explained to Lee Ann's parents what we'd just seen. Mrs. Dawson looked frightened and pulled Lee Ann to her in a tight embrace.

"Let us know if we can do anything, Kirk," Mr. Dawson said, shaking Daddy's hand. "Anything at all. I still have friends in the army. Maybe they can find out something."

"Thanks, Dave. If you hear anything, will you give me a call?"

"Sure thing."

Lee Ann's family stood on their porch, watching us walk back to our house. Mrs. Dawson kept her arm wrapped tightly around her daughter.

"Daddy, is that where Mama wanted to take me?" I asked.

"I'm not sure, baby. I'm not sure of anything right now. But you're safe. You don't have to be afraid. You're safe here with me."

But I didn't feel safe. I didn't feel safe at all. I thought about the nightmare I'd had about Mama coming to take me away, and I felt vaguely guilty. What if she was dead, and I'd had that dream about her? I held Daddy's hand tightly, my eyes darting from bush to bush, afraid at any minute that someone might appear with a gun, just like in the TV report.

When we got home, Grandma and Grandpa were waiting on the front porch. Grandma hugged me, telling me everything was okay.

All afternoon, the telephone rang. People called, asking what we knew, what they could do to help. Daddy called information to get the telephone number of the Peoples Temple church in San Francisco, but nobody answered the phone there.

In the early evening, a news report came on the television. Daddy turned the sound up, and we heard the reporter say there were reports of a mass suicide in Jonestown, the place where Peoples Temple had built a compound in the jungle. Some people who had escaped told the police in Guyana that people in Jonestown had drunk poisoned Kool-Aid.

"Oh my God," Daddy whispered.

I started to cry, and Grandma pulled me onto her lap. "Now you listen to me, Judy," she said firmly, stroking my hair. "Your mother is fine. I'm sure she's fine. She probably wasn't even down there."

"But why . . ." I began.

"Honey, we don't know why or how or anything for sure. But I don't believe your mama would kill herself. She's got too much life in her. She wouldn't do that."

"Grandma's right," Daddy said. "Your mama loves you too much to kill herself. I'm sure she's all right."

I nodded, but I wasn't sure at all that Mama was all right. If she loved me too much to kill herself, then why had she left me? Why hadn't she called on my birthday? I felt guilty again, thinking those things. But I couldn't help it. I thought about how Mrs. Dawson had hugged Lee Ann on the porch and felt tears sting my eyes.

"Why don't you help me get some supper ready?"

Grandma rose and took my hand. "Come on, we'll make spaghetti."

We sat down to supper with the television blaring from the living room, listening for more news. My stomach churned, rebelling at the spaghetti and meatballs Grandma had made. After a few attempts, Grandma stopped trying to persuade me to eat.

By ten o'clock, we knew nothing more than we'd heard on the news earlier. Daddy sent me to bed, and Grandma came upstairs with me. She sat on the edge of my bed, holding my hand and promising that everything would be okay.

"Don't leave, okay?" I asked. I did not feel at all sleepy, and I didn't want to lay there all alone in my room.

"Okay, honey," she promised. "I'll stay right here."

"And wake me up if you find out anything about Mama, okay?"

"Of course," she said, her voice quiet and firm.

"Grandma?"

"Yes, Judy?"

"Do you think it will help if we say a prayer?"

I don't remember ever praying before then, but it seemed like the right thing to do.

"Yes, honey." She smiled at me, squeezing my hand. "I think that's the best thing we can do right now."

I got out of bed and knelt on the floor, like I'd seen Susan do sometimes. Clenching my hands together, I squeezed my eyes shut and said my first prayer.

"Dear God, please let my mama be okay. Please don't let her be dead. She's done some bad things, but she's not a bad person. And she's a Christian now," I added, thinking that might close the deal. "So please let her be okay."

I sat a moment longer but couldn't think of anything else to say.

"Amen," Grandma said firmly. "Now, climb back into bed and try to sleep. You've done the best thing you can right now."

I didn't sleep for a very long time. Downstairs I could hear the television drone on, and the phone ringing, and Daddy's voice. When I finally dozed off, I saw in my dreams the men in the truck, shooting at people. I heard Mama's voice cry out. *Please, God,* I prayed in my dream, *please let her be okay.*

When I woke in the early morning, Grandma was still there, curled around me in the bed, snoring softly. I tried to climb out of bed without waking her, but I guess she was sleeping badly, too.

"Are you okay?" she asked.

"I have to pee," I said.

She smiled at me as I walked to the door. I didn't have to pee, actually. I just wanted to get up.

"Let's go have some cereal," she said, sitting up and rubbing her eyes. Her clothes were wrinkled. She'd slept in them.

When we got to the kitchen, Daddy and Grandpa were already there, drinking coffee.

"Did she call?" I asked as soon as I saw them.

"No, honey, not yet." Daddy rose and hugged me. "She's probably really upset right now, and she needs some time to calm down."

I saw Grandpa shake his head briefly at Grandma.

"Okay, then," Grandma said firmly. "We're up, so let's have breakfast."

Grandma's solution to any crisis was food.

She poured cereal into a bowl for me and coffee into a mug for herself. I ate my Cheerios quietly, watching them all intently, trying to figure out if they knew something they weren't telling me.

At eight, the phone started ringing again. Everyone, it seemed, had heard about the shooting in Guyana and wanted to talk about it. But no one had anything new to offer about Mama. Daddy decided I should stay home from school for the day. I was glad of it. I couldn't imagine sitting in my class trying to pay attention, wondering if Mama was alive or dead. And I couldn't bear to have my classmates watching me, whispering again about my crazy mother.

At ten, Grandma rose, put her hands on her ample hips, and said firmly, "Judy, go get dressed. We're going to church to say some prayers."

I looked from her to Daddy, startled. I'd been to church sometimes with Grandma when we lived with her, but I hadn't been since Daddy and I had moved into our own house. I didn't have a new dress to wear.

Daddy smiled at Grandma and then said, "I think that's a good idea. Get dressed, sweetie, and go to church with Grandma."

"But, Daddy," I said, "what if . . ."

"If we hear anything, I will come and get you. I promise," he added.

Still, I hesitated.

"Judy." Daddy rose and took my hands in his. "Right now is exactly the time when you should be in church. The very best thing you can do for Mama right now is pray."

I stood a moment longer, letting this sink in. Grandma always said the answer to everything was prayer. But I'd never heard Daddy say anything like that. It scared me.

Finally, I nodded. "Okay, Daddy. I'll go pray."

If I prayed in a church, maybe that would be more helpful than praying in my room. God knew about church, after all. But he might not know about my room.

A little while later, Grandma and I walked into the sanctuary at Irvington United Methodist Church. I hadn't been there in a long time, and never on a Monday. The sanctuary was empty, except for Grandma and me.

We sat down in a pew near the front and Grandma patted my hand. "Go ahead, now," she said softly. "Say a prayer for your mama."

I squeezed my eyes closed and leaned toward the huge cross at the front of the church. "Please, God. Please, God. Please," I prayed over and over again. "Please let Mama be okay."

I didn't pray for the dead congressman or anyone else. I prayed for only Mama. I hoped that was okay with God.

When I opened my eyes, Grandma was leaned forward in the pew, her head resting on her hands. Her lips moved silently. I sat quietly, just watching her. Grandma went to church every Sunday. Surely, God would listen to her prayers.

When we got home, Daddy and Grandpa were in the living room.

"Did you hear . . ." Grandma started to say, but Daddy shook his head firmly.

He gave me a hug and told me to go upstairs and change clothes. I heard them whispering behind me as I climbed the stairs.

"Daddy," I said, turning back. "What's going on?"

He looked at me a long minute, then gestured for me to come back down. Pulling me into his lap, he said softly, "They're saying now that a lot more people died in Guyana."

I stared at him, searching his eyes carefully. "Mama?"

"No, honey, we don't know that. We don't even know if she was down there. So let's keep a positive attitude, okay? Unless we hear otherwise, we'll assume your mama didn't go to Guyana, and that she's okay."

"But why doesn't she call?" I asked.

"Probably she's upset, Judy, and scared. But she'll call. You'll see, it will be okay."

Daddy kept the television on all day, with the sound off, turning it up whenever the news came on. At first, he and Grandma tried to keep me from watching it, but after a while they gave up. And so I saw the pictures of bodies—men, women, and even some children, lying facedown on the ground, some with their arms around each other. At first, it was hard to watch, but then I began looking carefully, searching for Mama. I didn't see anyone who looked like her.

The news reporter said that more than four hundred bodies had been found. But several hundred people were missing. No one knew where they were. Had Mama escaped into the jungle? Was she lost somewhere, trying to get home to me? Why did she want to go to Guyana, anyway? Why did she belong to a church where people killed themselves? My head ached from so many questions.

In the middle of the afternoon, the doorbell rang and I ran to answer it. Standing on our front porch was a tall, thin woman with short, blond hair. Behind her stood a bald, paunchy man.

"Hello, Judy," the woman said. "Do you remember me?"

I shook my head.

"I'm your Grandma Pat . . . your mother's mother. We met once before, when you were a little girl."

"Pat." Daddy put his hand on my shoulder and opened the door wider. "Have you heard anything?"

The woman shook her head.

"Hello, Kirk," said the bald man, shaking Daddy's hand.

"Come in," Daddy said. "We've been watching the news, but so far we haven't heard anything about Cassie."

In the living room, Grandma and Grandpa shook hands with Mama's parents.

"Can I get you anything, Pat?" Grandma said. "You must be worried sick."

"No, thank you, Anne. I'm fine," the woman said. She didn't smile or return Grandma's quick hug. "Leave it to Cassandra to get involved in a mess like this."

Grandma took a step back and stared at her. "We don't know for sure if she is involved."

The woman shrugged and sat down in Daddy's chair. The bald man paced the living room floor.

"I called Senator Lugar's office yesterday and again today, but they don't know if she was there," he said.

"You called the senator's office on a Sunday?" Grandpa looked surprised.

"Hell, yes, I did," the man said. "That lunatic, Jim Jones, he started out here in Indianapolis. A lot of people followed him to California when he went. And I'm betting a lot of the ones dead are from Indiana. Lugar's office was open, all right. They just don't know anything yet."

"John knows the senator, actually," Mama's mother said, smiling. "They've played golf together."

Daddy just looked at her, then shook his head.

"When's the last time you heard from Cassie?" he asked, looking from her to the man.

"Not since John's stroke," the woman said. "She hasn't written or called since then. Of course, she wouldn't. She's never been concerned about our feelings. She's never even sent a Christmas card."

Daddy simply stared at her.

"We haven't done the best job," the bald man started to say, but his wife cut him off.

"We've done everything we could for her, John. She's just impossible. She always has been. She's never worried about anyone but herself. She's a spoiled, selfish brat."

"Get out!"

Everyone stared at Daddy.

"I mean it, Pat. Get out of my house! Cassie might be . . . She's in trouble, and all you can do is bitch about how selfish *she* is? God! No wonder she's such a mess." Daddy was shaking.

The woman rose gracefully and brushed her sleeve with one manicured hand.

"Well, I see that some things have not changed," she said, gazing steadily at my father. "Come on, John. We're obviously not welcome here."

With that, she walked out the front door and down the steps. Her husband stood a moment watching her, then reached for Daddy's hand again.

"I'm sorry, Kirk," he said. "She is worried about Cassie, she just doesn't know how to show it. I'll call you if I hear anything."

"Thanks, John. I'll call you if we hear anything, too."

Daddy closed the door behind them and turned to me. "I'm sorry, honey, that you had to hear that. She's an awful woman."

I nodded. "Mama said she was mean."

Daddy hugged me. I could feel him still shaking. "She *is* mean. And I think that's why your mama has such a hard time. She never felt safe or loved."

"Not even with us, Daddy?"

He sat down and pulled me onto his lap. "Well, I think for a while she did. But your mama . . . she's always looking for something that she can't find."

I nodded again, even though I didn't really understand.

"Come on, Judy." Grandma held out her hand. "Let's start dinner. Do you want to make a meat loaf?"

Like I said, Grandma's solution to everything was food.

I went to bed that night with Grandma holding my hand. We still hadn't heard anything from Mama. I prayed as I lay in bed, my eyes squeezed shut, *Please, God. Please. Please let my mama be okay.*

❧ 12 ❧

I didn't go to school the next day, either. Daddy went into his office because he had a client who needed to see him. Before he went, he walked with me to Grandma and Grandpa's house. I held his hand tightly. As we walked down Ohmer Avenue, we heard a lot of noise, far more noise than we usually heard in our quiet neighborhood. In front of the Missions Building across the street from my grandparents' house, several large vans were parked on the lawn. Men with cameras and microphones jostled for position in front of the building's sign.

"What's that?" I asked, staring.

"Those are news people," Daddy said, grimacing. "They want to know if the people at the Missions Building know anything about what happened in Guyana."

"Do you think they do?"

"What?" Daddy wasn't paying attention to me. He was watching the camera crews.

"Do you think the people in that building know what happened?"

"I doubt it, honey," he said. "They're probably just as confused as the rest of us."

Grandma opened her front door before we even knocked. "Come in," she said, glancing across the street at the crowd of reporters.

She'd made pancakes for breakfast. I tried to eat one, but my stomach felt like I'd swallowed a big rock.

"Don't let her go over there," Daddy said, nodding his head toward the chaos across the street.

"As if I would." Grandma sounded indignant. "We're going to bake cookies today. And maybe we'll do a jigsaw puzzle."

"Thanks, Mom." Dad kissed her cheek, then bent to kiss my head.

"I won't be gone long," he said. "I should be back before noon."

I nodded.

"It's going to be okay, Judy." He'd said that about a million times now, as if saying it would make it so.

"I know, Daddy."

After he left, Grandma bustled around the kitchen, pulling bowls and spoons and baking sheets from cabinets. "How about we make chocolate chip?" she said, nodding at me.

I shrugged. I didn't want to make cookies. I didn't want to be there. I wanted . . . Mama. I wanted her with the sharp, painful longing I hadn't felt in a long time. I remembered dancing in the rain with her, the way she sang while we kneaded bread dough, how she kissed my nose and called me her Sweet Judy. I wanted my mama back, even just for a little while. I wanted to know she was okay, not dead in a jungle in Guyana with a bunch of crazy people. I wanted to sit in her lap and smell her hair and be safe again.

Instead, I helped Grandma make cookies. I stirred as she measured flour and sugar and butter into the bowl. When the first batch was in the oven, the phone rang. Grandma went to her bedroom to answer it, even though there was a phone in the kitchen. I knew she was afraid it might be bad news and didn't want me to hear.

I tiptoed down the hall and stood outside her bedroom door, listening. But apparently, it was someone who didn't know any more than we did.

"I don't know," Grandma was saying. "We're still waiting to hear something . . . anything."

I walked into the front room and stared at the men standing on the lawn in front of the Missions Building. Then I walked out the front door and across the street to the big glass door of the building. I pulled open the door and walked inside. If someone here knew what was going on, I would make them tell me.

A smartly dressed black woman sat at the reception desk, her eyes trained on the herd of reporters out front.

"Excuse me," I said.

She started, then smiled at me.

"What can I do for you?" she asked.

"My mama was in that church," I said. "And I want to know if she died."

The woman stared at me, wide-eyed. Then she rose and walked from behind her desk to kneel before me.

"What's your name?" she asked.

"Judy Webster," I said.

"And your mother was in Peoples Temple?"

I nodded.

"Well, Judy, my name is Clara. And I wish I could tell you what you need to know. But right now, we just don't know very much. We don't know who was there and who wasn't. I'm very sorry."

Tears stung my eyes and I tried to blink them back.

"Do you live around here?" The woman took my hands in hers.

"I live on University," I said.

"How about I walk you home?" she asked. "Your family must be worried about you."

She stood and took my hand, leading me out the glass door to where the news people were.

"Judy!"

Across the street, my grandmother stood on the porch, waving.

"That's my grandma," I said.

Clara walked with me across the street to Grandma.

"Where have you been? You scared the life out of me!"

"Judy came to ask if we knew anything about her mother," Clara said softly. "I told her that we just don't know anything yet."

Grandma stared at her, holding my hand tightly.

"Your daughter belongs to Peoples Temple?" Clara asked.

"My daughter-in-law," Grandma said. "That is, my former daughter-in-law. Judy's mother."

"What is her name?" Clara asked.

"Cassie Webster," Grandma said.

"Well, if I hear anything, anything at all, I'll come tell you."

"Oh, thank you!" Grandma took Clara's hand and shook it. "Thank you so much. We're just so worried."

"I understand." Clara shook her head sadly. She leaned down to look me in the face. "If I hear anything, Judy, I'll come tell you right away. And I will pray for your mother, okay?"

I nodded. The lump in my throat kept my voice inside.

Grandma and I watched as she walked back across the street, past the crowd on the lawn, and into the building.

"What a lovely woman," Grandma said. "And just what did you think you were doing?"

"Daddy said the news people are here because they think the people in the building know what's happening."

"Oh, honey." Grandma knelt and hugged me. "Don't you worry, okay? Your mother is going to be fine."

I nodded, but I didn't believe her.

After lunch, Daddy still hadn't come back. Grandma had the television on, with the sound off. Every time a news bulletin aired, we watched silently. The number of dead grew all day . . . first four hundred, then six hundred, then more. After a while, she stopped telling me that Mama was okay. I think she stopped believing it, too.

Just before two, someone knocked on the door. Grandma rose to answer it. Then she gasped.

"Cassie! Thank God! Oh, thank God! Are you okay?"

She opened the door wide and pulled Mama in from the front porch. "Oh my God! Oh my God! Oh, thank God!"

Mama stood still as Grandma hugged her tightly. I sat on the couch, watching. Mama was here. Mama was alive. Mama was okay, just like I'd prayed for. But I couldn't make myself get up, run to her, or say anything. I just sat and watched while Grandma hugged her and cried.

"Where's Kirk?" Mama asked, pulling back from Grandma's embrace.

"He's downtown. Cassie, we've been out of our minds. Where have you been? Are you okay?"

Mama's eyes found me, huddled on the couch. "Judy? Oh my God, Judy! My Sweet Judy."

She ran and dropped to the floor in front of me, scooping me into her arms.

"Sweet Judy," she crooned, again and again. "My Sweet Judy." I felt her tears fall onto my neck. "Thank God you're okay. Oh, thank God."

I clung to her, trying hard to understand that she was really here. Mama, who I hadn't seen for so long, who I thought was dead or lost in a jungle in South America, Mama was here, holding me tight and crying and shaking all over.

"Mama," I whispered finally, touching her gold hair.

"Cassie," Grandma said, pulling at Mama's shoulder. "Are you all right? Where have you been?"

Finally, Mama sat back on her haunches, still holding my hand tightly, and looked up at Grandma.

"I've been in hell, Anne," she said.

Grandma stared at her in silence. Then she asked, "Were you in California? We thought maybe you'd gone down there ... to Guyana. And we thought ... oh, Lord, Cassie! We thought you might be dead!"

Mama's eyes darted around the room. "I might still be dead, Anne," she said. "If they find me, I *will* be dead."

"Who? If who finds you?" Grandma's eyes widened.

"The government, the CIA," Mama said. "They're killing us all." Grandma sank into a chair. "What are you talking about?"

"They're killing us, Anne," Mama insisted. "They sent down that congressman, and then they killed him to make us look crazy. And then, oh, God, Anne. They killed us! They killed everyone down there, even the babies."

Grandma just looked at her as if she was crazy.

"You have to hide me," Mama continued. "They're after us, all of us. They want us all dead."

"Hush, now," Grandma said softly. "You're scaring Judy."

And that was true. I was scared. Why was the government after Mama? Were they after me, too? Why did they kill those babies?

Mama's eyes were huge, staring at the wall above my head. Tears spilled down her cheeks as she shook her head.

"You don't know," she said. "You just don't know."

"Come on." Grandma pulled Mama up by her arm. "Let's go in the kitchen and have some coffee. You look like you could use some."

Mama allowed herself to be pulled into the kitchen, but she clung tightly to my hand. Her eyes darted about the room as if she was looking for something, or someone.

We sat at the kitchen table and Grandma poured two cups of coffee. She set out the plate of cookies we'd made and told Mama to eat some.

"We were so worried," she said, eyeing Mama cautiously. "Why didn't you call us and let us know you were okay?"

"I couldn't, Anne. My phone was probably bugged. All our phones are bugged."

"What's 'bugged'?" I asked.

"Never mind," Grandma said, giving Mama a firm look. "I'm just glad you're here."

We sat in silence for a moment, while Mama ate a cookie. Then Grandma rose. "I have to call Kirk," she said. "He's been out of his mind with worry."

Mama just nodded and reached for another cookie. She was eating like she was half starved. I sat watching her while Grandma dialed the phone.

"Kirk? It's Mom. And everything is okay. Cassie is here. . . . Yes, she got here a few minutes ago. She's fine. . . . Yes, honey, she's fine. . . . Okay, we'll wait for you. Drive carefully."

She smiled as she hung up the phone. "He's coming right away. Oh, Cassie, he's been so worried. We've all been so worried."

Mama didn't answer. She seemed nervous, like she was waiting for something bad to happen. It made me nervous, just watching her.

"Good gracious, honey. You look starved," Grandma said as Mama took another cookie. "Let me make you a sandwich. You need something more than cookies."

Mama smiled at her then. "Thanks, Anne. I guess I forgot to eat this morning."

So Grandma made a grilled cheese sandwich and found some potato salad in the fridge. Mama ate everything Grandma put in front of her. I simply watched her eat. It had been years since I'd seen her. I'd forgotten how pretty she was, even now, with her blond hair hanging limp around her face and dark circles sagging under her eyes.

"Mama?"

"Yes, Sweet Judy?"

"I prayed for you."

Mama's green eyes filled with tears and she took my hand. "Thank you, sweetie. I'm sure what kept me safe were your prayers."

"Mom?" Daddy's voice rang from the front room.

"In here," Grandma called back.

Daddy rushed into the room and stood, staring at the three of us. Then he dropped to his knees, right there on the linoleum floor, and cried. I ran to him and put my arms around his neck. I'd only seen Daddy cry once before.

After a minute, he ran his hand across his eyes and hugged me. Then he walked to the table and draped his arms around Mama.

"Thank God," he whispered. "I was so scared."

Mama leaned into him, letting her head rest on his chest. "Hey, Kirk," she said softly. "I'm sorry I worried you."

Daddy sat down at the table and took Mama's hands. "Where have you been, Cassie? Why didn't you call?"

Before Mama could answer, Grandma rose and said, "Come on, Judy. Let's let your folks talk for a bit."

"But, Grandma . . ."

Daddy smiled at me and said, "Go on, honey. Your mama and I have some things we need to talk about."

So I went back to the living room with Grandma and she turned on the television to afternoon cartoons.

"You wait here," she said. "I have to call Grandpa and let him know your mother's okay."

She walked back to her bedroom and closed the door. I sat for a minute, staring at the television without really seeing it. Then I got up and tiptoed down the hall toward the kitchen. I stopped outside the door and listened.

"It was the most beautiful thing I've ever been part of," Mama was saying. Her voice sounded tired. "A truly integrated community, everyone helping everyone, it was just beautiful. And Jim Jones was the most wonderful man, Kirk. Honestly, he was the most loving man I've ever known. He would never have done this. It had to be the CIA. They've been after us for so long."

"But, Cassie," Daddy said. "They're saying on the news it was a mass suicide."

"No!" Mama's voice was sharp. "I don't believe that. You don't understand, you just don't know how bad it's been. The government planted spies in the church, they were watching us all the time. We knew when that congressman went down it would be bad. He took a bunch of defectors with him, troublemakers is what they are. And now look what they've done."

She started to cry. I could hear her soft sobbing. So I ran to her and put my arms around her neck.

"Don't cry, Mama. Please don't cry. Daddy and I still love you."

She clung to me and cried harder.

"Have you called your parents?" Daddy asked, patting her back.

She shook her head. "Hell no," she said. "They'd probably turn me in to the feds."

"They were here yesterday, Cassie. They . . . well, your dad was really worried. You should call him."

She just shook her head again.

"What am I going to do now?" she asked. "Where will I go? Everyone I knew, my whole family is gone."

"We're not gone, Cassie," Daddy said. "Judy and I are right

here. And my folks, they'll help. You'll stay with us until you get things sorted out."

She stared at him, tears dripping from her chin.

"Really, Kirk? You'd let me stay with you?"

"Of course you'll stay with us. You're Judy's mama and . . . and you'll stay with us."

"Thank you," she whispered, covering his hand with hers.

Grandma came into the kitchen and announced that Grandpa was on his way home. "He's closed the garage for the day, and he's stopping at the store to get some things for dinner. We're going to have a nice welcome-home dinner, just the five of us. Unless you want to invite your parents, Cassie?"

"Thank you, Anne. That's sweet of you, but I don't think . . . I can't tell you . . ." She started crying again.

Grandma patted her back and said, "There, now. It's okay. Why don't you lie down for a while? You look exhausted. Now, don't argue, you need some rest. You look like you haven't slept in days."

Mama let herself be pulled toward the bedroom that had been mine once, when Daddy and I had moved in with my grandparents after Mama left. At the door, she stopped and turned.

"You won't leave, will you?" she asked, looking at Daddy.

"No, Cassie. I'll stay right here. It's going to be okay. You get some rest."

I sat at the table next to Daddy and he took my hand.

"She's going to be okay," he said. "She's just tired and upset, and she needs to rest."

"Daddy, what's the CIA?"

Daddy grimaced and shook his head. "It's like the president's police force, honey. But don't worry, they're not after Mama. She's not thinking clearly because she's so upset. She'll calm down once she's had some rest."

13

Daddy was right about the CIA. They did not come for Mama. But he was wrong about Mama. She didn't calm down, not even after she'd rested a lot.

She came to stay at our house with Daddy and me after dinner that night. I showed her the yard and the tree where Daddy was building me a tree house. I showed her my room and played some records for her on my record player. Then Daddy showed her the guest room, where we had a daybed and a television for company.

Mama smiled and nodded and looked at everything, but she seemed like she wasn't really hearing anything we said. Her eyes darted constantly. She startled at every little noise. She didn't sit in one place more than a few minutes before moving someplace else.

At nine o'clock, she said she was so tired she thought she might just die. That scared me. So when she went to bed in the guest room, I went with her. And I held her hand until she fell asleep, just like Grandma had held mine while we worried about whether Mama was okay. Then I sat for a long time just watching her sleep. Finally, Daddy told me it was time to go to bed.

"Will she be okay?" I asked as he closed the door to the guest room.

"Yes, honey," he said. "She'll be fine."

Daddy stayed home from work the next day, and I stayed home from school again. Daddy made pancakes and I went to wake Mama. She was whimpering in her sleep, and when I touched her shoulder, she sat up like she'd been hit by lightning and swung her arm at me. "No!" she yelled.

I jumped back, my hands in front of my face, afraid she would hit me. But she dropped her hands when she saw me. "Oh, Sweet Judy," she said. "I'm sorry! Mama is so sorry. I was having a bad dream and I thought . . . well, I'm just really sorry. Are you okay?"

I nodded. "Daddy's making pancakes," I said cautiously.

She smiled at me and held open her arms, but I backed out of the room, turned on my heel, and ran back down the stairs and into the kitchen.

"Hey, what's wrong?" Daddy asked when he saw me.

"I don't . . . I . . . What's wrong with her, Daddy?"

He knelt in front of me and took my face in his hands. "Your mama has been through a terrible, terrible experience, honey. She needs some time to rest and heal. But she'll get better, you'll see. Are you okay?"

I nodded.

Mama padded barefoot down the stairs. "Judy? Honey, are you okay? I'm sorry I scared you."

"It's okay, Mama," I said, leaning into Daddy's chest.

"No, it's not okay, and I'm sorry." Mama sat on the floor in front of me and reached for my hand. "I was having a really bad dream, and I didn't know it was you."

"It's okay," I repeated.

Her beautiful green eyes filled with tears and she shook her head. I felt bad for her then, so I put my arms around her neck cautiously. She pulled me into her lap and held me so tight I could hardly breathe.

"How about some breakfast?" Daddy stood and waved toward a plate piled high with pancakes. After a long minute, Mama let me go.

We ate at the kitchen table. Daddy and I both watched Mama as she ate her pancakes. Her eyes constantly strayed toward the back door. Finally, Daddy patted her hand and said, "It's okay, Cassie. You're safe here. No one is coming after you."

She simply shook her head again.

"I called Rhonda last night," Daddy said. "She's coming over this afternoon to see you."

"Oh no, Kirk," Mama said. "I can't. I don't feel like seeing anyone. Not yet."

Daddy talked to her the way he talked to me sometimes when I was afraid. "Come on, Cassie. It's Rhonda, she's your best friend. Or, at least she was your best friend. She's been really worried about you, and she just wants to see you."

Rhonda did come that afternoon, carrying a bunch of daisies, a bottle of wine, and her two-year-old son, Jason. She hugged Mama, the baby squished between them.

"God, Cassie, we were so worried about you. Are you okay?"

Mama pulled back slightly and tried to smile. "I'm okay," she said softly. She reached out to touch Jason's cheek. "He's beautiful," she said.

"Yeah, he is, isn't he?" Rhonda smiled. "He's my angel."

She turned to me then. "Hey, squirt," she said. "How are you doing? I'll bet you're glad your mom is home."

I nodded and tried to smile.

Daddy walked into the kitchen and smiled at us all. "I'm heading for the store," he announced. "Is there anything you want, Cassie?"

Mama shook her head. "I'm okay, Kirk. Thanks."

"Okay, well, I won't be gone long. Are you staying awhile?" he asked Rhonda.

"Sure." She grinned. "I'll be here awhile. We have lots of catching up to do."

Daddy kissed the top of my head, then he kissed Mama's head, too. That surprised me.

"Back in a bit," he said, closing the back door behind him.

Rhonda handed Mama the bottle of wine. "I brought refreshments," she said, laughing.

"Oh, no, thanks." Mama shook her head. "I don't drink anymore."

Rhonda stared at her in disbelief. "Not at all?"

"No," Mama said. "Father says it's a waste of time and money."

"Father?" Rhonda looked confused.

"Reverend Jones . . . Jim," Mama said. "We call him Father. Or, well, we did call him that."

She sat down at the table and put her head in her hands. Rhonda looked at me, her eyes wide, then sat down beside her and draped her arm over Mama's shoulders.

"It's okay, Cassie," she said softly. "You're going to be okay now."

Jason squirmed on her lap, then reached for one of Mama's dangly earrings.

"No, baby," Rhonda said, pulling his hand away. "Those aren't for you."

She put the baby on the floor and he toddled toward me, his hands stretched out in front of him.

"He loves coming to see you," Rhonda said, smiling at me.

"Can I give him a cookie?"

Rhonda nodded. "But just one, okay?"

I got an Oreo cookie for Jason, and he sat down on the floor and began eating it at once.

"So, no wine for you? Do you mind if I have a glass?" Rhonda asked Mama.

"No, I don't mind." Mama rose and began looking through the cabinets for a glass.

"They're here," I said, pulling a wineglass from a shelf. Then I got the corkscrew from a drawer. Mama smiled as she took it from me. "Thanks, sweetie."

She poured red wine into the glass and set it on the table. Then she stood a minute, looking at the glass.

"Oh, what the hell," she said. She took another glass from the cabinet and poured herself some wine, then sat at the table with Rhonda.

"Good girl," Rhonda said, smiling. "You deserve a drink, after everything you've been through."

Mama took a sip and closed her eyes, smiling slightly. Then she took a long drink from the glass. "God, I'd forgotten how much I love a good cabernet," she said. She seemed to relax in her chair a bit, and smiled at Rhonda.

"So," she said, "how old is your angel?"

"He turned two in August," Rhonda said, smiling at the blond toddler whose face was now smeared with chocolate.

"He's really beautiful," Mama said. "Are you married?"

Rhonda nodded. "I married Pete Granger; do you remember him? He played in that band we used to go see at the Vogue. Tall, blond, very good-looking . . ."

Mama shook her head. "I don't remember," she said. "But good for you. Are you happy?"

Rhonda nodded and sipped her wine. "I'm really happy," she said. "Life is good."

They sat in silence for a minute. I looked from Mama to Rhonda, remembering how we used to play in the cardboard houses they made. Rhonda was the same as always, but Mama was . . . different now.

"How about you, Cassie? How are you? We were so scared for you."

Mama shook her head. "I don't know how I am, Rhonda," she said softly. "I feel like I'm in a bad dream and I can't wake up."

"Well, God knows, it's a nightmare," Rhonda said, patting her hand. "But it's over now, and you're okay. I just thank God you weren't down there. I just . . . I don't understand how all those people could kill themselves like that. And the babies . . ." Her voice trailed off as she watched Jason with his cookie.

"I don't think they killed themselves," Mama said. "I don't believe that."

"But the news said . . ."

"I don't care what the news says," Mama said firmly. "I knew those people. They wouldn't just kill themselves. Good Lord, Rhonda, they were building a paradise down there. Honestly, I saw the pictures. I talked to people who were there. It was beautiful, everyone living and working together. And they had a school and a nursery and . . . they didn't kill themselves," she finished, her voice flat. "They just couldn't have."

Rhonda didn't answer at first. She sipped her wine and watched Mama carefully.

"So, what do you think happened?" she finally asked.

"It was the government," Mama whispered. "The CIA or the special forces or something. They were after us for a long time, because we were socialists, you know. And if enough people learned the truth, the government wouldn't stand."

Rhonda stared at Mama. "Is that what you really think?"

Mama nodded, then reached for the wine bottle and poured more wine into her glass and Rhonda's.

"They bugged the church," she said. "They bugged our phones. They spread lies about us. It was terrible. And now . . ." She shook her head again. "Now, they're all gone, all my friends, my family. They're all dead."

Rhonda reached out and held Mama's hand. "Not all your friends and family are gone, honey. I'm here. Judy's here. Kirk's here. We're here for you."

"Thanks," Mama said, her voice so soft I could hardly hear her.

"More!"

Jason's demand made us all jump.

"More cookie?"

"No, sweetie," Rhonda said, pulling a wet wipe from her bag to wipe his face. "No more cookies."

"More cookie! More cookie!" His voice rose an octave.

Rhonda sighed. "Oh, all right. One more," she said, handing him another Oreo.

"Cassie," she said as she sat back down at the table, "how did you get involved in that church? I mean, you never went to church when you were here."

Mama took a long drink from her glass and stared at a spot on the wall behind Rhonda's head.

"I was pretty much a mess when I hit San Francisco," she said. "After I lost Judy, I went back to the farm, but it wasn't the same without her there. And Glen . . . well, he turned out to be a pig. So,

I left the farm with a guy named Noah, a really interesting guy. He was smart and funny, and we did okay at first. But, we were doing a lot of acid. And Noah started with heroin. And then, he over-dosed."

"Oh, God, Cassie, I'm sorry," Rhonda said.

"I was a mess," Mama said. "I didn't know very many people out there and I didn't have a job. I didn't know what I was going to do. And one day, I thought, *Fuck it. It's all over anyway. Just end it and be done.*"

Rhonda stared at her and then turned to me. "Judy, why don't you take Jason into the living room and play?"

Mama nodded. "That's a good idea, honey. Why don't you do that?"

I didn't want to leave. I wanted to stay and hear what Mama would say next, what she wanted to end. But I knew better than to argue. I pulled Jason up by the hand, got him another cookie, and led him into the living room. I sat down in the doorway, listening as best I could to Mama and Rhonda.

"So, did you try to . . . Oh, Cassie, honey, I'm so sorry."

"I took a whole bottle of pills," Mama said, "and woke up in the emergency room."

"Why didn't you call me?"

"I was a mess, Rhonda. I didn't want anyone to see me like that."

"So, what happened?"

"Well, when I woke up, there was a woman sitting by my bed, a black woman about my age. She told me her name was Yolanda and said if I wanted help to get off the drugs, she knew someone who could help me. Then she started talking about this church, Peoples Temple, and all the work they were doing with drug ad-dicts and homeless people. God, Rhonda, it sounded like heaven on earth. And I wanted to be part of that. I wanted to be part of something. So, when I was released from the hospital, Yolanda took me up to Ukiah to meet Jim Jones."

"What was he like?"

"Oh." Mama's voice sounded far away. "He was the most amazing man. Really, you just wouldn't believe it. He took my hands and looked me right in the eyes and promised me that I could get well. He said they had work for me to do, so I had to get well. And honest, Rhonda, it was like he knew me. He really knew me. Like he could see my whole fucked-up life and all the stupid things I'd done, and he loved me anyway.

"So, I moved into one of the church houses and I went cold turkey."

"Wow," Rhonda said. "That must have been really hard."

"It was awful," Mama agreed. "But Yolanda stayed with me the whole time. And not just her, other people stayed, too. And they helped me. They held my head while I threw up. They fed me and took care of me. They never left me alone, and they just kept telling me I could do it. And one day, I knew I could. I just knew I could do it.

"After I got clean, I moved into an apartment in San Francisco with Yolanda and three other girls. We worked at the San Francisco temple. At first, I spent a lot of time on cleaning crew. Sweeping and mopping, doing dishes, helping in the kitchen. After a while, I got promoted to answering the phone and doing office work.

"It was so great, Rhonda. Really, it was so great. I mean, I didn't get a lot of sleep . . . sometimes we'd go two or three days without sleeping. But it was great just being part of it all."

"How did everyone end up in Guyana?" Rhonda asked.

Jason was toddling around the living room now, leaving chocolate handprints on everything he touched. I pulled some old magazines from the coffee table and found a pen, and let him draw on the magazines, all the while listening carefully to the conversation in the kitchen.

"Some people in the media were out to get us," Mama said. "They hated Jim for what he stood for, for helping the poor and having blacks and whites living together. It's such a racist world." She sighed.

"So they started printing all these lies about the church in the newspapers, and then some people who used to be part of the church and left, well, they got involved and started telling more lies. Honestly, it was awful. Scary, really. They just lied and lied, and the media ate it all up.

"So Jim decided it was time to move the church down to Guyana. They started working on a place down there a few years ago, and Jim decided it would be safer for us to be there."

"How come you didn't go?" Rhonda asked.

"I wanted to," Mama said. "But Jim wanted me to stay and work at the church in San Francisco for a while longer. He knew I wanted to bring Judy with me when I went down, and he said he was working on making that happen."

"Thank God it didn't happen!" Rhonda said.

"I guess so." Mama's voice was soft.

"You guess so? God, Cassie, think about it! If you'd taken Judy down there, you'd both be dead."

I leaned my head back against the wall and watched Jason scribbling furiously. I felt like I might throw up. I'd been so worried about Mama being there, but I'd never thought about being there myself. I closed my eyes, trying to imagine what it would have been like to live in the jungle, to be so far away from Daddy and Grandma and Grandpa and Lee Ann, to drink poisoned Kool-Aid and die like all those other people.

"I might still be dead."

"What?" Rhonda sounded alarmed.

"If the CIA finds me, they'll kill me, Rhonda. They're killing all of us." Mama's voice was tired.

"Oh, Cassie, come on. You don't really believe that, do you?"

"It's true," Mama insisted. "They killed hundreds of people already, don't you think they'll finish us all off if they can?"

I heard Daddy's car pull into the driveway, and then the back door opened.

"How are you girls doing?" he asked.

"We're okay," Rhonda said. But she didn't sound very sure of that.

"Good," Daddy said. "Where's Judy?"

"She's in the living room with Jason," Rhonda said. "Speaking of which, I'd better be getting him home for his nap."

She appeared in the hallway and stopped when she saw me sitting there. She shook her head and put a finger to her lips, then reached for my hand to pull me up.

"Don't you worry about what she says," she whispered, hugging me close. "She's being kind of paranoid, but she'll come out of it."

She picked Jason up and carried him back into the kitchen. "Let's wash your hands, kiddo," she said. "I'm afraid he's left a cookie mess in your living room."

"That's okay," Daddy said. "We've had cookie messes before."

I followed Rhonda into the kitchen and watched as she rinsed Jason's hands and face. Mama still sat at the table, her wineglass empty, her eyes dull.

"What are you guys doing tomorrow?" Rhonda asked. "You're welcome to join us for Thanksgiving dinner. I even bought a turkey."

"Thanks, Rhonda, but we're going to my folks'," Daddy said.

"Well, let's plan on getting together soon, okay?"

Mama just nodded. She didn't look up when Rhonda and Jason left. She simply turned the empty wineglass in her hand and stared at the table. She looked very sad.

"Mama?" I touched her hand gently. "I'm glad you didn't go down there."

She smiled at me then and pulled me into a hug. "Me too, honey."

I don't know if she meant it or not, but I did. I was glad she hadn't gone.

Daddy ordered Chinese takeout for dinner, and I ate cashew chicken while Mama picked at her plate.

"Do you have anything to drink?" she asked Daddy.

"I've got some wine," Daddy said. "It's white, is that okay?"

Mama nodded and smiled as he poured a glass for her.

After dinner, she went to bed, even though it wasn't even eight o'clock.

"Is she okay, Daddy?" I asked, watching her walk unsteadily up the stairs. She seemed so tired, so old, so different from the Mama I remembered.

"She'll be okay," Daddy said. "She just needs lots of rest right now."

The phone rang, and Daddy answered it.

"Hey, John," he said. "Yes, she's doing okay. She's already gone to bed. No, I don't think so. She says she's clean. Yeah, I believe her. I think she's just exhausted. Yeah, that sounds okay. Sure, I'll talk to you tomorrow.

"That was your Grandpa John," he said. "I think he's coming tomorrow evening to see your mama."

"Is that woman coming, too?" I asked. I thought that probably wouldn't make Mama very happy.

"No, honey." Daddy smiled. "Your grandmother isn't coming with him. John and I thought it would be better if she didn't."

"Daddy, is Mama going to live with us?"

"No, baby." Daddy sat down on the floor beside me. "She'll stay with us until she gets better."

"What will happen then?"

"Well, then I guess she'll get a job and an apartment and . . . and she'll be better."

I nodded. "Maybe she can live with Rhonda."

"Is it okay, having her here?" Daddy asked.

"It's okay," I said. But it wasn't, really.

For so long, I'd wanted Mama to come home. I'd wished for it, dreamed about it, wanted it more than anything. But now that she was here, I wasn't sure if I wanted it anymore. She wasn't like I remembered. The Mama I knew had smiled and laughed a lot. She'd told funny stories and danced around the living room. Not like the fragile, scared woman she was now. This was a Mama I didn't know.

～ 14 ～

We went to Grandma's in the morning to help cook Thanksgiving dinner. Daddy and Grandpa sat in the living room watching television while Grandma bustled around the kitchen, giving orders.

"Cassie, will you put those cranberries on to boil? Judy, where are you? Come here and help me with these plates."

Grandma chopped onions and celery and mixed them with bread crumbs. Then she poured chicken broth from a can over the entire mess and began smashing it together with her hands. Finally, she took a large spoon and began ladling the stuffing into the huge turkey sitting on the counter. Mama watched for a minute, then excused herself.

"Cassie? Are you okay?" Grandma called after her.

"I'm fine, Anne." She didn't sound fine.

"Oh, Lord, I forgot she's a vegetarian," Grandma said, wiping her hands on her apron.

I followed Mama into the living room. "Are you a vegetarian, Mama? What's a vegetarian?"

She smiled at me. "A vegetarian is someone who doesn't eat meat. I used to be one. I do eat meat sometimes now, but . . . but I can't stand looking at that carcass!" She shivered as if she were cold.

Daddy laughed and said, "You don't have to eat it, Cassie. Not if you don't want to."

Mama smiled at him. "I'll be okay once she puts the damned thing in the oven."

After we'd watched the Macy's parade on TV for a while, we returned to the kitchen, where Grandma was boiling potatoes and stirring the cranberries. Her cheeks were flushed.

"Oh, Cassie, I'm sorry about the bird. I forgot."

"It's okay, Anne." Mama smiled. "What can I do to help?"

When everything had come out of the oven and off the stove, we sat down at a table loaded with food. Grandpa asked us to hold hands and said grace.

"Dear Heavenly Father, we are so grateful to be gathered around this table today as family. We are so thankful to have Cassie back with us, and so thankful to have enough food to eat and a safe place to live."

I peeked at Mama, sitting next to me. Her eyes were open and she stared at her plate. She looked like she might throw up.

"We ask your blessings, God, on those who aren't as fortunate as we are, and especially on those who . . . on those who left us this week. We ask that you accept them into your heavenly arms and comfort them and their families. Amen."

"Amen," we all said.

"Thank you, Earl," Mama said. Grandpa reached across the table and took her hand, patting it.

Grandma chattered away while we ate, talking of the weather and the coming Christmas holidays and anything else she could think of.

"Of course you'll be with us on Christmas," she said, smiling at Mama. "We'll do Christmas morning at Kirk's house, and then come here for a big lunch. Just think, it will be Kirk and Judy's first Christmas in their new house. Before . . ." Her voice trailed off.

"Before that, Kirk and Judy lived here," Mama said, "after I left. It's okay, Anne, I'm not going to break if you talk about it."

"Oh, well." Grandma rose and took the mashed potato bowl into the kitchen to refill it.

"What did you do at Christmas while you were gone?" I asked, hoping it was the right thing to say.

"Well, let's see." Mama laid down her napkin and thought for a minute. "When I was at the farm in Kentucky, we didn't really celebrate Christmas. And then in San Francisco the first year, I had dinner with some friends. And the next year, we had Christmas on New Year's Day at the church."

"Why on New Year's?" Daddy asked.

"Because everything goes on sale after Christmas," Mama said. "So we could get the kids a lot more presents the week after Christmas. Every child in the church got presents. We spent the same amount on each one. It was beautiful." She sighed then and picked up her napkin.

"That is beautiful," Grandma said, walking into the room with a bowl heaped with steaming potatoes.

We sat in silence for a minute, then Grandma continued. "But it will be so good having you here this year, Cassie, especially for Judy."

Mama patted my hand.

"And if you'd like, we can ask your folks to join us," Grandma said.

Mama laughed, but it didn't sound like a happy laugh. "Thanks, Anne. I don't think so."

"Oh, okay," Grandma said. "Whatever you think is best."

The telephone rang and Grandma walked back into the kitchen to answer it.

"Yes, this is Mrs. Webster," she said. "Yes, she is my daughter-in-law. Why do you ask?"

Mama sat up straight, her eyes wide.

"No!" Grandma's voice was sharp. "No, you cannot talk to her. This is a holiday, young man. It's Thanksgiving. . . . Yes, I'll tell her. But I'm sure she won't want to talk to you."

Grandma walked back into the dining room, wringing her hands. We all stared at her.

"That was a reporter from the *Star*," she said, not looking at Mama. "He wanted to talk to Cassie."

"No!" Mama yelled. "How did he know I'm here?"

"I don't know," Grandma said. "But I told him you weren't interested in talking to him."

"Oh, God," Mama said, dropping her head into her hands. "They know where I am. How do they know? What am I going to do now?"

Daddy rose and walked around the table, draping his arms around her. "You're going to finish eating Thanksgiving dinner, and then we're going to do the dishes, and then we'll go home and maybe eat some more pie. And then we'll go to bed. And you'll be fine. Do you hear me? You'll be fine."

Mama was shaking so hard she rattled the table. I stared at her, frightened.

"Cassie?" Daddy dropped to his knee beside her chair and took her chin, forcing her to look at him. "I will *not* let anything bad happen to you. Do you hear me? I promise you, I won't let anyone hurt you."

She stared at him with wide eyes. Finally, she nodded her head and leaned against him.

"Judy and I are here, and Mom and Dad are here, and we're going to take care of you. I promise we're going to take care of you."

"But what if . . ."

"Cassie, you're not in Guyana, okay? You're in Indianapolis, Indiana, in the United States of America. Nobody is going to come get you and take you away. Nobody is going to hurt you."

Mama started to cry, her shoulders shaking.

Grandma rose and motioned for me to follow, which I did gladly. I wanted to be away from where Mama sat sobbing. We began clearing dishes from the table.

"Why don't you lie down for a little while?" Grandpa said to Mama. "You look like you could use a nice nap."

"That's a good idea," Daddy agreed, pulling Mama up from her chair. "Lie down and rest for a bit. I'll stay with you, I promise. I won't leave you alone."

I watched him take her hand and pull her toward the back hallway, watched her follow him like a child, holding his hand tightly. My eyes stung with tears.

"Now, missy." Grandma's voice was firm. "No tears from you. Come on, we've got a job to do."

But then she pulled me into a hug and kissed my head. "It's okay," she said. "Your mama just needs some rest."

I leaned into her ample chest and rested my head on her shoulder. Grandma always seemed sure of things. And when I was with her, I felt surer, too.

After we had cleaned up the dishes, Daddy and Mama and I walked back to our house. Daddy carried most of a pecan pie. I carried a big bowl of whipped cream. Mama chewed her fingernails and held Daddy's hand tightly.

We hadn't been home long when the doorbell rang and I ran to answer it. Standing on the porch was the balding, paunchy man who was Mama's father.

"Hello, Judy," he said, smiling. "Do you remember me?"

I nodded and held open the door.

"They're in the kitchen," I said, then followed him down the hall toward the light.

"Cassie!" The man's voice broke when he said it, like he was about to cry. Mama looked up in surprise and smiled at him.

"Hey, Dad." She rose and opened her arms. They hugged for a long time.

"Oh, honey, we were so worried about you."

"I'm okay," Mama said, pulling back slightly. She looked toward the doorway, then back at her father.

"Mother didn't come," the man said. "We thought it might be best for now."

Mama nodded and sat back down at the table.

"Have you eaten, John?" Daddy asked. "We've got some great pecan pie."

"No, thanks, Kirk. I've eaten."

"How about a glass of wine then?"

Daddy poured a glass for the man and set it on the table in front of him. The man smiled and took a sip.

"How are you, honey? Are you okay?" he asked Mama.

"I'm okay," she said again.

"We were worried sick when we heard. . . . We're just so glad you're all right. Karen wants to come see you this weekend, if that's okay. She's been out of her mind."

"Who's Karen?" I asked.

The man turned to me and smiled. "Why, she's your aunt, Judy. She's your mother's sister. Don't you remember her?"

I shook my head.

"All the more reason for her to come, then. It's time to start putting this family back together."

"How's Mom?" Mama asked, not looking up from the table.

"She's all right. She's been so worried about you. Honestly, she has. She just . . . well, you know, she's your mother." His voice trailed off.

"I'll bet she wishes I'd died in Guyana." Mama's voice was dull and flat.

"Oh, Cassie! Don't say that. Don't even think that. Your mother loves you."

"Yeah, right."

"She does, honey. We both do. It's just, she has a hard time showing it. She's . . . well, she's your mother."

He sat quietly for a minute, watching Mama. Then he took a long drink from his glass and set it on the table.

"Actually, Cassie, we—that is, your mother and I—we want you to come home and stay with us, for as long as you need to. Your old room is just like you left it and we have plenty of space and . . . well, you can't stay here forever."

Mama stared at him for a minute and grimaced. "Thanks, Dad, but no thanks. I'll be fine."

"Of course you will," Daddy said, putting his hand on her shoulder. "And you can stay here as long as you need to get back on your feet."

Mama looked from her father to Daddy, then rose and walked out of the kitchen without saying anything.

"Is she all right?" my grandfather asked.

"She's pretty shaken up, John. She's really upset and not think-ing clearly. Give her some time, she'll be okay."

"Well, if there's anything we can do, anything at all, will you call us? Seriously, Kirk, she's my daughter and I want to do right by her. And she can't stay with you all forever."

"I know," Daddy said. "But for now, we're okay. Cassie needs some time and space to figure things out. She's got to do some grieving. I think it's good for her to be with Judy and me."

"You're a good man, Kirk," my grandfather said. He stood and shook Daddy's hand. "She's lucky to have you in her corner."

"And you," he said, turning to look at me. "You're probably the best medicine in the world for her right now. You be good to your mother, okay?"

I nodded. He wasn't mean like his wife.

After he left, I went to Mama's room and knocked on the door. She didn't answer, so I just went in anyway. Mama was lying on the daybed, curled up like a little kid. Her eyes were open, but she didn't look at me. I stood a minute, uncertain what to do, my stom-ach clenched. Then I climbed onto the bed and curled myself into the curve of her body. She put her arms around me and sighed deeply.

"I love you, Mama," I whispered.

"I love you, too, my Sweet Judy."

⤳ 15 ⤳

We spent a quiet weekend at home, just the three of us. Mama slept a lot. Daddy worked at the kitchen table on some papers. I read, watched television, and worked on a jigsaw puzzle. I was bored, but I didn't want to leave Mama alone. I was afraid she might leave again, or maybe that she would die.

On Sunday, Lee Ann called and asked me to come to her house. Carol was coming to visit. We hadn't seen Carol since summer vacation, now that she went to a different school.

"I can't," I said.

"Why not?"

"Well, my mama is still here and . . ."

"Judy?" Daddy put his hand on my shoulder. "It's okay for you to go to Lee Ann's. Your mother will be fine. I'll be here. You go on and see your friends."

So I walked to Lee Ann's house. Her mother hugged me tight and kissed my forehead.

"Are you okay?" she asked, smiling at me.

"Yeah," I said.

"Well, if you need to talk about anything, anything at all, you know I'm here, Judy. You can come anytime and I'll be here." She hugged me again.

"Okay."

Mrs. Dawson said stuff like that. Sometimes it made Lee Ann roll her eyes, but I liked it, because I knew she really meant it.

She made us some hot chocolate. Then Lee Ann, Carol, and I went to Lee Ann's room and flopped on the bed. None of us spoke at first. Carol stared at me as if I were an alien. She twirled her long black hair around a finger and watched me from beneath a fringe of bangs.

"Are you glad your mom is home?" Lee Ann asked.

I shrugged.

"What's she like?"

"She's different than she used to be," I said, sipping my cocoa.

"Like how?" Lee Ann asked.

"Well, she used to be fun, you know? But now . . . she's really scared. And she sleeps a lot. And she cries a lot. She's just different."

Lee Ann took my hand. "Well, she's still your mom. So you have to love her."

"I guess so. I mean, I do . . . I think."

Carol snorted. I stared at her. Finally, she set down her cocoa and brushed the hair from her face.

"Your mother is crazy," she pronounced. "My mom says she's crazy and she's been brainwashed and she's probably going to hell."

I stared at her in silence.

"What's 'brainwashed'?" Lee Ann asked.

"Well"—Carol smiled slightly—"it's like in voodoo, how the witch doctor can make people do whatever he wants them to, because he has control over their minds."

"But if that man had control over their minds, then he's the one who should go to hell, right?" Lee Ann said softly.

"Oh, but they let him have control," Carol said. "So that means they're going to hell."

Lee Ann said nothing as Carol picked up her cocoa and began sipping from the mug.

"She is not," I shouted.

Both of them turned to look at me now.

"She's not crazy and she's not brainwashed and she's not going to hell!"

Carol smiled at me like I was a toddler.

"Then why did she belong to that church? My mother says . . ."

"She went to that church because they were helping people." I rose from the bed and stood over her, my hands on my hips. "They were helping poor people and . . . and lots of things." I didn't want to mention the drug addicts.

"They were a bunch of nigger lovers," Carol said firmly, as if that proved her point. "My daddy says that black men were sleeping with all the white women. I bet your mother had sex with lots of niggers."

Without warning, without even planning to, I slapped her hard across the face.

"Hey!" Carol put her hand to her cheek and stared at me, her eyes wide.

"You're just hateful," I said, "and prejudiced. And . . . and you don't know anything!"

I slammed the door behind me when I left the room and ran down the stairs toward the front door.

"Judy?" Mrs. Dawson emerged from the kitchen. "Is everything okay?"

I didn't even stop to answer her. I grabbed my jacket from the coat tree and left the house, running down the sidewalk toward the safety of home.

"Hey," Daddy said when I came into the house. "You're back."

I nodded, keeping my head bowed so he wouldn't see the tears pooling in my eyes.

"Judy?" he said as I ran up the stairs toward my room. The phone rang then, and he went to answer it. A few minutes later, he appeared at my bedroom door.

"Honey, are you okay?"

I nodded again.

"Mrs. Dawson called. She told me what happened, what Carol said."

"She said Mama is going to hell." I was sobbing now. "And that she probably slept with lots of men . . . black men."

"Oh, honey." Daddy sat on the bed and scooped me into a tight hug. "Carol's parents have filled her head with lots of nonsense. They're just ignorant, stupid people. They don't know anything about your mother, or anything else."

He held me while I cried. Neither of us heard Mama come into the room. I saw her first, standing just inside the doorway, holding a coffee cup, tears dripping from her chin.

"It's okay, Mama," I said.

Daddy rose and wrapped his arms around her.

"Don't worry about it, Cassie. The Millers are just ignorant bigots. They moved out to New Palestine when the schools integrated. That tells you just what kind of people they are."

"I'm sorry," Mama whispered, reaching for my hand. "I'm so sorry, Sweet Judy. I never wanted to hurt you."

I took her hand and Daddy wrapped his arm around me and the three of us stood together, just holding one another for a while.

Finally, Daddy stepped back and took my chin in his hand. "Mrs. Dawson says that Lee Ann told Carol off after you left."

"She did?"

"And Carol called her mother to come get her."

"I slapped her," I said, not meeting his eyes.

"You did what?"

"I slapped her right in the face." I could feel my cheeks reddening. I had never hit anyone before in my life. I knew I was probably in trouble now.

"Oh, my Sweet Judy." Mama dropped to her knees beside me and pulled me into a hug. "Oh, honey, you should never, ever hit anyone."

"I know." My voice came out in a whisper.

"Well," Daddy said after a minute, "she deserved it."

Mama stared at him in surprise, and then both of them began laughing. I watched them in disbelief. They laughed until Mama started crying again. I wondered if I would ever understand grown-ups.

Later that afternoon, Mama's sister arrived. I'd never met my Aunt Karen, but I could have told you who she was if I saw her on the street. She looked just like Mama, except her hair was short and she wore high heels.

"Cassie!" she cried, pulling Mama into a hug. "Oh, good Lord, honey, I'm so glad to see you."

We all sat at the kitchen table. Daddy poured coffee for the adults and cider for me. Mama smiled at her sister, but she seemed nervous. She kept shredding paper napkins on the table.

"How are you?" Karen asked.

"I'm okay," Mama said. She glanced at Daddy and he nodded and smiled at her.

"Well," Karen said firmly, "you need a haircut. When's the last time you cut that mane?"

She reached out and pulled a lock of Mama's hair. "I mean, it's beautiful hair, but you need some shape, some style."

Mama smiled at her and took a deep breath, then relaxed into her chair.

"I'll take you to my stylist down in Greenwood," Karen said. "No, don't argue. She's a miracle worker and you'll love her. Don't worry, I'll pay for it. Now, what's your clothes situation?"

Mama laughed then. "Oh, Karen, you just never change, do you? I'm glad you're here."

"Me too, honey." Karen patted Mama's hand. "Now, about your clothes . . ."

I followed them into Mama's room, where Karen surveyed the meager wardrobe Mama had brought with her.

"Okay," she said, eyeing a dark blue sweater. "We've got some serious shopping to do. No, don't argue. Just get your jacket and let's go to the mall."

She turned to me. "Do you want to come, Judy?"

I shook my head. The idea of trailing along behind this power shopper held no appeal.

"Okay, then." She nodded. "That's probably best. You stay here with your daddy and leave the shopping to the pros."

Soon they were gone, leaving Daddy and I alone in the kitchen. Daddy smiled at me. "So, what do you think of your aunt?"

"She's kind of . . . bossy," I said.

"She is that," he agreed. "But I think she's just what your

mother needs right now. She won't ask a lot of questions. She won't make Cassie talk about it. Karen is always focused on the here and now. I think she'll help your mother."

I nodded, but I wasn't sure I agreed.

"She's so different than Mama," I said.

"Yeah," Daddy said. "She's a whole lot like her father, very take-charge. But she's also really kind, and when they were little, she and your mama were pretty close."

"How come I never met her before?"

Daddy sipped his coffee for a minute, then set the cup down on the table.

"Okay," he said. "Okay . . . it's kind of an ugly story. But I think you're old enough now to understand it."

I stared at him. What ugly story?

"Your mama grew up in a pretty wealthy family. Her father, that's your Grandpa John, he's a very successful businessman. He traveled a lot when Cassie was growing up. And Pat, your grand-mother, she didn't really . . . she wasn't . . . well, you've met her. You've seen how she is. She wasn't a very good mother.

"So Karen took care of Cassie a lot. She's a couple years older, and like you saw, she's a take-charge kind of person. But she was good to your mama. When Cassie had bad dreams, Karen would sit with her till she fell asleep again."

"But then why . . ." I started.

"Okay, so when your mother was sixteen, she went to a party with Karen. Most of the kids were older, but Karen knew them. They were her friends. Anyway, there was alcohol at the party, and Karen had some to drink. And she lost track of Cassie."

He paused to take a drink of coffee and stared at the table. Then he shook his head.

"So, some guy at the party gave your mama some drugs that made her very sleepy. And when she went to lie down on a bed, he followed her and . . . and he raped her. Do you know what that means?"

I nodded, my eyes wide. Lee Ann's father had been a soldier in Vietnam. One time when he'd had a couple beers, we overheard him telling Lee Ann's mother about a man from the army who had raped a woman in the village. He could still hear her screams in his sleep, he said.

And that happened to Mama?

"Afterward, Karen came looking for Cassie and found her passed out. She got her home, and they didn't talk about it. Cassie was too embarrassed to talk about it, and I think Karen felt guilty for taking her to the party and then leaving her.

"Anyway . . ." Daddy's voice trailed off.

"That's why they're not friends anymore?" I asked.

"That's part of it," he said. "And that's enough for now." He rose and gathered the coffee mugs, rinsing them in the sink.

"I think Aunt Karen will be good for your mama right now," he said. "She won't pry and she won't judge. And she won't let Cassie slip away."

I nodded. If she kept Mama from slipping away again, I was prepared to love my aunt.

"Now," Daddy said, "what should we make for dinner?"

❦ 16 ❧

The next day, I walked to school with Lee Ann. We didn't talk about Carol or what she'd said. Instead, we talked about what we wanted for Christmas.

Daddy took Mama to spend the day with Rhonda while he went to work. So after school, I walked to Grandma's house to do my homework until Daddy came to get me. Then we went home.

When we got there, the lights in the house were on and we heard the stereo before we even opened the door.

In the kitchen, Rhonda and Mama were singing along with John Lennon, "Imagine all the people living life in peace." Jason sat on the floor surrounded by plastic measuring cups and spoons. It looked like every pot, pan, and dish we owned was out.

"Hey!" Daddy said, smiling. "How are you girls doing?"

"We're good, Daddy-O," Rhonda sang. "Just cooking up a storm."

"Cassie, you okay?"

Mama turned to smile at him. Her face looked relaxed, more like the Mama I remembered. Her eyes were bright and glassy.

"I'm better," she said. "Today, I feel like I'm going to be better." She shook her head and her newly styled hair swung at her shoulders.

She draped her arms over Daddy's shoulders and swayed to the music. "It's just really good to be home."

Then she turned to me. "Hey, my Sweet Judy," she said, holding open her arms. "Give me a hug."

She wrapped her arms around me tight and I could feel her heart beating against my cheek. It felt like she had really come home at last.

"I'm making lentils and rice," she announced. "I hope you're hungry."

I set the table while Daddy showered and Mama cooked. It smelled heavenly.

"How was your Thanksgiving?" Rhonda asked.

Mama smiled. "It was okay. Anne made a big turkey and all the trimmings. It was good."

She sighed then and took a long drink from her glass of wine. "Last year on Thanksgiving we served a big meal at the church. We cooked for days. More than four hundred homeless people came. I just can't believe . . ." Her voice trailed off and she stared out the window.

Rhonda hugged her, wiping a tear from her cheek. "It's okay, Cassie. It'll be okay. You're home, you're safe, and we love you."

Mama nodded and began stirring the pot on the stove.

"That smells great!" Daddy walked into the kitchen and grinned at us. "It's been a long time since we've had lentils and rice. I'm afraid my cooking is pretty limited, right, Judy?"

I smiled at him. "But you make good pancakes, Daddy."

We sat down at the table and Rhonda pulled Jason onto her lap. He began stuffing handfuls of rice and lentils into his mouth.

"His table manners can use some work," Rhonda said, smiling down at him.

"He's precious," Mama said.

The food was good and I ate two platefuls. But Mama only pushed hers around on her plate, although she did drink her wine. Daddy talked about a client he was helping who'd been charged with assault.

"He hit a cop," he said. "The cop was beating the hell out of him and he took one swing back and now he's going to jail." He shook his head.

"We worked with a lot of former prisoners at the church," Mama said softly. "We helped them get back on their feet. Jim helped them find jobs."

We sat in silence for a minute, until Jason dropped a fork to the floor.

"How about a little more?" Daddy asked, holding his hand out for my plate. I shook my head. I was stuffed to the gills.

Rhonda took Jason home after dinner, and Daddy and I cleaned the kitchen. It took a while. Mama and Rhonda had made quite a mess.

Mama sat at the kitchen table, sipping her wine and staring at nothing. I wished I could think of something clever to say, something that would make her smile. But I couldn't.

The phone rang and we all jumped. I ran to answer it.

"Hello, Judy," a woman's clipped voice came through. "This is your Grandmother Pat, and I would like to speak to Cassie."

I stood there a minute, holding the receiver in my hand, uncertain what to do. I knew Mama would not want to talk to her mother.

"Excuse me?" The voice on the phone was impatient now. "I want to talk to my daughter."

"Mama," I called. "There's a phone call."

She walked into the living room and looked at the phone as if it were a snake that might bite her.

"Who is it?"

"It's that woman," I whispered. "The one who's your mother."

Mama grimaced and wrung her hands together.

"Cassie." Daddy walked into the room. "You don't have to talk to her if you don't want to."

Mama sighed and reached for the phone.

"Hello, Mother," she said.

A long silence followed, then Mama said, "I'm fine. No really, I'm fine.

"No, Mother," she said. "I don't think that's a good idea. . . . No, I don't think so. . . . Mother, I said no!"

Her voice exploded into the room, shaking me to the core.

"I will *not* come and live in that house again. I never want to set foot in that house again. Frankly, I'd rather be dead!"

She slammed down the receiver and sank into a chair, her whole body shaking.

Daddy put a hand on her shoulder. "It's okay, Cassie. You don't ever have to go back there, not if you don't want to. You can stay here as long as you need to. It's okay."

I held Mama's hand that night when she went to bed. I sat on her bed and held her hand until I was sure she was asleep. Then I tiptoed down the stairs to the living room, where Daddy was watching television.

"Is she asleep?" he asked.

I nodded and curled up next to him on the couch. My head and stomach both hurt, and I felt more tired than I ever remembered being.

"Is she gonna be okay?" I asked.

"I think so, honey," he said. "I hope so. I'm thinking it might be a good idea for her to see a counselor, so she can talk about what happened and work through it all."

We watched television in silence for a few minutes and then he said, "Just be patient with her, Judy. She's been through an awful experience and she needs us to be very patient right now."

I sighed, and he squeezed my shoulder.

"Are you okay?" he asked.

"Yeah," I said. "I just wish . . ."

He waited for me to finish. I took a deep breath and swallowed hard.

"What if she doesn't get better, Daddy? What if she's like this always?"

He hugged me and kissed the top of my head.

"She'll get better, Judy. I promise you, she will. In the meantime, have I told you how much I appreciate everything you're doing?"

I shook my head. What was I doing?

"You are really helping her," he said. "Staying close and being patient and just loving her. That's the best medicine in the world for your mama right now."

I hoped he was right. I hoped it would be enough.

The next morning I woke early.

I padded barefoot down the hall to the guest room, thinking I might crawl into bed with Mama, so she wouldn't be alone when she woke up.

The bed was empty.

I stood staring for a minute, then ran to Daddy's room.

"Daddy, Mama's gone," I said as I pushed open the door.

But Mama wasn't gone. She was curled up next to Daddy in his bed. She opened her eyes and smiled at me.

"Hey, Sweet Judy. Good morning. Climb in here with us."

Daddy sat up, looking at me. I just stared at them. Then I turned and ran back to my room, closing the door behind me. I heard Mama's voice, then Daddy's. Pulling the covers over my head, I turned away from the door and closed my eyes tight.

"Hey, honey." Daddy's voice was soft. I felt his hand on my shoulder.

"Hey," he repeated, pulling the covers back. "Are you okay?"

I nodded, keeping my eyes shut.

"Judy, look at me," he said, turning me to face him. "It's okay, honey. Your mama had a bad, bad dream last night and came to sleep in my bed because she was scared. That's all. It's okay."

I nodded again, fighting the tears that were stinging my eyes.

"I'm going to make some eggs and toast," he said, stroking my forehead. "Does that sound good?"

I could only nod. My voice was stuck somewhere in my throat.

"Okay, well . . . you get dressed and come down when you're ready," he said.

I lay there feeling sick to my stomach. I wasn't even sure why I was crying. Mama and Daddy used to sleep together every night, all those years ago in our attic apartment. I remembered climbing into bed with them when I was little and snuggling down between them. I remembered Mama's breath on the back of my neck and Daddy's soft snoring.

But back then, we were a family and that's what families did. Now . . . what were we now?

"Hey, sweetie." Mama stood in the doorway, pulling a robe closed about her. It was one of Grandma's robes that she'd borrowed.

I turned to face the wall. I didn't want to see her there, in my room, wearing Grandma's robe. I didn't want to see her sleeping in Daddy's bed.

"Judy?" Her voice was soft and anxious.

"I'm sleepy," I said, not turning to look at her.

"Okay, honey. You rest, then."

I could hear her breathing as she stood silently a minute.

"Your daddy's making scrambled eggs," she said. "Your favorite."

"How do you know?" I asked.

"Well, because he said that's what he's making, silly."

"How do you know it's my favorite? You don't know anything."

And she didn't, she didn't know anything about me or about Daddy or about our life together. She didn't even know where we kept the wineglasses in the kitchen until I showed her. She'd left us, left me, and gone away. She'd bought presents for other kids on Christmas, but not for me. She hadn't even called on my birthday. And now here she was, standing in my bedroom, wearing Grandma's robe, sleeping in Daddy's bed, acting like she belonged, but she didn't. She didn't belong here at all.

"Oh." Her voice was so soft I could barely hear her.

"Oh," she said again.

I heard her close the door as she left my room.

I lay there a long time, even after I smelled the tempting aroma of bacon. I didn't want to go downstairs and sit at the table with them. I didn't want to pretend everything was just like it used to be, because it wasn't. Mama was different. I was different. She'd been gone a long time, and just left me behind. Then she wanted to take me to the jungle, and people there died. She could have died there. I could have died there. What kind of mother did that?

Nothing was the same as it used to be, and I couldn't pretend it was.

Finally, Daddy knocked at my door.

"Hey, peanut," he said. "Come eat breakfast before it gets cold."

I trudged downstairs and sat at the kitchen table, where Mama sat watching me, her eyes wide. She was shredding a paper napkin again.

"Hey, honey," she said, smiling anxiously. "Daddy made some good eggs for you."

I ate my eggs in silence. Each mouthful felt like sawdust. My stomach churned. I wanted to walk away from the table, away from her, just like she'd left me, to see how she felt then. I wanted to slap her and hurt her as much as I hurt when she left. I wanted to scream at her and tell her I didn't want her to be my mama. I wanted a real mother who stayed and who wasn't crazy and who took care of me, instead of me taking care of her.

Instead, I chewed and swallowed and kept my eyes on my plate.

Mama and Daddy drank their coffee. I could feel them watching me. I knew I should say something to make them feel better, but I didn't. I just didn't.

Finally, I excused myself from the table, half my eggs and both slices of bacon untouched on my plate. I just wanted to be away from them both.

I dressed and sat on my bed, watching the clock, waiting until I could leave for school.

After school, I walked to Grandma's house. She looked up in surprise when I came in.

"Hi, Judy. What are you doing here?" she asked, rising to hug me.

"I always come," I said, dropping my school bag on the couch.

"But, I meant . . . I wasn't sure if you were coming now that your mother's here."

I shrugged my shoulders and walked into the kitchen. I poured a glass of milk and got a cookie from the cookie jar. When I went back into the living room, Grandma was sitting in her rocker, snapping green beans. "Everything okay?" she asked.

"Sure," I said, turning on the television.

We watched cartoons for a little while, then Grandma said, "Okay, why don't you tell me what's wrong?"

Grandma always knew when something was wrong. It was like she had radar or something, she could just tell. Like the time in second grade when Carol's mother invited all the girls in our class to a mother-daughter tea party at their house—every girl except me.

"Well, you don't have a mom," Carol had explained, not meeting my eyes.

I didn't tell Grandma about it at first. I thought she'd be mad at Carol, and Carol was my friend. But of course she knew something was wrong. And of course eventually I told her about the party. She was Grandma. She always found out.

She had been mad, all right. Not at Carol, but at Carol's mom.

"If I weren't a Christian woman, I'd have a few words for her!" she said, when I told her about the tea party. "I'm going to call that woman right this minute."

"No!" I'd shouted. "Please, Grandma, don't."

She didn't call, in the end. Instead, she and Grandpa took me to Chicago for the weekend on a shopping trip. We stayed in a hotel and ate in restaurants, and I came home with lots of new clothes.

And then Grandma organized her own party and invited all the girls in my class, even Carol. We wore our Easter dresses and patent leather shoes and rode the bus downtown to the Tea Room at the L. S. Ayres department store, where we sat at a long table with a white linen cloth, and waiters in white shirts and black vests brought us chicken velvet soup and Monte Cristo sandwiches. For dessert, each of us got a Snow Princess—a scoop of ice cream decorated with whipped cream and sugar flowers to look like a hoop skirt, topped with a china-doll figure holding a paper parasol. Girls in my class still talked about that tea party.

I looked at Grandma now and remembered the tea party and all the times she'd held my hand until I went to sleep after Mama left. I remembered the school field trips she'd chaperoned and the snacks she always had ready after school and how she'd made my costume for the school play the year before. I remembered all that and bit my lip, thinking how I'd always wished it was Mama there, instead of Grandma. I hoped she didn't know that. But she was Grandma, so probably she did.

I sighed and shrugged again.

"Don't you shrug your shoulders at me, young lady." Grandma set aside the pot of green beans and leaned forward. "I taught you better manners than that. Now, what's wrong?"

I sat a minute, trying to put into words what was wrong. Finally, I said, "I don't want her here."

"Who?" she asked. "Your mama? You don't want your mama here?"

I nodded, feeling the tears stinging my eyes again.

"Oh, honey, of course you do. That's all you used to talk about, having your mama home again. Of course you want her home."

I could only shake my head and blow my nose.

"Come here," she said, opening her arms so I could sit on her lap. "What happened?" she asked.

I shook my head again.

"Judy Bug," she said—she hadn't called me that in a long time—"you tell your grandma what happened to upset you. Did your mother do something? Say something? What happened?"

"She slept in Daddy's bed," I finally said, and burst into tears. Once I started crying, I couldn't stop. I sobbed into Grandma's soft body until my stomach ached.

"Oh, honey," she crooned again and again. "It's okay. It's okay, Judy."

But it wasn't okay. Nothing was okay.

"Your mama has been through a terrible time," she said, wiping tears from my cheeks and rocking me gently. "She needs our help now. She needs us very much."

I shook my head and cried harder.

She let me cry for a while, then handed me a tissue and patted my cheek.

"Judy, I know it's hard for you to understand. You shouldn't even have to understand, because it's a grown-up thing. But you have to try, honey. Your mother has had such a scare, and she's afraid and she needs . . ."

"I was scared, too!" I shouted, pulling away from her. "I was scared and Daddy was scared and you and Grandpa were scared. And it's her fault!"

There, I had said it.

Grandma looked at me for a long minute, and then she smiled.

"I can see why you think so," she said, handing me another tissue. "She's your mother, and she's supposed to take care of you. Instead, you're taking care of her. It's hard, honey. I know it's hard. But . . . well, sometimes life is hard. That's all."

"Why did she go away?"

I blurted it out before I could stop myself, then clapped both hands over my mouth and shook my head. It's what I'd always wanted to ask, ever since I could remember, but I never did. Because inside I knew the answer, I always knew. Mama left because she didn't love me enough to stay. I ducked my head as if I could ward off the answer I didn't want to hear.

"Oh, Judy," Grandma said softly. "I don't know all of it. I know she was unhappy. She was unhappy before she met your daddy. She had a terrible time growing up. You've met her mother. . . ." Her voice trailed away.

"But then she seemed to be happy when she married Kirk. And when she had you, she was over-the-moon happy. She loved you so much."

"But she left," I said.

"Yes, she did. And that was wrong for her to do," Grandma said. "It was very wrong, and I had a hard time forgiving her for it."

"Did you forgive her?" I asked.

"Mostly," she said. "I'm still working on it."

She hugged me tight and kissed my cheek.

"I don't know why she left, Judy, I'm sorry. I don't think even Cassie really knows why she left. Except I think . . . well, I think she's always looking for something that will make her feel better about herself. I think that's why she joined that church."

I blew my nose again.

"I know it's hard to understand, but your mother does love you," Grandma said. "She's always loved you. And now she's home, and she needs us. She needs you, Judy."

I didn't answer. I thought about all the times I had needed Mama, and she wasn't there. It wasn't fair now that she needed us.

"And, honey, just because she's back, that doesn't mean your daddy doesn't love you just like always. You know that, too, right?"

I shrugged again.

"Judy Webster, don't you shrug your shoulders at me! And don't you start thinking your daddy doesn't love you, because he loves you more than anything. You are his whole life."

Maybe that was true, or maybe it had been true just because Mama wasn't there. Maybe now, with Mama back, he wouldn't love me so much. Maybe the next time Mama left, instead of taking me with her, she'd take Daddy away.

Grandma tilted my chin to make me look at her.

"Doesn't your daddy make you breakfast and get you ready for school every day? Doesn't he tuck you in and read to you every night? Doesn't he take you to the movies and buy you popcorn? Isn't he building you a tree house? Your daddy loves you so much, and nothing in the world is going to change that.

"Do you understand me?" She took my hand and held it tight. "Nothing will ever change the way your daddy loves you."

"I guess so," I said. I hoped so, anyway.

"No, you don't guess so," she said, squeezing my hand. "You *know* so."

She rose from her chair and picked up the pan of beans.

"Now," she said, "if I don't get these beans on to boil, your grandpa won't eat till eight. Come help me get supper started."

She held out her hand and I took it and followed her into the kitchen.

✎ 17 ✎

Daddy picked me up after work, just like always. But when we got home, the house was dark and quiet.

"Cassie?" Daddy yelled up the stairs. "Are you home?"

No one answered.

"Maybe she's at Rhonda's," he said. "I'll just call over there."

He reached for the phone and then stopped. A white envelope was sitting by the telephone. His name was written on it in blue ink.

Daddy sat down and tore open the envelope, then read the note inside. He said nothing for a very long minute. Then he ran his hand over his eyes and stood, putting the note back into the envelope.

"Well," he said at last, "your mama has decided to go stay with her sister for a while, with Aunt Karen."

He walked into the kitchen, never looking at me. I followed him.

"Where is that?" I asked.

"What?"

"Where does Aunt Karen live?"

He sighed and sat down at the table. "She lives in Bloomington, just about an hour away."

He pulled the note from the envelope again and read it, his lips moving silently. Then he sighed again.

"I'm sorry, Daddy."

"It's okay. It's probably the best place for her right now. I just wish . . ."

"I didn't mean to make her go away," I whispered.

"Oh, honey! It's not your fault." Daddy opened his arms and pulled me close. "It's nothing you did or said. It never was. You know that, right? You know when she left before it wasn't because of anything you did. And it's not this time, either."

I leaned into him and cried then. I cried because she'd left us again and I was sad, but I was also relieved, and that made me cry even more.

I cried because I knew this time it *was* my fault. I had been so mean to Mama that morning. I'd wished her gone, and now she was gone. And no matter what Daddy might say, I knew the truth.

"It's okay, Judy," Daddy crooned in my ear. "It's gonna be okay. We'll be okay, just like we were before. You and me, kiddo, we're gonna be fine."

When I stopped crying and went to wash my face, I heard Daddy on the phone.

"Hey, Karen, it's Kirk. Is Cassie there with you? Okay, good. . . . No, that's all right. I understand. I just wanted to make sure. . . . Okay, sure. Good. Well, thanks."

We ate leftover lentils and rice for dinner, then washed the dishes together, just like always. And even though I knew Daddy was sad, and even though I was sad, it was nice being just the two of us again.

Me and Daddy, we would be okay.

PART 3

MAMA'S NEW LIFE

∽ 18 ∾

"Hey, wait up!" Lee Ann called as I wheeled my bike from the school parking lot. She ran to meet me, her cheeks pink and round.

"What are you gonna do tonight?" she asked.

"I don't know." I shrugged.

"Want to go to the mall?" she asked. "My mom said she'll drive us."

Washington Square Mall was to Lee Ann what Mecca is to the Muslims. My dad said that once, and I think it was true. She loved the mall, she worshiped all the stuff there, and she was always dragging me along on her shopping trips. Well, actually they were shoplifting trips. Neither of us had any money, but that didn't stop us from bringing home things we liked. Usually I took small stuff like lip gloss and hair bands. Lee Ann, though, could walk out of a store with almost anything and no one ever suspected her. She smiled at the clerks and asked about perfume, all the while she had a sweater or a blouse stuffed under her jacket. I admired her, really. She was very good at it.

But I was getting tired of the mall. It was spring, finally. The mountains of snow had melted and daffodils were poking their heads through the ground. I wanted to be outside after the long winter.

"I don't know," I said. "I was thinking about riding to the park."

For my twelfth birthday, Dad had bought me a ten-speed, and I loved it. It was pure freedom to get on that bike and ride. I'd missed it during the long, cold days of winter.

Dad let me take my bike out, as long as I told him where I was going. Ellenberger Park was a good place to hang out. I almost always saw someone I knew there. And even if I didn't, I liked riding along the creek, watching the squirrels chitter away at each other.

"Oh, come on," Lee Ann said, holding my arm. "They're having a big sale at Penney's."

"Like it matters if stuff is on sale," I said, grinning at her. "You never pay for anything anyway."

"But a sale means lots of people. That makes it easier, you know? And there's a really cute sweater I saw there. Bright red and cut down to here." She made a deep V with her fingers.

She grinned back at me. "I'll get you one, too."

"No," I said. "I can't wear the stuff you can." I glanced at her chest, which had grown a lot since we started junior high.

"You could if you stuffed your bra," she said. "Marilyn Kucher does that, and no one even knows."

"Yeah, right. Everyone knows Marilyn stuffs her bra," I said.

"Well, come anyway and we'll find something else for you."

"Maybe," I said.

What I really wanted just then was to be on my bike, riding as fast as I could go. Instead, I was walking it home beside Lee Ann. She didn't like to ride her bike to school. She didn't want to get sweaty or mess up her hair. Sometimes I wondered why she was my best friend. We were so different. But, Lee Ann had been my friend since the first day of kindergarten. She knew all about Mama. She'd hold my hand when I cried and stick up for me when other kids laughed about my crazy mother. She loved me.

We turned onto University Avenue and Lee Ann stopped, taking my arm. "Who's that on your porch?" she said.

Even from a distance, I knew who it was. Mama's blond hair

blew about in the wind as she gazed up the block, looking in the opposite direction from where we were.

"Oh no," I whispered. "What's she doing here?"

"Is that your mom?"

"Yeah," I said. My stomach turned flip-flops and I had to stop and steady myself against the bike. I hadn't seen Mama since she left us after Thanksgiving when I was nine. I'd talked to her on the phone sometimes and she'd written letters. A couple times she said she was going to come visit, but she never did.

And now, here she was, sitting on my front porch, just as if she belonged there.

"Shit," I said.

"What are you gonna do?" Lee Ann looked from me to the house.

"I don't know."

"Come to my house." She pulled at my arm. "We can walk around the other way and she won't see us."

But just then, she turned and looked directly at me. And she smiled.

"Shit," I said again.

She waved at me.

"Look, you go home and tell your mom she's here, okay? Ask her to call my dad and tell him. I'll . . . I guess I'll go talk to her."

"Are you sure?" Lee Ann's eyes were wide.

"Yeah, it's okay. She can't do anything to me now."

I squared my shoulders and we walked toward the house, where Mama still sat on the porch swing. When I parked my bike in the yard, she stood up. And then I could see her belly, huge and swollen, like she'd swallowed a basketball.

"Judy? Oh, God, my Sweet Judy! Look how much you've grown." She reached out and pulled me to her, squishing me against her belly.

Behind me, I heard Lee Ann's feet pounding down the sidewalk toward her house. I knew Daddy would be home soon.

"What are you doing here?" I asked, pulling away from her.

"I wanted to see you," she said, sitting back down on the swing and patting the seat beside her. I did not sit down.

"Where have you been?"

"Oh, Judy, I've been all over," she said. "You know where I've been. I've called you, I've written."

I simply stared at her.

"Okay, well, I was in Bloomington for a while, and then I went back to San Francisco. But that was just too sad. There was no one there I knew anymore. So I moved to Los Angeles. I wanted to be someplace warm and sunny. I got a job in a bookstore, and that's where I met Navid. I've told you about him, remember? He's my . . . well, I guess you'd say he's my boyfriend. But that just sounds so . . . anyway, we live together now and . . ." She patted her stomach and smiled. "We're going to have a baby!"

Still I said nothing. I couldn't think of anything to say.

Actually, that wasn't true. I could think of lots of things, like, "Why didn't you ever come back after you left?" And, "Why the hell do you think you can show up again, just like that?"

But those weren't things she'd want to hear.

"Navid and I got into town yesterday," she continued. "We're staying at the Ramada Inn. You'll meet him later. I thought it might be best to tell you first myself."

She paused, looking at me, waiting for me to say something. Finally, she plowed on.

"So, the baby is due in June—just two more months! You're going to be a big sister. What do you think of that?"

"I don't know," I said. And that was true. I did not know what I thought of that.

"Let's go inside," she said, glancing at the house next door, where old Mrs. Gagen was peeking at us from behind her lace curtains. I figured she'd probably already called my father.

I shook my head. "I don't think you should come inside," I said. "I don't think Daddy would like it."

"Oh," she said, looking down at her hands. "Well, then, we can sit here until he gets home, I guess."

I stood where I was, my back to the door, watching her.

"How's school?" she asked.

"It's okay."

"I can't believe you're in the sixth grade already."

"Seventh."

"What?"

"I'm in the seventh grade."

"Oh, right . . . I'm sorry, I lose track sometimes. You're just growing up so fast."

She smiled at me, but I could see her lip trembling. Her green eyes were too bright. I knew she was trying not to cry. Still, I didn't sit down by her.

"What . . . what's your favorite class?" she asked.

"History," I said.

"Oh, good. That's good. History is important."

A long silence followed.

"And do you . . . do you have a boyfriend?" She smiled at me again.

"God, no!"

"A pretty girl like you? I don't believe that."

I stared at her. Lee Ann was pretty. Lots of girls in my school were pretty. I was not one of them. I was too skinny and too awkward to be pretty.

"Who was that with you?" Mama nodded down the block where Lee Ann had gone.

"Lee Ann."

"Oh, you're still friends. . . . That's nice. She's a nice girl."

"Yeah."

What I wanted to say was, "How would you know?" The same way I'd asked it three years earlier when she'd talked about scrambled eggs being my favorite. But, I didn't. Whatever she was going to do next, I sure as hell didn't want it to be my fault . . . again.

Daddy's car screeched around the corner and into our driveway.

"Cassie?" he said, screening his eyes against the late-afternoon sun.

"Hey, Kirk." She smiled at him and held out her arms. But he only stood on the steps.

"What are you doing. . . . Are you pregnant?"

"Yep," she said. "Seven months. I'm due in June."

"Who's . . . I mean, oh."

"His name is Navid," Mama said. "I told Judy about him. We've been living together for a while and . . . well, now I'm pregnant."

"Well, congratulations, I guess." Daddy shifted his weight from one foot to the other. "What are you doing here?"

"Well, goodness, you're the second one who's asked me that."

She smiled at me, then at him. "Can't I come and see my daughter if I want to?"

Daddy just looked at her for a long minute. Then he turned to me. "You okay?"

I shrugged.

"Why don't you go inside and start your homework," he said. "I need to talk to your mother."

He handed me his house key. I took it, but I wondered why he didn't just let me use the key I always did, the one we hid in the planter by the door. And then I understood—he didn't want Mama to know the key was there.

I went inside and up to my room. I didn't even try to stay close to hear what they were saying. I didn't want to know.

After a while, I heard the front door open and Daddy's steps on the stairs.

"You okay, kiddo?"

He was leaning against the doorframe, running his hand through his hair.

"I'm okay," I said.

"Are you sure?"

"Yeah."

"Well, she's gone back to the hotel," he said, sitting on the bed beside me. "I told her if she wants to see you, she'll have to call first and let us know she's coming. It's not okay for her to just show up like that."

I nodded.

We sat for a minute, and he said, "So, she's going to have a baby. What do you think about that?"

I shrugged.

"Judy? It's okay if you're upset or angry or . . . whatever. Whatever you're feeling is okay."

"Whatever," I said. I wanted him to leave me alone. I needed time to think about it all.

He kissed my cheek and walked to the door. "Okay, well, I'm here if you want to talk."

"Okay."

"How about tacos for dinner?"

I nodded. I wasn't hungry at all. In fact, I felt sick, like I'd been sucker punched.

"Dad?"

He stopped at the top of the stairs. "Yeah?"

"Can I go to the mall with Lee Ann tonight?"

He looked at me for a long time and said, "Sure you can, if you want to."

"Okay."

"Judy?"

"Yeah."

"I love you."

"I love you, too, Daddy."

19

"I can't believe she just came without telling you first." Lee Ann was trying on lipstick at the cosmetics counter in JC Penney.

"Yeah," I said, watching her carefully frame her lips and then fill them with color.

"How long is she staying?"

"I don't know."

"Are you going to see her again?"

"I don't know," I said again. "Maybe."

"And she's living with an Indian or something? What's his name?"

"Navid. I don't know if he's Indian. It sounds Indian, doesn't it?"

"It's something foreign, that's for sure." Lee Ann pursed her lips and pouted at the mirror.

"Can I see that eyeliner?" she asked the lady behind the counter, as she slipped the lipstick into her pocket.

"And she's gonna have a baby. Wow, that's . . . I don't know, that's weird."

I nodded, glancing around to see if anyone was watching while I shoved a bottle of perfume into my jacket.

"So, does she think you're gonna come live with her and Navid and the baby?"

I laughed. "Well, if she does, then she's crazier than we thought."

We wandered down the mall to the Orange Julius and bought drinks, then sat down to watch the crowds of shoppers.

"Judy?" she asked, staring intently at something on the other side of the mall.

"What?"

"Do you miss her still?"

I took a long drink and thought about it.

"Sometimes," I said. "When I think about how she was when I was little, how she used to dance and build cardboard castles, then I miss her. But when I think about how she was last time she was here . . . not really. I don't really miss her at all."

"I don't know what I'd do without my mom," she said.

"Well, that's different. Your mom is great. I mean, I know she nags at you sometimes, but, God, she's great."

Mrs. Dawson was my idea of the perfect mom. She came to all of Lee Ann's activities, cooked good food, volunteered at school. She did all the things my Grandma did, but she was an actual mom. She looked like a mom. She didn't stand out like Grandma. And she wasn't crazy like Mama. She was just a normal, good mom.

Sometimes she yelled at Lee Ann and me, but she was always there when Lee Ann needed her. And when I needed her, she was there, too.

The year before when a boy in my class kept grabbing my butt and pinching me, it was Mrs. Dawson I told. I just couldn't talk to Grandma about something like that.

Mrs. Dawson marched into the principal's office and told him exactly what had happened. And Mark Meyers got suspended for three days. He hadn't bothered me since then.

"I wish your mom was great, too," Lee Ann said, squeezing my hand.

"Yeah," I said. "I guess I kind of miss the idea of her more than I miss her, you know? I mean, I wish I had a mom like yours. I miss that, even though I never really had it."

"You can always come live with us," Lee Ann said. "Mom would be okay with that."

"Yeah, but what would my dad do then?" I asked.

And then I wondered, what would Daddy do without me? Would he be lonely? Or would he just be free to get on with his life? When he looked at me, did he see me, or just a reminder of Mama?

"Come on," I said, throwing the last of my drink in the trash. "Let's go to Spencer's and get some earrings."

Later that night, I lay awake for a long time, wondering what it would be like to have a mother like Lee Ann's. What it would be like if Mama was normal. I thought about the birthday parties she'd thrown when I was little and how we used to make bread together and how she ran behind me, holding the seat of my bike when I learned to ride without training wheels, her hair streaming behind her as she called out encouragement. Had Mama been happy then? Or did she know, even then, that she would leave?

What if she wanted me to go with her to Los Angeles? She couldn't make me go. I was twelve now. She couldn't just take me away like she'd done before. But what if she asked me to go with her? Would I want to go?

Definitely not if she was the Mama who'd come home after Jonestown. But what if Mama was really back? The Mama who had played with me and brushed my hair and did fun things—what if that Mama wanted me back? Would I go then?

What would Daddy do without me?

It gave me a headache just wondering about it all.

I put on my slippers and went downstairs to get some aspirin, walking softly so I wouldn't wake Daddy. But he was already awake, sitting in the kitchen, his head in his hands.

"Daddy?"

"Oh, hey, peanut." He smiled at me. "What are you doing up?"

"I have a headache."

He poured me some water and handed me two aspirins, then sat back down at the table.

"Are you okay?" I asked. Probably it was the first time I'd ever asked him that. At least it's the first time I remember.

He shrugged and smiled at me. "I'll be okay."

"Do you miss her?" I asked, sitting down beside him.

"Yeah, honey, I do. Sometimes I miss her like hell."

"Are you sad she's going to have a baby with someone else?"

He looked at me for a minute, then reached out and touched my cheek.

"I guess it makes me a little bit sad," he said. "And it worries me."

I nodded. It worried me, too. What if she loved the baby like she'd never loved me? Worse, what if she left the baby like she'd left me?

"Do you think she's happy now?"

He sighed. "I don't know, Judy. I don't know if your mother will ever be really happy."

"Do you think she'll leave that man and the baby like she did us?"

He shook his head. "I don't know. I hope not, but . . . I just don't know."

We sat in silence for a while. I wished I could say something to make him happy. But there was nothing to say.

Finally, he looked at the clock and said, "Okay, it's past eleven and it's a school night. You need to be in bed."

I kissed his cheek and put my glass in the sink.

"Daddy?"

"Yeah."

"Do you think I should see her while she's here?"

"If you want to, then yeah, you should. But you don't have to."

"I don't know if I want to or not."

"That's okay, Judy. You don't have to decide right this minute. Get some sleep and see how you feel tomorrow."

I lay awake for a long time, staring at the ceiling and thinking about my dad missing her. I hadn't ever thought about that. I'd never even thought about how it must have hurt him when she left. And then left again. And now, here she was, back . . . and pregnant. Poor Daddy.

I heard the clock downstairs chime midnight, but I wasn't sleepy at all. I wanted something to make Daddy feel better. But what would that be?

And then I remembered what Grandma had said the night we heard about the congressman being shot in Guyana. That praying was the best thing we could do. I hadn't prayed in a long time. But I knelt by my bed and prayed as hard as I could. I prayed that Daddy would be happy again and that he would stop missing Mama so much. Finally, I crawled back into bed and fell asleep.

❧ 20 ❧

The next morning the phone rang while I was eating breakfast. Daddy answered it, then called to me.

"It's your mother," he said, covering the receiver with his hand. "She wants to see you after school, to take you out for dinner. Do you want to do that?"

"Are you coming, too?"

He shook his head. "No, honey. It will be you and your mom and her . . . friend."

I sat down on the stairs, trying to decide.

"Judy, it's okay if you want to go. She's your mom. If you want to spend some time with her, that's okay."

"But why can't you go with us?"

He smiled. "I don't think that would be a good idea. And, to tell you the truth, I don't really want to. But you can go if you want to."

He watched me for a minute, then said, "I promise you, Judy, it won't hurt my feelings if you want to see your mother."

"Okay," I said.

"Okay, what?" he asked.

"Okay, I'll go with her for dinner."

"You sure?"

I nodded. I wasn't really sure. I wasn't sure at all. But part of me wanted to see her again, to ask her some things I needed to know.

Daddy told Mama she could pick me up at five. That would give me time to come home and do homework before dinner.

He kissed me on the forehead when I left for school.

"I think it's a good thing for you to spend some time with her," he said. I'm not sure he meant it.

"I love you, Daddy."

"I love you, too."

The day dragged on for what seemed like forever. I watched the clock in every class, wishing I could just go home and crawl into bed.

At lunch, Lee Ann and I sat with Vernita, and Lee Ann told her about Mama coming back and being pregnant. Vernita squeezed my hand.

"My dad has kids with his new wife," she said. "Two girls. They're five and three."

"Do you like them?" I asked.

"They're okay," she said. "I don't see them very much."

"But . . . does it feel like they're your sisters?"

She shrugged. "Not really. More like cousins or something, I guess."

It was hard to imagine having a brother or sister. For most of my life it had been just Daddy and me.

"I wish I had a sister," Lee Ann said. "Or even a brother, maybe."

Lee Ann's mother couldn't have any more babies after Lee Ann was born.

"My brothers are pretty cool," Vernita said. "Malcolm's kind of a pain, but Mike drives me places sometimes. He's okay."

"Well," I said, "I probably won't even know this baby. Mama lives in Los Angeles now."

"Maybe you can go visit her," Vernita said.

I shook my head. "I don't think so. I don't think Daddy would let me go out there. And . . . and I don't know if I would go, even if I could."

"But she's your mother," Vernita said. "Don't you miss her at all?"

I shrugged. "Not really."

Lee Ann caught my eye and smiled. She knew me better than anyone else, and she knew when I was lying.

When Daddy brought me back from the farm in Kentucky all those years before, Lee Ann had simply accepted me back into the group, no questions asked. Carol had been kind of mean at first, because she said Mama was a bad person and maybe I was, too. But Lee Ann had overruled her then and many times after.

When Mama had come back and everyone thought she was crazy and brainwashed, Lee Ann stood up for me again, daring anyone to say something bad about me or about Mama. After Carol said those nasty things about Mama sleeping with black men and going to hell, Lee Ann cut her off completely. In fact, we never saw Carol after that.

When Mama left again, Lee Ann held my hand while I cried and listened while I talked and nodded while I spewed about how awful Mama was and how glad I was that she'd gone. She never argued with me about it, even when I went from crying sad to spitting angry in a heartbeat. She just let me talk or cry or rage as much as I wanted to.

And she shared her mom with me. Sometimes I wondered if she resented sharing her mom, especially when Mrs. Dawson bought me things—little things like a silver frame for a picture she had taken years before of Mama and me, or a funny music box that played Arlo Guthrie's "Garden Song," after I told her once that Mama used to sing it to me.

If Lee Ann ever did resent it, she never said so. She just loved me like I loved her. She was my best friend.

After school I sat in my room, watching the clock. At four, Daddy came home. It surprised me; usually he didn't get home until after five.

"You okay?" he asked.

I nodded.

He handed me a quarter. "If you want to come home, you just call me and I'll come get you."

"Okay."

"I mean it. If you feel uncomfortable or scared or your mother . . . does anything that upsets you, you find a pay phone and call me."

"I will."

The doorbell rang and Daddy went to answer the door.

I stared at myself in the mirror, willing my stomach to settle down.

When I walked downstairs, Daddy was standing in the hallway with Mama and a tall, olive-skinned man.

"Where are you going to eat?" he asked.

"Wherever Judy wants to go," she said.

"Hey, you!" She turned to me and pulled me into a hug. "You look beautiful."

I pulled away, not wanting to feel her belly against me.

She smiled and turned to the man standing behind her.

"Navid, this is my Sweet Judy."

The man extended his hand to me. I hesitated, then shook hands with him.

"I'm glad to finally meet you, Judy," he said. His eyes were the darkest I'd ever seen, darker even than Vernita's. "I've heard so much about you."

I couldn't think of anything to say. I hadn't heard hardly anything about him, after all.

"Where do you want to go for dinner?" Mama took my hand.

"I don't know. Wherever."

"Well, it's up to you," she said, smiling brightly. "Just choose a place."

"She likes the Oriental Inn," Daddy said.

"Oh, that place on Arlington? That sounds good. Is that where you want to go, Judy?"

Daddy nodded at me. We knew all the waiters at the Oriental Inn. We ate there a lot. We even knew the owner. I would be safe there.

"Yeah, I like that place."

Mama chattered in the car, her hand resting on Navid's shoulder as he drove.

"Honestly, Judy, I can't believe how much you've grown. You're as tall as I am."

I nodded.

"And you're so beautiful. Navid, isn't Judy just beautiful?"

"She is," he said, smiling at me in the rearview mirror. "Just like her mother."

I looked out the window. I didn't look anything like Mama. She was blond and pretty and graceful. I was brown-haired like Daddy. My eyes were brown like his. I was his daughter.

"Hello, Judy." Mr. Tan, the owner of the Oriental Inn, smiled at me as we came in. "How are you?"

"I'm fine, Mr. Tan."

"And this is your mother?"

Mama looked surprised, but she smiled at him. "Yes, I'm Judy's mama. I'm Cassie."

"Okay," he said, ignoring Navid's outstretched hand. "I have a good table for you right here."

We sat in the booth Daddy and I always sat in, by the wall with a huge silk painting of a tiger.

"This is nice," Mama said. "Don't you think so?"

"Very nice," Navid said. "Do you come here a lot?" he asked me.

"Daddy and I come almost every week," I said.

Navid smiled and nodded.

"What do you like to eat?" Mama asked.

"I like the kung pao chicken. Daddy always gets mu shu pork."

"That sounds good. Let's order both of those."

Mama smiled and smiled at me.

When the waiter came to take our order, he grinned at me. "You have the usual?"

"Sure."

"And you?" He turned to Mama.

"Oh, I'll have whatever she has."

"Okay. You?"

Navid looked at the menu for a long time, then ordered the seafood deluxe.

We sat there looking at each other for an awkward minute, and then Mama said, "Judy is in the seventh grade now. Imagine . . . she's so grown up."

Navid smiled at me. "Do you like school?"

"It's okay."

"She likes history," Mama said.

Navid nodded.

"Navid is a teacher," Mama said. "He teaches at a college in Pasadena. It's called CalTech, the California Institute of Technology. It's one of the best science schools in the country."

"Cool," I said, watching for the waiter to bring our soup.

"He teaches political science," Mama said. "There's a lot about history in that, isn't there?" She turned to Navid.

"Well, you have to understand history to understand where we are now. So yes, I'd say there is."

"There." Mama looked at me expectantly, as if this should mean something.

"Oh," I said.

The waiter brought our soup and I started eating mine immediately. I didn't know how to talk to these people, Navid and my mother. What was there to say?

"Once the baby is born, you have to come see us in LA," Mama said. "I really want you to be part of the baby's life."

"I don't know if Daddy will let me go to California."

"Well, he can always come with you. That would be fine, wouldn't it, Navid?"

"Sure." He nodded. "That would be fine."

"It's such a beautiful place. You'll just love it. We can go to the beach and the mountains. And there's a really good zoo in San Diego. And the desert is close by, so we could go hiking. Would you like that?" She smiled at me, almost like she was begging me to say yes.

"Sure," I said. "That sounds okay."

"Good," she said. "I'll talk to your dad about it. Maybe you can come in July. We have an extra room and it's all made up and ready for you."

"What about Daddy?"

"Oh, well . . . I guess your dad can sleep on the couch."

"Or he could get a hotel room," Navid said.

"Yes, he could do that," Mama agreed. "We'll have so much fun, Judy. I just can't wait for you to see our house and the city . . . and your new little brother or sister." She patted her tummy.

"What are you naming it?" I asked.

"Well, if it's a boy, we'll call him Kamran. That's a Persian name that means lucky. And if it's a girl, her name will be Parvaneh. That means butterfly. Don't you love it?"

"Sure," I said. "It's okay."

"You don't sound like you like it." She looked disappointed.

"Well, it's kind of a different name. And she might not like it once she gets to school. Other kids might tease her about it."

"Why on earth would they tease her about a beautiful name like Parvaneh?"

"The same reason they used to tease me about being Sweet Judy—it's just weird."

"Oh," she said, looking down at her soup. "I didn't know that. . . . I'm sorry, Judy."

"It's okay," I said. "No one calls me that anymore. They just call me Judy now."

The waiter arrived with our food. Kung pao chicken for me and Mama, seafood deluxe for Navid. He put a set of chopsticks beside my plate. I grinned at him.

"Can you use those?" Mama asked.

"Sure," I said. "Daddy and I use them all the time."

I picked up a peanut with my chopsticks and popped it into my mouth, pleased with myself for being able to do it.

"Well, look at you," Mama cooed. "Isn't that something, Navid?"

He smiled and nodded. "When you come to visit us, I'll cook you something from my country," he said.

"Where's that?"

"Persia," he said. "That's in the Middle East, between Iraq and Afghanistan."

"Are you a Muslim?" I asked. It would be cool to know a Muslim.

"No, not Muslim," he said. "My family are Bahá'ís. That's a faith that was born in Persia in the eighteen hundreds."

"Oh," I said. I'd never heard of that.

"We are going to have a Persian Bahá'í wedding," Mama said, "after the baby is born. Maybe we can do that while you're out there with us. I would love that."

"That would be cool," I said. I meant it, too. I thought it would be very cool to see a Persian Bahá'í wedding. It sounded very exotic.

Mama smiled and seemed to relax a little. She took a bite of her chicken and her eyes widened. Immediately she reached for her water.

"That's hot!" she said.

I giggled. "It's these little red peppers," I said, picking one up with my chopsticks. "Just put them on the side of your plate if you don't like them."

"Are you eating them?" she asked.

"Sure," I said, putting the pepper in my mouth. I tried to chew it without gasping. I did eat the peppers, but usually I cut them into tiny pieces and ate them with other stuff. I swallowed the pepper and smiled at her, my mouth on fire. "They're good."

"You like to try new foods?" Navid said. "That's good. You'll like my food, then. Your mother . . ." He looked at her and laughed. "She likes Persian food some, but when I make Indian food, she doesn't like it so much."

"Hey, I'm learning," she said, swatting at him playfully. "I just can't eat it right now because of the baby."

He laughed again. "When the baby comes, he will eat my food."

"Oh no, you are not giving our baby curry. At least not until she's older."

Navid just smiled.

"How long have you lived in the States?" I asked. "You don't sound like you come from someplace else."

"I came here when I was ten," he said. "Iran is not such a good place for Bahá'ís now. My mother and father came to Los Angeles and opened a yogurt shop."

"Oh." For some reason that disappointed me.

"But my grandparents and aunts and cousins still live in Iran."

"Have you been?" I asked Mama.

"No," she said. "It's not safe for Bahá'ís in Iran now. But Navid has lots of family in the States, so the baby will learn about Persia from them. She'll be a proper little Persian girl," she said, smiling.

"I want him to know where he comes from," Navid said.

"You guys are funny," I said. They looked at me, puzzled.

"You keep calling the baby *him*," I said to Navid. "And Mama keeps calling it *her*."

They both laughed.

"Navid would really like to have a son," Mama said. "And I always just assume it's a girl like you and . . . well, like you."

"Do you want another girl?" I asked.

"Oh, I just want the baby to be healthy," she said. She was picking at her food with her fork, carefully pushing all the peppers into a pile at the side of her plate.

"And that," Navid said, covering her hand with his, "is exactly why you should have this baby at the hospital, just to be safe."

Mama smiled at him. "Oh, honey," she said, "I had Judy in a tent at Woodstock, for God's sake. Giving birth is a natural process. Millions of women give birth at home. It's just the way it should be."

"And countless women die in childbirth," Navid said. "In my country, it happens all the time. Even here it happens more than you'd think. Besides, when you had Judy, you were nineteen years old. You're thirty-one now. That puts you at a higher risk for complications."

I watched them talking, thinking how much they seemed like a married couple. It made me happy and sad, all at the same time.

When we'd finished our dinner, Mama asked if I wanted to come back to their hotel and swim in the indoor pool.

"I don't have my swimsuit," I said.

"We can get you one in the gift shop," she said. "Come on, it'll be fun."

But I thought about Daddy, sitting at home waiting for me. And how he'd said not to go anywhere but the restaurant.

"No," I said. "I have homework."

So they drove me home. Navid waited in the car while Mama walked with me to the door.

"Thanks for coming, honey," she said. "It's just so good to see you."

She hugged me and I could feel a wet spot on her cheek.

"It was fun," I said.

"We'll be here until Sunday," Mama said. "I'll call your dad and set up something for tomorrow."

"I can't tomorrow," I said. "I have a test on Friday I have to study for."

"Okay, then, how about Friday? We can go to dinner again, and maybe you can come back and swim with me. I'm quite a sight in my swimsuit, you know."

She patted her swollen belly and laughed.

"Maybe," I said.

"Well, good night, Sweet Judy. I love you."

"Good night, Mama." I kissed her cheek and went inside.

Daddy was sitting in the living room, watching television. He smiled at me when I came in.

"So, how was it?"

"It was okay."

"Are you okay?"

"Yeah, I'm good. It was all right."

I sat beside him on the couch.

"Mama got the kung pao chicken," I said, smiling.

"No way! She doesn't like spicy food."

"She didn't know it was spicy. She just ordered it because I did."

Daddy laughed. "Was she surprised?"

"Yeah, she was. I don't think she liked it very much."

"I bet she didn't."

We sat a minute, and I said, "Navid is nice. He's from Persia."

"Persia? You mean Iran? How did Cassie meet someone from Iran?"

"He came here when he was a kid. He's a teacher at a college in Pasadena."

"Oh," Daddy said.

"He wants the baby to be a boy."

Daddy said nothing.

"Did you want me to be a boy before I was born?" I asked him.

He smiled at me. "No, honey. I just wanted you to be healthy."

"That's what Mama says, too."

He nodded.

"They're going to get married after the baby's born," I said. I wasn't sure it was right to tell him, but I figured he'd find out sometime anyway. "It's gonna be a Bahá'í wedding."

"He's a Bahá'í?"

"Yeah."

"So, a Bahá'í wedding. That will be different, I guess."

"Mama wants me to come."

"To the wedding? Where will it be? Not in Iran!"

"No, in Los Angeles. She wants me to come after the baby is born and stay for the wedding."

"And what do you think about that?" He was watching me closely.

"I don't know," I said. "I mean, I think it would be cool to see a Bahá'í wedding, but . . . I don't know."

"Well, if you want to go, I guess I could take you. To Los Angeles, that is, not to the wedding. I don't think I want to go to the wedding."

I nodded. I understood why he wouldn't want to go.

"She wants me to go out again on Friday," I said.

"Well, if you want to go that's okay."

"She said I could bring my swimsuit and swim at the hotel pool."

"Okay." Daddy leaned back and sighed.

"Is it okay? Really?" I had to ask. He didn't seem okay.

"Yes, honey, it's okay. She's your mother and you haven't seen her in a long time. It's okay for you to spend some time with her."

"Okay." I leaned over and kissed his cheek. "I'm gonna go call Lee Ann."

I'd promised to call her after dinner. She wanted to know everything.

"A Persian wedding? How cool. Are you going?"

"Maybe," I said. "Daddy said he'd take me to Los Angeles if I want to go."

"Can I come?"

"I don't know. Maybe. I can ask, anyway."

"I really want to see a Persian wedding."

"I'll ask Daddy," I promised.

"So, it was okay?" she asked.

"Yeah, it was okay. Mama seems happy and Navid's nice. They're like a married couple already."

"I can't believe your mom is going to marry a Persian."

"Yeah, pretty weird."

"Is she going to become a Bahá'í?"

"I don't think so."

I thought about that for a minute, then said, "Lee Ann, don't tell anyone at school, okay?"

"What . . . that your mom is back, or that she's marrying a Persian?"

"All of it. Just don't tell anyone about it, okay?"

"Not even Vernita? You have to tell her. She already knows your mom is here."

"Okay, but just Vernita. No one else."

"Okay," she agreed. "But I still think it's pretty cool."

We did tell Vernita about it the next day at lunch. Her eyes widened when she heard about the wedding.

"That sounds cool," she said. "Will she have to wear one of those veils over her face?"

"I think that's Muslim," I said. But I wasn't sure. I'd have to ask Mama.

I made her promise not to tell anyone else about Mama. Moving from grade school to junior high had given me a measure of anonymity. Some of the kids from my grade school remembered about Mama and how she'd tried to take me and then how she almost went to Guyana. But most of the kids in my junior high didn't know any of that. If they bothered to ask, I just told them my parents were divorced. Sometimes I made up stories about where my mother was—she was an artist and had moved to the desert to paint or an archaeologist on a dig in Egypt.

I didn't tell the truth, which was that my mother had been crazy and kidnapped me and taken me to a commune and almost died of a drug overdose and then joined a cult. And that it was my fault she left the second time, because I was so mean to her. That last part I hadn't even told Lee Ann.

Junior high was hard enough without everyone knowing about Mama.

On Friday at five, Mama and Navid arrived to pick me up for dinner. I carried an overnight bag with my swimsuit and beach towel. We went to Gringo's Taco House and ate, then drove to the Ramada Inn. Mama emerged from the bathroom in a bright red maternity swimsuit, her huge belly pushing its way into the room ahead of her. She waddled slightly and looked altogether ridiculous. I laughed when I saw her, but Navid kissed her cheek and told her she was beautiful.

Mama and I paddled around the pool for a while as Navid watched from the deck. He had not brought his swim trunks.

"I remember when I was pregnant with you, I loved to go swimming," Mama said, pushing wet hair back from her face. "I felt so light in the water. But this time"—she patted her stomach—"I just feel like a barge. I've gained so much weight with this pregnancy. Not like with you." She smiled at me.

"Are you really going to have the baby at home?" I asked.

"I hope so," she said. "Navid is worried about it, but I think I'll be fine. We'll have a midwife with us—that's a woman who knows all about birthing and stuff. And if anything happens that shouldn't, she'll know what to do."

She laughed. "It can't be any worse than with you. God, we were all just partying and then, whoosh, there you came two weeks early. We couldn't even find a nurse until after it was all over. Your dad was freaking out, but I knew it would be okay. . . . And it was. You were perfect."

"If I was perfect, then why did you leave?" I asked it before I could stop myself. It just came out of my mouth.

"Oh, my Sweet Judy, I didn't want to leave you. I wanted to take you with me. But they wouldn't let me."

I dove under the water and swam to the opposite side of the pool. After a minute, she paddled over to where I was.

"I'm so sorry, baby. I really didn't want to leave you. I just had to get out of Indiana. I felt like I was dying here. And your dad . . ."

"Daddy's great," I said. "He's the best dad in the world."

"Oh, I know that, honey. He loves you and he's taken really good care of you, and he's a good person. But I couldn't stay with him. It would have killed me. And eventually it would have killed him, too."

I hooked my elbows on the side of the pool and stretched my legs out behind me, my face turned away from her.

"Judy, I wish you'd look at me."

I stayed where I was and heard her sigh.

"Look, I was just too young. I was eighteen when I married your dad and nineteen when I had you. That's too young to be a wife and mother. I had to figure out what I wanted to be. I had to see other places. I was just too young. Don't you get that?"

I shook my head. "Daddy was too young, too. But he stayed."

She touched my shoulder. "Your daddy was a whole lot better at being a grown-up than I was." She sighed. "He probably still is. And . . . well, I might as well tell you, it's just that . . . I was messed up on drugs then. It didn't seem like such a big deal at first. I mean, everyone was doing it. But . . . it messed me up. It messed me up a lot.

"But I'm trying, Judy. I'm trying to be a better person. I've been clean for almost five years now, and I will never go back to that life. Never! I want to be a good mother to this baby. I want to make up for leaving you. I want . . . so much."

Her voice wavered, and when I looked at her, I saw tears in her eyes.

"Mama?"

"Yes, my Sweet Judy?"

"I'm sorry I made you go away last time."

"What?"

"When I told you that you didn't know anything and I was mean, and you left."

"Oh, honey." She pulled me to her in a hug. "Oh no, that wasn't your fault. It wasn't anything you did. Don't you ever think that, okay? I just . . . I felt like I was hurting you by being here. Your friends were so mean to you and then you got upset and . . . I thought it would be better for you, and for your dad, too, if I went to Karen's. I didn't want to cause any more chaos in your life. I didn't want you to have to take care of me. I just wanted you to be happy. Oh, Judy, it wasn't your fault."

I let her hug me while I thought about that. Had she really left because she thought she was hurting me? That was something I hadn't thought of before. I remembered how sad she looked when she heard what Carol had said.

"You know that, right?" she said finally, taking my face in her hands. "You know it's not your fault that I left?"

"I guess so."

"And I know you didn't like the farm, and it was wrong of me to take you there without your dad." She was talking faster now.

"I just felt like I had to leave Indiana, baby, to go somewhere and be part of . . . something. But I didn't want to leave *you*. I couldn't bear to leave you. That's why I took you with me, because I couldn't stand the thought of leaving you, of being away from you."

Her eyes never left mine; her hands stayed on my face so that I had to look at her.

"I never wanted to leave you, Sweet Judy. And I never stopped loving you."

Was that true? Did Mama really love me, after all?

The door to the pool area opened and a family with a bunch of little kids came in. The kids were shrieking and running and jumping in the water. It was time to leave.

Navid and Mama drove me home and Mama walked me to the door.

"Well," she said, "tomorrow we're going to Bloomington to see Aunt Karen and my dad. Do you want to come with us? I know they'd love to see you."

I shook my head. Daddy and I had already made plans for Saturday. We were going to a movie and out for pizza.

"I can't," I said. "I've got stuff to do."

"Oh," she said. "Well, then, I guess this is good-bye."

She hugged me and held me for a long minute. We'd never actually had a good-bye before. She'd always just left.

I chewed on my lip and felt tears stinging my eyes. Just when she seemed like a real mom, talking about stuff with me like moms do, she was leaving again.

"Hey," she said, smiling at me and touching my cheek. "This is not good-bye forever. You're coming to California in July, right?"

I nodded. "Daddy said he'd bring me."

"Okay, then it's just good-bye for a couple months. And the next time you see me, you'll be a big sister. Won't that be fun?"

I nodded again.

"And don't forget, Sweet Judy, not even for a minute, that I love you so much."

"I love you, too, Mama."

And I did. It surprised me, but I knew it was true. I loved Mama still. Knowing that she loved me, hoping that she loved me, opened some kind of door in my heart. And all the love I'd forgotten or pushed away came flooding back in.

I clung to her then, crying on her shoulder, feeling her tears on my neck.

The front door opened and Daddy appeared.

"Is everything okay?" he asked quietly.

"Yeah," I said, pulling back from Mama and wiping the back of my hand across my eyes. "It's good."

Mama smiled at Daddy and then at me, then kissed my cheek again.

"I'll see you soon, my sweet girl. Real soon, okay?"

I nodded and tried to smile as she walked down the steps toward the car where Navid was waiting. Then I followed Daddy back into the house.

"You sure you're okay?" he asked, watching me closely.

"I'm okay," I said. "She said she loves me."

I sat down on the couch and he sat beside me.

"Of course she loves you. Didn't you know that?" He took my hand in his and held it for a minute.

"I guess so."

"Do you want some tea?" he asked.

"Okay.

"Daddy?" I said as he rose.

"Yes, Judy?"

"I want to go to the wedding."

He stood a minute just looking at me, then he smiled and nodded.

"Okay, honey. If you want to go to your mom's wedding, then we'll go."

"Thanks," I said, smiling at him.

"And, Daddy?"

He turned to look at me again.

"I love you."

❦ 21 ❦

"Judy, are you ready? We've got to go or we'll miss our flight," Daddy hollered from downstairs.

"I can't get my suitcase closed," I yelled back, staring hopelessly at the overstuffed bag on my bed.

"Oh, for Pete's sake!" Daddy laughed as he pulled the suitcase onto the floor. "Are you taking your entire closet? Here, you sit on it and I'll zip it."

I sat on the suitcase and Daddy zipped it, then he lugged it downstairs.

I followed him to the car, where his small suitcase was already in the trunk.

"I wasn't sure what to bring," I said. "I've never been to a Persian wedding before."

We drove to the airport and waited in line to pass through security. My stomach churned. I'd never been on a plane.

"You'll be fine." Daddy smiled at me. "It's safer than riding in a car."

We found our row and I buckled myself into the window seat.

"Are you okay?" Daddy asked. "You look like you're going to be sick."

I nodded, holding his hand tightly as the plane taxied onto the runway, then picked up speed and rose into the air.

After a while, I relaxed enough to let go of his hand.

"See, it's not so bad," Daddy said. He pulled a magazine from his briefcase and began reading. I stared out the window, remembering all the times I had looked up at airplanes in the sky and wondered who was on them and where they were going. I wondered if anyone was looking up at this plane, wondering about me.

Almost four hours later, the pilot announced that we were coming into Los Angeles. Far below, I could see the city spread out in all directions. It seemed to go on forever. Somewhere in that huge city, Mama lived with Navid and Kamran, her new baby boy.

As we walked into the airport terminal, I held Daddy's hand again. The airport was huge, much bigger than the one in Indianapolis. And it was filled with people, all kinds of people. A woman in a veil passed by, carrying a huge covered basket. A man with the darkest skin I had ever seen sat with an equally dark child on his lap. By the airport bar, several people with shaved heads and bright orange robes handed out marigolds to passersby. It was like a whole different world.

"There he is," Daddy said, pointing to where Navid stood. He waved and Navid smiled and waved back.

"Welcome," Navid said, shaking Daddy's hand. "How was your flight?"

"Fine," Daddy said. "I don't think Judy liked it very much."

"No?" Navid looked at me.

"It was okay," I said. "Where's Mama?"

"She's at home with the baby," he said. "I didn't think it would be good to bring him out around so many people. Come on, let's get your luggage."

We found our suitcases and followed Navid across an enormous parking lot to his car. Daddy rode in the front seat with Navid and I sat in back. I stared out the window as we pulled onto the freeway, all twelve lanes of it. So many cars buzzed around us, it almost made me dizzy.

"It will take a little while," Navid said. "We moved up to

Pasadena six weeks ago. It's closer to my work, and it's a better place to raise children."

I couldn't even imagine raising children in such a big city.

"How is the baby?" Daddy asked.

"He's fine." Navid smiled. "A big, strong boy."

"And Cassie?"

"Oh, she's fine, too. A little tired, but she's okay."

We passed palm trees and tall buildings and everywhere more cars. By the time we pulled off the freeway, I felt as if we'd traveled halfway across the universe.

Navid parked in front of a big cream-colored stucco building. "We're on the fourth floor," he said, pulling my suitcase from the trunk. "It's a good thing we have an elevator." He grinned at me.

"Cassie Joon," he called as he opened the door to the apartment. "We're home."

She walked into the living room carrying a tiny baby wrapped in a blue blanket.

"Oh, Sweet Judy," she said, "welcome home!"

She hugged me, then pulled the blanket back from the baby's head. He had thick, dark hair and huge black eyes.

"This is Kamran," Mama said, smiling proudly, "your new baby brother. Isn't he beautiful?"

I touched his small cheek. "Yes, Mama. He's beautiful."

I stared at the baby, looking for something familiar, some sign that he was my brother. But all I saw was a miniature Navid staring back at me.

"Hey, Cassie." Daddy leaned forward and kissed Mama's cheek. "How are you?"

"I'm fine, Kirk," she said. "I'm better than fine. I'm . . . well, I'm blessed." She smiled at him.

"Good," he said, shifting from one foot to the other. "That's good."

"Here," Mama said, pulling me toward the sofa. "Sit down and you can hold him."

I sat and she laid the baby carefully in my arms. I cradled him, staring down at his brown face. He didn't look like me at all. He didn't even look like Mama.

"Navid Joon," Mama said, "get the camera and take a picture of Judy and Kamran."

Navid snapped several photos of me holding the baby, then several more with Mama sitting beside me. Daddy stood by the front door, watching in silence.

Finally, Navid set the camera aside. "Are you hungry?" he asked, looking from me to Daddy. "Can I get you something to eat?"

"No, thanks," Daddy said. "We ate on the plane."

"Ah." Navid shook his head. "That's not real food. I made Indian food—curry. You must eat."

He strode into the kitchen and Mama laughed.

"You have to eat something," she said. "He was up half the night cooking. And please, Kirk, sit down. Sit down and relax. You've had a long trip." She smiled at him.

Daddy sat down in a chair by the door, beneath a huge framed picture of a kind-looking old man with a white beard.

"Who's that?" I asked, pointing to the picture.

Mama smiled. "That's 'Abdu'l-Bahá," she said. "He's the son of Bahá'u'lláh, the founder of the Bahá'í faith. It was a gift from Navid's parents. They gave it to us when we moved in as a housewarming present."

"So," Daddy said, eyeing the picture, "Navid's family is Bahá'í. Will you raise the baby as a Bahá'í?"

"Oh," Mama said, "it's funny. Before Kamran was born, Navid didn't seem to care so much about religion. But now . . . well, now he'd like to raise the baby in his faith. So yeah, I guess we'll raise him as a Bahá'í."

Daddy smiled. "And what do your folks think of that?" he asked.

Mama sighed. "I talked to them after Kamran was born," she said. "They sent that." She pointed to a stroller sitting by the door. "I asked them to come to the wedding, but of course they won't."

"I'm surprised you even asked," Daddy said.

"It was Navid's idea," Mama said. "Family is really important to him. He wanted them to come. He met Dad when we were in Indiana. And they seemed to hit it off. But . . . well, you know my mom."

"I'm sorry, Cassie."

"It's okay," she said. "Karen is coming."

Daddy smiled. "Good for her."

"You know, Kirk, you're welcome to come to the wedding." Mama smiled at him.

"Thanks, Cassie. I don't think so. But thanks."

"Here we are!" Navid emerged from the kitchen carrying a big platter stacked with plates, glasses, and silverware. In the center sat a huge pile of rice and a bowl filled with a yellowish sauce. "This is from India," he said. "I know you like spicy foods, Judy. You will love this."

He piled rice onto a plate and ladled sauce over it, then handed it to me. He filled another plate for Daddy. He looked at Mama and she laughed and shook her head. "No, thanks," she said. "I can't handle your sauces. Especially while I'm breastfeeding."

As if on cue, the baby whimpered and squirmed, then let out a cry that sounded like a kitten yowling for its mother.

Mama smiled and lifted her blouse, raising the baby to her bare breast. Daddy looked away.

"Ah," Navid said. "But that's exactly why you should be eating it. So Kamran Joon develops a good, strong stomach."

Mama just shook her head again. "I've already eaten."

I took a cautious bite and then another. The wonderful, complex flavor of the curry filled my mouth, and then I began to feel a slow, steady burn building. Navid watched me, smiling. He poured a large glass of water from a pitcher and handed it to me.

"Do you like it?" he asked, watching me gulp down the cold water.

I nodded, taking another bite.

"There," he said, smiling at Mama. "You see? Even Judy eats my food. What are we to do with you?"

Mama just laughed.

After we had eaten, Daddy asked if Navid would take him to the car rental place, so he could rent a car. But Navid only smiled.

"No," he said. "While you are here you must drive Cassie's car. She is not driving. She is not going anywhere. So the car is free."

"Oh no, I can't," Daddy said. "What if she wants to go someplace?"

"Then I will take her," Navid said, putting his hand on Mama's shoulder. "She should not drive so soon after the baby."

Mama sighed and patted Navid's hand. "He thinks I'm as fragile as a china doll," she said, smiling. "I can't make him believe that I'm fine. Just fine."

"You are more than fine," he said, leaning down to kiss the top of her head. "You are perfect. And it is my job to keep you safe that way."

Mama laughed and laid the baby in a bassinet by the couch, touching her finger to his nose lightly.

"Well," Daddy said, looking toward the front door. "I really can't use your car. I'll rent one. That's what I'd planned on."

But Navid would not be moved. After much discussion, he finally pressed the car keys into Daddy's hand. Daddy sighed and gave up.

"You are staying at the Holiday Inn?" Navid asked. "It's not far from here. I will make you a map."

"Okay," Daddy said, kissing my forehead. "I'll call you later. You gonna be okay?"

I nodded, holding his hand. I would be staying at the apartment with Mama and Navid and the baby.

"Are you?" I asked, softly, so Mama wouldn't hear.

"Yes, honey. I'll be fine. I'm going to check in, unpack, and hit the hay. It's been a long day."

He left with Navid's map tucked into his pocket and Mama's car keys in his hand.

"Well," Mama said, putting her arm around my shoulders. "Let me show you your room. We fixed it up just for you."

The room was small, with a bed placed under the window. It was decorated in peach and green, just like my room at home.

"I hope you like it," Mama said. "I tried to make it like I remember your room at your dad's."

"It's nice," I said. I felt a huge lump in my throat, thinking about her decorating this room for me. "Thank you."

She smiled and hugged me. "I'm so glad."

"Where does the baby sleep?" I asked.

"Well, right now he sleeps in our room. But when he gets older, I suppose we'll move him in here."

"Oh." I swallowed hard. The peach and green wouldn't stay then.

"But for now, it's all yours," Mama said brightly. "You can put your things in here." She pointed to a dresser. "Goodness." She laughed, looking at my suitcase. "You brought a lot of things."

She began pulling clothes from the suitcase and laying them in drawers.

"Probably too much," I said softly. After all, I would only be staying a week.

"That's okay," she said. "We have lots of room. Oh good, you brought your swimsuit. We have a pool, you know. It's on the roof."

"Really?" I'd never heard of a pool on a roof.

"Sure. Tomorrow we'll go up there and swim. Would you like that?"

I nodded.

"Oh, Sweet Judy," she said, plopping down on the bed. "I'm so glad you're here."

I sat down beside her and she pulled me into a hug.

"I feel like I've been waiting forever to have you with me. And now, here you are." She smiled, but I could see tears in her eyes.

"We're going to have so much fun," she continued. "Tomorrow we'll swim and maybe take a walk. And one day Navid is going to take us to the beach. And then there's the wedding, of course. That will be fun, too. On Friday, we're going to have dinner with Navid's family. They can't wait to meet you. You'll love them, they're so great. And we'll have a big dinner. And then Saturday . . . well, that's the wedding."

She leaned back against the pillow and smiled. "It's going to be beautiful, Judy. A beautiful Persian wedding. And wait till you see my dress. It's gorgeous! And I have a dress for you, too."

She rose and walked to the closet, pulling out a green and gold silk gown.

"Look," she said, holding it out to me. "Isn't it beautiful?"

I could only nod. It was indeed beautiful, like a shimmery scarf.

"Try it on," Mama said. "Come on, try it on and let's make sure it fits you."

So I undressed and Mama slipped the gown over my head. The soft, light fabric fell gently around me until it touched my feet.

"And look," Mama said, pulling at a fold of fabric. "You use this to cover your head. Oh, honey." She sighed, smiling at me. "You're gorgeous! Look!" She led me to a mirror and I gazed at myself. I looked different in the dress, exotic almost. My dark hair contrasted nicely with the gold of the scarf.

"Navid," Mama called. "Come look at my Sweet Judy in her dress."

Navid stood in the doorway and smiled at us. "You look almost like a Persian, Judy Joon," he said, nodding at me. "Beautiful."

"Why do you call everyone Joon?" I asked.

"It's a Persian term of endearment," he said. "It's like saying Judy dear."

I wished Daddy could see me in the dress.

After I'd dressed in my normal clothes, Mama took me up to the roof to look at the swimming pool. It was surrounded by potted palm trees and lounge chairs. It looked like a Hollywood movie set. To the north, the San Gabriel Mountains rose, barely visible through the brownish haze.

"You should see it in the winter," Mama said. "When the smog's gone, the mountains are amazing."

She pointed out some Mediterranean-looking buildings a few blocks away. "That's CalTech," she said. "That's where Navid works. Tomorrow we'll walk over there and you can see it. It's beautiful. It looks more like a spa than a college campus. You'll love it."

Before I went to bed that night I called Daddy, just to say good night. And to make sure he was okay.

"I'm fine," he said. He sounded tired. "Don't worry about me. Just have a good time with your mother and the baby."

"Okay, Daddy," I said. It made me sad thinking of him alone in a hotel room. "Do you have a pool there?"

"Yes," he said. "I think there's a pool."

"Okay," I said, knowing he would not use the pool. "Good night."

"Good night, Judy."

"Daddy?"

"Yes, honey?"

"I love you."

"I love you, too, peanut."

After I got off the phone, Mama tucked me into bed and kissed my forehead. "Good night, my Sweet Judy. I'm so glad you're here."

"Good night, Mama."

She turned out the light and closed the door behind her. I stared out the window at the lights of the unfamiliar city. I felt a million miles away from my home in Indiana. I wished Lee Ann could be here with me. She would love the pool and the silk gown, although I thought she probably wouldn't like Navid's curry very much.

After a long time, I fell asleep.

22

The next few days passed in a blur. We walked around Pasadena, Mama pushing Kamran in his stroller and buying us ice cream on Lake Street. We swam in the pool on the roof while the baby slept in a little basket under an umbrella. One day Navid drove us to Malibu Beach. Mama and I splashed in the ocean while he watched us from the shore, cradling the baby. Daddy came for dinner a couple times, but mostly he stayed at the hotel. I called him every night to say good night.

On Friday afternoon, I put on the dress I had brought with me for the wedding. We were going to have dinner with Navid's family.

Mama brushed my hair and pulled it back into a French braid.

"When we get there, be sure to shake their hands," she said. "And be very polite, okay? Navid's parents are very traditional."

I nodded.

"And you should call them Mr. and Mrs. Ghorbani. They probably wouldn't like it if you called them by their first names. And Navid's sister will be there with her husband and their kids. They're so cute, you'll love them. Samira is five and Farid is two. They're just precious."

I nodded again.

After she had surveyed me in the mirror, she smiled and rested her hand on my shoulder. "My Sweet Judy, you are getting to be so beautiful," she said.

I stared at myself in the mirror, wondering what she saw that I didn't.

I closed my eyes as we drove on the freeway. Watching all the cars made my head ache. In his car seat beside me, Kamran slept, sighing now and then, his mouth making small sucking motions, his tiny hand wrapped around my little finger.

We pulled into the driveway of a big stucco house with a fountain in front. I stared in silence. Navid's family must be very rich.

Before we could even knock, a woman opened the door and stepped onto the porch. She wore a black dress and very high heels. Her dark hair had golden highlights and was coiled around her head. Silver earrings sparkled against her neck.

"Cassie Joon, come in. Come in. Welcome."

She held the door wide for us. We stepped into a two-story entryway. A huge crystal chandelier dangled above us.

"And this is your daughter," the woman said, smiling at me and holding out her hand. "Welcome, Judy. Welcome to our family." She shook my hand, still smiling.

"Judy, this is Mrs. Ghorbani," Mama said. "She's Navid's mother."

"Hello," I said.

"And this is Mr. Ghorbani, Navid's father."

A tall man leaned down to shake my hand. Then he smiled. "You are pretty like your mother," he said.

"And these are Maryam and Azad."

I shook hands with each of them. Maryam was a beautiful woman with full lips and long, dark hair. Her husband was older, short, and round, with a kind face.

"And here are your new cousins," Maryam said, pulling her children forward for me to meet. "This is Samira and that's Farid."

Samira smiled shyly, but Farid simply stared and put his fingers in his mouth.

"Come in, please. Be comfortable." Mrs. Ghorbani waved us into a sitting room. Ornate furniture was grouped near a large marble fireplace. Beautiful cushions were scattered across a soft, intricately woven carpet.

We sat down on the sofa and Maryam served us small, clear glasses of tea. Mrs. Ghorbani took the baby from Navid and nuzzled him with her mouth. "Aziza," she crooned, smiling at the baby. "Kamran Joon, it's Maman Bozorg. I'm Grandmama. And here is Baba Bozorg, your grandfather. Oh, Joonam, such a beautiful boy." She was clearly delighted with the baby.

Samira sat down beside me on the sofa. "I'm five," she said, folding her hands neatly in her lap. "How old are you?"

"Twelve," I said, smiling at her.

"That's pretty old," she proclaimed. Everyone laughed.

"So, Judy, what grade are you in at school?" Mrs. Ghorbani asked.

"I'm going into eighth grade."

"Ah." She smiled, then resumed her nuzzling of the baby.

"Your mother says you like history," Mr. Ghorbani said.

"Yes, sir," I answered.

"That's good, very good," he said. "History is important. It's important to know about the past. I have some books about Persian history. You will like them." He rose and walked into the next room, returning with an armful of books.

"Don't worry, they are in English," he said, smiling proudly as he handed them to me. "So you can learn about your new family's history."

"Thank you," I said, eyeing the pile on my lap. I didn't know when he thought I was going to read all those books.

"Here." Maryam rose. "Let me put those by the door, so you don't forget them. Azad Joon, will you give Judy some cookies?"

Her husband passed a silver platter to me, heaped with cookies.

"These are very good," he said, pointing to what looked like small brown flowers. "Nan-e Nan-Nokhochi, made with chickpea flour. You will like them."

I took a small bite and smiled at him. "It's good," I said. "Thank you."

"Cassie Joon, she has lovely manners, your daughter." Mrs. Ghorbani smiled at Mama. "And she's beautiful like her mother."

"Thank you, Farzaneh," Mama said. She sat at the edge of the sofa and seemed nervous in this grand house.

"Judy, do you like Persian food?" Maryam asked.

"I don't know," I replied. "I don't think I ever had it."

"Navid Joon." His mother clucked. "What have you been feeding this girl?"

"Judy likes spicy food." He grinned. "I've been making curries this week."

Mrs. Ghorbani shook her head. "What have you been eating, then, Cassie Joon?" she asked, laughing. Apparently everyone knew that Mama did not like spicy foods.

"Well, tonight we have the Persian food," Mrs. Ghorbani said, turning back to me. "We have rice and yogurt and kebabs and fesenjan. You will like it, I think."

I nodded. If it was anything like Indian curry, I knew I would.

We gathered around a huge table. White china plates rimmed in gold gleamed against the dark wood. On the table was a huge platter with dried fruits. Another plate held bread, feta cheese, vegetables, bunches of herbs, and a bowl of yogurt.

"Okay, you try this," Mr. Ghorbani said, spearing a radish and putting it on my plate. "And this is good, too."

He handed me a piece of flat bread, then spooned a small scoop of brown paste onto my plate. "Hummus," he said. "Not Persian, but very good. You dip the bread, like this." He scooped some hummus onto a piece of bread and popped it in his mouth.

I did the same, savoring the creamy texture of the dip and the chewy bread.

Next came platters piled with rice—some yellow with saffron, some speckled with herbs and lima beans. A silver tray held skewers of grilled lamb. And in the center of the table sat a big tureen filled with a dark, lumpy-looking sauce that smelled like heaven.

"You try the fesenjan," Mr. Ghorbani said, ladling the sauce over rice on my plate. "It is chicken and walnuts in pomegranate sauce. Very good."

It was very good. Everything was very good. Across the table from me, Farid was eating rice by the spoonful. His cheeks bulged so that he looked like a chipmunk.

"So, tomorrow we have a wedding," Mr. Ghorbani said.

"Finally a wedding," Mrs. Ghorbani said.

Mama and Navid exchanged glances.

"We are doing this all backwards," she continued, smiling at me. "First the baby, then the wedding. Ah, well, better a late wedding than no wedding."

I nodded, unsure what to say.

"Have you ever been to a Bahá'í wedding, Judy?" Mr. Ghorbani asked.

"No, sir."

"You will like it, I think. Very simple and beautiful."

"And after, a wonderful party," Mrs. Ghorbani said. "With a lot of Persian foods for you to try . . . and dancing."

"Oh," I said. I wondered what kind of dancing there would be. I didn't know how to dance very well.

"How many people are we expecting?" Mama asked.

I was surprised by the question. It was her wedding, after all.

"Oh, not so many," Mrs. Ghorbani said, smiling. "Maybe two hundred."

Mama's eyes widened. Navid patted her hand.

"That's not so many, really," he said. "Just family and friends."

Mama managed a small smile and nodded.

"We had to invite people from the Bahá'í community," Mr. Ghorbani said. "We don't want to insult anyone."

"People want to meet you, Cassie. And they want to meet your daughter. You are joining our family, our community. It's important," Mrs. Ghorbani said.

I watched Mama carefully as she wrung her napkin in her hands.

"It's fine," she said, smiling. But her voice didn't sound very sure.

After dinner, Maryam took Mama's arm in hers and patted it. "Don't worry, Cassie Joon," she said, smiling. "It really isn't such a big wedding. If Maman had her way, she'd have invited all of Los Angeles."

It was quiet on the drive back to the apartment. Kamran had fussed before we left, but he fell asleep as soon as the car started. Mama was quiet, too.

"So, Judy," Navid said finally, "what do you think of Persian food?"

"It's good," I said. "But I think I like Indian better."

Navid laughed and patted Mama's shoulder. "You see, Cassie Joon? Judy likes my curry even better than Maman's fesenjan."

Mama smiled but said nothing.

Later, when I was in bed staring at the city lights out the window, I heard them arguing in the living room.

"Okay, yes," Navid said, "it's a lot of people. But you have to understand, Cassie. This is my family, my culture. They can't have just a small wedding."

"But we agreed on a small ceremony." Mama's voice trembled. "You promised just family and a few friends."

"And that's what it will be," he said. "For Persians, two hundred is a small wedding."

"I won't even know anyone," Mama said.

"You will know me," Navid said softly. "And you will have Judy with you, and your sister. That's all that matters . . . right?"

"I guess so," she said. "It's just a lot more than I wanted."

"It's our marriage," he said. "Don't you want to celebrate that with the people who love us?"

"Who love you," she said. "They don't even know me."

"That's why they're coming, Cassie. They want to know you. You are going to be my wife. They want to know who you are."

I heard her sigh, then say softly, "It's okay, Navid. If it's what you want, then it's okay."

They were quiet after that and I fell asleep to the sounds of traffic far below.

23

Saturday dawned hot and clear. Navid drove to the airport to pick up Karen while Mama bustled around the apartment, worrying over her dress and mine. I sat on the couch holding Kamran on my lap, watching her. She seemed very nervous.

"Now, part of the service will be in Farsi," she said. "That's the Persian language. But mostly it will be in English. It's pretty simple, really. And you will sit with Karen, is that okay?"

I nodded.

"And don't worry about the dancing," she said, smiling at me. "It's Persian dancing, and it's really easy. Here, I'll show you."

She took Kamran from me and put him in his pumpkin seat on the table. Then she turned on the tape player. Exotic music filled the apartment.

"See, you take your hands like this and move them back and forth. Good, that's good."

I tried to copy her movements, but it wasn't easy. They didn't exactly match the music. Mama really had no rhythm.

"And then you move your feet like this."

I watched her, copying the movement of her feet, trying not to laugh. She looked kind of ridiculous.

"Good, honey. That's good. You've got it!"

We were both dancing and laughing when the apartment door opened. Navid grinned at the two of us, then stepped into the apartment. Behind him was Mama's sister, Karen. She took one look at us and burst into laughter.

"Oh Lord, Cassie," she said. "You dance just like you did in high school."

Mama ran to hug her.

"Oh, Karen, I'm so glad you're here!"

Navid put his hand on my shoulder and smiled at me. "You've picked up our dance very well, Judy Joon. You're a natural."

I felt my cheeks redden and shook my head.

After Karen had cooed over Kamran and admired his dark hair and eyes, his tiny fingers and toes, Navid wrapped the baby in a blanket and bundled him into his car seat.

"I am taking Kamran Joon to my parents' house," he said. "I will dress for the wedding there, and Maman will watch the baby for us."

He kissed Mama on the forehead. "I will see you at the wedding," he said, smiling down at her.

"Okay," she said. "Drive carefully."

Navid left with the baby, and Mama made coffee for Karen. I sat and watched the two of them in the kitchen. They looked so much alike, but they were so different. Karen was dressed stylishly, with short spiky hair and very high heels. Mama looked just like she always had. Her blond hair hung long and straight down her back. She was wearing a white gauzy dressing gown and her feet were bare.

"Okay," Karen said when she'd finished her coffee. "What are we doing with your hair?"

"Well, I thought I'd brush it," Mama said, smiling.

"Oh, God." Karen sighed. "It's a good thing I'm here."

She sat Mama in a chair and began brushing her hair. "We'll French braid it and twist it up around your head," she said, demonstrating. "What kind of veil are you wearing?"

"No veil." Mama laughed. "This isn't the middle ages."

Karen frowned. "Then what are you wearing?"

Mama rose and pulled a beautiful, pale pink silk gown from the closet. Karen inspected it, then smiled. "It's beautiful, Cassie. It looks just like you. But what are you wearing in your hair?"

"Nothing," Mama said.

Karen stared at her for a long minute, then shook her head. "No," she said firmly. "You need something in your hair. The dress demands it."

"Well, it's a little late now," Mama said. "We have to be at the hotel by four."

"That's plenty of time," Karen said. "Where's the nearest flower shop?"

So we drove to a shop and Karen told the florist exactly what she wanted, choosing pink roses with dark greenery and white baby's breath. Then she watched while the florist wove the flowers into a beaded tiara, making suggestions now and then. When the piece was done, she set the tiara on Mama's head and pronounced her fit to be seen. Mama just laughed.

We returned to the apartment and dressed for the wedding. Then Karen braided Mama's hair and wound it around her head, topping it with the flowered tiara. Really, it was perfect.

"Oh, Cassie." Karen smiled. "You're beautiful."

Mama examined herself in the mirror.

"It doesn't look like me," she said softly. "What do you think, Judy?" She turned to look at me.

"I think you're beautiful, too." I was telling the truth. She really did look beautiful.

"And now for some makeup." Karen reached for a cosmetic bag she'd brought.

"Oh no, Karen, absolutely not! I am not wearing makeup." Mama shook her head fiercely.

"Come on, Cassie. It's your wedding. You need something. Just a little lipstick and blush, maybe some eyeliner."

But Mama would not be moved. Sighing, Karen turned to me.

"How about you, Judy? Can I put some lipstick on you?"

"Absolutely not!" Mama said again. "Sweet Judy is beautiful just the way she is."

She pulled me to stand beside her in front of the mirror. "Just look how beautiful she is," she said so softly I could hardly hear her.

I looked at the two of us in the mirror, Mama in her pale pink gown and tiara, me in my green and gold silk. I wondered yet again why she thought I was beautiful.

Finally, Karen gave up arguing and went to make up her own face, emerging from the bathroom looking polished and chic.

"Are we ready?" she asked.

Navid had sent a car to pick us up, a long white limousine. Karen gave a low whistle when she saw it. "Now, this is the way to travel," she said as we settled into the car. "Look," she said, opening a tray. "Refreshments!"

She poured a glass of champagne and held it out to Mama. Mama smiled and shook her head.

"I can't," she said. "It's a Bahá'í wedding. Bahá'ís don't drink."

"Well, you're not a Bahá'í," Karen said, holding the glass out to her again.

"No, but I can't show up with alcohol on my breath, Karen. Navid's mother would just die. Besides, I'm nursing."

"Oh well," Karen said, smiling. "More for me."

She poured a soda for me, and I sipped it carefully. I didn't want to spill anything on my beautiful dress.

We pulled up in front of a huge pink hotel in Beverly Hills. Peacocks strutted across the lawn. A man wearing a dark uniform and white gloves opened the car door and ushered us inside.

"Ah, Cassie Joon, here you are at last! We were beginning to worry." Mrs. Ghorbani enveloped Mama in a hug, kissing both her cheeks.

"Judy Joon, you look so beautiful," she said, kissing my cheeks.

"Farzeneh, this is my sister, Karen," Mama said, pulling Karen forward.

Mrs. Ghorbani took a long look at Karen, taking in the stylish haircut, elegant gown, and stiletto heels. She nodded approval and kissed Karen, too. "Welcome, Karen. Welcome to Los Angeles. Welcome to our family.

"Now," she said, taking Mama's arm. "We go upstairs for some pictures. Karen, you take Judy just down there." She pointed down a long hallway. "At the end on the left." With that, she pulled Mama away, talking the entire time. Mama looked over her shoulder and smiled at us. She looked scared.

"Okay, kiddo," Karen said. "Let's check this place out."

We wandered through the lobby into a lounge where several people sat drinking from fancy glasses. Karen ordered a martini for herself and another soda for me. "We've got plenty of time before the service," she said, sitting down in a plush chair.

We watched people come and go, Karen commenting from time to time on someone's clothes or hair.

"Look at that suit," she said, pointing to a man in black. "That's an Armani. Probably worth more than my car."

I nodded.

"So," she said, turning her gaze to me, "what do you think of Navid?"

"He's nice."

"Yeah, my dad liked him, too," she said. "But you know he's Persian. And those Middle Eastern men, they can be pretty old-fashioned."

I nodded, not understanding exactly what she meant.

"I mean, their culture is pretty patriarchal. The man is the head of the house and all that. I don't know how Cassie's going to deal with that."

She took a sip of her martini and said, "And that mother-in-law, what a piece of work. I'll bet she's a real control freak."

"She was nice last night," I said, feeling like I ought to defend Navid's family.

"Oh, I'm sure she's nice, hon. But I'll bet she likes to run the show. I mean, look at this place." We both gazed around the ornate hotel lobby. "This just isn't Cassie at all."

"There are going to be two hundred people at the wedding," I said.

Karen laughed. "That's not Cassie, that's the mother-in-law. Oh well." She took another drink. "I hope she'll be happy. God knows your mom's had enough unhappiness to last a lifetime."

I hoped Mama would be happy, too. She seemed happy at home with Navid and the baby.

"Okay, come on, kiddo." Karen rose and took my hand. "Let's go see what a Persian Bahá'í wedding looks like."

We walked down the long hallway and into a huge room festooned with garlands of white roses and candles. White chairs stood in neat rows facing a small stage surrounded by white pillars, each topped with roses and candles. A man in a black tuxedo ushered us to the front row, where the bride's parents usually sat.

Eventually the room filled with elegantly dressed people. All around us conversations buzzed in a lyrical language I couldn't understand. Finally, a hush fell over the crowd as a string quartet began playing music.

Mr. and Mrs. Ghorbani arrived, sitting across the aisle from Karen and me. Then Navid walked into the room from a side door, followed by Azad, his brother-in-law. They stood on the stage, smiling and handsome in their black tuxedos.

Samira and Farid walked slowly up the aisle. Samira sprinkled flower petals in her wake. Farid held a small white pillow and stared solemnly ahead. When she saw me, Samira smiled.

After them came Maryam, dressed in a long gown of pale green with gold accents, the same colors as the dress I wore.

Finally, Mama appeared in the doorway. The string quartet began playing Pachelbel's "Canon in D" and everyone rose. Mama walked up the aisle, looking nervous at first, then smiling when she saw Karen and me. So far, the wedding was just like an American wedding. It was fancier than anything I'd seen before, but still . . .

Once Mama reached the stage, we all sat down and I waited to see what would happen next. A man rose and read a prayer by Bahá'u'lláh, the founder of the Bahá'í faith. Then Karen stood and read from the Bible about love being patient and kind. When she sat down, another man rose and began singing. It was a prayer, I learned later, chanted in Arabic, and it was hauntingly beautiful. Another man rose when he was finished and chanted in Farsi, another prayer.

Mama and Navid faced each other and said in turn, "We will all, verily, abide by the will of God." Then they lit a candle and kissed.

The string quartet played again and they walked back down the aisle. The wedding was over.

Karen looked at me and smiled. "Well, that wasn't so bad," she said. "I wasn't sure what to expect, but that was all right."

We followed the wedding party down the aisle and into the hallway.

"Judy, how beautiful you are!" Maryam was smiling at me. She kissed both my cheeks and turned to Karen. "You must be Karen," she said, shaking Karen's hand. "I am Maryam, Navid's sister. I'm so glad you could be here."

She introduced Karen to Azad and Mr. Ghorbani, then led us back into the wedding room. "We will take some family pictures now. Samira, come away from the candles!" She strode away from us toward her children, who were leaning against one of the white pillars on the stage.

"Hey," Mama said, scooping me into a hug. "Did you like the service?"

I nodded. "It was nice."

"I'm so glad you're here," she said. "You, too, sis." She hugged Karen.

"We have to take pictures now." She grimaced. "I can't believe how many pictures they want."

A photographer spoke rapidly in Farsi, pointing this way and that. Maryam took my arm and led me to where he pointed, Karen trailing behind. We stood and smiled for what seemed like an hour, moving when the photographer told us to. Finally, he released us and we walked back to the hallway. My face hurt from smiling so much.

"Now," Mrs. Ghorbani said to Karen, "you and Judy go in, and we will follow you."

A man in white gloves opened the door to an even bigger ballroom that was filled with round tables covered in white cloths. Candles sparkled on each table, surrounded by garlands of white roses. Beautifully dressed people sat at the tables, talking in that bewildering, beautiful language that is Farsi.

The man led us to an empty table right up front, where we sat down and waited to see what would happen next. Soon, we were joined by Maryam, Azad, Samira, and Farid. Then Mr. and Mrs. Ghorbani entered the room, and everyone clapped. After they had been seated at the table with us, the door opened again and Navid led Mama into the room. Everyone clapped again.

Mama and Navid stopped by our table and kissed us all, then began circulating through the room. I watched as Navid introduced Mama over and over again, and people kissed her cheeks. She smiled, but I could see she was nervous.

People began filling their plates at the buffet tables, and still Navid and Mama circled the room, shaking hands and kissing cheeks. Karen and I followed Maryam and the children to the buffet and stared at the array of foods laid out.

"That is morasa polo," Maryam said, pointing to a platter of rice that seemed to sparkle with berries and nuts. "And this is khoresht ghormeh sabzi. It has herbs and red beans and dried lemons. You will love it."

There were kebabs and rice dishes and fruits and platters of vegetables. I'd never seen so much beautiful food in my life.

We returned to our table, our plates full, and ate until we could eat no more. And still Mama and Navid circled the room. Would they ever sit down and eat?

Finally, Mama plopped down in the chair beside me. She looked exhausted.

"Where's Kamran?" she asked Maryam.

"He's with Aunt Goli," Maryam said. "He's okay."

"I need to nurse him," Mama said. "My milk just let down."

After a week with Mama and Kamran, I knew what she meant.

Maryam led Mama from the room.

A few minutes later, Mrs. Ghorbani came to the table. "Where is Cassie Joon?" she asked.

"She went to nurse the baby," Karen said.

"Oh no." Mrs. Ghorbani shook her head. "But it's time to cut the cake."

She walked purposely toward the door where Maryam had just led Mama.

Karen raised an eyebrow to me, as if to say, "See?"

After a few minutes, Mama returned, looking flustered and unhappy. She let herself be led to the huge wedding cake and smiled for the camera as she and Navid cut the cake.

Then, they walked to the dance floor. A band began playing a waltz, and Navid tried to lead Mama through their first dance. He was whispering the beat in her ear; I could see it from where I sat. Mama just laughed as she tried to follow him. Eventually other couples arrived on the dance floor and Mama came back to our table.

"Jesus Christ," she hissed to Karen, leaning heavily against her shoulder. "Is this ever going to end?"

But the evening was only beginning. After the cake was eaten, the Persian dancing began and all of us ended up on the dance floor. Mama had taken her shoes off by then. I saw Mrs. Ghorbani frown at that, but Mr. Ghorbani patted her arm and whispered something to her, and she let it go.

The dancing was fun. I picked up the steps easily, and before long, I could follow even the most intricate patterns. Navid laughed and patted my shoulder. "We'll make a real Persian of you, Judy," he said, looking proud.

Finally, sometime long after midnight, the last of the guests said their good-byes, kissing cheeks with Mr. and Mrs. Ghorbani, then with Navid and Mama, Maryam and Azad, and Karen and me. I'd been kissed more in one night than I had been in my whole life.

Navid retrieved Kamran from his Aunt Goli and ushered Mama into the limo. Karen and I followed. As soon as the car pulled away from the hotel, Mama pulled the strap of her pink gown down and began nursing the baby. She sighed deeply and seemed to relax into the plush leather seat.

"Thank God that's over," she said, smiling at the baby's head.

"Oh, it wasn't so bad, was it?" Navid kissed her cheek.

Mama just smiled at him.

"Does anyone else want a drink?" Karen opened the tray, pulling out a fresh bottle of champagne.

"No, thank you," Navid said. "But you go ahead."

So Karen drank champagne while Mama nursed, Navid smiled, and I fought to keep my eyes open. The wedding was over. Mama was married.

* * *

The next morning, Daddy arrived at the apartment and handed Mama's car keys to Navid.

"Congratulations," he said, shaking Navid's hand. "I hope you'll be very happy."

"Thank you, Kirk," Navid said. "I will do my best to take good care of her."

Karen was flying back to Indianapolis on the same flight, so we all packed our suitcases into Navid's car. Mama stood on the front step of the apartment building, holding Kamran, fighting back tears.

Daddy kissed her cheek and told her to be happy. Karen hugged her tightly and told her to call if she needed anything, anytime.

Then it was my turn.

Mama hugged me tightly, and I felt her tears falling on my head.

"Oh, my Sweet Judy," she crooned. "I love you so much. Thank you for coming."

I simply clung to her, my words stuck somewhere deep in my throat.

"Maybe you can come back at Christmas," she said, kissing my forehead. "Would you like that?"

I nodded, not trusting my voice.

"Okay, then, we'll plan on that. You be good now, okay? And take care of your dad. And . . . and I love you."

"I love you, too, Mama."

She kissed me once more and then I climbed into the backseat of the car with Karen and we drove away. I looked out the back window until we turned the corner, watching Mama as she stood crying on the step, cradling Kamran and waving good-bye.

≈24≈

I did not go to California for Christmas. First Daddy said it would cost too much. When Mama and Navid offered to buy my airplane ticket, he said no to that, too.

"Why not?" I asked.

"Because I said so," he replied.

"But, Daddy, that's not fair."

"Judy, drop it, okay? Maybe we can go next summer. But I can't afford to take off work again, and I'm not letting you fly out there by yourself."

"Well, I think you're just being mean," I yelled as I stomped up the stairs to my room.

When I talked to Mama on the phone that night, she sounded sad but said she understood.

"I wouldn't want you flying by yourself, either," she said. "Your dad's right about that. I just wish he could come with you."

"He says he can't take off from work," I said.

I heard her sigh. "Kirk has always been a workaholic," she said. "It's just who he is. Well . . . maybe you can come in the spring."

"Maybe," I said, "if he'll let me."

"It's all right, Sweet Judy," she crooned. "Don't worry about it, and don't be mad at your dad. We'll work something out. Here, talk to Kamran."

I heard the baby gurgling at the other end of the line. "Hi, Kamran. It's Judy, your sister. Hi, baby."

I felt stupid talking to a six-month-old who couldn't even talk back.

"Oh, Judy, you should see him. He gets so excited when he hears your voice."

I wondered if that was true, or if she was just saying it to make me feel better.

Later that night, I sat on the couch watching television and feeling grumpy.

"Do you want some popcorn?" Daddy asked. "I'll make some if you do."

That was a peace offering on his part.

I shook my head and said nothing.

"Okay, look, I'm sorry it's not going to work out for you to go see your mom. I really can't take off another week right now, and I can't let you go by yourself."

"You're just a workaholic," I said under my breath.

"What?"

"Nothing."

"What did you say?" He sat down on the couch beside me.

"Mama says you're a workaholic," I mumbled, knowing I shouldn't have said it.

"Oh," he said softly, running his hand through his hair. "Well, I know that's what your mother thinks, but I hope that's not what you think."

I shrugged my shoulders.

"Judy, look at me," he said, taking my chin in his hand. "I do work hard. And I'm proud of the work I do. I help people when they need it the most. I know your mom has never understood that, but I thought you did. And I always, always make time to spend with you. You know that, right?"

His eyes were fixed on mine, unwavering.

I sighed and said, "Yeah, Daddy. I know that."

"Okay, good," he said.

"I just wish we could go to California again."

"We will, honey. Just not right now. Maybe this summer we can go."

"But Kamran is growing up," I said. "Mama says he's getting bigger every day. And he's sitting up now and rolling over. And I'm missing it all."

"I'm sorry about that," Daddy said. "But there's not much I can do about it. I can't make your mother move back to Indiana. I could never make her do anything she didn't want to do. I don't think anyone could."

We sat in silence for a minute. Then he said, "I really am sorry, honey. I just can't go right now."

"It's okay," I said.

"So, do you want some popcorn?"

"Sure," I said. "I'll melt the butter."

For Christmas, Daddy gave me a beautiful brown puppy with soft fur and long ears. I named him Rufus. Grandma and Grandpa gave me a new coat with a fur-lined hood. Mama sent me two albums—*Vacation* by the Go-Go's and Crosby, Stills, and Nash's *Greatest Hits*. The note she sent with them read, "I thought you'd like something fun, and the Go-Go's are nothing but fun! And I wanted you to have some CSN to remember your mama, who loves you so much."

I played the albums at Lee Ann's house the day before New Year's Eve while we ate tortilla chips with salsa and compared our Christmas gifts.

"Your mom is so cool," she said. "My mother would never buy me albums. Or, if she did, they'd be totally lame."

"Yeah," I said. "She's into music and all that. But still, I wish she was more like your mom. I wish she was . . . here, you know?"

Lee Ann nodded, dipping a chip into salsa. "Maybe someday she'll move back to Indiana," she said.

"I don't think so," I said. "She seems pretty happy in California. Plus, Navid's family is there. I don't think he'd leave them."

"It sucks that you didn't get to go for Christmas."

"Yeah," I said. "But Daddy says maybe we'll go this summer."

"I wish I could go with you."

"Maybe you can, if your parents buy your ticket."

"They won't," she said, sighing. "They won't ever let me do anything fun."

Just then, Lee Ann's mom knocked and opened the bedroom door. "Do you girls want some cocoa?" she asked.

"No, thanks," we said in unison.

"Okay, well . . . can you turn the music down a little bit? I can hear it all the way downstairs."

Lee Ann sighed heavily and rolled her eyes at me as she turned the dial a tiny bit to the left.

"See what I mean?" she asked after her mother had closed the door again.

"Yeah," I said. "But it's nice she wanted to make us cocoa."

Lee Ann just shook her head. "Sometimes I wish she'd just disappear," she said. Then she stopped, her cheeks reddening. "I'm sorry, Judy. I didn't mean that."

"It's okay," I said. I knew she was just venting. Lee Ann loved her mom. I could see that, even if she couldn't always.

"Want to come to my house?" I said. "We can play with Rufus."

"Sure," she said. "And your dad will let us play the records however loud we want."

We walked back to my house, albums in hand and the rest of the chips in a plastic bag.

"Whose car is that?" Lee Ann asked.

A small brown Toyota was parked in the driveway. It sported a bumper sticker that read, "Nurses are angels in comfortable shoes."

"I don't know," I said, opening the front door of the house.

"Oh, Judy, hi." Daddy was sitting on the couch in the living room beside a woman I'd never seen before. Two wineglasses sat on the coffee table, a half-empty bottle of chardonnay between them.

"Hi," I said, looking from him to the woman. Daddy had never had a woman visit before.

"This is Treva," he said, gesturing to the woman. She smiled at me, a dazzling smile of red lips and white teeth.

"Hi, Judy," she said, rising and extending her hand to me. "I'm so glad to meet you. I've heard so much about you."

I remembered Navid saying the same thing when he met me, and I thought the same thing I'd thought then. *I've heard nothing about you.*

"And this is Lee Ann," Daddy said, smiling. "She's been Judy's best friend since kindergarten."

"That's great," the woman said, smiling now at Lee Ann. "Old friends are the best friends. I've known my best friend since we were in first grade."

She sat back down on the couch, still smiling at us. She was very pretty, with shoulder-length curly red hair, blue eyes, and freckles.

"We're going to listen to albums," I said. "Where's Rufus?"

"I put him out back," Daddy said.

"He had a little accident," Treva said.

"On Treva's shoes," Daddy said, pointing to a pair of white tennis shoes sitting by the door.

"But it's cold outside," I said.

"He's okay," Daddy said.

"I'm going to take him up to my room."

Lee Ann followed me to the kitchen, where Rufus was scratching frantically at the back door. I scooped him up from the back porch.

"Poor baby," I said, snuggling him close. He was shivering all over.

"He's so cute," Lee Ann said, scratching his ears.

"I can't believe they left him outside. It's so cold out." I squeezed the puppy so hard he let out a small yelp.

"Yeah," Lee Ann agreed. "Just because he peed on her shoes. Geesh."

I carried Rufus up to my room, Lee Ann following with the albums and the chips. Once we settled in, she began feeding chips to the dog.

"Look." She smiled. "He likes tortilla chips."

"Don't give him too many. I don't want him to throw up."

We turned on the stereo and began singing along. "Vacation, all

I ever wanted. Vacation, had to get away." Lee Ann danced around the room with Rufus in her arms while I flopped on the bed. "Vacation, meant to be spent alone."

"Judy!" Daddy's voice called up the stairs, loud enough so that we could hear him above the music. "Turn that music down, please."

Lee Ann's eyes widened as I reached for the volume on the stereo. "Wow," she said, "I never heard your dad yell before."

She dropped onto the bed beside me, Rufus in her lap.

"He does sometimes," I said.

"But never over your music." She shook her head. "Who is that woman, anyway?"

I shrugged. "I never saw her before," I said.

"Do you think they're dating?"

I shrugged again, then shook my head. "No, Daddy would've told me if he was dating someone."

She looked at me doubtfully.

"Really," I insisted. "Daddy tells me everything."

"Well, he didn't tell you about Treva." She drew out the name in a high, fake voice. "Oh, Judy, it's *so* nice to meet you. I've heard *so much* about you."

We both giggled.

"Probably she's just a client," I said. "Someone he's helping."

"Maybe she murdered someone," Lee Ann whispered. "Or stole something."

"I doubt my dad would have a murderer over for wine," I said.

"She's really pretty," Lee Ann said, feeding Rufus another chip.

"I guess so." I sat for a minute listening to the Go-Go's. "She's not as pretty as my mom."

By the time Lee Ann left, Treva was gone and Daddy was washing the wineglasses in the kitchen.

"Hey, kiddo," he said, smiling as I opened the fridge. "What do you want for dinner?"

"Let's make spaghetti," I said, pulling out onions and sausage.

I chopped onions while he browned the meat.

"So, what did you think of Treva?" he asked.

I shrugged.

"She thought you were really nice," he said.

I shrugged again.

"Why was she here?" I asked as I pulled out a pan to boil water for the pasta.

"She's a friend," Daddy said. "I met her a couple months ago at a benefit and we've gone out a couple of times."

I stared at him, holding the pan before me like a shield. "You're dating her?"

"Well, I wouldn't call it dating, exactly. It's just been a couple times. She's a friend," he repeated.

"Oh."

I poured water into the pan and set it on the burner.

"She's a nurse at the hospital," Daddy said. He tasted the spaghetti sauce, then added oregano. "She works in the maternity wing, helping deliver babies."

"Oh."

I watched the water in the pan, waiting for it to boil.

"A watched pot never boils," Daddy said. That was something Grandma said a lot, and not just about cooking.

I set the table, eyeing him now and then when I thought he wasn't looking. He was smiling at the sauce.

"She's a lot younger than you," I said.

"A few years, yeah," he said. "She's twenty-five."

Daddy was thirty-two. That seemed like a lot younger to me.

"Does she have kids?"

"No," he said. "She's never been married. She paid her own way through nursing school and has an apartment near the hospital."

"Oh."

I wasn't sure what I thought about Treva being in our house. But I was impressed that she had her own apartment.

"I was thinking," Daddy said as he put the spaghetti into the now-boiling water. "Maybe I should ask her to join us tomorrow night?"

On New Year's Eve, Daddy and I always watched the Dick Clark countdown on television. At midnight, he opened a bottle of champagne and poured a glass for himself and a tiny bit into a glass for me, filling the rest with orange juice. Then we'd toast and make

184 • *Sherri Wood Emmons*

our predictions and resolutions for the year. We'd done it ever since we moved into our house. We'd never had anyone else join us.

"What do you think?" he asked. I could feel him watching me as I poured milk into our glasses.

"Whatever," I said, shrugging.

"And you can ask Lee Ann to spend the night, if you want."

I said nothing, just returned the milk to the refrigerator.

"Would you like that?"

I turned to look at him. He was smiling at me, looking hopeful.

"Sure," I said. "I'll ask Lee Ann."

And so we welcomed 1983 watching Dick Clark with Treva and Lee Ann. Daddy and Treva sat on the couch, sipping champagne long before midnight. Lee Ann and I sprawled on the floor, playing with Rufus, eating popcorn, and studiously ignoring Daddy and Treva.

As the countdown began, Daddy poured a bit of champagne into glasses for Lee Ann and me, then filled the glasses with orange juice. At midnight, I turned to toast with him, but his eyes were on Treva, smiling at her as they clinked glasses. Then, as I watched, he leaned forward and kissed her on the mouth.

"Hey!" Lee Ann shouted as my glass dropped into her lap, soaking her with orange juice.

The glass rolled from her lap onto the floor and shattered.

"Uh-oh," Treva said, smiling.

Daddy went to the kitchen for a towel.

"Don't worry, sweetie," Treva said to me. "Accidents happen."

Lee Ann drained her glass and smacked her lips. "I gotta go change," she said, dabbing her pants with the towel Daddy handed her.

"I'll go, too," I said, following her from the room.

"Judy?" Daddy's voice followed us up the stairs. "Don't you want to toast?"

I didn't answer, just stomped up the stairs to my room, slamming the door behind me.

"What's wrong with you?" Lee Ann asked as she stripped off her wet jeans.

"Nothing," I said, dropping onto my back on the bed. Rufus yipped and jumped, trying to reach me. I scooped him up and sat him on my stomach.

"You want to go back down?" Lee Ann asked. She had put on her pajama pants—bright pink with red hearts that contrasted starkly with her green and yellow striped sweater.

"No," I said. "Let's just hang out up here."

"Okay." She put a John Cougar album on the stereo and began bouncing around the room to "Jack and Diane."

"Did you know John Cougar is from Indiana?" she asked.

I nodded, scratching Rufus's soft ears.

"He lives in Bloomington," Lee Ann continued. "Maybe if we go to IU for college, we'll meet him. Maybe he'll put us in one of his music videos."

Lee Ann was nothing if not optimistic.

She dropped onto the bed beside me, breathing heavily from her dancing. Rolling onto her side, she propped her head on her arm and asked again, "What's wrong?"

I said nothing for a minute, but she just kept waiting. Lee Ann was also persistent.

"Didn't you see them kiss?" I finally said.

"Who? Your dad and Treva?"

"Duh, who else? Right at midnight, they kissed."

Rufus was squirming to be released. I let go of him and he ran to the bottom of the bed and began chewing on my sock.

"I didn't see that," Lee Ann said. Then she smiled. "That's nice for your dad."

"Humph." I didn't think it was nice at all.

"Seriously, Judy, it's nice for him. He's been alone ever since your mom left. She got married, but he's been all alone."

"He hasn't been alone," I said. "He has me."

She laughed, then stopped when I glared at her.

"Okay, you know what I mean. He hasn't had a girlfriend or anything since your mom. I bet he's lonely."

"Well, he could've waited to kiss her until I wasn't around."

Lee Ann laughed again and shoved me with her elbow. "Oh,

God, Judy, get over it. My mom and dad kiss all the time, and you don't see me throwing a fit."

"But that's your mom and dad," I said. "She's not my mom. She's . . . nothing."

"Well," Lee Ann said, rolling onto her back, "I think she's nice. And she's really pretty."

She was right about that. Treva was pretty, in a Kewpie doll kind of way. But she wasn't as pretty as Mama.

"Hey, did you hear who Heather Johnson is dating?" Lee Ann's conversations often veered from one topic to another, with little to no apparent connection. "Kevin Harding! Isn't that gross?"

25

Over the next few weeks, Treva became a fixture in our household. Sometimes she cooked dinner for Daddy and me. Sometimes Daddy cooked for us. Sometimes we ordered Chinese takeout or pizza. Always, she stayed long after I went to bed.

Treva was nice enough, but she was pretty annoying. She was always perky, like an overgrown cheerleader, for one thing. I never heard her raise her voice or sound angry. She was always smiling. Sometimes I wanted to say something hurtful to her, just to see if I could wipe that smile off her face. But I didn't.

Daddy seemed happy when she was around. He smiled a lot and sang silly songs while we washed dishes or folded laundry. Lee Ann was right about that, I guess. Daddy had been lonely. And now he wasn't. I tried to be happy about that, but mostly I just felt annoyed.

Still, life in the eighth grade was going pretty well. Lee Ann, Vernita, and I were all on the student council, so we got to help decide on the decorations for the Valentine's Day dance. Lee Ann was going to the dance with Michael Day, and she was excited about it. Vernita and I did not have dates. We would go together and help with the refreshments.

A week before Valentine's Day, Treva came for dinner. Daddy had made chili. Treva had brought a salad and bread.

"So, what are you wearing to the dance, Judy?" Treva asked.

"I don't know," I said. "Probably my blue dress." I had only three dresses. The blue was the nicest.

"Oh, you need a new dress for a dance!" Treva nodded her head at me emphatically. "It's your first dance, right? You have to have a new dress."

"Would you like a new dress, honey?" Daddy was looking at me now, smiling.

"It's okay, Daddy. I can wear my blue one."

"No, it's not okay!" Treva was nodding at Daddy now. "She has to have a new dress for her first dance. In fact"—now she turned back to me—"I'll go shopping with you this weekend, if you want. We can go to the mall. L. S. Ayres has beautiful dresses. What do you say?" She was smiling at me, still nodding.

"That's a great idea," Daddy said, covering Treva's hand with his own. "I'm sure you'll do a much better job helping her find something than I would."

"Well, it's a girl thing," Treva said, smiling at him. "So"—she turned back to me—"how about Saturday morning? I can pick you up at ten, and after we find a dress, we can have lunch." She seemed very pleased with the idea.

"Judy, what do you say?" Daddy was watching me closely.

Well, what I wanted to say was, "Hell no!" I did not want to go shopping with Treva. I did not need her help picking out clothes. And I sure as hell did not want to spend a whole morning with her, and then have lunch.

Instead, I mustered a smile. "Sure," I said. "That sounds like fun."

"You are so lucky!" Lee Ann said when I told her about it. "My mom took me to Sears for my dress. God! L. S. Ayres has such great stuff. And Treva has really good taste."

I slouched on the couch at her house, watching as she ironed clothes. Lee Ann's mom believed that everything should be ironed—even jeans and underwear. We didn't iron anything at my house. Daddy and I did laundry every Sunday, and we hovered over the dryer waiting for it to stop so we could pull out the clothes before they wrinkled.

"I like the dress you got," I said. "It looks nice on you."

"It's okay." She sighed. "But I'll bet someone else shows up wearing the same thing. Everyone shops at Sears. But, man, I bet you get something completely original."

And that, in a nutshell, was what I was afraid of. I did not want anything completely original. I wanted to just blend in, like everyone else. God only knew what kind of outlandish dress Treva would want me to buy.

"Where are you going for lunch?" Lee Ann asked, folding a newly ironed T-shirt neatly into the laundry basket.

"I don't know."

"Maybe she'll take you to Farrell's!"

Farrell's Ice Cream Parlor and Restaurant was Lee Ann's favorite place at the mall. In addition to huge hamburgers, chili dogs, and fries, they served an enormous assortment of ice cream desserts.

"God, I wish I could go," she said, pulling another shirt from the pile.

"Me too," I said, and I meant it. Lee Ann liked Treva and could talk to her. I never knew what to say when Treva was around.

On Saturday morning, promptly at ten, Treva knocked at the front door.

"Hey, you," I heard her purr to Daddy when he answered the door.

"Hey, yourself," he said softly.

I watched from the top of the stairs as they kissed, then cleared my throat loudly.

"Hey, Judy!" Treva's voice was bright, like a new penny. "Are you ready to go?"

I shrugged and clomped down the stairs.

"You all have fun," Daddy said, kissing my forehead and then Treva's. "And don't break the bank!"

"Don't worry, Kirk." Treva laughed. "I know how to shop on a budget."

We climbed into Treva's little Toyota and pulled away from the house. I switched on the radio, so we wouldn't have to talk.

"Billie Jean is not my lover," Treva sang along with the radio. Jeez, even with music on, she couldn't be quiet.

"So, do you have any ideas about what you want?"

I shrugged my shoulders again.

"Oh, come on, you must have something in mind. Long or short?"

"I don't know," I mumbled.

"Well, I'm thinking short," she said. "Save the long dresses for prom."

"Whatever."

"What do you think about something a little out there?" she asked. "Maybe a short skirt with a big blouse and a great big belt?"

I simply stared at her.

"Okay, maybe not," she said. "A nice dress then, maybe something in red, to bring out your dark hair."

I said nothing. I couldn't imagine wearing a red dress to the dance, or anywhere else, for that matter.

At the mall, we wandered through the department store, Treva pulling dress after dress from the racks and me rejecting each and every one. Finally, she put her hand on her hip and said, "Okay, look. I'm really trying here. And I think you're not. Do you want to get a dress? Because if you don't, let's just go home."

It was the first time I'd ever heard her lose her cool. I felt just a little bit proud of myself. Then I thought of what Daddy would say if we came home without a dress, and Treva telling him I'd had a bad attitude.

"I want a dress," I said.

"Okay, then, what do you want?"

I gazed around at the racks and racks of dresses, overwhelmed. "I don't know."

"Well, who at school dresses the way you like? Whose style do you like?"

"Well, Casey Cochran dresses nice."

"Okay, what kind of stuff does she wear?"

"She wears . . . um, I don't know. Nice stuff."

Treva sighed. "Does she dress preppy? Or valley girl? Or like Madonna?"

I stared at her again. Madonna? Seriously?

"I guess she's just kind of casual. You know, like skirts and tights. And she has these cute boots."

"Okay." Treva smiled. "Now we have some direction. Are the skirts long or short?"

"Longer," I said. "And she has this little hat she wears."

"Got it," Treva said. "We're definitely in the wrong store. Come on."

She led me back to the car and we drove to Broad Ripple, a neighborhood I had heard of but never actually been in. Small shops lined narrow streets that were filled with college-age kids.

"Here," Treva said, pulling into a parking spot in front of a store called Grateful Threads. Inside I stopped and stared. It was like stepping back to the years when Mama lived with us. Broomstick skirts, tie-dyed tops, and woven shawls hung from the walls. And there, in the back, I saw a pair of granny boots even better than the ones Casey Cochran wore.

I tried on several outfits before settling on a green, ankle-length skirt, an off-white gauze blouse, pink tights, and the beautiful black boots. As I stood staring at myself in the mirror, Treva plopped a small, crushed velvet cap on my head.

"Perfect," she proclaimed. "Now you need some jewelry."

She draped a long strand of beads around my neck.

"What do you think?"

I could only nod. I looked so stylish, so much older. And, I realized with a jolt, I looked like Mama. Not in the face, of course. But this was how Mama dressed. Well, except for the hat.

"Good," Treva said. "You look great. And no one else will have anything like this at the dance, trust me."

And that was okay, actually. I didn't mind having this outfit, one that no one else would have.

Treva paid for the clothes using Daddy's credit card. Then we walked out onto the busy street.

"Let's go to the Parthenon," she said. "You'll like it."

We sat by the window in the little Greek restaurant, watching people go by. I stared at the menu, unfamiliar with the choices.

"Have you ever had Greek food?" Treva asked.

I shook my head.

"Try the gyro," she said. "It's a sandwich with beef. You'll love it."

So I ordered a gyros sandwich and Treva ordered something called a falafel, which looked like a hamburger but was made with garbanzo beans instead of meat.

"I wish we lived here," I said absently, gazing out the window at the busy neighborhood.

"Yeah, Broad Ripple is fun," Treva agreed. "But it's not really safe at night. Not like Irvington."

"Do you hang out here a lot?" I asked.

"I used to," she said. "I used to date a guy who lived not far from here."

"Why'd you stop dating him?" I asked.

"Well . . . I guess we just wanted different things," she said, dabbing at her mouth with a napkin. "We started dating in college and had a lot of fun. But then I was ready for a more serious relationship, something with a future, you know? And he just wanted to keep on the way we were."

I sat for a moment, thinking, then said, "Do you think you have a future with my dad?"

She smiled at me. "I'm not sure, Judy. We haven't been dating very long. But, I like your dad a lot. He's such a good guy. So, maybe, I just don't know yet."

"You know he still loves my mom," I said, not looking at her.

"I'm sure he does," she said softly. "You don't have a child with someone and then just stop loving them."

She sat quietly for a minute, then said, "But your mom has re-married. And your dad has been pretty lonely. I think there's room in his life for someone new, don't you?"

I shrugged, wishing I hadn't started this whole conversation.

"I'm not trying to replace your mom," she said. "You know that, right?"

I nodded. "I guess so."

"And like I said, it's too soon to know what the future will bring for me and your dad. Right now, we just like being together."

"I'm done," I said, not hungry anymore. "Can we go home?"

Treva took a last bite of her falafel and went to pay the bill while I sat staring out the window.

~ 26 ~

In June, Daddy and I flew back to California. I wasn't so afraid on the airplane this time, relaxing enough to enjoy watching out the window as we landed. Mama was waiting in baggage claim, holding Kamran on her hip. She waved as we came down the escalator.

"Oh my God, Judy. Look how much you've grown up!" She scanned me from head to toe. "I love your new haircut!"

Treva had taken me for a haircut before the dance and my long curls were gone, replaced with a stylish bob.

"Hi, Kirk." She kissed Daddy on the cheek.

"Hey, Cassie." He smiled and then touched Kamran's cheek. "Hey, look at you, big guy!"

Kamran was now a year old and cuter than ever. He hid his face in Mama's shoulder and peeked shyly at us.

"I can't believe how big he is," I said.

Mama laughed. "He's getting huge, isn't he? But he's a good boy." She nuzzled the baby. "Aren't you a good boy? Yes, you are Mommy's good boy."

Kamran smiled then, revealing four small teeth.

We drove to Pasadena in Mama's car, Daddy sitting in front, me in the backseat with Kamran, who stared at me with huge dark eyes, as if I might just bite him.

"How are you, Cassie?" Daddy asked.

"I'm okay," she said. She was frowning at the traffic. "I hate the traffic here."

I watched as she switched lanes, glaring at a driver in another car who tried to cut her off.

"Jackass," she muttered. Daddy smiled at her.

"Sorry," she said, smiling into the rearview mirror. "I just get so mad at people when they act like jerks."

"Do you have to do a lot of driving on the freeway?" Daddy asked.

Mama sighed. "You have to get on the freeway to go anywhere here," she said. "To get to Navid's parents' house or visit friends or go to the movies. Everything is an hour away. Not like home."

She sighed again. "I really do miss the pace of things back home."

We drove to Pasadena and she parked the car in front of the apartment building. When I climbed out of the car, the heat was stifling.

"It's so hot!" I said, pulling my suitcase from the trunk.

"Yeah," Mama said, unstrapping Kamran from his car seat. "It's pretty miserable in the summer."

The air-conditioned lobby felt like bliss. I was dripping with sweat from the short walk to the building.

In the elevator, Kamran began tugging at Mama's shirt. "Nus," he said.

"Yes, baby, just a minute. We'll nurse when we get inside."

"Nus!" he said again. "Nus!"

Mama was fumbling in her purse for the key to the apartment. She looked hot and flustered, her cheeks red.

"Nus!" Kamran was yelling now. "Nus!"

"Damn it, Kamran," Mama said sharply. "Just hold on."

The baby began to cry as Mama dropped her purse.

"Well, shit," she said.

"Here." Daddy bent to pick the purse up. "I'll get it."

He unlocked the door and opened it. Mama went in with Kamran and I followed her inside, then stood staring. The apartment that had been so bright and clean the summer before was a mess.

Laundry spilled from the couch, dirty dishes sat in the sink, and toys lay strewn across the floor.

"Sorry about the mess," Mama said, pushing clothes from the couch and setting Kamran down. "I can't seem to keep up with it all."

She flopped down onto the couch and pulled the baby into her lap, then raised her shirt for him to nurse. Daddy stood by the doorway, looking away from her.

"Do you want something to drink?" she asked. "There's Coke in the fridge. Or tea?"

"I'm okay," Daddy said.

I walked into the kitchen to get a Coke.

"Sit down," Mama said to Daddy. "Just push those toys off the chair, it's okay."

Daddy perched on the edge of the chair, his eyes fixed on a point far above Mama's head.

"Do you want a Coke, Mama?" I asked.

"No, honey. But you know what I would like? A beer. Would you get me a beer from the fridge?"

I pulled a bottle of Corona from the refrigerator and searched for a bottle opener. The kitchen was a disaster. Dirty dishes filled the sink and counters. The dishrag I picked up to wipe away a spill smelled sour.

"Here you go." I handed the bottle to Mama, and she took a long drink.

"Thanks, honey," she said.

"Should I put my stuff in the bedroom?" I asked.

"Sure," she said. "It's a little bit different from last time you were here."

And it was. The room was now a nursery, with a crib and changing table and more toys strewn about. My bed sat along one wall, opposite the crib.

"Will Kamran mind me sleeping in his room?" I asked.

"He'll be fine," Mama said. "He hardly ever sleeps in there anyway. Mostly he sleeps with us." She sighed again.

"I'd like him to get used to sleeping in his own bed, but he just cries and cries and I can't stand it."

"Are you okay, Cassie?" Daddy asked softly. "You look . . . tired."

"I am tired," she said, moving Kamran to her other breast. "I don't remember being this tired with Judy."

"Well, you were younger with Judy," Daddy said, smiling.

"Yeah, I know. But . . . Kamran just never sleeps. I mean it, he never sleeps. He doesn't take naps, he won't sleep in his own bed, and when he sleeps in our bed he's always kicking and rolling and he wakes up every two hours and wants to nurse. I'm just exhausted all the time."

I sat down beside her on the couch and leaned my head on her shoulder. "Maybe I can watch him for a little while and you can take a nap," I said.

"Oh, honey, that's sweet, but I'm okay," she said, smiling at me.

"No, Cassie, I think that's a very good idea. I'll stay a while with Judy, and between the two of us, we can keep the little guy busy. You go take a nap. You'll feel better."

Mama started to protest again, then gave a sharp yelp.

"Ouch," she said, pulling Kamran from her breast. "Don't you bite me!" she said, shaking her finger in his face. He smiled at her and touched her face.

"Seriously, Cassie, go lay down. We'll take care of him." Daddy reached for the baby, who buried his face in Mama's lap.

"But you just got here," Mama said. "I want to visit, not nap."

"We'll be here for a week, and there's plenty of time to visit. You need a nap." Daddy's voice was firm. He picked Kamran up and held him high in the air. "We'll be fine, won't we, buddy?" He grinned at the baby, and finally Kamran smiled back.

"Go now," Daddy said softly, still grinning at the baby. "Before he notices."

Mama hesitated for a moment, then rose and walked to her bedroom, carrying her beer. "Just fifteen minutes," she said. "Then I'll feel better."

She closed the bedroom door behind her.

"Okay," Daddy said, bouncing Kamran in the air, "let's get this place in shape. Do you want to hold the baby or wash dishes?"

I watched him as he bounced the baby. He knew exactly what to do.

"I'll wash dishes," I said.

Half an hour later, the kitchen was clean. I sat down on the floor in the living room and pushed cars across the carpet with Kamran while Daddy folded laundry, stacking everything neatly in a laundry basket. Then Daddy read books with Kamran while I dusted the furniture and picked up toys. By the time Mama emerged from her bedroom an hour and a half later, the apartment had been transformed.

"Oh my God," she said, standing in the middle of the living room. "You guys didn't have to do that. Wow!" She walked into the kitchen. "It's like a whole new place."

She sat down at the kitchen table and Kamran toddled toward her, arms outstretched. She scooped him into her lap and smiled, but her eyes sparkled with tears.

"Thank you, Kirk," she said softly. "And, my Sweet Judy, thank you. Thank you both so much."

She gazed around the room again, then said, "Navid will be thrilled." She sighed heavily.

"Where is Navid?" I asked. I knew he didn't teach classes on Saturdays.

"He's at the Bahá'í Center," she said. "They're doing a service project downtown, so of course he *had* to go." She sighed again. "I think he goes just to get away from me and this." She gestured around the apartment. "He can't stand the clutter. But does he ever lift a finger to help? No, of course not."

"When will he get home?" Daddy asked, sitting at the table with Mama.

"God knows," she said. "He said he'd be home by five, but I'll believe that when I see it."

I looked at the clock. It was four thirty.

"Well," Daddy said. "When he gets home, maybe you can drive me to the car rental place?"

"Sure, Kirk," she said. "That's the least I can do after you did all this." She waved her arm around the room. "Honestly, it's like a whole different apartment, isn't it? And I feel so much better. Thank you guys so much."

"No problem," Daddy said.

"Now I can even get to the stove to make us something to eat."

She rose, Kamran on her hip, and began moving about the kitchen, pulling out bowls and pans. "How about stir-fry?"

"That sounds great!" I said. "Can I help?"

"Sure," she said. "You chop and I'll fry."

I chopped broccoli and onions and carrots and tofu while Mama cooked rice and made the sauce. Then she dumped all of the vegetables and the tofu into a big wok and began stirring them around in the oil. Kamran, perched on her hip, played with her necklace for a while. Then, without warning, he leaned forward and put his hand into the wok.

"No!" Mama shouted, but it was too late. His shrill cries filled the apartment.

"Oh, baby, oh no!" Mama ran to the sink and turned on the water, putting Kamran's hand beneath the flow. His fingertips were red. He howled with pain.

"Is he okay?" Daddy asked.

"I don't know," Mama said, her voice shaking. "Look at his fingers."

Daddy held Kamran's tiny hand beneath the water and looked carefully at his fingers.

"He'll be okay," he said after a minute. "It doesn't look like he burned himself very badly. No blistering."

Still the baby cried, great gulping sobs, tears and snot running down his face.

"Shhhh," Mama crooned. "It's okay, baby. You're okay. It's all right."

"Do you have any first aid cream?" Daddy asked.

"I don't know," Mama said. "Maybe in the medicine cabinet in our bathroom."

Daddy went in search of first aid cream while Mama shushed the baby. I stood helplessly in the kitchen, unsure what to do.

"Oh, damn!" Mama said suddenly, "Judy, will you turn off that wok?"

Smoke was rising from the wok, the vegetables now burned black. As I reached for the pan, the smoke detector started blaring, which made the baby scream even louder.

"Got it." Daddy reappeared with the medicine, which he smeared onto Kamran's hand. Then he reached overhead to pull down the smoke detector. With the sudden silence, even Kamran stopped crying for an instant, then began again. Daddy began opening windows to let out the smoke.

"So much for dinner," Mama said. She looked as if she might start crying herself. "I'm really sorry, guys."

"It's okay," Daddy said. "Here, you sit down and put his hand in here." He placed a bowl of cool water on the table. "Judy and I will make something, right, peanut?" He turned to me and grinned.

"Okay," I said. I wanted to do something to help.

"Oh, Kirk, you can't do that." Mama smiled weakly. "You don't cook."

"I will have you know that I have become quite a decent cook," Daddy said. "Well, at least an adequate cook."

"He makes good spaghetti," I said.

Daddy dumped the burned vegetables into the trash, then opened the pantry. "You've got pasta, you've got spaghetti sauce, you've got tomatoes and onions and garlic. Do you have any sausage?" he asked.

Mama smiled and shook her head.

"Well, then we'll have vegetarian spaghetti," Daddy said.

I chopped more onions and some tomatoes and mushrooms while Daddy started the water to boil. Then he made the sauce while I set the table. This was a routine we had down pat.

By the time Navid arrived home, Daddy was putting dinner on the table.

"Hello, Kirk. Hi, Judy." Navid shook Daddy's hand and gave me a quick hug.

"Hi, Navid. You got here just in time. Dinner is ready." Daddy gestured toward the spaghetti and sauce on the table.

"Kirk and Judy cooked," Mama said, smiling at us.

Navid kissed Mama's forehead, then reached for the baby. But when he lifted Kamran into his arms, the baby began to cry again, his fingers removed from the cool, healing water.

"What happened?" Navid asked, looking from the baby to Mama.

"I was making stir-fry, and he touched the wok," Mama said, reaching for Kamran.

"Let me see," Navid said, still holding the baby. He examined Kamran's red fingertips and frowned.

"We should take him to the doctor," he said.

"I think he's okay," Daddy said softly. "No blistering, just a little burn."

"And are you a doctor now?" Navid's voice was sharp.

"Navid!" Mama said. "Kirk is only trying to help."

Navid gave her a cold look. "How could you be so careless?" he asked. "Look at him." He held Kamran's hand toward Mama. Kamran was screaming.

"It was an accident," Mama said, reaching again for the baby.

"It was a careless accident," Navid replied. "I am taking him to the emergency room."

"Navid, I don't think that's necessary," Mama said.

I stood wide-eyed, watching them argue.

"I don't care what you think, Cassie. It's your carelessness that caused this, and now I am taking care of it."

He wrapped a wet dishcloth around Kamran's red fingers and pulled his keys from his pocket.

"Well, then." Mama rose. "If you insist on taking him, I'm coming, too."

"Do as you like." Navid's voice was cold.

"Judy, why don't you stay here with your dad and eat." Mama kissed me briefly. "We won't be gone long." She followed Navid from the apartment, closing the door behind her. We could hear Kamran's cries as they waited for the elevator. Then, it was quiet.

"Daddy, why is Navid so mad?" I asked.

"He's just scared about Kamran," Daddy said, sitting down at the table. "It's scary when your kid gets hurt, especially when he's so little. Navid will be fine once he realizes Kamran is okay."

"He was mean to Mama," I said.

"It'll be okay, honey," he said. "He's just worried. He'll calm down."

He ladled sauce over my spaghetti and then served himself. We ate in silence for a few minutes. I wondered if Kamran was all right. I wondered even more if Mama was all right.

By the time we had finished, Mama and Navid still weren't home, so we cleared the table and put the rest of the spaghetti into the refrigerator. Then we washed the dishes.

"Well," Daddy said, "let's see what's on the news."

He flipped on the television and we sat on the couch watching the news. Then we watched *T. J. Hooker* and *The Love Boat*. At ten o'clock, as *Fantasy Island* was coming on, we finally heard the key in the front door.

Navid walked in, carrying Kamran, who was asleep on his shoulder. Behind them came Mama. She smiled when she saw us.

"Hey, guys," she said. "Kamran is fine. It's nothing serious."

Navid carried the baby into his nursery, then reappeared in the living room.

"I'm sorry, Kirk," he said, extending his hand to my father. "I shouldn't have snapped at you like that."

"It's okay," Daddy said, shaking his hand. "I understand how it is."

Mama flopped down on the couch beside me and put her arm around my shoulder.

"What have you guys been up to?" she asked.

"Just watching TV," I said as Daddy turned off the television.

"There's spaghetti in the fridge," Daddy said. "You guys must be starving."

"Thank you, Kirk, for making dinner, and you, too, Judy. Thank you both for cooking and for cleaning the house." Navid smiled at me. "It looks one hundred percent better."

"That's okay," I said.

Mama rose and walked to the kitchen. "I'll make you a plate," she said, touching Navid's arm as she passed him.

"Thank you, Cassie Joon," he said. But he didn't look at her.

We sat back down at the table while Mama and Navid ate re-heated spaghetti. Mama chattered away while Navid ate in silence.

"Good Lord," Mama said, "the emergency room is a zoo. I mean, it's a complete zoo. It took them three hours to even get to us. Poor Kamran was asleep by then, and of course they had to wake him up to look at his hand."

"What did the doctor say?" Daddy asked.

"It's just a little burn," Mama said. "Just like you said." She smiled at Daddy.

"Well, it's always good to play it safe," Daddy said.

Mama sighed and sat back in her chair. "Good Lord, I'm tired."

Navid raised his eyebrows at her. "I thought you had a nap today," he said.

"Well, I think I could sleep for a year and still not be caught up," Mama said. "It's exhausting keeping up with the baby."

Navid folded his napkin and set it on the table. "I don't know why you complain so much," he said softly. "My mother had three children in four years, and she still managed to keep the house clean and cook proper meals."

With that, he rose and walked into the bedroom, leaving his dishes on the table.

Mama sighed again.

"Well," Daddy said, his voice soft. "I guess it's too late to rent a car tonight."

"Oh, Kirk, I'm sorry," Mama said. "I forgot."

"It's okay," he said, smiling at her. "Maybe you can just drive me to the hotel and I can rent a car tomorrow."

"Sure," she said, rising. "Let me get my keys."

She disappeared into the bedroom, reemerging with her purse. "Judy, do you want to come with us, or are you ready for bed?"

"I'll come," I said. I didn't want to stay in the apartment with Navid. He was in such a bad mood.

We drove Daddy to the Ramada Inn and left him with his suitcase at the front door. Mama was quiet as we drove back home.

"I'm sorry, honey," she said as we turned onto her street. "This isn't how I pictured your first night here."

"It's okay," I said.

"Mama?" I asked as she pulled into a parking spot. "Are you okay?"

She smiled at me and touched my cheek. "I'm fine, Judy. Just tired, that's all."

"Are you and Navid okay?"

She looked at me steadily for a minute, then sighed. "We'll be okay, I think. It's just hard, adjusting to being parents."

"Did you and Daddy fight a lot when I was born?"

"No," she said. "But we were a lot younger then. I don't remember being so tired all the time. And your dad . . . well, your dad had a lot of patience."

We locked the car and walked to the apartment building. Even though it was almost eleven, it was still stiflingly hot.

"Hey," Mama said, smiling at me. "Do you want to take a swim?"

"Isn't it too late?" I asked, remembering the pool hours listed on the roof.

"Not if we're quiet," she said. "Remember, my Sweet Judy, rules were meant to be broken."

We changed into our swimsuits and took the elevator to the roof. The pool lights were out and the water was dark and still. Leaving our towels on the deck, we slipped into the cool water.

"Oh, that feels good," Mama said. "And look, you can even see some stars." She pointed to the sky, where a few tiny specks glistened. There weren't nearly as many stars as we had at home.

"In the winter, you get a better view," she said, leaning back into the water and stretching out her arms. "In the summer, you can't see the stars at all most of the time. Too much smog."

We floated on our backs, watching the stars.

"Do you like California?" I asked.

"It's okay," she said. "I like it better in the winter than in the summer. It's too hot in the summer, and too smoggy. And it's always too crowded."

She sighed again. "Sometimes I really miss Indiana."

She laughed then. "God, I never thought I'd hear myself say that. But it's true. Sometimes I really miss being back there."

"Do you think you and Navid will ever move?"

She laughed again, but it was a sad little laugh. "No," she said. "Navid will never leave his family. They're really close."

"Navid said his mother had three children, but I only met Maryam at the wedding."

"Navid had a brother who died a long time ago," Mama said. "He lived in an apartment building in Tehran and there was a fire." She paused. "I think that's why he got so upset about Kamran's burn."

"He wasn't very nice to Daddy," I said, remembering Navid's response when Daddy said Kamran's burn wasn't bad.

"I know," Mama said. "He was just worried. And then he felt bad about it."

"He wasn't very nice to you, either."

Mama was quiet for a minute. A plane flew overhead and somewhere on the street below a car honked its horn.

"Navid is a good man, Judy," she said finally. "He tries to do the right thing. He just . . . he gets frustrated sometimes . . . with me."

She sank beneath the water then, reemerging a foot away, her hair dripping.

"But we'll be all right. Don't worry, okay?"

We toweled off and walked back to the elevator, dripping on the floor as we went.

"I put towels in your room, if you want a shower," she said, unlocking the apartment door. "Do you need anything else?"

"No, I'm good." I was shivering in the air-conditioning.

Mama kissed my forehead. "I'll see you in the morning, my Sweet Judy. Sleep well." Then she tiptoed into the bedroom, closing the door behind her.

A minute later, I heard the shower running in her bathroom.

I toweled my hair partly dry and pulled a nightgown from my

suitcase. Then I lay in my bed by the window, listening to Kamran's steady breathing from the crib.

I wondered if Mama was happy, after all. She didn't seem as happy as she'd been the summer before. But maybe she was just tired, like she said.

As I drifted off to sleep, the baby woke up and began to cry. A minute later, Mama walked into the room.

"Sorry," she whispered, as she lifted Kamran from his crib. "He never sleeps through the night in here."

She carried the baby from the room, closing the door behind her. After a long time, I fell asleep.

27

The next morning I found Mama sitting alone in the kitchen, drinking coffee. She smiled when she saw me.

"Good morning," she said, rising. "Do you want some juice?"

She poured orange juice into a glass and set it before me.

"Where is everyone?" I asked.

"Navid took Kamran to Bahá'í school," she replied. "It's like Sunday school for Bahá'ís. They go every week."

"Do you go with them?"

Mama shook her head. "No, Sunday morning is my quiet time. It's the one time in the week that I have just to myself."

"Does Navid mind that you don't go?"

"Well." She walked to the refrigerator and opened the door, pulling out eggs. "He'd like it if I went, I think. But I really need the time alone."

"Is it weird that Kamran is going to be a Bahá'í and you're not?"

"It's important to Navid," she said. "And I don't think it really matters what religion you belong to."

"That's what Daddy says, too."

Mama broke eggs into a bowl and whisked them with milk.

"Do you believe in God?" I asked.

She stopped whisking for a minute, then poured the eggs into a skillet.

"I'm not sure," she said. "But I think if there is a God, he is much bigger than anything we can imagine. And he's certainly bigger than any one religious group can claim."

She stirred the eggs in the skillet, adding salt and pepper.

"I think most Western religions have it all wrong, in a way," she said. "They all claim that their way is the only way to God. I think God must be bigger than that. Do you want Tobasco sauce on your eggs?" She smiled at me and I nodded.

"There's a guy I know who teaches a different way of thinking about God," she said, scooping eggs onto a plate and setting it on the table in front of me. "He says that God is in everything and in everyone. I kind of like that idea."

"Is he a Christian or a Bahá'í?" I asked.

"Actually," she said, sitting down at the table with her coffee, "he's a Hindu. He's from India, and he studies under a guru— that's a kind of spiritual teacher. It's pretty cool."

"Does he believe in heaven?" I asked.

She smiled. "In a way, I guess. He believes in reincarnation, that we don't just live one time on earth. We keep getting reborn until we learn everything we need to know. And then, we stop getting reborn and that's nirvana, which is kind of like heaven in a way."

I thought about this while I ate my eggs. Had I lived in the world before?

"Does that mean that Kamran was somebody else before he was born?"

"Yeah," she said. "And now he will grow up in this life and learn what he needs for the next time around."

"That's kind of weird," I said.

"I guess it seems weird to us because we aren't raised with it," she said. "To the Hindus, it seems weird that people believe they only live once."

"What does Navid think about him, your Hindu friend?" I thought Navid probably didn't think too much of Mama's friend.

Mama laughed. "He thinks Arjun is behind the times. He says

that Hinduism was a valid path to God in its time, but now it's out-moded. Bahá'ís believe in progressive revelation."

"What's that?"

"The idea that God sends prophets down every few hundred years to update things. So, Jesus came in his day with teachings that were right for his day. And Muhammad came with teachings right for his day. And now, Bahá'u'lláh has come with teachings right for this time."

"What do you think?" I asked, trying to take in what seemed like a very complicated thing.

"Well," she said, "like I said, I just don't know. I like some of what the Bahá'ís teach—like the equality of men and women and the unity of mankind. But . . . there are things I don't agree with, too."

She rose to pour more coffee into her cup. "I guess you could say I'm still looking for a faith that fits. So far, what Arjun tells me about Hinduism makes more sense to me than anything else. But, I'm not sure what I believe.

"How about you?" she asked, sitting back down at the table. "What do you believe, Judy?"

"I don't know," I said, sighing. "Grandma says prayers can fix things, but sometimes I pray and nothing happens. Daddy says it doesn't matter if you're a Christian or a Hindu or a Jew, as long as you're trying to do the right thing."

"Well, I'm with your dad on that one. I think if there is a God, he doesn't give a rat's ass what your religion is, as long as you're doing good things in the world."

I finished my eggs and put my plate and fork in the sink.

"What should we do today?" Mama asked. "We could go to the beach or take a picnic up to the mountains. Or, if you'd rather, we can just hang out."

"Let's go to the beach," I said. "Will Navid and Kamran come, too?"

"I don't know," she said. "They should be home in about an hour and we can ask if they want to come."

I showered while Mama drank more coffee; then she showered

while I watched MTV. By the time Navid arrived with Kamran, we were packing a picnic lunch.

"Hey," Mama said, reaching for the baby. "We're going to the beach for a picnic. Do you want to come?"

Navid smiled at me. "That sounds like fun," he said. "But I can't go today. I'm helping Azad at the Bahá'í Center. We are soundproofing the youth room, so they can play their music without driving everyone else crazy."

"Oh, Navid," Mama said, "you can do that next week. Judy's only here for a little while. Come to the beach with us."

He shook his head. "I'm sorry, Cassie, but I made a commitment and I cannot just break it."

Mama sighed and took Kamran into the nursery to change his clothes. When she reemerged, he was dressed in little swim trunks and a T-shirt, wearing sandals and a sun hat.

"We'll see you at dinner then," she said, not looking at Navid.

"Okay," he said, kissing the baby's head. "Be careful, and don't let him get too much sun."

We drove to Malibu and Mama pointed out places along the way while Kamran slept in his car seat. By the time we got to the beach, he was awake and fussing.

"Okay," Mama said, lifting Kamran from the car, "you get the bag and I'll carry the cooler."

We spread a blanket on the white sand and Mama raised a large umbrella above it, so we could sit in the shade. We stripped to our swimsuits and sat down. I was wearing my first two-piece, and I felt self-conscious and proud at the same time. Mama wore a low-cut white one-piece. She had lost all of her pregnancy weight, but her breasts were swollen from nursing. I noticed several men watching her as we undressed.

We ate our sandwiches while Kamran happily shoveled sand into and out of a little bucket. I thought Malibu was probably the prettiest place in the world, with the ocean in front of us and the mountains behind.

After lunch, we took Kamran into the water and Mama held him while he splashed and laughed.

"Look at those houses," I said, pointing up the beach, past a large fence that extended far out into the water. Huge, beautiful homes sat along the water, their windows glistening in the afternoon sun.

"Yeah," Mama said. "Aren't they hideous?"

I stared at her. I thought they were beautiful.

"Really rich people live there," she said. "And they put up that big fence to keep everyone else out." She looked at the fence in disgust. "It's disgraceful that the city lets them do that. The beach belongs to everyone."

"Do you think anyone famous lives there?" I asked.

"Sure," she said. "Lots of Hollywood people have houses here."

"I wish we could go over there . . . just to walk on the beach."

The strip of beach in front of the houses was pristine and empty, unlike the crowded public beach where our blanket lay.

"Okay," she said, grinning at me. "Let's do it."

She started walking through the water toward the fence, holding Kamran on her hip.

"No, Mama, it's okay," I said, struggling to keep up with her. "We don't have to. I mean, we're not supposed to, right? That's why they have the fence."

"To hell with the fence," she said, laughing over her shoulder. "Like I said, the beach belongs to everybody."

She waded deeper into the water, holding Kamran aloft. The waves crashed against us, nearly knocking me over.

"Mama," I said, reaching for her hand. "I want to go back."

"Oh, come on, Judy," she said, taking my hand. "It's okay. It's just a little bit farther."

She pulled me along as she pushed into the waves. Each one seemed bigger than the last, threatening to push us under. My heart pounded. I held tight to her hand.

"Here," she said triumphantly, as we reached the end of the fence. "Come on."

She pulled me around the fence and turned to smile at me, then her eyes widened. I turned just in time to see a huge wave crashing down on us. I was pushed under the water and felt Mama's hand slip from mine. I closed my eyes and held my breath. I couldn't tell which way was up or down, or where I would end up. My lungs felt like they were going to burst and I opened my mouth and gulped down seawater. *Dear God,* I prayed. *Please. Please. Please don't let me drown.*

I hit something solid then, the fence. I grabbed on with both hands and held tight, feeling the wave pushing me forward. Then suddenly, I could breathe. I was several feet from the end of the fence, holding on for dear life, coughing and sputtering. I felt like I might throw up.

My eyes scanned the water, searching for Mama and Kamran. Then I heard her.

"Oh, Judy, thank God!" She was behind me, a few feet closer to the beach. She still held Kamran tightly. He was soaked and whimpering.

She struggled toward me through the water, then grabbed me into a fierce hug.

"Are you okay?"

I nodded. I couldn't seem to find my voice. All I could do was hold her with one arm, and clutch the fence with my other hand.

"Come on," she said, pulling me forward. "We're almost there."

We let ourselves be pushed toward the forbidden, empty beach. When we reached the sand, we dropped to our knees and sat a moment. Kamran splashed in the shallow water, happy again.

"Are you okay?" Mama asked again.

"I guess so," I said. "I swallowed water."

"You'll be okay," she said, smiling at me. "And look, here we are!"

She waved her hand at the empty white sand. But all I could look at was the fence extending far into the water. I didn't want to go out there again.

"Come on," Mama said, rising and extending her hand. "Let's take a walk."

I allowed myself to be pulled along, still feeling sick to my stomach.

"God," she said softly, "look how big these houses are. Who needs a house that big?"

I looked at a house she pointed to far down the beach and saw a man standing on the deck. He was watching us with binoculars.

"Mama, I don't think we should be here."

"It's all right, Judy. No one cares if we walk on the beach."

She was wrong about that, as it turned out. We hadn't walked more than a few yards when a dune buggy appeared on the beach, its yellow light flashing as it drove toward us.

"Excuse me, ma'am," a young man said as he stopped the buggy in front of us. "This is private property, and you're trespassing."

"Oh pish," Mama said, smiling brightly at the man. "We're just taking a walk. The beach belongs to everybody."

"No, ma'am," the man said firmly. "This beach belongs to the homeowners, and you will have to leave now."

"Come on, Mama," I said, pulling at her hand. "Let's go."

"No," Mama said, the smile fading from her face. "I am a tax-payer, and the beach belongs to everybody. We're just taking a walk, for God's sake. It's not like we're staking the place out."

The man took out a radio and raised it to his mouth, but before he could speak, another man appeared on foot, a tall, blond man wearing shorts and a white shirt. He was very handsome and very tanned.

"It's okay, Luke," the newcomer said. "They're my guests."

He smiled at Mama. After a moment, she smiled back.

"You sure, Mr. Jenson?" The security guard looked from the man to Mama and back again.

"Yes, it's okay. I'll vouch for them." Mr. Jenson smiled at the guard, then again at Mama.

"Okay." The guard climbed back into his dune buggy. "You know how to get in touch if you need anything." He gave us one last, long scowl and drove away.

We stood in awkward silence for a minute, then Mama said, "Thank you. That was very kind of you."

He grinned at her, his blue eyes crinkling at the edges.

"He's just doing his job," he said, nodding toward the retreating buggy. "But he takes it a little too seriously sometimes."

"Well," Mama said, smiling back at him. "We really appreciate your help. And . . . we don't want to keep you."

"You're not keeping me from anything," Mr. Jenson said. "I saw you come around the fence. Looks like you got banged up a little bit."

He was looking at my knees, which were scraped and bloody.

"Oh, Judy," Mama said. "I didn't see you were hurt. Are you okay?"

"I'm okay," I lied. I wasn't okay at all. My knees stung, my shoulder hurt from crashing into the fence, and my stomach was full of the ocean.

"Here," the man said, gesturing toward the huge house we'd been looking at. "I've got some first aid cream."

"Oh no," Mama said. "We can't impose on you like that."

"It's no imposition," he said, turning to walk toward the house. He looked over his shoulder and smiled again. "Can't have your little girl wandering around like that."

Mama took my hand and we followed him toward the house. It was peach-colored stucco with huge windows facing the ocean. We climbed the stairs to the deck where he'd been watching us with the binoculars.

"Here," he said, gesturing toward a table. "Have a seat and I'll find the first aid kit."

He disappeared into the house. Mama sat down on a brightly cushioned chair at the table, Kamran on her lap. She shaded her eyes and gazed out at the water, smiling. After a minute, I sat down, too.

Mr. Jenson reappeared with a small bag, a wet washrag, and some soap. After Mama had washed my knees, he handed her some ointment from the bag and she smeared it on the scrapes.

"There," she said, smiling. "You'll be as good as new."

"Really, I can't thank you enough, Mr. Jenson," she said, handing the ointment back to the man.

"It's no problem," he said. "A little bit of excitement in an otherwise boring day. And please, call me Jack."

"Well, thank you, Jack. I'm Cassie, this is Judy, and this little guy is Kamran." Mama waved the baby's hand at the man.

Just then a woman appeared in the doorway. She was dark-skinned with jet-black hair, wearing an apron and sensible-looking shoes. She carried a tray with a pitcher and three glasses.

"Thank you, Martina," Mr. Jenson said as she sat the tray on the table. "Lemonade?" he asked, turning to Mama.

Martina poured lemonade into the glasses and handed them around.

"Well, thank you," Mama said again. "This is very nice."

Martina disappeared into the house without a word.

"So." Mr. Jenson leaned one elbow on the table. "Are you from LA or just visiting?"

"I live in Pasadena," Mama said. "But Judy is here visiting from Indiana."

He turned to look at me. "I grew up in Michigan," he said, as though that might mean something to me. I nodded and took a sip of lemonade.

"And what do you do in Pasadena?" he asked Mama.

"I'm a stay-at-home mom," she said, bouncing Kamran on her knee.

"And is there a husband at home?"

Mama laughed. "Well, there is a husband, but he's not at home very much."

My mouth dropped open slightly. She was flirting.

"Doesn't sound like a very smart husband," Mr. Jenson said.

"And is there a Mrs. Jenson?" Mama asked, smiling at him.

"There is a soon-to-be-ex-Mrs. Jenson," he said, smiling back at her.

"Ah, I'm sorry," Mama said.

"Well, I'm not," he replied, laughing.

We sat on the deck for almost two hours, Mama and Mr. Jenson chatting away while Kamran dozed on her lap and I stared at the ocean, willing Mama to get up so we could leave.

Finally, I said, "We better go home now. Navid's gonna wonder where we are."

Mama glanced at me and I saw she was annoyed. But she quickly smiled. "I suppose you're right," she said, rising from the chair and moving Kamran from her lap to her shoulder.

"Already?" Mr. Jenson rose, too. "Well, let me at least drive you back to your car. I can't let you go around the fence again. That really is a dangerous thing to do."

As we walked through the house to the garage, I gazed around me, trying to take it all in, every detail, so I could tell Lee Ann about it. The house was beautiful inside, all gleaming light wood and white furniture. A huge grand piano sat in a corner. On it were dozens of framed photographs.

"Is that Johnny Carson?" Mama said, stopping in front of the piano and pointing to a photo.

"Yes," Mr. Jenson said. "He lives a couple doors down. Nice guy."

I recognized several other famous faces on the piano. Mr. Jenson must be some kind of celebrity himself, I guessed.

In the garage, we climbed into a jeep, Kamran sitting on Mama's lap, because there was no car seat. Mr. Jenson drove us back to the public beach and smiled at Mama as she climbed out of the car.

"Come back sometime," he said, holding her eyes for a minute. He reached into his pocket and pulled out a card, which he pressed into her hand. "Or call."

Then he turned and smiled at me. "Enjoy your visit, Judy."

With that, he drove back toward the gated community.

"Well," Mama said, sighing softly. "Wasn't that something?"

I didn't answer her as we trudged back across the public beach to retrieve our things.

We packed up our things and drove back to Pasadena in silence. Kamran ate graham crackers and played with a set of keys. Mama smiled and hummed softly as she drove. I stared out the window, wishing I was back in Indiana.

"Judy," Mama said as she parked the car in front of her apartment building. "Let's not mention what happened today to Navid, okay?"

I pulled the cooler from the trunk, saying nothing.

"It's just . . . he wouldn't understand," she said, catching my hand. "He'd get all freaked out and . . . well, let's just not tell him, okay?"

I remembered suddenly the time all those years before when she'd asked me not to tell Daddy I had been sick after I ate the brownies. And just as suddenly I had a vivid picture of Mama and

Derrick rushing from the bedroom, half dressed, right before I threw up that day.

"Whatever," I said, pulling my hand from hers.

When we got into the apartment, I headed for my room, ready for a shower. Ready to be away from Mama. When I emerged from the bathroom, she was sitting on the couch, looking at the business card Mr. Jenson had given her.

"You should throw that away," I said.

"Oh, God!" She jumped. "You startled me."

She laughed and slipped the card into her wallet. "I'm not going to call him. It's just . . . nice that someone finds me interesting, you know?"

"Navid thinks you're interesting," I said. "Daddy thought you were interesting, too."

I didn't mean to say the last part. It just came out.

Mama sighed. "Someday, you'll understand, sweetheart."

She rose and walked to the kitchen. "I'm making lentils and rice for dinner. Does that sound good?"

Navid noticed my skinned knees as soon as he walked into the apartment.

"What happened?" he asked.

"Oh, she fell on the sand," Mama said, kissing his cheek. "It's nothing, just skinned knees."

After dinner, I called Daddy.

"How are you doing?" he asked.

"I'm okay."

"You sure? You don't sound okay."

"I'm just homesick, I guess."

He laughed. "Already? We've only been here two days."

"Daddy? Can you come over tomorrow?"

"I guess that depends, honey. What are you and Cassie doing?"

"I don't know. But can you come anyway?"

"Judy, are you all right?"

"I'm okay," I repeated. "I just miss you."

"Okay, honey," he said softly. "Tomorrow, I'll come see you."

"I love you," I said, closing my eyes against the tears.

"I love you too, peanut."

I lay in bed that night wishing I was back in my own room in Indiana, just Daddy and me . . . or even Daddy and me and Treva, for that matter. I wished we hadn't come to California again. I wished Mama was like she'd been the last time we were here, laughing and dancing in the living room. She'd been happy then, hadn't she?

Now she seemed frustrated and restless, antsy . . . almost like she was spoiling for a fight. Mama was messing up again, and I didn't want to be here to see it happen. I wanted to remember her just the way she was last summer. I didn't want to see the way she was now.

I sighed unhappily, thinking again about how she'd asked me to lie to Navid, just like she'd asked me to lie to Daddy all those years ago.

Why couldn't Mama ever just be happy?

28

The next morning, Daddy knocked on the door just after Navid left for work.

"Kirk," Mama said, pulling her robe closed. "I didn't know you were coming over."

"I was hoping I could hang out with you and Judy today," Daddy said. "Is that all right? My ten o'clock call fell through, so I'm free for the day."

"Well, sure. I guess so." Mama walked into the kitchen. "Do you want coffee? Have you had breakfast?"

"I've eaten," he said. "But coffee sounds good. Hey, peanut!" He kissed the top of my head. "How are you doing?"

"I'm okay," I said. I was eating pancakes.

Mama poured a cup of coffee for him and sat down at the table next to me.

"I was just asking Judy what she wanted to do today," she said.

"Well, I was thinking maybe we could all go to Disneyland," Daddy said, smiling at me. "I know that was on Judy's wish list."

"Oh, I don't know," Mama said.

"My treat," Daddy said. "Come on, Cassie, it'll be fun. I bet Kamran will like it, too."

"He's too little," Mama said. "And it's such a long drive. And it's expensive, Kirk. You can't believe how much it costs."

"We're on vacation," Daddy said. "And I brought some extra cash. You want to go, don't you, Judy?"

"Yes," I said, nodding at him. "That sounds like fun."

Mama said nothing for a minute. She sipped her coffee and looked at Daddy, then at me. Finally, she sighed.

"Oh, all right," she said. "It's not my kind of place, but if Judy wants to go, then I guess we'll go."

"Thanks, Mama," I said, rising and putting my plate in the sink.

Daddy drank his coffee while Mama and I dressed. Then we waited while Mama got the baby ready to go. After what seemed like an hour, we were ready.

"I'll drive," Daddy said.

"You don't know how to get there," Mama protested.

"I got directions at the hotel," Daddy said. "There's a map in the car. And you know the way, so you can navigate if we get lost."

Daddy opened the door of the red Honda he had rented. "All we need is Kamran's car seat."

We moved the car seat from Mama's car into the Honda, then Mama climbed into the front seat beside Daddy and I sat in back with the baby. After a two-hour drive, during which we sat for long periods on the freeway not moving at all, we arrived.

"Wow," I said, climbing out of the car. The parking lot was even bigger than the one at the airport. "It must be a mile just to get to the gate."

"Don't worry," Mama said, pulling Kamran from the car. "There's a little train that takes us."

We waited at a covered kiosk, then boarded a train that dropped us at the front gate.

"Wow," I said again, as we entered the main street. "It's just like in the pictures."

Daddy rented a stroller for Kamran and we let ourselves be pushed along by the crowd.

"Look at all the shops," I said. "I have to get something for Lee Ann."

"Oh, you don't want to buy anything here," Mama said. "Everything here is overpriced junk."

"I have my own money," I snapped. "And I told her I'd get her something."

Mama sighed and rolled her eyes at Daddy. He just laughed.

"Let's wait till the end of the day to buy stuff," he said. "That way we don't have to carry it around all day."

Kamran began fussing in his stroller.

"I think he needs a change," Daddy said, bending over him and holding his nose.

"I'll get him," Mama said sharply. She pulled the baby from the stroller and scanned the street for a bathroom. "You guys wait here. I'll be right back."

Daddy and I sat on a bench, the stroller in front of us.

"You sure you're okay?" he asked.

"I'm okay," I said. "She just gets on my nerves sometimes."

He laughed. "Well, that's probably the first normal mother-daughter moment you've had with her in a long time."

I shrugged.

"Seriously, honey, it's pretty normal for mothers and daughters to get on each other's nerves sometimes."

"I guess so."

I thought about telling him about Mr. Jenson, but I didn't want to ruin the day. I'd never been to Disneyland, after all.

Mama waved as she walked toward us. She was so pretty, her blond hair hanging straight down her back, green eyes sparkling, hips swaying in her tight, hip-hugging jeans. For the millionth time, I wished she was more like Lee Ann's mom and less like . . . well, like Mama.

Mrs. Dawson wasn't much older than Mama, I realized with a start. But she would never wear such tight jeans and such a low-cut top. And she wouldn't flirt with other men . . . especially not in front of Lee Ann. Not like Mama had done yesterday with Mr. Jensen. Mrs. Dawson was a mom. Even though she only had one kid and Mama had two, Mrs. Dawson knew how to be a mother in a way Mama didn't seem to get.

Mrs. Dawson was a grown-up, I thought, and Mama was still like a kid—immature and pretty irresponsible. After all, even I knew better than to trespass on a private beach, or to go so deep in the ocean with a baby. Mama just did whatever she wanted to, even if other people got hurt.

"Here," Daddy said when Mama reached us. "Before you put him back in the stroller, let me take a picture of you guys in front of that fountain."

We stood smiling at him, Mama's arm around my waist.

"Good," he said, snapping away.

"Would you like me to take one of all of you?" An older woman tapped Daddy's shoulder.

"Sure," he said, smiling at her. He showed her how to use the camera and then came to stand beside me, his hand on my shoulder.

"You have a beautiful family," the woman said as she handed the camera back to him.

"Oh, we're not . . ." Mama started.

"Thank you," Daddy said, smiling first at the woman, then at me.

Mama stared at him as the woman walked away, arm in arm with her husband.

"What was that?" she asked.

"Oh, come on, Cassie." Daddy laughed. "We don't have to give our whole life story to everyone."

Mama just shook her head.

"Now," Daddy said, taking my hand. "Let's head to Fantasyland first."

Daddy and I had fun, but Mama did not enjoy herself. She trailed along behind us, pushing the stroller and complaining about the heat, the crowds, and how expensive everything was. The only part she seemed to like was the It's a Small World ride. Kamran sat in her lap and gazed wide-eyed at the singing, dancing dolls. Even Mama relaxed in the cool of the boat.

"Who's hungry?" Daddy said after we'd been on every ride in Fantasyland.

"Me!" I said. "Let's eat."

We found an outdoor table at a busy restaurant and sat down.

"Good God," Mama said when the waitress brought the menus. "Look how much everything costs. This is ridiculous."

Daddy just grinned at her.

"Seriously, Kirk, we shouldn't eat here. It's awful how much they charge, just because they can. Capitalism at its absolute worst."

"You're not even paying," I said before I could stop myself.

Mama looked at me in silence for an instant, then opened her mouth to say something, but Daddy interrupted her again.

"It's okay, Cassie. Just order whatever you want. I've got it covered."

We ate hamburgers and fries while Mama complained about the food.

"I can't believe they serve this kind of junk. You'd think they'd at least offer something healthy."

I wanted to slap her.

After lunch, we headed to Tomorrowland, where Daddy and I stood in line for more than an hour to ride Space Mountain. Mama, thankfully, did not wait with us, choosing to sit on a bench under a tree with Kamran.

"She's not having much fun, is she?" Daddy said.

"I don't care," I said. "I love it."

"Well, maybe next we should ask her what she wants to do."

"Whatever," I said. "She'll probably just want to go home."

By four o'clock, Mama was done.

"We need to go," she said firmly. "We're going to hit rush hour traffic as it is. It's going to take us all night to get home."

"Well, then, why don't we stay late?" Daddy said. "We can have dinner at the Tahitian place. They have hula dancers." He winked at me.

Mama shook her head.

"And then we can stay for the parade," Daddy continued. "That way we won't have to deal with the traffic at all."

Mama simply pushed Kamran's stroller toward Main Street.

"Oh, come on," I whined. "I've never been to Disneyland before and I'll probably never get to come again, and you want to go home? That's not fair."

Mama stopped abruptly and turned to me.

"I was under the impression that you came to California to visit with me."

"Yeah, well, you didn't seem to even notice I was there yesterday," I said loudly.

Daddy stared at both of us.

"Oh, I see," Mama said, her hands planted firmly on her hips. "This is your way of punishing me for something I didn't even do. Nice, Judy. Very nice."

She began pushing the stroller again. Daddy took my hand and we followed her down Main Street and out the gate, into the parking lot. We waited in tense silence for the train to take us back to the car.

Mama had been right about the traffic. It was almost eight by the time we got back to her apartment.

"Hey." Navid smiled at us when we came in. "I didn't expect you back so early. You didn't stay for the parade?"

Mama simply carried Kamran into the nursery.

"What happened?" Navid asked, looking from Daddy to me.

"I don't think Cassie likes Disneyland very much," Daddy said.

"She complained the whole time," I spat.

Daddy patted my shoulder.

"Well," he said, "I guess I should probably get going."

I grabbed his hand.

"Judy, are you all right?" Navid looked confused.

"I . . . I think I'm going to stay with Daddy tonight," I said. "That's okay, right, Daddy?"

I stared at him, willing him to say yes.

"Well, I guess it's okay, if that's what you want. Is that what you really want?"

"Yes," I said. "Wait just a minute while I get my stuff."

I ran into the nursery, where Mama sat in a rocking chair, nursing Kamran.

"What are you doing?" she asked as I pulled my suitcase from under the bed.

"I'm going to stay with Daddy tonight," I said, not looking at her.

She didn't say anything at first. I could feel her watching me.

"Fine," she said softly. "If that's what you want."

I shoved my pajamas into the suitcase, locked it, and dragged it from the bedroom, never once looking back at Mama.

"Judy, what has happened?" Navid asked. "Did you and your mother have a fight?"

"No," I said. "I just . . . I really just want to be with my dad. That's all."

"Well, then, I guess we'll see you tomorrow," he said. He put his hand on my shoulder and squeezed slightly. "Okay?"

I nodded and took Daddy's hand. We walked to the car in silence. Inside the car, I began to cry, softly at first and then harder, my face pressed against the side window. Daddy sat beside me, his hand on my shoulder.

"What happened?" he asked when I had finally snuffled to a stop.

"She ruins everything," I said. "That's probably the only time in my whole life I'll get to go to Disneyland, and she ruined it."

"Okay, I get that she spoiled the day today," he said. "But what happened yesterday? What did she do?"

I shook my head. I didn't want to talk about Mr. Jenson to Daddy. And I definitely didn't want to talk about what I had remembered about Mama and Derrick.

"Judy." Daddy took my chin in his hand so I had to look at him. "I can sit here all night if I have to, but you are going to tell me what happened."

"I just . . . Why does she have to be so selfish?" I said softly. "She never thinks about anyone but herself."

Daddy just nodded, like he understood.

And so I told him about the fence and the huge wave and the man in the dune buggy. And then I told him about Mr. Jenson, and his business card pressed in Mama's hand. When I had finished, we sat in silence for a long minute. Then Daddy sighed.

"Okay," he said. "You're right, that was a selfish thing for her to do, a very selfish and stupid thing. And it was wrong of her to put you in the middle of it. I'm sorry, honey."

He turned the key in the ignition and sighed again.

"Maybe bringing you out here was a bad idea," he said softly.

"It's okay, Daddy," I said. "I mean, I wanted to come. I just wish . . ."

"I know," he said. "Me too."

He pulled into traffic and smiled at me, a sad kind of smile. "Let's go back to the hotel, get something to eat, and watch a movie. Does that sound okay?"

I nodded, torn between relief at having told him the truth and guilt at betraying Mama.

~29~

I woke the next morning with a stiff neck. The rollaway cot Daddy had asked for at the hotel wasn't very soft. I heard Daddy talking softly on the phone. His back was to me. I lay still and listened.

"It was stupid, Cassie," he whispered into the phone, "and dangerous. Judy was scared when she got hit by that wave."

He was quiet for a minute, then said, "I know she's all right, but she could have been killed. When are you going to learn that you can't just break the law anytime you want to?"

More silence. I saw him turn to look toward me so I closed my eyes and pretended to be asleep.

"And taking her to a stranger's house? What were you thinking? She could tell you were flirting with him. She's not a little kid anymore."

I could hear Mama's voice rise, but I couldn't make out what she was saying.

"Like hell it's not my business." Daddy sounded really angry. "Anything to do with Judy is my business. I'm surprised you didn't have her watch Kamran while you and Mr. Malibu had sex."

I stiffened, listening intently.

"Look, Cassie, what you do with your life is up to you. I gave up trying to help you a long time ago, and frankly, I don't give a damn anymore what you do. Cheat on Navid. Leave him and the baby. Go make another mess of things, but not with my daughter. Do you understand me? I will *not* let you drag Judy into another one of your messes."

More silence. Then he said, "Look, I'm going to take her sight-seeing today. She needs a break and so do I. I'll call you tonight."

With that, he hung up.

He walked into the bathroom and closed the door. I stared at the ceiling, wishing again that I was in my own room in our house in Indianapolis.

By the time Daddy emerged from the shower, I was dressed and watching television.

"Hey," he said. "Did you sleep okay?"

"Yeah."

"I was thinking today we'd do some sightseeing; how's that sound?"

"Okay."

"I called your mom and told her we're spending the day together, just you and me."

"Was she mad?"

Daddy smiled at me. "Well, she wasn't thrilled, but she'll get over it."

We ate breakfast in the hotel restaurant. I watched people in the pool while Daddy looked at a huge map.

"The one thing I have to do while I'm here is visit Marilyn Monroe's grave," he said.

I looked at him and he grinned, but his cheeks were red.

"Why?" I asked.

"Treva is a huge fan of hers. I promised her I'd take a picture of the grave. I know"—he ran his hand through his hair—"it's silly. But she really wants a picture."

"Okay." He was right. It was beyond silly. It was ridiculous.

"Look"—he pointed to a spot on the map—"she's buried in Westwood. That's right near Santa Monica. We can go to the cemetery and then to the beach. Santa Monica has a big pier and lots of shops. Maybe you can find something there for Lee Ann."

"Sounds good," I said, wiping syrup from my chin. "Should I bring my swimsuit?"

"Sure," he said. "If you want to, we can swim."

Then I remembered that my swimsuit was at Mama's apartment. She'd rinsed it in the sink when we got back from the beach and hung it in her shower to dry.

"I don't have it," I said. "It's at Mama's."

"Well, I guess we could swing by there and get it."

"No," I said. "Let's not. We don't have to swim."

We drove west on the Ventura Freeway, then cut south through the mountains and drove through Beverly Hills, passing the huge pink hotel where Mama and Navid had gotten married. I pointed it out to Daddy. He nodded but said nothing.

When we got to Westwood, we parked and asked directions to the little cemetery where Marilyn Monroe was buried. Only she wasn't actually buried in the ground, as it turned out. She was in a white crypt; that's what the little booklet we had called it. Beside her name plaque was a little vase, holding fresh flowers. I sat on a bench while Daddy took several pictures of the plaque and flowers.

The booklet said several other famous people were buried in the cemetery, and that surprised me, because it wasn't very big. Daddy asked if I wanted to look at any of the other graves, but I said no. I would have liked to see someone famous alive, but I thought it was kind of creepy to go visiting graves of people we didn't even know.

We walked around Westwood for a while, then got back in the car and drove to the Santa Monica Pier. It was crowded, even though it had been badly damaged by a storm several months earlier. We watched men fish from the pier and then wandered to the shore, where a group of guys had set up a stage and were break-dancing to very loud music. People flew by us on roller skates and bikes. Everyone looked tan and lean and healthy.

"Let's get something to eat," Daddy said, scanning the board-walk. "Do you want to try a falafel? It's a Greek sandwich."

I remembered the sandwich Treva had eaten in Broad Ripple. It had smelled really good.

"Okay."

We bought sandwiches at a little kiosk and sat on a bench to eat them. The falafel tasted as good as it smelled, spicy and warm with cool yogurt sauce on top. When we'd finished, we got back in the car and drove south to Venice Beach.

"Wow," I said, taking in the scene. "Mama would love it here."

I'd never seen such an assortment of people. It was like stepping onto a movie set. All along the boardwalk, entertainers performed. A man in a torn T-shirt sang reggae, backed by a small band and a steel drum. Farther along, we saw more break-dancers and then a man playing the saxophone. Women in hot pants and bikini tops skated by. Kids on bikes were everywhere. And on the beach itself, a big man with lots of tattoos was juggling chainsaws. We stood and stared, and then Daddy started taking pictures.

We saw people playing basketball and beach volleyball, a group of college kids were dancing on the sand to music from a boom box, and out in the water were several surfers.

We spent a couple hours just wandering, stopping now and then to look in the shops. I bought Lee Ann a necklace made of little conch shells and a tank top that read "Venice Beach . . . another day in paradise." Daddy bought a small painting of the beach for Treva and a set of ceramic coffee mugs for Grandma and Grandpa.

Finally, exhausted, we plopped down on the sand and watched the seagulls dive-bomb the shoreline, snapping up bits of food that people threw into the air.

"I wish we lived here," I said, leaning back on my elbows and letting the cool ocean breeze waft over me.

"That would be fun," Daddy agreed. "But it's expensive, and you'd have to deal with tourists all the time."

"Like us," I agreed. "That would be okay. We're not so bad."

Daddy laughed. He seemed relaxed and happy.

"Treva would love this place," he said.

I nodded. Who wouldn't love this place, after all?

We sat in silence for a while. I watched Daddy watching the people.

"Thanks, Daddy," I said.

"For what?"

"For bringing me here today."

"You're welcome, peanut. I'm glad we came."

"What do you want to do tomorrow?"

He sat for a minute, staring out at the ocean. Finally, he turned to look at me. "I'm not sure, Judy. Do you think you should go to your mom's tomorrow?"

I shook my head. "No, let's do something just you and me again."

He put his hand on my knee. "Look, I know you're mad at her right now. I get that. I'm kind of mad at her, too. But she is your mom, the only one you've got. And after we go home, who knows when you'll see her again?"

I stared at the water, watching a seagull circling high overhead.

"You don't have to see her if you really don't want to," he said softly. "But I'm afraid you'll get home and regret it if you don't."

"Maybe I'll see her on Wednesday," I said. "Is that all right?"

"Sure," he said, smiling. "If that's what you want."

"Daddy, do you think she's going to cheat on Navid?"

He looked at me like he was surprised, then he cleared his throat. "I don't know, honey. That's between Cassie and Navid. It doesn't have anything to do with you."

"Did she cheat on you?"

Daddy rose and held out his hand, pulling me up, too.

"Judy, there are some things that are private, between married people. And they should stay private."

"She slept with Derrick, didn't she?"

He dropped my hand and looked out at the ocean, silent for a long minute.

"How do you know that?" he finally asked.

"When she asked me not to tell Navid about Mr. Jenson, I remembered one time when I was little . . ." My voice trailed away. I was sorry now that I'd brought it up.

"Oh, Judy." His voice sounded tired. "Oh, honey, come here."

He pulled me into a hug and we stood like that on the beach for a long time.

"I'm sorry, Daddy," I whispered.

"You don't have anything to be sorry for," he said, tilting my chin up. "You didn't do anything wrong. You know that, right?"

I nodded.

"But I'm sorry she cheated on you."

"Me too," he said quietly.

We walked back to the car, holding hands. I wished I knew how to make things better for him, but I couldn't think of anything to do or say.

"Look, Judy," he said as we pulled onto the busy freeway toward Pasadena. "I know your mom has disappointed you. And she's hurt you. But I hope you know she never meant to do that."

I stared out the window at the passing cars.

"Cassie had a really hard time growing up," he said. "It made her not trust people."

I looked at him in surprise.

"She trusts everybody," I said, thinking of Jim Jones and Mr. Jenson and Derrick.

"She wants to trust everybody," he said. "She tries to trust everybody. But I think deep down, she can't ever really trust anyone, not even herself. She's always waiting for people to leave her. I think that's why she left us. And I think if she leaves Navid, it's the same thing. She leaves before she can get left. She's trying to protect herself."

"She's nuts," I said.

Daddy smiled. "She is a little nuts," he agreed. "But she's not mean. She doesn't mean to hurt people. She just . . . she's your mom."

"That's what you used to say about her mom," I mused.

He paused then, staring at the traffic ahead.

"Yeah," he said finally, "I guess you're right. Cassie has tried so hard to not be like her mom, but in the end, she's done the same thing to you that her mom did to her."

We inched forward in the bumper-to-bumper mess, breathing in exhaust from the car ahead of us.

"What about Kamran?" I asked. "Will she leave him, too?"

"I don't know," he said. "I hope not."

"Me too," I said, thinking of Kamran nestled at Mama's breast, twisting her blond hair in his small brown hand as he nursed.

"So, tomorrow how about we drive out to the desert?" Daddy

asked. "Would you like that? Or maybe we could go to the wild animal park in San Diego."

"Let's do that!" I'd read about the wild animal park, where the animals roamed free and the people were enclosed.

"Okay," he said. "And maybe on Wednesday, you can spend at least a little time with your mom?"

"Okay." I sighed. I knew he was right, that I should see her again. I just really didn't want to.

❧ 30 ❧

On Wednesday morning, Daddy woke me up at nine. I was tired and sunburned from our adventure the day before in San Diego, and what I really wanted to do was go back to sleep. Instead, I got up and took a shower, wincing as the water hit my reddened skin. Then we had breakfast.

"Okay," he said as I ate my eggs and toast, "I'll take you to your mom's when you're done, and I'll pick you up about five. Is that okay?"

I shrugged. I didn't really want to go to Mama's. I didn't want to see her, knowing what I did about her and my dad. Still, like Daddy said, she was the only mother I had. And I knew he was right, that I'd regret it if I didn't see her again while we were here.

"What are you going to do?" I asked.

"I've got some reading to do for a case," he said.

"But you're supposed to be on vacation," I said.

"Well, maybe I'll do my reading at the pool." He smiled. "It's okay, Judy. I'm fine."

He drove me to Mama's and walked up to the apartment with me.

"Here," he said before we knocked on the door. He pressed a quarter into my hand. "Just in case you need to call."

He knocked on the door and Mama opened it. She smiled at me and opened her arms.

"Hey, honey," she said, wrapping me in a hug. "I'm so sorry about Monday. Disneyland just isn't my thing, you know?"

I didn't hug her back and stepped away as soon as she released me.

"Okay," Daddy said, "I'll be at the hotel if you need me. You have the number, right?"

"Yeah," I said. "I have it."

Daddy left, and I sat down on the couch. The living room looked like it had the day we first arrived—a total mess.

"Where's Kamran?"

"He's taking a nap," Mama said. "Sorry about the mess. I just can't seem to keep up with everything."

She began picking up dishes and carried them into the kitchen.

"Do you want something to eat? I can make eggs."

"I ate at the hotel."

"How about some juice?"

"No, thanks."

She walked into the living room carrying a cup of coffee and stood looking at me for a moment.

"I really am sorry, honey," she said. "I'm sorry about Disneyland, and I'm sorry I upset you at the beach."

I shrugged. "It's okay."

She sat down beside me on the couch and patted my knee.

"I told your dad he was overreacting," she said, smiling. "He's always been such a worrier."

I said nothing.

"So, what do you want to do today? Kamran should be up soon, and then we can do whatever you want."

"I don't know," I said.

"We can drive up to the mountains and have a picnic. Or, hey, I know! We can go to Venice Beach. It's a funky, fun place, one of my favorite places. I bet you'll love it."

"Daddy and I went there on Tuesday," I said, not looking at her.

"Oh." She sounded disappointed. "Well, how about we stay here this morning and go to the pool?"

"I'm sunburned," I said, pulling my sleeve up so she could see.

"I've got some heavy-duty sunscreen," she said. "You'll be okay."

"Whatever."

I reached for the remote control and turned on the television to MTV. Mama sat watching me watch TV.

Finally, she said, "Okay, I get that you're mad at me. But, God, Judy, it's not like I did anything wrong. We had lemonade with a nice man who rescued us from the beach Gestapo. There's nothing wrong with that."

On the television, Michael Jackson's "Beat It" blared. Mama reached over, took the remote from me, and turned it off.

"Hey," I said, "I was watching that."

"You didn't come all the way from Indiana to watch television," she said. "You came to see me. And damn it, Judy, you are going to look at me."

Her eyes were tearful and she blinked several times.

"Just tell me what was so wrong with having lemonade with Mr. Jenson," she demanded. "It's not like we had an affair."

"Then why didn't you want me to tell Navid?" I asked, knowing the answer already.

Mama sighed. "Navid is just . . . He's very proper about things. He wasn't that way so much before the baby, but now . . . well, he just wouldn't get it."

"I think he'd get it exactly," I said.

"And what is that supposed to mean?"

"I think he'd know you were probably going to cheat on him."

"Judy!" Mama's eyes widened. "Why would you say something like that?"

"You cheated on Daddy," I yelled. "With Derrick and probably with Glen, too. I know you did, so don't even deny it."

"Who told you that?" she said, her voice soft.

"I'm not a baby anymore," I said. "I remember . . . things. I didn't know then, but now I do. I know what I remember, and I know what you did."

Mama sat quietly for a minute, staring at me and wringing her hands in her lap.

When she finally spoke, her voice was quiet.

"It was a long time ago," she said. "And I was just a kid. God, Judy, I was eighteen when I met your dad and nineteen when I had you. I wasn't old enough to be a wife or a mother. And . . . well, it was the sixties. Things were different then. When your dad and I got married, neither of us worried too much about stuff like . . . well, like sex."

"He didn't cheat on you," I said.

She sighed. "No, he didn't. But if he had slept with someone else, I'd have been cool with that."

I stared at her, my mouth open, before I finally said, "I don't believe you. And anyway, it doesn't matter, because he didn't cheat on you. You cheated on him with Derrick and Glen and . . . probably lots of other men. You're just a whore!"

She drew back from me as if she'd been slapped, her eyes wide. She rose and walked from the room. I could hear her crying in the bathroom. I felt bad for calling her a whore. But I was still mad at her. After a few minutes, she walked back into the room, clutching a handful of tissues.

"All right," she said, sitting down again. "Let's get something straight right now. You can be as mad at me as you want. You can even hate me. But don't you ever, *ever* call me that again. Is that clear?"

I nodded.

"I don't expect you to understand, Judy. It was a different time, and I was a different person back then. I wasn't a good wife to Kirk. And I wasn't a very good mother to you. I tried, but I was just too young."

She paused, waiting for me to respond. I didn't say anything.

"But I wish you could see that I've changed," she continued. "I've grown up a lot since then. And I'm trying so hard to be a good wife and mother now. Sometimes it's hard and I don't always get it right, but I really am trying."

She paused again.

"Then why did you take Mr. Jenson's phone number?" I asked.

"Oh Lord," she said, flopping back on the couch. "I don't even know how to explain it to you."

"Try," I said.

She sighed deeply and sat back up. "Okay, it's like . . . I love Navid, you know that, right? He's kind of uptight, but he's a good man and I love him. But he's changed so much since Kamran was born. He used to be fun and now he's just so . . . rigid, I guess. He fusses all the time about the house and the laundry and how I take care of the baby. He's gotten to be a lot like his mom. And that's hard to deal with."

She took a drink of coffee and stared at the wall for a minute.

"And then a man like Jack is interested, and that's flattering, I guess. It's really nice to know I'm still attractive. That's all. It's just nice to know I'm still alive.

"I don't expect you'll understand that. You probably won't get it until you're my age. I'm not eighteen anymore. I'm over thirty and I've had two babies and my body is changing. And sometimes, Judy, it's just nice to know that someone like Jack thinks I'm attractive."

I said nothing.

"I'm not going to call him," she said firmly. "I threw his card away that night."

"Really?" I hoped she was telling me the truth.

"Really," she said. "I promise. I threw the card away. I'm not going to call him. I'm not going to cheat on Navid. I'm really trying to be a good wife and mother. Do you believe me?"

"I guess so," I said.

"Okay. Then, let's make a pact." She took both my hands in hers. "From now on, I promise you that I will try hard to be a better mom to you. And I promise not to put you in the middle of things. And I promise . . . God, I don't know. I just promise to try. Will you?"

I nodded, and she squeezed my hands.

"Thank you, honey."

She kissed both my cheeks. "You know I love you, right?"

"I know, Mama."

"Good. So, let's stop talking about all this stuff and decide what we're going to do today, okay?"

Just then we heard Kamran crying in the nursery.

"Here we go," Mama said, rising. "I'll get him up and change him, and you think about what you want to do."

She walked into the nursery and I went to the kitchen for a glass of water. The phone rang, and I answered it. "Hello?"

"Hey, beautiful, how are you doing this morning?" a man's voice said.

"What?" His voice sounded familiar, but it wasn't Navid.

"Cassie?" the voice said.

"No," I said, "it's Judy."

"Oh, hey, Judy, it's Jack Jenson. You remember, from the beach?"

I stood staring at the receiver for a minute, then dropped it and backed away from the phone.

Mama emerged from the nursery with Kamran on her hip. "Hey, did I hear the phone?"

She stopped when she saw me. "Judy, what's wrong?"

She saw the receiver dangling down the wall. "Who's on the phone?"

"It's Jack Jenson." I spat the words at her. "Your new boyfriend."

"Oh," she stammered, her face going white. "I . . . Judy, I didn't . . ."

"You said you threw the card away!" I was yelling now. "You promised me you did. You lied."

She stepped toward me. Kamran began whimpering. "Honey, I just . . ."

"You're not trying to be a good wife and mother. You're just doing what you always do. You're leaving."

She grabbed at my wrist and I pulled away.

"No," she said loudly. "I am not leaving."

"Yes, you are," I yelled. "You're leaving. It's what you always do. You leave."

Kamran began crying in earnest. Mama ran her hand over his hair.

"Stop it," she said. "You're upsetting him."

She turned toward the phone then, reaching for the receiver. "Hey," she said as I opened the front door. "I can't talk now."

I was on the elevator before she realized I was gone. I heard her calling for me as the car descended.

I walked quickly to Lake Street, remembering the phone booth outside the ice cream store. My fingers shaking, I put the quarter into the phone and dialed.

"I'm at the corner of Lake and California," I said when Daddy answered. "Come get me."

I sat down on the curb to wait for him, my stomach churning. She'd lied to me, right to my face. She'd looked me right in the eyes and promised me, and that was just a lie. Everything about Mama was a lie. She didn't love Navid, just like she hadn't loved Daddy. She didn't love me or Kamran, either. How could she love us and act like she did? You didn't lie to people you loved. You didn't promise and then just lie. And you didn't leave.

I shook my head, blinking back tears, thinking of Kamran again, his small hand touching Mama's cheek. What would happen to him when she left? Who would take him for his first day of school and pick him up every day? Would he lie in bed at night wondering what he'd done wrong? Would he think it was his fault that she'd left?

I had a sudden, vivid memory of lying in my bed at Grandma's house as she stroked my forehead and shushed me while I cried. I was just a little kid, for Christ's sake! I was six! And she just left. Mothers didn't do that to their kids, not real mothers. Mothers were supposed to take care of you and know what grade you were in and help with your homework. Mothers were supposed to take pictures when you went to your first dance and go to PTA meetings and . . . and just be there.

Mama did none of those things. Mama was none of those things. She was a liar and a cheater and a whore. I felt my cheeks redden at the thought, ashamed that she was my mother. Ashamed that I had believed her lies. Ashamed that I had loved her.

I leaned forward and vomited on the street. A homeless man stopped to stare at me and then shuffled away.

Wiping my hand across my mouth, I rose, stepped back from the curb, and caught sight of myself in the window of the ice cream store. My dark hair hung to my chin, my dark eyes were wide and red. I looked nothing like her, and I was glad of it. For the first time ever, I was glad I didn't look like her, glad I wasn't anything like her, glad she had left and never come back.

Finally, I was done with Mama.

PART 4

MAD WORLD

❧ 31 ❧

I wasn't even there when the garage burned down, but of course I got blamed for it.

Downstairs, I could hear Piper Watkins yelling at my dad.

"This is just not something my children would do!"

Her children—God, if she only knew. Luce was a thirteen-year-old kleptomaniac who'd steal anything that wasn't nailed down. And Trent . . . well, he was probably in mourning about now. He'd stashed all his *Playboy*s in the garage. Now they were just ashes. That made me smile.

"Look, I'm sorry her mother is dead, but you have to do something about her. Judy is a wild thing. She's headed for trouble. And she is *not* taking my children along for the ride!"

The front door slammed. I heard Daddy coming up the stairs.

"You told Piper Watkins your mother is dead?"

I nodded.

"Why would you say that?"

I shrugged. "It's easier."

Easier than explaining that my mother had left two marriages and two children behind, and was now living in an ashram somewhere in India with her guru/lover. Somehow, I couldn't see telling that to Piper Watkins.

Daddy shook his head and sat down on the bed beside me.

"What were you guys doing in that garage? And don't hand me some load of crap about melting crayons into candles. Piper might believe that, but I sure as hell don't."

I shrugged again. "It's just a place to hang out."

"And the fire started on its own, just like that?"

"Probably Luce was smoking."

"Luce smokes?" Daddy looked surprised.

"Everybody smokes."

He looked at me closely.

"Everybody but me." I smiled at him.

"Judy, if I catch you smoking . . ."

"God, Dad. I don't smoke. That's just stupid."

He took my chin in his hand and tilted my head so I was looking straight into his eyes.

"Honest, I don't smoke."

"I hope not," he said. "What are you doing tonight?"

"Hanging out with Lee Ann."

"Well, be home by ten."

"I thought you were going out with Treva," I said, looking away.

Dad had been dating Treva for over two years now. She still annoyed me, but I had to admit that sometimes having her around was handy. She took me shopping in Broad Ripple and bought me clothes. She took me to her hair salon to get my hair cut. Once I stayed overnight at her apartment when Daddy was on a business trip. She let Lee Ann stay over, too. We ate pizza, watched videos, and gave each other manicures.

Other times, though, I wished she would drop off the face of the earth. Like when she tried to give me advice about guys, or when she told Daddy I was too young to hang out in Broad Ripple on Friday nights, even though all my friends did.

"I am," he said, rising. "But I want you home by ten, anyway. I'll call the house at ten, and I expect you to be here."

"Whatever." I sighed.

"There's some leftover Chinese food in the fridge," he said.

"Okay."

He closed the door behind him. A few minutes later, I heard the shower down the hall.

As pleased as I was about Trent's *Playboys* burning, the loss of the garage was a problem. At least I hadn't left the stash there. That would have been a disaster.

I checked the shoe box in the back of my closet. Almost a quarter-pound of pot, neatly divided into nickel and dime bags. I shuddered at the near miss. All that money, all that pot could have gone up in smoke. Lord, Piper Watkins would've had a heart attack if she'd smelled pot burning. What would she think about her precious angels if she knew what they'd been doing in the garage?

Luce was fairly useless, of course. We wouldn't have cut her in at all if she hadn't found the stash. The only way to keep her mouth shut was to pay her off—and not in money. She really didn't need the money. All she had to do was bat her eyes at her parents and they'd buy her anything she wanted. Or, she'd just steal it. Instead, Trent and I gave her a constant supply of weed. I was pretty sure that's how the fire started. Luce always smoked in the garage . . . stupid bitch.

Trent wasn't a whole lot better, but at least he was big. When I decided to start the business, I'd gone alone to the first meeting with my supplier. Mitch was a big-time dealer, an eighteen-year-old dropout, and he creeped me out. After that first meeting, I always took Trent along. He might be stupid, but he was built like an ox and fast on his feet. Plus, he had keys to his grandmother's garage, the perfect place to conduct business. At least it had been. Now we'd have to find someplace new.

I flopped down on my bed to think about that. We needed someplace private but close to home, someplace where no one would notice the traffic. We did a lot of business.

The phone rang downstairs and I ran to answer it.

"Hello?"

"Hi, Judy!" Treva's voice still bugged the hell out of me. She was always so damned perky. "Is your dad home?"

"He's in the can."

"Oh." She sounded disappointed. "Can I leave him a message?

Will you tell him I'm still at the office, and he can just pick me up here."

"Will do," I said, hanging up before she could say anything else.

Honestly, I couldn't see what Dad saw in her. Treva was pretty, I guess, in an obvious kind of way. But she talked all the time. I mean, *all* the time. It was enough to make my ears bleed.

Dad came down the stairs, tucking his shirt into his khakis.

"Who was on the phone?"

"Treva," I said, opening the fridge. "She says to pick her up at her office."

"Okay." He kissed the top of my head. "I won't be late. And remember, home by ten."

"Okay."

After he left, I heated the Chinese takeout in a pan on the stove and ate it with Doritos. I wondered if it would be safe to call Trent, and decided against it. No way Piper would let him talk to me today. According to Piper, I was the cause of everything her kids did wrong. Nothing was ever their fault. Like the time Trent got caught throwing mud balls at the Catholic school. Piper was sure I'd put him up to it, even though I was the last person on earth who'd do that. Nuns scared the hell out of me. Or when Luce stole a bike from the kid up the block. Piper told my dad that must have been my idea, too.

I wondered, for about the millionth time, what it might be like to have a mom like that. A mom who made breakfast and came to school meetings and thought I could do no wrong. A mom who stuck around. A mom who wasn't a lunatic. Probably it would be worse to have Piper as a mom.

I sighed as I put my dish in the sink. It would at least be nice to have someone at home who cooked. Dad's repertoire included pancakes, scrambled eggs, and spaghetti. Mama may have been nuts, but she was a good cook. Sometimes I could almost taste her stir-fry with tofu, if I tried hard.

The phone rang again. Lee Ann sounded slightly stoned.

"Has your dad gone?"

"Yeah, he won't be back till after ten."

"I'm coming over."

She arrived a few minutes later, clutching a bag of potato chips. Her eyes were bloodshot and glassy.

"Geez, you started without me," I said.

"Just a couple tokes," she said. "I couldn't wait. My mom is driving me crazy."

We opened my bedroom window and lit a joint. Rufus curled up at the foot of the bed, watching us with his sad dog eyes.

"I mean it," Lee Ann said. "She's making me nuts. You can't believe how bad it is. She's on me for every little thing. 'Lee Ann, your room's a mess.' 'Lee Ann, why can't you cut your hair?' 'Lee Ann, you need to make more of an effort at school.'" She lit a cigarette and dragged deeply, blowing smoke out the window. "You're so lucky."

"How's that?"

"Your dad's really cool," she said, leaning heavily against the wall. "And you don't have to deal with a mom."

"Yeah, I guess." My head felt heavy, like my neck couldn't quite hold it up.

"Seriously," she said. "You have it made."

"For now, at least."

"What do you mean, for now?"

"What if Dad marries Treva?" I stubbed out the last of the joint and popped the remainder in my mouth.

"Oh, God, do you think he's going to?"

"I don't know. He's out with her all the time. And when they're not out, she's here, trying to be my new best friend."

Lee Ann giggled. "Well, if they get married at least you could borrow her clothes."

I stared at her, aghast. "Like I'd be caught dead in her clothes. Geez, Lee Ann, you're wasted."

"What are you gonna do about the garage?" she asked.

"I don't know. We'll have to find a new place, I guess."

"Bummer."

We sat in silence, watching the smoke from her cigarette curl through the screen in the window. It's funny how interesting smoke can be when you're stoned.

"Hey," she said suddenly. "I have an idea. What about that

house by the railroad tracks, the one that's boarded up? Carla told me there's a window in back that's broken. I'll bet we could get inside."

"Maybe," I said.

"Seriously, Judy, that could work. No one goes down there anymore."

"That's because the little kids think it's haunted."

We laughed at that. Everything's funny when you're stoned.

"Let's go," she said, rising from the bed and steadying herself against the wall.

"What, now?"

"Sure, let's go see it."

"Okay." I pulled myself to my feet and swayed. "In a minute. First, let's eat something."

We ate the entire bag of chips in the kitchen. Then we headed for the house. It wasn't a long walk, only a couple blocks. When we got to the tracks, we followed them another block to where the little house sat back from the road, its windows boarded, graffiti on its siding. We walked around to the back and there, indeed, was an unboarded, broken window.

We dragged an old lawn chair from the neighbor's backyard and climbed onto it to open the window. Then we climbed in, brushing broken glass aside and giggling like idiots.

It was dark inside. We waited for our eyes to adjust to the dim, then looked around the room.

"Damn, we should have brought a flashlight." Lee Ann swore as she stumbled on a loose floorboard.

The house had been empty for a long time, as long as I could remember. It smelled musty, like wet leaves.

"Let's go," I whispered, pulling at Lee Ann's hand. "It's too dark. Let's come back tomorrow, when it's light out."

"Chicken!" She laughed, pulling her hand from mind. "Let's just see what's in the other rooms."

"Seriously, Lee Ann, let's go. We can't see anything without a flashlight."

She sighed heavily.

"Let's go get some ice cream." I knew that would get her attention.

"Okay," she said. "But tomorrow we're coming back. And we're bringing a light."

We climbed out the way we'd come in, balancing on the rickety lawn chair and then jumping to the ground.

I looked back at the house as we walked down the railroad tracks and shivered. The place looked dark and creepy. No wonder the little kids thought it was haunted.

You're being paranoid, I said to myself. *It's the pot.* Sometimes that happened.

But in the gathering dark, the house looked spooky, like something dead and forgotten.

"I'm gonna get strawberry," Lee Ann said. "And maybe hot fudge on top."

I laughed. Lee Ann was so predictable. My best friend since the first day of kindergarten, she was funny and outgoing and fiercely loyal. She struggled with her weight and complained that she was fat. She wasn't, really, just a little pudgy. Too much ice cream, too many chips. Still, the boys seemed to like her. Her boobs were huge.

Since Vernita had moved away the year before, Lee Ann was the only person who knew everything about my mom, everything about me. And she loved me anyway.

We didn't go back to the house the next day. Lee Ann's mother made her stay home to clean her room. I didn't mind, really. I wasn't anxious to go back. I sat in my room, doodling for a while, until I couldn't stand the boredom. Then I walked to Lee Ann's house and rang the bell. Her mother answered the door.

"Hi, Judy." She smiled at me.

"Hi, Mrs. Dawson. Can I help Lee Ann clean her room?"

She laughed and said, "Of course, you can, sweetheart. Go on upstairs."

I loved Mrs. Dawson. She was always nice to me. When I started my period, she took me to the store to buy pads. She bought my first bra for me. And whenever I came for dinner, she made meat loaf, because she knew it was my favorite.

Lee Ann was sitting on the floor in her bedroom, surrounded by piles of clothes, papers, books, and photos. She grimaced at me. "What the hell am I supposed to do with all this junk?"

"We could throw it out the window and burn it in the backyard," I suggested.

She laughed. "And then roast marshmallows on the fire?"

"Come on," I said, holding out a trash bag. "Let's start with the stuff you can throw out."

This proved harder than it sounded. Lee Ann was kind of a pack rat. She argued over every item that went into the bag.

"Not those! Those are my favorite overalls."

I held them up and traced my finger down a long tear in the seam. "They're two sizes too small, and they're torn," I said, tossing them into the bag.

We went through clothes first, tossing some, setting others aside for Goodwill, and folding the rest back into her drawers. After an hour or so, we had waded through the clothes, books, and papers. A huge pile of photographs remained on the floor. There must have been a thousand of them. I sighed. This would be the hard part.

"Here," I said, shoving the photos into the space between us. "Let's start by making two stacks. 'Definitely keeping' and 'maybe keeping.'"

Forty-five minutes later, the definite stack was so tall we had to start a second pile. The maybe stack had all of seven pictures.

Finally, I gave in. "Okay, let's just put them all in a box for now and you can do them later. I'm hungry."

Lee Ann smiled, relieved, and ran downstairs for a box. I sat on the floor, flipping idly through the pictures. Lee Ann on the first day of junior high, grinning at the camera and giving the thumbs-up. The two of us at the pool, sporting our first bikinis, the summer I'd gone out to California, the last time I saw Mama. Lee Ann and Susan, maybe eight years old, pulling a tiny cake from an Easy-Bake Oven. I smiled, wishing my dad had taken more pictures when I was a kid.

Lee Ann returned with a shoe box. "That's not going to be big enough," I said.

"Let's just see," she replied.

"Hey, look at this one," she said, holding a photo out to me. "It's all of us and our moms at the Christmas pageant in kindergarten."

I took the photo and stared at it. My own face stared back at me, smiling and holding my mother's hand. Mama smiled at the camera. She wore a long broomstick skirt with a fuzzy blue sweater. Her blond hair cascaded around her shoulders like a veil. She looked so much younger, so much prettier than the other moms in the photo. She didn't look much older than I was now.

"Do you want to keep that one?" Lee Ann asked, watching my face closely.

"No," I said, "that's okay."

I put the picture into the shoe box. Lee Ann promptly retrieved it and shoved it at me.

"Keep it," she said. "You don't have that many pictures of your mom."

She was right about that. Daddy had a small album with a handful of photos from the time he was married to Mama—a couple pictures of their wedding at a state park, one of Mama in the kitchen holding a wooden spoon and covered in flour, one of the three of us taken shortly after my birth. When I was younger, I often spent entire afternoons looking at those pictures, staring hard, searching for some trace of what went wrong, why Mama left us. I hadn't done that in a long time.

I put the photo in my pocket to take home.

After we'd boxed all of the photos, made the bed, and swept the floor, Lee Ann's mom inspected the room and pronounced it clean. Then she made grilled cheese sandwiches and tomato soup for lunch.

"What do you want to do now?" Lee Ann asked, wiping bread-crumbs from the table to the floor below.

"I don't care. What do you want to do?"

This was our mantra for the summer. Like the vultures in *The Jungle Book*, we were constantly bored, unable to come up with anything fun or interesting. Sometimes we played cards or rode the bus to the mall. Sometimes we walked to the park to swim or plopped down on the grass to watch other people play tennis. We sighed and longed for the day when we gained the glorious freedom that came with having wheels. We had both taken driver's ed in June, but neither of us was sixteen yet. I was marking days until my birthday—just twenty-three to go before I could get my license. For now, though, we were stuck with our bikes.

"Want to see a movie?" I asked.

"Can't," she said. "I'm broke."

"I'll pay."

"No." She shook her head. "You always pay."

That was true. Lee Ann always spent her allowance the minute she got it on ice cream and chips. I, on the other hand, had plenty of money. Dealing pot was very lucrative.

"Let's go to Smoots," she said, standing.

Lee Ann had a crush on the guy who worked behind the counter at the little grocery store. His name was Denny, he was seventeen, and he had his own car.

"Okay." I shrugged my shoulders.

"But first do my hair," she said.

I braided her hair into a French twist and watched her apply eye shadow.

"I don't know why you wear that stuff," I said. "You look good without it."

She just sighed and combed mascara onto her lashes.

"Someday you'll meet someone you'll want to look good for," she said, smiling at me in the mirror.

"Whoever I like is just going to have to like me the way I am," I said, rolling my eyes. "I'm not going to waste my money on make-up."

We snuck out the back door so Lee Ann's mom wouldn't see the eye shadow and walked to the grocery.

"If he's there, you go back to the frozen foods and let me talk to him, okay?" Lee Ann patted her hair.

"I know." I nodded. Personally, I didn't think Denny would ever ask her out. We'd been in the store almost every day this summer. If he hadn't asked by now, he probably wasn't going to. Of course, I didn't say that to Lee Ann. She was my best friend. I wanted her to be happy.

"Hi, Denny!" Lee Ann's voice was breathy and soft.

"Oh, hey," he said, looking up from the magazine he was reading.

"My mom needs a few things for dinner. She's always running out of stuff." Lee Ann laughed.

"I need something in back." I looked over my shoulder as I walked toward the frozen foods. Lee Ann was leaning against the counter, smiling brightly. Denny looked bored.

I wandered through the store, idly picking things up and putting them back on the shelves.

"Judy?"

I looked up from the box of macaroni I was holding. I didn't recognize the guy standing in front of me. Then he smiled.

"Matt?"

"Yeah, it's me."

I hadn't seen Matt Carmichael in years. His parents had divorced when we were in the fifth grade, and he and his mom had moved away. I'd always liked Matt. He was nice.

"I thought you moved to Kentucky or somewhere."

"We did," he said, grimacing. "We moved in with my mom's parents for a while. But now we've moved back to Indy."

"Cool," I said. "Are you going to Howe this fall?"

He nodded. "Yeah, we're renting a place on Butler until Mom finds something she wants to buy."

"Wow." I was impressed that his mother would buy a house on her own.

"Yeah," he said. "Mom went back to school while we were in Lexington. She got her teaching license. So she's gonna teach at 57."

I laughed. "Aren't you afraid she'll hear all those stories about you?" Matt had been the class clown at School 57.

He shrugged. "It's been a while. I doubt anyone there even remembers me now."

We stood a minute, just looking at each other. He had grown up a lot. But I guess I probably had, too. It had been four years since he moved away. He was tall now and kind of cute, with shaggy brown hair and dark eyes. I became acutely aware of my ratty T-shirt and unbrushed hair.

"You look good," he said. His eyes crinkled at the corners when he smiled. He was very cute.

"I'm a mess." I laughed. "I've been helping Lee Ann clean her room."

"Lee Ann Dawson? Is she still around?"

"Yeah, and we're still best friends. She's here." I gestured toward the front of the store. "Come say hi."

We walked to the counter, where Lee Ann was still leaning, smiling at Denny.

"Hey, look who I found," I said.

Lee Ann looked at Matt for a long minute before she recognized him.

"Matty O'Patty!" she said, grinning. "Where the hell have you been?"

Matt's grin faltered for a second. He sighed. "No one's called me that for a long time."

Then I remembered how, in the second grade, Matt had played a leprechaun in the class St. Patrick's Day play. And how, for years after, Lee Ann and Susan had called him Matty O'Patty. God, he'd hated it!

Lee Ann's eyes scanned quickly up and down Matt's lanky form. "You've turned into a hunk!" she proclaimed.

Matt laughed, and I saw a blush on his cheeks.

"And look at you." He smiled at Lee Ann. "You're a hottie."

She laughed and made a small curtsy. "Law, sir, now you're just turning my head."

Lee Ann was good at flirting. It seemed to come naturally to her. Why couldn't I ever think of anything clever to say to a boy? Maybe it was something you were supposed to learn from your mom.

Denny cleared his throat then. He was eyeing Matt with distaste. Maybe I'd been wrong about his attitude toward Lee Ann. Or maybe he just didn't like not being the center of attention.

Lee Ann introduced the boys, then put her hand on Matt's arm and said, in her soft, breathy voice, "How 'bout you walk me and Judy home?"

And so we left, the three of us, without buying a thing. Matt strode along between Lee Ann and me, smiling the whole time.

"Matt's going to Howe this fall," I said. It was the only thing I could think of.

"Oh, good!" Lee Ann cooed. "You'll love it. And everyone will be so glad to have you back."

"If anyone even remembers me," he said.

"Oh, trust me. We all remember you." Lee Ann laughed. "Remember when you poured sugar in Miss Warren's gas tank, and her car wouldn't run?"

"Oh, and when you left the bottle of mouthwash on Mr. Barr's desk?" I laughed. Matt had been a prankster back then.

He laughed. "Yeah, those were good times."

"Well, I can't wait to see what you're going to do now," Lee Ann purred, touching his arm.

Matt shook his head and grinned. "Nope," he said. "I'm strictly on the straight and narrow these days. No pranks for me."

Lee Ann laughed again, as if he were joking. But I could see from his face he was being serious.

"Why?" I asked. "What happened?"

"It's a long story," he said. "Let's just say I found religion."

Lee Ann stared at him blankly. "Seriously? You've gotten religion?"

He smiled and shoved at her shoulder. "Still Miss Literal," he said. "I mean I had to grow up while we were in Kentucky. My mom was in school, and she didn't have time to spend in the principal's office every week because of some stupid prank I'd pulled."

"His mom is going to teach at 57," I told Lee Ann.

"Oh, God." She grimaced. "That's just what the world needs . . . another goddamned teacher."

She was joking. I knew that. But Matt didn't. His smile faded.

"She's worked really hard to be a teacher," he said. "She's gonna be a good one."

Lee Ann just laughed again. "If you say so," she said.

I could see that she'd hurt his feelings. But I didn't know what to say to make it right.

At the corner, Matt stopped and said, "Well, I gotta go home."

Lee Ann made a pouty face. "Really? I thought you were going to walk us home."

He stood a minute, undecided. Lee Ann touched his arm lightly.

"Come on," she said. "Come to my house and hang out with us for a while."

He shrugged and grinned, then continued walking with us. Lee Ann chattered happily on about Howe High School, where we would all be sophomores in the fall.

"Judy and I will show you all around. It's pretty big, but you'll be okay. Just don't let anyone try to sell you an elevator pass. There is no elevator."

"Yeah," I said. "But Lee Ann paid ten bucks for a pass last year."

She shoved my shoulder. "You told me to."

We sat on Lee Ann's front porch, drinking lemonade and talking until late afternoon.

"I gotta go home," I said finally.

"Yeah, me too," Matt said. "I'll walk you."

Lee Ann's eyes widened, and she smiled at me.

"Well, don't be a stranger," she said. "Now you know where I live."

Matt and I walked to my house in silence. I couldn't think of anything to say.

"Lee Ann hasn't changed much," he said after a while.

"Yeah, same old Lee Ann."

"But you've changed."

"Me? How?" I asked.

"You used to be real shy," he said. "Like you were afraid of everything. You don't seem like that anymore."

I smiled at him. "Well, you know what it's like. I mean, I was practically the only person I knew whose parents were divorced. And my mom . . ." I faltered, unsure what to say.

"I know," he said. "I felt that way, too, after my dad left. In Lexington, I didn't know anyone whose parents were divorced, either."

"Do you ever see your dad?" I asked.

"No." He shook his head. "Not in a long time. He moved to Florida and got married right after the divorce. Now he's got a new kid."

"I'm sorry," I said. "That sucks."

"Yeah." He sighed. Then he smiled. "But Mom is doing great. I'm really proud of her, finishing school and all."

"This is my house," I said, stopping at the driveway.

"Is it just you and your dad?" he asked.

"Yeah, at least for now. My dad's been dating this woman for a while, though. I'm afraid he's gonna marry her."

"You don't like her?"

"She's okay, I guess. But she's kind of like an overgrown cheerleader." I sighed unhappily.

"Well," he said. "I'd better go home. I'll see you around."

Just then my father pulled his car into the driveway, honking and waving.

"Hey, kiddo, how was your day?" he asked as he closed the car door.

"Okay," I said. "This is Matt. He used to be in my class at 57. He just moved back from Kentucky."

"Hi, Matt." Daddy shook his hand.

"Hey," Matt mumbled.

"Judy and I are getting pizza for dinner. Do you want to join us?" Daddy said.

"No, thanks," Matt replied, his cheeks reddening slightly. "I've got to get home. My mom's expecting me."

"See you," I said.

"Yeah, bye," he said, turning and loping down the sidewalk in long strides.

"So"—Daddy grinned at me—"is he anyone special?"

Now it was my cheeks turning red.

"No, Dad, geez, he's just a guy I used to know. He moved away in the fifth grade when his parents got divorced and now he's back. Lee Ann and I ran into him at Smoots."

"Ah, Smoots," Daddy said, shaking his head. "Did Lee Ann make any progress today?"

I laughed. Daddy knew all about Lee Ann's crush on Denny. I told him most things. Not everything, of course, but definitely more than Lee Ann told her parents.

"I didn't think so," I said. "But Denny didn't seem real thrilled when Matt showed up, so maybe he'll start noticing her now."

Daddy shook his head and laughed. "She's a little bit boy-crazy, isn't she?"

"Yeah," I said. "But she's not slutty or anything."

He raised his eyebrows at me. "I wish you wouldn't talk like that. It makes you sound . . . trashy."

"Sorry. I just wanted you to know that she's not like that."

"I know she's not," he said. "If she was, you wouldn't be hanging around with her, right?"

"Right," I said.

I wondered what he would think if he knew about the pot in my closet. Like I said, I told him most things, but definitely not everything.

"How 'bout that pizza?" he asked. "I'm starved."

≈ 33 ≈

Two days later, Lee Ann and I returned to the abandoned house by the railroad tracks. We brought along a flashlight and a stepladder from Lee Ann's garage.

The house didn't look so scary in the daylight, just sad and abandoned. We perched the ladder beneath the broken window and climbed inside. Lee Ann switched on the flashlight and swept it around the room. It was mostly empty, with broken glass scattered beneath the window and an old mattress on the floor.

"What's that?" Lee Ann whispered, focusing the light on the mattress. Something dark stained the surface.

"I don't know, maybe blood?"

"Gross!" She took a step backward, moving the light along the walls. "Let's see what's in the other rooms."

We wandered through the house, whispering in the empty rooms.

"This could work for your business," Lee Ann said. "No one ever comes down here."

"I don't know," I said. "I'm not sure I want to hang out here. And the neighbor might notice people climbing in and out the window."

"Maybe," she agreed. "But you don't have anyplace else. You

can't deal out of your house. Your dad would figure that out pretty fast, I bet."

"Yeah," I agreed. "But I still don't think this place will work. It's creepy."

"You should bring Trent and see what he thinks."

When we had wandered through every room, we walked back to the bedroom with the old mattress. Lee Ann knelt in front of it, training the light on the dark stain.

"It looks like blood," she said.

"No, I don't think so. More like pee."

"Gross," she said again. "If you set up shop in here, you're gonna have to get rid of that."

We climbed out the window and headed toward home, carrying the stepladder.

"Hey!"

Matt waved from across the street. "What are you guys doing?"

"Nothing," I said quickly. I did not want to tell him about the house or my business. I didn't think he'd approve.

"What's with the ladder?"

"Uh," I stammered.

"We rescued a kitten from a tree," Lee Ann said, smiling. She was good at coming up with lies on the spot.

"Cool," he said, falling into step with us. "I have a cat."

"Aw," Lee Ann said. "Can we see it?"

"Sure, I guess." Matt smiled at her. "Do you want to come now?"

"Okay." She smiled back. We walked to his house, a little bungalow on Butler Avenue.

"Hey, Mom," he called as we walked in. "I'm back."

A woman emerged from the kitchen, dish towel in hand, and smiled at us.

"Hello," she said.

"This is Judy and Lee Ann," Matt said. "They went to school with me at 57."

"It's nice to meet you," she said. "You'll have to excuse the mess; we're still unpacking."

The living room was filled with boxes, some open and others still taped shut.

"They want to see JoJo," Matt said.

"I think he's upstairs," his mother said. "He hasn't come downstairs since we moved in. I think he's freaked out. Do you guys want a Coke?"

"No, thanks," Lee Ann said.

"Okay, well, I have to get back to unpacking the kitchen."

We went upstairs and Matt began calling, "Here, JoJo. Here, kitty, kitty."

After a minute or two, a small gray cat emerged from a bedroom. He stared at us with unblinking eyes, then meowed. Matt scooped him up and scratched his head.

"Mom got him for me when we moved to Kentucky," he said. "So I wouldn't be lonely."

He laughed, but it sounded like a sad laugh.

"Were you lonely?" I asked.

"Yeah, at first. I missed my friends and my dad."

"You said your dad's in Florida, right?" Lee Ann asked. "Do you ever go see him? I love Florida."

"I went once," he answered, holding the cat while I scratched its ears. "That was right after the divorce, before he got married again."

"Do you like his new wife?" Lee Ann asked. I stared at her, wishing she would stop asking questions. I was sure Matt didn't want to answer them.

"She's okay, I guess. She's got two kids, and then they had a kid together. I've only seen him once."

"Judy's mom got remarried and had a baby, too," she said. "A boy."

"Yeah?" He looked at me. "How old is he?"

I had to think a minute. How old was Kamran now?

"I guess he's three now," I said finally. "I haven't seen him since he was one."

Matt nodded his head. "So you don't see your mom much?"

I shook my head, wishing to God Lee Ann hadn't started this conversation.

"She's in India," Lee Ann announced. "She lives in a commune or something. What's it called, Judy?"

"It's an ashram," I muttered. I wanted to strangle her now. She knew I didn't like to tell people about Mama.

"Wow," Matt said. "So she's like a Hindu?"

"Yeah," I said. I was surprised he would know that.

"Well, at least she's something," he said. "My dad's just a prick."

We all laughed, but I could see it hurt Matt to say that.

"We'd better go home," I said. I wanted to stop the conversation.

"Why?" Lee Ann said. "It's not even four."

"I've got stuff I have to do," I said, edging toward the stairs.

"Okay," Matt said. He put the cat down and it ran up the hallway and into the room it had come out of.

We walked downstairs and he held the front door open for us.

"I'll see you around," he said.

"Come by sometime," Lee Ann said, smiling.

"Why did you want to go?" she hissed at me as soon as we were out of the house.

"Why did you tell him all that stuff about my mom? You know I hate that!"

"I didn't think you'd mind," she said. "His dad did the same thing, you know."

I kept walking, not looking at her.

"Okay, I'm sorry," she said, touching my arm. "I shouldn't have told him."

I slowed my pace and took a deep breath.

"It's okay," I said. It wasn't okay, but I knew she really was sorry.

We walked in silence. A car drew alongside us.

"Hey, Lee Ann!"

It was Denny, leaning out the driver's side window, grinning at her.

"Oh, hi, Denny," she purred, smiling back at him.

"Want a lift?"

She looked at me, clearly delighted.

"Go ahead," I said. "I'm gonna walk."

"You sure?"

"Yeah," I said. "You go ahead."

She gave me a quick hug and climbed into the car. She waved as they pulled away.

I walked half a block and stopped. We had left the stepladder at Matt's. I knew Lee Ann's dad would be mad if he realized we'd taken it.

Sighing, I turned around and walked back toward Matt's house. We had left the ladder on the front porch. Maybe I could retrieve it and leave without even seeing him.

"Hi," he said, walking toward me on the street. He was carrying the ladder. "You guys forgot this."

"Thanks," I said, taking the ladder from him. "I was just coming back for it."

"Where's Lee Ann?" He looked around.

"She got a ride with a friend."

"The guy from the store?" He smiled as he asked it.

"Yeah, how'd you know?"

"I saw him parked across the street when you guys left. I think he was waiting for her."

I shook my head. "I guess he finally noticed her, after all."

He fell into step beside me.

"I'm sorry she asked you all that stuff about your dad," I said, not looking at him.

"It's okay," he said. "I used to get uptight about it, but now I figure it's his problem, not mine. I mean, I'm not the one who screwed up. He is."

I looked at him then, and he smiled.

"You don't like to talk about your mom, do you?" he asked.

"Not really," I said. "It's just so weird, you know? I mean, she left us and moved to some commune in Kentucky. Then she almost went to Jonestown, you remember? The commune with all the crazies who killed themselves? Yeah, she was part of that church. And now she's left her second husband and kid and is living on an ashram in India. It's just . . . weird."

"Yeah," he agreed. "But that's her problem, not yours. You didn't do any of that stuff."

"I guess."

"And your dad seems normal." He smiled. "I mean, he seems like a nice guy."

"He is," I agreed. "Your mom seems nice, too."

"Yep, she's great."

We walked in silence for a minute, then turned the corner onto University.

"Do you want to come in?" I asked when we reached my house.

"I can't," he said. "I've got to help Mom with unpacking."

"Well, thanks for walking me home."

"No problem," he said. He smiled at me. "It beats unpacking."

I laughed and set the stepladder down on the porch.

"So, I'll see you around," he said, turning to leave.

When I opened the door, I saw Daddy sitting in a chair by the window, watching Matt walk away. He smiled at me.

"No one special, huh?"

"Shut up, Dad."

He grinned as I walked up the stairs to my room.

∼ 34 ∼

On the first day of our sophomore year, Lee Ann arrived at my house early so she could change her clothes and put on makeup. Then I twisted her hair into a French braid.

She studied herself critically in the mirror.

"God, I'm so fat," she said, frowning at her image.

"No, you're not," I said, slapping at her arm.

She turned to look at her profile, sucking in her stomach.

"I wish I had your figure," she said, putting her hand on her belly. "Or at least your flat belly."

"Yeah, but you wouldn't trade those boobs for anything, and you know it."

She laughed then, exhaling deeply.

"Let me put some makeup on you," she said.

"No way," I replied.

She just sighed and shook her head.

"You know, you'd be really pretty if you did something with your hair and wore a little makeup. Not much, just a little blush maybe, and some mascara. And if you got some new clothes."

Lee Ann wore skin-tight jeans and a baby-doll top with a low neckline. I had on my usual cargo pants and T-shirt.

"Let's go," I said, glancing at my reflection in the mirror. "I don't want to be late."

Matt met us at the corner to walk together. His eyes widened when he saw Lee Ann.

"You look like you're going on a date," he said, grinning.

"You like?" She spun around, her hands on her hips.

He laughed and nodded.

"Good," she said, tucking her hand through his arm. "Now if you could just help me convince Judy to doll herself up a little bit."

"Naw," he said, smiling at me. "Judy looks good just like she is."

He offered his other arm to me and I took it, feeling my cheeks grow warm.

"Don't forget," Lee Ann said as we walked in the glass doors of the high school, "meet me at three in the lobby so we can sign up for tryouts."

"What are you trying out for?" Matt asked.

"We're gonna be Hornet Honeys," she proclaimed confidently. Howe High School's sports teams were called the Hornets.

He looked at her blankly.

"You know," she said, "pom-pom girls, the ones who dance at halftime at the football and basketball games."

At this he laughed, looking from Lee Ann to me.

"Seriously?" he asked. "You guys want to be pom-pom girls?"

I dropped my eyes to the floor. I actually did not want to be a pom-pom girl. But Lee Ann really, really wanted to be a Hornet Honey. And she had pretty much coerced me into doing tryouts with her. I didn't expect either of us to make the squad. I was not the pom-pom girl type. And Lee Ann, although she looked the part . . . well, Lee Ann was a terrible dancer. She didn't know that, of course. And I wasn't about to tell her. But I didn't want her to fail on her own. I figured if we tried out together and neither of us made it, that would be easier on her.

"Oh, trust me," Lee Ann said, crooking her finger under Matt's chin and smiling, "we are gonna be the best Honeys ever."

He just laughed. "Here's where I get off," he said when we

reached the front office. "I've got to register for classes. See you guys later."

I watched him walked into the office, thinking how nice he was. When I turned, Lee Ann was watching me carefully, a smile on her lips.

"So," she said, shoving me with her elbow, "you and Matty O'Patty?"

I shook my head and tried to smile.

"You could do worse," she said. "He's kind of a hottie."

"He's okay," I said.

The first bell rang and we headed in separate directions toward our lockers and a new semester.

At three o'clock, I stood in the gym in a huge crowd of girls, looking for Lee Ann and feeling completely out of place.

"Boo!" she said, putting her hands over my eyes.

"Where have you been?" I asked. "I've been here for ten minutes."

"Oh." She smiled. "I was having a little talk with our friend Matt."

I stared at her, saying nothing. Matt was in three of my classes, and we'd talked several times during the day. And now Lee Ann was probably going to announce that they were seeing each other.

"Don't give me that look," she said, "we were talking about you."

"Oh." This was even worse.

"And . . ." She drew the word out.

"And what?" I finally asked.

"And he likes you!" She sounded triumphant, as though she herself had made this possible.

"Really?" My voice sounded strangled in my throat.

"Really," she said. "He told me so himself. He asked if you were dating anyone, and I said no, and then he asked if I thought you would go out with him."

"What did you say?"

"I told him I didn't know; he'd have to ask you himself."

"Oh, God, Lee Ann, why did you say that?" I felt my cheeks reddening. "Do you think he will?"

"Uh, yeah." She said this as though it were perfectly obvious. But it wasn't at all obvious to me.

"Attention, girls! Attention, please!"

Miss Harrison, the teacher in charge of the Hornet Honeys, waved her hand in the air. Eventually, the chatter stopped and two hundred pairs of eyes focused on her. She smiled brightly.

"Welcome to auditions for the Hornet Honeys," she said. "We have thirty-two spots available, so there will be a lot of competition this year."

I gazed around the gym at all the girls, wondering which of them would take those coveted spots. Several had been on the squad the previous year and were practically guaranteed a place. Poor Lee Ann, I thought, stood no chance at all.

We divided into groups of twenty, each group under the direction of a senior Hornet Honey. Together we worked on marching steps, with our knees high and our toes pointed. Then we began learning the dance to the school song. I didn't think it was terribly hard, but a lot of the girls kept getting the steps confused. Lee Ann looked completely lost.

As we walked home after practice, Lee Ann was mostly silent.

"Ugh," I said as we neared home. Treva was just pulling into our driveway. She smiled and waved when she saw us.

"Hey!" she called. "Come help me with these bags."

She had been to the grocery and it seemed like she'd bought the entire store. When we had deposited the bags on the kitchen counter, she turned to beam at us.

"So how was the first day?" she asked.

"Okay," I said.

Lee Ann shrugged.

"You're kind of late getting home, aren't you?" Treva looked up at the clock and then at me, like she was my mom or something.

"We stayed for tryouts," I mumbled.

"What are you trying out for?"

"Hornet Honeys," Lee Ann said. "But we're not going back."

I stared at her.

"Why not?" Treva asked. "Being on the drill team is fun. You'll love it!"

"I don't think we'll make it," Lee Ann said, looking at the floor. "It's really hard, and some of the others just seem to get it so fast."

"It's okay," I said. "We'll do something else." I wasn't sure what, but I was relieved she had given up on the pom-pom-girl idea.

"Oh, no!" Treva sounded emphatic. "You can't just give up after one practice. Everyone has a hard time at first. You have to stick with it, and it'll come."

Lee Ann raised her eyes then to look at her. "Do you think so?"

"Yes," Treva said, nodding. "I'll tell you what, I was on drill team in high school and in college. I can help you, if you want."

"Really?" Lee Ann's face brightened.

Oh, hell, I thought. Just what I wanted, to audition for the Hornet Honeys *and* spend a bunch of time with Treva. Perfect.

For the next week, we practiced every evening in our backyard under Treva's careful eyes.

"Get those knees higher, Lee Ann," she'd call. "Pop that hip out. Point your toes!"

I was surprised at how easily the steps came to me, how quickly I picked up even the most complicated routines, and most of all, how much fun I was having.

Lee Ann struggled mightily, but by the end of the week even she had learned the basic steps of the dance, if not the flourishes.

"You know what, Judy," Treva said after dinner one night, "you're really good at dancing. I think you're going to make the squad."

"Really?" Daddy smiled at me. "I didn't know you could dance. That's great."

"What about Lee Ann?" I asked, regretting it almost as soon as the words were out of my mouth. I already knew the answer.

"Well," Treva said, rising from the table. "She's trying really hard."

"Yeah." That about summed it up.

The next afternoon, we waited in the gym for our turns to display our marching skills, numbers pinned to our fronts and backs.

Then we performed the school song in groups of twelve. This was the first cut. Half of us would not be asked to come back to perform the jazzy dance routine.

I watched Lee Ann march with her group. She was concentrating hard. I could see her lips moving, counting out the patterns. She forgot to smile. I didn't watch her perform the school song routine. I couldn't.

Oh well, I thought when it was my turn. It was fun and now it's over.

I didn't feel nervous at all. I wasn't coming back for the second audition, after all. I was just doing this to help out Lee Ann.

I marched and spun and remembered to point my toes. I danced to the school song with confidence, smiling at the sheer fun of the dance. When I had finished, I went to sit on the bleachers beside Lee Ann to watch the last of the groups audition.

We waited on the bleachers for forty-five minutes after the last group, while the seniors and Miss Harrison retreated to another room. When they returned, they had a list of numbers—the girls they wanted to return for the second audition. Everyone in the room leaned forward a bit, each girl waiting to hear her number called. There were cries of triumph and tears of despair. Lee Ann clutched my hand so hard it hurt, then released it as they passed by her number without calling it.

"Let's go," she said, pulling me to my feet.

"Seventy-four," Miss Harrison called just then.

Lee Ann froze and turned to look at the number seventy-four pinned to my chest. She turned and walked straight down the steps and across the floor, toward the door. I stood where I was, frozen. I knew I should follow her. But I had no idea what I would say to her. How could I make it better for her, if I had been chosen and she hadn't?

"Congratulations, Judy!"

Sarah Martinson hugged me and smiled. "I knew you'd make it. Do you want to come to my house tonight and practice?" She had made the first cut, too.

"Uh," I said, not sure, my eyes following Lee Ann as she left the gym.

"I know," she said. "Heather didn't make it either." She pointed to the retreating figure of her best friend. "But you did. And I did. And . . . well, we should practice. Right?"

"Okay," I said.

Okay? Really? What was I doing, agreeing to practice for an audition I wasn't going to?

"Come to my house at seven," she said.

"Actually," I heard myself saying, "why don't you come to my house? My dad's girlfriend is a really good dancer. She's been helping me."

Good Lord. Had I really just said that?

"Great!" Sarah hugged me again. "I'll see you at seven."

I walked home alone. Lee Ann was nowhere to be seen.

Treva was waiting on the front steps.

"Hey!" she called. "How did it go?"

"I made first cut," I said.

"Lee Ann?"

I shook my head.

"I'm sorry, hon," she said. "I know that sucks. But . . . you made it. That's great! When is second cut?"

"On Friday."

"So, we have three days to get that routine down pat," she said, smiling. "That's plenty of time. You've already got most of it."

"I'm not sure I'm going," I said.

"What? Oh, Judy, you have to. You're good at this! And you like it. I can tell you like it."

I shrugged.

"Look," she continued, "I know you started out just because Lee Ann wanted you to, but you are really good at this. You can do drill team and still be her friend, right?"

"I don't know," I said. "Maybe."

"Of course you can," she said. "You and Lee Ann have been friends too long to let something like this get in your way. Besides, once she gets past the disappointment, she'll be happy for you. She's your best friend."

"Maybe," I said again.

"So," she said, rising, "do you want to start practicing?"

"Can we do it after dinner?" I asked. "I think another girl is coming to practice with us."

She smiled at me. "Sure," she said, "the more the merrier."

Sarah arrived at seven and we began practicing the jazz routine in the backyard while Treva and Daddy sat on the back porch, watching. Treva called out suggestions from time to time. Daddy just watched us and smiled.

When we had finished the entire dance, Treva switched off the boom box.

"Nice work," she said. "You guys are both doing a terrific job!"

"Thanks, Treva!" Sarah beamed back at her.

"So, same time tomorrow?" Treva asked.

"That would be great, thanks," Sarah said.

"Judy, is that okay for you?"

"Sure, I guess so."

Sarah gathered her things to go home.

"So, I'll see you tomorrow," she said.

"See you."

I walked with her to the front of the house, where her bike was parked. She waved as she pedaled away. I waved back.

And then I saw Lee Ann, standing in the next-door neighbor's yard, watching us.

"Hey," I called.

She didn't say anything, just turned and began walking up the block toward her house.

"Hey!" I called again, running after her. I grabbed her arm and she turned to face me.

"So," she spat, "you and Sarah are practicing together. How nice for you both."

"Come on," I pleaded. "Don't be mad at me. It's just . . ."

"It's just what? You made it and I didn't. And now you and Sarah can be Hornet Honeys together and best friends and whatever. I don't care!"

"Lee Ann," I started, but she cut me off.

"You didn't even want to do it! I had to drag you to the tryouts. And now . . . you get to do it and I don't. It's not fair!"

"I'm sorry," I said. "I'm sorry you didn't make it."

"Then quit!" she yelled.

I stood still, just staring at her. Her eyes were red, her skin blotchy. She was my best friend, the only one who'd known me for so long.

"I can't," I said. The truth was, I didn't want to quit. I loved the dancing. I loved feeling the beat of the drums in my feet. It was exciting and natural at the same time.

"Then fuck you!" she yelled, pulling her arm from my grasp.

She walked away from me, not looking back.

"Hey, you okay?" Daddy's hand was warm on my shoulder.

I shook my head, feeling my throat constricting.

"It'll be all right," he said. "She's just upset, but she'll get over it. You guys are best friends. She can't stay mad at you."

We walked into the house, where Treva was settled on the couch with a cup of tea.

"So, that was fun," she said. "You and Sarah both did really well."

I stared at her, then ran upstairs to my room.

35

The next morning, Lee Ann did not come by on the way to school, so I walked alone.

"Hey," Matt called to me as I passed his house. "What's up?" he asked as he fell into step beside me.

I shrugged.

"Where's Lee Ann?"

"She's mad at me."

"What for?"

"She didn't make first cut for drill team."

"So why is she mad at you? That's not your fault."

"I made first cut."

"Oh," he said. "Still, that's no reason to be mad at you."

I shrugged again.

"She doesn't want me to do it," I said. I glanced at him to see if he agreed with her.

"That's crazy," he said. "Just because she didn't make it doesn't mean you shouldn't do it if you want to. Do you want to?"

"Yeah," I said. "I kind of do. I didn't think I would, but it's fun. And I'm pretty good at it."

"Well, she needs to get over it, then."

He smiled at me. I smiled back.

"What are you doing after school?" he asked.

"I have to stay for practice. Second cut is on Friday."

"What about after dinner?"

"Sarah Martinson is coming over to practice. She made first cut, too."

"So, you're going to be pretty busy this week?"

"Yeah, I'm sorry."

He stopped and took my hand. "Well, how about Saturday? Are you busy on Saturday?"

"No," I said. "I don't think so."

"Do you want to go see a movie?"

"Sure," I said. "That sounds like fun."

"Okay." He grinned at me and I felt light-headed, like I was a little high.

Lee Ann didn't sit with me at lunch, so I sat with Sarah and her friends. I could see Lee Ann across the cafeteria, sitting with some other girls. She never once looked in my direction.

After school, I walked to her house and knocked on the door. Mrs. Dawson answered.

"Hi, Judy," she said, smiling. "Lee Ann's up in her room. But I have to warn you, she's in a foul mood."

"Thanks, Mrs. Dawson."

I climbed the stairs and knocked on her bedroom door.

"What?" she yelled.

"It's me," I said.

Silence.

I knocked again.

"Lee Ann? Can I come in?"

The door swung open and she stood in the doorway, blocking the way in.

"What do you want?" she asked, glaring at me.

"I want to talk to you."

"Are you still doing tryouts?"

"Yes, but . . ."

She slammed the door in my face.

"Come on, Lee Ann," I called, banging on the door.

"Go away!" she shouted from inside the room.

Sighing, I turned and walked downstairs. Mrs. Dawson was waiting at the bottom.

"Don't worry," she said, patting my arm. "She's pretty disappointed, but she'll get over it. I told her she's being ridiculous, but she's in a mood."

"Thanks," I said, looking back up the stairs.

I walked home slowly, wondering if I should just not go to the tryout on Friday. I hated having Lee Ann mad at me. But I really did want to make the drill team.

At dinner that night, Daddy asked me about practice and then about Lee Ann. He smiled and hugged me and told me what everyone else was telling me, that Lee Ann would get over it. I hoped he was right.

As we cleared plates from the table, I took a deep breath and said, "So, Matt Carmichael asked if I want to go to a movie on Saturday."

Daddy grinned at me. "What did you say?"

"I said yes." I bent my head down so he couldn't see my reddening cheeks. "If it's okay with you."

"Sure, it's okay," he said, still grinning. "I mean, I need the details. What movie are you going to see? Who's driving? When will you be home? But . . . it's okay with me."

"Thanks, Dad."

"You said his mom is a teacher?" he asked.

"Yeah, she just started teaching at 57."

"Where is his dad?"

"He's in Florida. He's got a new family."

"Ah." Daddy nodded. "Well, he seems like a nice kid."

I nodded.

The front door opened and Treva breezed into the kitchen.

"Hey," she said, kissing Daddy on the cheek. "I hope I'm not late."

"You're right on time," Daddy said. It was five till seven.

"I'm gonna go change." I went to my room to put on shorts and a T-shirt for practice.

When I came back into the kitchen, Treva smiled at me.

"So," she said, "you have a date!"

I glared at Daddy. He grinned and Treva laughed.

"That's great," she said. "I can't wait to meet him."

Sarah arrived and we went to the backyard to practice our dance. After an hour, we were finished rehearsing and drinking Cokes on the front porch.

"Is Heather mad at you?" I asked her.

"No," she said, looking puzzled. "Why?"

"Lee Ann is really mad at me," I said. "She doesn't want me to be on the drill team."

"Well, too bad for her," Sarah said. "She's supposed to be your best friend. She should be happy for you."

"Yeah." I nodded unhappily. "I guess so."

"Heather was upset at first," she continued. "But she didn't ever get mad at me because I made it."

"That's good."

Treva walked out carrying a plate of chocolate chip cookies.

"Fresh from the oven," she proclaimed.

"When did you have time to make those?" Sarah asked, clearly impressed.

"She buys refrigerated dough," I said.

"Beats baking from scratch!" Treva set the plate down between us. "So, have you told Sarah about your big date?"

Sarah's eyes widened. "You have a date? With who?"

I wanted to kill Treva.

"Matt Carmichael," I mumbled.

"The new guy in Mr. Lawson's class?"

I nodded.

"He's cute," she said.

Sarah had collected a string of boyfriends since junior high.

"Where are you going?" she asked.

"To the movies."

She nodded. "That's a good first date. You don't have to talk too much."

I hadn't thought about that.

"What are you gonna wear?" she asked.

"I don't know." I hadn't thought about that, either.

"Well," she said, "if you want, I can come over and do your hair for you. And your makeup." She smiled at me.

"That sounds like fun!" Treva trilled. "I'll bring the camera!"

"Um," I said. "I wasn't going to wear any makeup."

"Oh, you have to wear makeup," Sarah insisted. "Just a little mascara, maybe? You have really pretty eyes."

"That's a good idea," Treva agreed. "And if you want, we can go to Broad Ripple Saturday morning and get you a new outfit, something fun and a little bit flirty."

"I love Broad Ripple!" Sarah said.

"Well, you should come with us," Treva said. "We'll make a day of it."

"Okay," Sarah said. "Thanks."

And so it was settled, without my ever agreeing to any of it—a day with Treva and Sarah, lunch and shopping in Broad Ripple, and a makeover. I felt like I might throw up.

What I really wanted to do was call Lee Ann. But, of course, I couldn't.

By the time I got to school the next day, it seemed like everyone knew about my date with Matt. Three people stopped me to talk about it before first period had even begun. Sarah was nice, but she definitely didn't keep things to herself.

In the cafeteria, Lee Ann appeared behind me in the lunch line.

"So," she said, "you're going out with him?"

"Yeah," I said.

"Good!" she said, smiling. "I told you he'd ask you."

A huge wave of relief flooded through me.

"Yeah," I agreed. "You did."

We inched forward in the line, choosing grilled cheese sandwiches and chocolate milk.

"So," she said as we sat at our usual table. "Do you want me to come do your hair?"

"Oh," I stammered. "Um, well, actually Sarah is coming."

Her smile faltered. "Oh," she said. "Okay."

"But you should come, too," I said. "I didn't even ask her to come. Treva did."

"Whatever," she said, her voice flat.

"Please come," I begged. "They've set up this whole day and I . . . I really wish you'd come."

She chewed her sandwich, her eyes on the table.

"Hey!" Sarah set her tray down beside mine. "Did you tell Lee Ann about the big date?"

"We were just . . ." I started.

"No, actually," Lee Ann snapped. "She did *not* tell me about it. I had to hear about it from Luce Watkins."

"Oh," Sarah said. "Well, maybe if you'd been acting like a friend instead of a jealous bitch, Judy would have told you herself."

Lee Ann's eyes widened; her cheeks grew red. She rose, picked up her tray, and stalked away from the table.

"Geesh," Sarah said. "What is wrong with her?"

"I don't know," I mumbled. But I did know. I knew just how she felt. She felt the way I did every time Mama let me down.

After school, we had one final practice before the next day's try-outs. I fumbled through the steps, turning at the wrong time and nearly knocking over the girl beside me.

"What's wrong?" Sarah whispered.

I shrugged, missing another step.

"Judy?" It was Miss Harrison. She waved to me. I left the line and walked to where she sat with a senior named Becky Wright.

"Are you okay?" Miss Harrison asked. "You seem . . . distracted."

I shrugged my shoulders.

"Look," she said, patting the chair beside her. I sat down. "I heard about your friend, Lee Ann, is that her name?"

I stared at her. How on earth did Miss Harrison know about Lee Ann?

Becky leaned forward and smiled at me.

"My sister is in Lee Ann's algebra class."

Ah, that explained that.

"I know it's upsetting when your friend is mad at you," Miss Harrison said. "But you are doing really well, Judy. You have a definite shot at making the squad."

"Really?" I looked up then.

"Really," she said, smiling. "So, rule number one of the Hornet Honeys is, no matter what else is happening, when you're on the field you're *on*. Put everything else out of your mind, and just dance. Okay?"

"Okay," I said.

"Good." She smiled again. "Now get back out there and show us what you can do."

I concentrated hard on the dance, feeling a rush of adrenaline when I completed the trickiest sequence without faltering. I could see Becky Wright and Miss Harrison watching me. I smiled until I thought my cheeks would crack.

The next day, Sarah and I made the squad. We were both officially Hornet Honeys.

❧ 36 ❧

On Saturday, Treva arrived at ten, Sarah just behind her. Both of them were more excited about the day, it seemed, than I was. We drove to Broad Ripple.

"Grateful Threads?" Treva asked as she parked the car.

"What's that?" Sarah asked.

"It's a great store," Treva said. "Judy likes it, don't you?"

"Sure," I said. Honestly, I just wanted to go home.

"Wow." Sarah sighed when we entered the shop. "This is too cool."

I tried on several outfits—hip-hugger jeans with a baby-doll top, skin-tight red pants with a colorful oversized blouse, a short skirt with a midriff-baring top. I looked ridiculous.

Then, Treva spotted a pair of acid-washed jeans. I tried them on and they fit like a glove.

"Good," she said, nodding. "Now we need a top to go with it."

"How about this?" Sarah held up a black-and-white striped tank-top with a scooped neckline and a short-cropped denim jacket.

I had to admit, the outfit looked good.

"It needs something," Treva said, looking at my reflection in the mirror.

"Here." Sarah draped a black lacey scarf around my neck.

"Perfect," Treva said, smiling. "What do you think, Judy?"

I stared at myself in the mirror.

"It's okay," I said.

"It's better than okay." Sarah laughed, pushing my shoulder lightly. "It's perfect. Matt won't know what hit him."

We bought a pair of dangly silver earrings to complete the outfit, then headed to the Parthenon for lunch.

"This is great," Sarah said, gazing around the restaurant. "I didn't even know this place was here."

We ate falafels while Treva and Sarah chattered away about Broad Ripple and clothes and drill team. Treva's college drill team had gone to a national competition. She'd even been the caption of the squad her senior year.

I sat listening to them, thinking how surreal it felt to be out with Treva again, and with Sarah. How much had changed since the first time we'd come shopping in Broad Ripple all those years ago. Suddenly, I wondered what Mama would think if she could see me sitting there. She'd probably die if she knew I was going to be a Hornet Honey—glorified Barbie dolls, she'd once called the pom-pom girls dancing during halftime of a football game on television. I smiled, thinking about how much she would hate me being one of them.

At home that afternoon, Sarah moussed my hair so it looked messy and a little bit spiky. Treva snapped pictures with her camera, stopping now and then to give advice. When my hair was done, Sarah brushed blush onto my cheeks and smoky gray eye shadow on my eyelids. Then she twirled my lashes around the mascara brush and ran lipstick across my lips. When she was done, I stared in the mirror at a young woman I barely recognized. Was that me?

I looked older and wilder and . . . well, kind of sexy. I hoped Matt would like the new me.

Sarah left before dinner, kissing my cheek and telling me to call her later and tell her all about it.

At seven, I was pacing around the living room, trying hard not to chew off the lipstick she had applied so carefully. Daddy and Treva sat on the couch, watching me.

"You look great," Treva said. "Doesn't she look great?" she asked Daddy.

He smiled. "She looks beautiful," he said. "All grown up."

The doorbell rang and I started toward the door.

"Oh no," Treva said, taking my arm and steering me toward the stairs. "Upstairs with you. We'll call you in a minute, and then you can make a grand entrance."

She seemed firm on this, so I walked up the stairs and waited in my room.

After what seemed like a very long time, Daddy called me. "Judy, are you ready? Matt's here."

I walked down the stairs, trying hard not to think about how stupid I felt. Matt stood with Daddy and Treva in the front hall. He grinned when he saw me.

"Wow," he said, "you look . . . great."

"Thanks," I mumbled.

"Okay," Daddy said, shaking Matt's hand. "The movie, then pizza, then home, right?"

"Yes, sir," Matt said.

"And you'll be back by eleven?"

"Yes, sir," Matt repeated.

"Have fun!" Treva leaned forward and kissed me quickly on the cheek.

"Yeesh," I said as we walked to the car Matt had borrowed from his mother. "Sorry about that."

He laughed. "It's okay. They're nice."

We saw several people we knew at the movie theater, and I felt awkward and very conspicuous in my new clothes and makeup. Matt bought the tickets and then got us Cokes from the concession stand. I was relieved to finally sit down in the darkened theater to watch *Back to the Future*. As the previews began, Matt reached over and took my hand in his. I sighed happily and relaxed into my seat.

We went to Pizza Hut after the movie. It seemed like half of Howe High School was there.

"Hey, Judy!" Sarah waved from a table in the back. "How was the movie?"

"It was good," I said. "Funny."

"Do you guys want to sit with us?" She smiled at Matt.

"Uh, that's okay," he said. "I think we're gonna sit over there." He pointed to a booth that had just been cleaned.

"Okay," Sarah said. "Have fun."

The girls giggled as we walked to the booth.

"Sorry," I said.

"What for?"

"I don't know." And I really wasn't sure what I was sorry about.

"You apologize a lot," he said. "Mostly for stuff that's not your fault."

"Do I?" I asked. "Sorry."

He laughed and so did I. We ordered a pizza and talked about the movie.

"I'd love to have a car like that," he said, pulling a slice of pizza onto his plate.

"One that could time travel?" I smiled.

"No." He laughed. "I mean, that would be cool, I guess. But I'd settle for a DeLorean."

"Me too." I laughed. "I'd settle for a used Pacer."

"You look really different tonight," he said. "Your hair and . . . everything."

"I know," I said. "Treva and Sarah went a little nuts."

"It's nice," he said. "You look good. Just . . . different."

"I feel kind of stupid."

"Why?" he asked. "You look really good."

"Thanks."

When we had eaten the pizza, we drove toward home. It was ten fifteen.

"We've got forty-five minutes," Matt said. "Do you want to go to the park?"

"Okay." I wasn't sure what we would do at the park. But I wasn't ready to go home.

We parked in a dark lot and sat for a minute.

Oh, God, I thought. *He wants to make out.*

Lee Ann had told me about making out. One time, we had even practiced kissing. But I hadn't ever actually kissed a guy.

Matt smiled at me. "Let's swing," he said.

He got out of the car and I sat for a second, torn between relief and disappointment. Then I followed him to the swings.

"Here," he said. "I'll get you started."

He pushed me until I was swinging high into the air. Then he took the swing next to mine and started pumping himself.

My hair whipped around my face. I knew that all of Sarah's careful handiwork would be ruined, but I didn't care. I felt free.

After a while, we slowed the swings to a stop and sat, just talking. We talked about school and his time in Kentucky and his mom's new job. He told me about the time he'd visited his father in Florida, and how weird that had been.

And then, I told him about Mama. Not everything, of course. I didn't tell him about Mr. Jenson or Derrick or any of that. But I did tell him how she left, over and over again. When I had finished, he stood and held his hand out to me, pulling me up from the swing.

"I'm sorry," he said softly. "That really sucks."

And then he kissed me. Softly at first, and then more firmly, pulling me close to him. I felt my mouth open to his, felt his tongue on mine. It was completely different than when I had practiced with Lee Ann. It felt . . . safe and thrilling all at the same time.

He drove me home, humming along to the radio. He parked in the driveway and walked me to the door. Then he kissed me again, lightly this time. I was acutely aware that my dad was on the other side of the door.

"I'll see you tomorrow, maybe," he said.

"Okay."

He walked toward the car.

"Matt," I called after him. "Thank you."

"Thank you, too," he said.

I watched as he backed out of the driveway, then took a deep breath and opened the front door. Dad and Treva sat on the couch, studiously pretending to watch whatever was on the television.

"Oh, hey, peanut!" Daddy said. "How was the movie?"

"It was good," I said.

"Did you have fun?"

"Yeah."

"What did he think of your new look?" Treva asked.

"He liked it."

"Good," she said, smiling.

"I'm going up," I said, heading toward my room and privacy and time to think about the night and the kiss and Matt.

❧ 37 ❧

Every afternoon for the next two weeks I spent on the football field, learning to march in precision step with the other girls and find my mark at just the right beat. We practiced with the band, and my spot was directly in front of the drum line. It was not the most visible spot—the premier places were held by the seniors—but it suited me just fine. I loved feeling the rumble of the drums up my spine. Besides, I wasn't ready to be front and center yet.

Sarah and I stood side by side, concentrating hard on hitting our marks.

"Smile!" Miss Harrison yelled through her megaphone. "Don't forget to smile!"

We smiled until our cheeks hurt. By the end of each practice, we were hot, sweaty, and sore. But the routine was looking good, and I was very proud to be part of it.

Sometimes the guys from the football team watched us as we finished up and they prepared to take over the field.

"Hey, Judy?"

I turned to see Trent Watkins standing behind me when I came off the field, holding his helmet in his hand. "You're a Hornet Honey?"

"Yeah," I said, smiling.

"Cool," he said, nudging me with his elbow. "Maybe you can sell to some of the other girls." He winked.

"I don't think so," I said, pulling away from him. I didn't want to get kicked off the squad for dealing pot.

"Oh, come on," he said, stepping toward me. "I know some of them smoke. Hell, probably most of them. It's a good market."

I shook my head, backing away from him.

"Well, if you won't do it, then just introduce me to some of them," he said. "I already sell to half the guys on the team."

"I'd rather keep that separate," I said.

"How the hell are we gonna make any money if you don't sell anything?" He was glaring at me now. I was acutely aware of just how big he was, especially with his shoulder pads on.

"I . . . I just don't want to sell here," I said.

"Hey, Judy!" Sarah waved to me from the gate. "Come on."

"I've gotta go." I edged away from Trent, turned, and ran toward the fence, not looking back.

"Who's that?" Sarah asked when I reached her. She pointed to Trent.

"He's just a guy who lives on my street," I said.

"He's cute."

I stared at her. Did she seriously think Trent Watkins was cute?

"He's a jerk," I said.

"Maybe you can introduce us," she said, smiling at Trent. He smiled back at her and waved.

"Trust me," I said, "you don't want to know him."

"Hey, who's your friend?" Trent had walked over to where we stood.

"Oh, um, this is Sarah," I mumbled. "Sarah, this is Trent."

"Are you new on the squad?" Trent asked her, eyeing her up and down.

"Yeah," she said, smiling at him. "My first year."

"I thought so," he said. "I'd remember you if you'd been here last year."

"We have to go," I said, pulling at Sarah's arm. "We're gonna be late for the meeting."

Sarah allowed herself to be pulled along toward the locker room, but she waved over her shoulder to Trent.

"He's really cute," she said again.

I rolled my eyes. "He's a jerk," I repeated.

After the meeting, I walked toward home. I hadn't walked even a block before Matt appeared, carrying a soda from Smoots. He met me most days after practice.

"Hey," he said, kissing me and handing me the soda. "How was practice?"

"It was good," I said. "I think we're gonna be ready by Saturday."

Saturday was the first home football game and our first performance.

"You're coming on Saturday, aren't you?" I asked. I'd asked him a dozen times already, but I just wanted to make sure.

"Yes, I'm coming," he said, grinning at me. "And after the game, we'll go to Gringo's and get something to eat. Okay?"

"Okay." I held his hand as we walked, listening as he talked about a project he was working on for biology. It felt so odd to be walking through my neighborhood, holding hands with Matt Carmichael. Odd, but very nice.

"Well," he said when we reached my house, "I'll see you tomorrow."

He kissed me again and left. I stood on the porch watching him walk down the street with that casual lope that had become so familiar and dear to me.

"Hey."

I turned to see Lee Ann standing on the sidewalk in front of my house.

"Hi," I said.

"So, you and Matt," she said, smiling at me shyly.

"Yeah," I said.

"I'm glad for you."

"Thanks."

We stood a minute in awkward silence, then she said, "Well, I'll see you later, I guess."

"Wait!" I called as she turned. "Do you want to come in?"

"Okay," she said. She smiled again. "For a little while."

We went up to my room and sat on the bed.

"So," she said, "how's drill team?" She asked it casually, but I could see her lower lip tremble a little.

"It's okay," I said.

"Good."

"It'd be a lot better if you were doing it, too."

"Thanks," she said.

We sat for a minute, then she sighed deeply and said, "I'm sorry I was such a bitch."

"You weren't," I said.

"Yes, I was."

"It's okay," I said. "I'm sorry, too."

"Do you want to come over tomorrow night? My mom is making meat loaf."

"Yeah," I said. "That sounds good. Thanks."

"Okay," she said, rising. "I'll see you tomorrow, then."

"Lee Ann?"

She stopped at the door and turned. I pulled her into a tight hug, and we both started crying.

"I'm really sorry you didn't make it," I said finally.

"Yeah, me too." She wiped her nose with the back of her hand. "But I'm glad you did."

"Thanks."

"So, I'll see you tomorrow."

"Okay."

She left and I flopped down on my bed, letting the relief wash over me. I felt like I'd been holding my breath for weeks, and now I could let it go. Lee Ann wasn't mad at me anymore. Everything was okay.

I stared at the ceiling, watching the ceiling fan spin slowly around. Could life get any better than this? Lee Ann and I were friends again. Matt was just about the perfect boyfriend. I was a Hornet Honey. Honestly, life seemed pretty much perfect.

"Judy?" Daddy's voice called from downstairs. "Are you home?"

"I'm up here," I yelled back.

He opened the door to my room and smiled at me. "How was practice?"

"It was good," I said. "Lee Ann came over. I'm gonna have dinner at her house tomorrow, okay?"

"Sure," he said. "I'm glad you guys are friends again."

He stood a minute, his hand on the doorknob. Then he stepped into the room and held something out toward me, an envelope, the thin, blue kind that meant a letter from Mama.

I took it from him and studied Mama's curvy, twirly handwriting of my name and address. It was postmarked in India.

"Thanks," I said.

"I'll be downstairs if you want to talk."

"Okay."

I put the letter on my desk and lay back on my bed, watching the ceiling fan. I felt like the light had been sucked out of the room. The air was heavy, oppressive. I rolled onto my side and stared at the envelope for a long time. Finally, I tore it open.

> *My dear Sweet Judy,*
>
> *I'm sorry it's been so long since I wrote, but I didn't know if you'd want to hear from me. It's been such a long time since I've heard from you and I miss you so much. I hope you are doing okay and that you're happy.*
>
> *I'm still in India—I guess you could tell that from the envelope. I'm still studying under my guru, and I'm learning so much all the time. Honestly, I have never been happier than I am now. I've never felt more at peace.*
>
> *But, I do miss you. I miss you and Kamran both so much that sometimes I almost can't breathe. My teacher says in order to be truly at peace, I have to make peace with my past—with you and your dad, and with Kamran and Navid. So, I am planning a trip to the States soon. I'm not sure of all the details yet, but I think I will be in Indianapolis in December. I'm going to Los Angeles first to see Navid and Kamran.*

*And then I will fly to Indy. And I really hope you will
see me.*

*I have so much to tell you, Sweet Judy. So much to
explain. I need to apologize, even if you can't forgive
me. And I need to see you and know that you're okay.*

*I'll write again before I come. Meantime, know
that I love you so much and I think about you and
pray for you every single day.*

Love, Mama

I read the letter a second time, then folded it back into the envelope and put it in my desk drawer. I lay there for a long time,
watching the fan circle overhead. When Daddy called me for dinner, I took the letter with me and put it in his hand. He read it
slowly, folded it, and pulled me into a hug.

"You don't have to see her if you don't want to," he said. "And
you definitely don't have to decide right now. You've got plenty of
time before December. And if you don't want her to come, I'll tell
her not to come. Okay?"

I nodded.

"Do you want to talk about it?" he asked.

I shook my head.

"Okay, then let's eat."

38

On Saturday night I stood at the end of the football field, my heart pounding so loudly I was sure everyone around could hear it. Miss Harrison walked down the line, stopping here and there to adjust a strap or hair bow.

"Okay, girls," she said brightly, "this is it! Remember to keep your lines straight, make your marks, and above all . . ."

"Smile!" we all called out in unison.

The drummers began the marching cadence and we high-stepped onto the field, under the glare of the huge lights. I couldn't make out faces in the stands at first, the lights were so bright, but there were thousands of people, all watching us. My palms were sweating. I was afraid I might drop my pom-poms.

Then the music began and I fell into the familiar rhythm and flow. I marched, twirled, hit my marks on time, and smiled my biggest smile. Somewhere in the stands, Daddy and Treva were watching. So was Lee Ann. And, of course, Matt. I concentrated on smiling just for them.

When we'd finished our jazz routine, the band began playing the school song, and everyone in the stands rose to sing along. We danced the dance, throwing our pom-poms high into the air at the end and catching them before we marched off the field. It was the most thrilling thing I'd ever done.

After the game, Matt and I went to Gringo's Taco House. We met Lee Ann and her current boyfriend, a junior named Steve who played on the varsity basketball team. Lee Ann hugged me and told me I had been the best Honey out there. I was so glad we were friends again.

"Seriously," she said. "I'll bet by the time you're a senior, you're captain of the squad."

I laughed and felt my cheeks burning.

"Oh my God," Lee Ann said then, touching my arm. "Look!"

I turned to where she was pointing and saw Sarah sitting in a booth with Trent Watkins and another couple. All of them looked stoned. When she noticed us looking at her, Sarah smiled and waved, then crawled over Trent to get out of the booth and walked toward us unsteadily.

"Hey," she said, dropping into the seat beside me. "How are you? Wasn't that just the most fun ever?"

"Yeah," I said, "it was fun."

"Are you here with Trent Watkins?" Lee Ann asked, her eyes never leaving Sarah's face.

"Well, yeah," Sarah said. "I am. What's it to you?"

"Nothing." Lee Ann sat back in the booth. "Just surprised, I guess."

"He's nice," Sarah said, smiling. "And cute. And . . . well, you know."

"I know what?" Lee Ann asked.

I shook my head slightly at her. I didn't want Sarah to go on.

"Well, he's got the goods." She giggled.

"You've been holding out on me," she said, turning to me. "How come you never told me about your . . . business?"

"I . . ." I had no idea how to answer her.

"What business?" Matt asked.

"It's nothing," I said, glaring into Sarah's bloodshot eyes.

"Judy and Trent have the best pot in Indy," she said, leaning over me to look at Matt. "Didn't you know? Or has she been holding out on you, too?"

"You're stoned," Lee Ann said flatly. "You don't know what you're talking about."

"And you're a fat pig," Sarah hissed at her. "No wonder you didn't make the squad."

She rose, steadying herself before walking back to her table.

We sat still for a minute. I wanted to sink right into the floor and disappear.

"She's stoned," Lee Ann repeated. "Don't listen to anything she says."

Steve was looking at me with new interest.

"So," he said, "do you deal?"

"No!" I said. "I don't . . . deal."

"Sorry," he said. "I just wondered."

"Judy's dad is a lawyer, for God's sake," Lee Ann said, shoving his shoulder. "She couldn't deal even if she wanted to."

She laughed. Beside me, Matt sat quietly.

When we'd finished our tacos, Matt and I walked back to his car in silence. Once inside, he turned to me and asked, "Do you really deal pot?"

I sat for a minute just looking at him.

"Yeah," I said finally. "That is, not anymore. But I did."

"That's not good, Judy," he said. "You could get in real trouble, and so could your dad."

"I don't do it anymore," I said. But at that very moment, I had several ounces in my closet at home.

"Good," he said. "Because I can't date a dealer."

He said it firmly, looking me right in the eyes.

"Okay."

"I mean it," he said, never taking his eyes from mine. "I had a friend in Kentucky who got into a lot of trouble over pot. And I won't be anywhere near it."

"Okay," I repeated.

He sighed then and relaxed a little.

"I know I sound like a narc," he said. "And I know it's just pot. But my friend ended up in juvenile detention. His mom was in school with my mom, and it just about killed her. I would never do that to my mom."

He smiled at me. "So, are we okay?"

"Yeah," I said, smiling back. "We're okay."

The next day I stuffed all of the pot into a padded envelope and tucked it into my backpack. Then I walked to Trent's house and knocked on the door.

"Hey," he said when he opened the door. "What's up?"

I shoved the envelope into his hand.

"I'm out," I said.

"Out of what?" He opened the envelope and his eyes widened.

"Out of the business," I said. "It's yours. You do it. You know where to get it. And I won't ever say a word. But I'm out."

I turned and walked down the sidewalk.

"Hey!" Trent called after me.

"What?"

"You're gonna miss the money."

I kept walking. He was probably right. I would miss the money. But I wanted Matt more than I wanted the money. And I wanted to not lie to him ever again. What he'd said the night before scared me, and I wasn't about to risk losing him. He was everything I'd ever wanted, I realized. Everything I never even knew I wanted.

Matt loved me. He hadn't actually said it, but I knew that he did. I just felt it. I felt safe with him, like I could be just who I was and nothing else, and that was okay.

I had finally told him everything about Mama. I did it one night while we were sitting in his car at the park. I told him about Derrick and Glen, and about Mr. Jenson. I wanted him to know. He was the first person I ever really wanted to know all about Mama. And after I told him, he kissed me and held me close and said it didn't matter. Her life wasn't my life. She was messed up, he said, but I was perfect. And in that moment, I felt loved like I never had before.

And I was damned sure not going to lose that because of Trent Watkins and some pot.

When I got home I scoured the closet, removing any remaining signs of my once lucrative business. Then I took a shower, dried my hair, and called Matt. I didn't have a reason, really. I just wanted to hear his voice.

Life was good.

Two weeks later, Trent knocked on my front door. It was late afternoon, and Daddy was still at work.

"Hey," I said, not inviting him inside. "What's up?"

"I need your help," he said, pushing his way into the house. "Is your dad home?"

"No," I said. "What's wrong?"

"Mitch won't deal with me," he said, pacing around the living room. "He's gotten all paranoid and he says he'll only deal with you."

"No," I said, shaking my head. "I told you, I'm out."

"Come on, Judy. All you have to do is go buy the stuff from Mitch. I'll handle everything else, and we'll split just like always."

I shook my head again.

"What's wrong with you?" His voice rose. "This is easy money. I'm doing all the work. All you have to do is go with me to get the stuff."

"No," I said. "I don't want to do it anymore. I don't want to get kicked off the squad."

"You're not gonna get kicked off the squad," he said. "You're not gonna get in trouble. I'm taking all the risks. I'm doing all the work."

I simply shook my head again.

He walked toward me, clenching his fists, and grabbed my arm.

"Look," he said, his face just inches from mine. "You have to do this. You owe me."

"No!" I shouted.

He shoved me backward and I hit my head against the wall. I raised my hands as he approached.

"Look, you stupid little cunt," he snarled, grabbing my wrists. "I'm not asking you, I'm telling you, you *are* going to do this."

"Stop it! You're hurting me."

He released my hands and took a step back.

"Okay, look," he said in a quieter voice. "I just need you to help me this one last time, that's all. Just so Mitch sees I'm okay. After this, I won't ask you again, I promise."

I stood still, watching him pace in front of me.

"Come on," he pleaded, "I have people I've promised stuff to. I can't back out on them now. Please, Judy? Just this one last time."

Still I said nothing.

"Okay," he said, his voice quiet and deadly, "then I guess I'll just have to tell your dad and Miss Harrison what you've been up to all this time."

"You wouldn't," I said. "You'd get in too much trouble."

"I will," he said. "And I'll swear it was all your idea. Because it was, you know, it was your idea.

"And," he continued, "Sarah will back me up."

"What does Sarah know about it?"

"She knows enough to be on my side," he said. "She'll swear that you tried to sell her acid."

I stared at him. "I did not!"

He laughed. "So, who do you think they'll believe? You, or me and Sarah? I mean, you're the one with the loony mother. Everyone will believe you're just like her."

I felt tears welling then, tears of frustration and anger and raw fear.

"Okay, one last time," I said. "But then I'm out."

He relaxed, his shoulders dropping, and let out a huge sigh.

"Okay," he said, smiling at me. "We'll go tomorrow after dinner."

I nodded.

"Don't worry so much," he said as he opened the front door to leave. "It's not like you haven't done it a million times before."

After he left, I called Lee Ann. Three minutes later, she was knocking at the door.

"What are you going to do?" she asked, watching as I paced around the living room.

"I have to go with him," I said. "I don't have a choice."

"Maybe you should tell your dad."

I stopped and stared at her. "Are you crazy? I can't tell my dad I've been selling pot for the last year and a half. He'd die!"

"Yeah." She nodded. "I guess so. Okay, so just go this one last time. You've done it before, and it's always been okay, right?"

I nodded miserably.

"It's because of Matt, isn't it?" she asked.

I nodded again.

"Well, he'll never know," she said. "And you won't have to do it again."

"I hope so," I said. But I wasn't at all sure she was right on either count.

39

Trent knocked on the door just after six and I slipped outside before my dad could rise from the table.

"I'm going for a walk with Lee Ann," I called, closing the door behind me.

We walked in silence, Trent smoking a cigarette.

"Not this way," I said as he started to turn onto Butler.

"Don't want your boyfriend to see you with me?" He laughed, throwing the cigarette butt into the street.

"Fuck you," I said.

He laughed again.

When we got to the park, we left the sidewalk and headed down the grassy slope toward the creek. It was getting dark already and cold. I shivered in my wool jacket.

"Here," I said, stopping just short of the bridge. "We'll wait here."

Trent lit another cigarette and we waited.

"Hey." Mitch's voice came from beneath the bridge. He sounded stoned.

We walked under the bridge and saw him crouched on the bank of the creek. He sat back and stared at us for a long minute, his eyes unfocused and glassy.

"What's he doing here?" He pointed at Trent, then glared at me.

"It's just Trent," I said softly, crouching down beside him. "He's okay. You've dealt with him before."

Mitch glared at Trent for a long minute, then turned his gaze to me.

"Where you been?" he asked, smiling at me. His breath stank of pot and beer. "I haven't seen you lately."

He reached out and touched my arm, and I steeled myself not to jerk away from him. Mitch creeped me out. He always had. Tonight he seemed more stoned, more out of it, more slimy than I'd ever seen him. I forced a smile.

"I've been busy with school and . . . stuff."

"She's got a boyfriend," Trent said, his tone mocking.

"Oh." Mitch's eyes ran over my face, his smile fading. "A boyfriend."

He turned from me and reached into his pocket, pulling out a gun.

"Shit," Trent hissed behind me. I heard him back away a few steps.

"Hey, Mitch," I crooned, putting my hand on his arm. "It's still me, just Judy. Everything's okay, right?"

He laid the gun on the ground in front of me and smiled.

"Sure, baby. It's cool. It's all good."

We sat in silence for a minute. Trent shuffled his feet behind us.

"So," I said softly, "do you have the stuff?"

"Oh, yeah." Mitch leered. "I've got the stuff, baby. You want it?"

"The pot, Mitch," I said firmly. "We've got the money. Do you have the pot?"

He laughed then and I inched farther away from him. He sounded . . . unhinged.

"'Course I do," he said. "Don't I always have the stuff? I'm the fuckin' candy man." He laughed again.

"Okay," I said. "Let's see it."

He pulled a bag from his jacket and held it out to me, holding on to it a moment before finally releasing it into my hands. I weighed it in my hands, then handed it to Trent.

"Okay, good. Here's the money." I handed him the three hundred dollars Trent had given me and watched him count it, counting out loud with him. When he'd finished counting, he smiled and picked up the gun from the ground.

A car's headlights swept along the bank opposite us and all of us froze, holding our breath. Mitch held the gun with his finger on the trigger. I felt beads of sweat dripping down my back, even though it was cold outside. All I wanted in the world was to finish this and be away from here, away from Mitch and Trent and the pot and the risk. All I wanted was to be at home, in my own room, safe.

The sound of the car faded and Mitch rose unsteadily. He stared at Trent, then raised the gun and pointed it directly at his chest.

"Bang," he said, smiling.

Trent just stared.

"Nice doin' business with you, baby," Mitch said, looking down to where I still crouched on the ground. "Don't be such a stranger."

With that, he lurched away along the creek, disappearing around a bend.

I heard Trent exhale at the same time I did. Then I rose and climbed the bank toward the street and the streetlights and safety.

"Hey, Judy," Trent called after me.

I turned.

"That wasn't so bad, was it?" He smiled.

"Go to hell," I spat.

I walked home with my hands shoved in the pockets of my jacket, relieved to be away from Trent, and even more relieved to be away from Mitch. He'd always been weird, but I'd never seen him so creepy, so paranoid, so out of it. Whatever he was on, I wanted no part of it.

"Home," I called as I came in the house.

"Okay," Daddy called from the kitchen.

I walked to my room, closed the door, and lay down on the bed, staring at the ceiling, and began to shake all over.

I would never do that again. I would never let Trent force me to. I would never put myself in danger like that. And I would never, never risk losing Matt. Not ever again.

40

As Thanksgiving approached, I fell into my usual blues. I hated Thanksgiving. It reminded me of the time Mama came home from California after we thought she'd died at Jonestown.

This year, instead of going to Grandma and Grandpa's, they were coming to our house. Daddy and Treva were preparing the meal, and Treva's parents were coming, along with her brother and his wife. The whole day sounded pretty gruesome to me.

"It won't be so bad," Matt said, as we walked home from school.

"Easy for you to say," I grumbled. "You get to go to a restaurant."

Matt and his mom had a tradition of having their Thanksgiving dinner out, since it was just the two of them. I thought that sounded like a great idea.

"Honestly," he said, "I'm kind of jealous. You get to have a big dinner with family. I remember when I was little we used to do that."

I squeezed his hand. "I'm sorry."

"It's okay," he said. "It is what it is."

"Well, come over when you get back from dinner," I said.

"No, I can't. I don't want to leave my mom alone on Thanks-giving."

I sighed. He really was protective of his mom.

"But you can come to my house," he said.

"Maybe, if my dad will let me. I don't know how late everyone is staying."

He kissed me good-bye on the porch and I went inside to the sound of the vacuum.

"Hey!" Daddy said, switching off the sweeper. "I'm glad you're home. You can take over with this while I work on the kitchen."

He kissed my head as he walked by. A minute later I heard him whistling in the kitchen. He seemed pretty excited about the whole dinner thing.

I vacuumed and dusted and took the rugs outside to shake them. It was chilly but sunny, a lot like that Thanksgiving week in 1978 when we thought Mama was dead. I sighed as I shook out the rugs, wondering if they celebrated Thanksgiving on the ashram where she lived.

"Do you want to help with the pies?" Daddy asked when I came back in. "I've got the pumpkin done but you could chop the pecans."

I chopped while Daddy brought the syrup to a boil. He had Grandma's recipes scattered across the counter.

"I hope these turn out like Grandma's," he said, stirring the syrup.

"I'm sure they'll be good," I said.

He grinned at me.

"You're in a good mood," I said, smiling back.

"Yep, I'm happy."

We had Chinese takeout for dinner, so we didn't mess up the kitchen, which fairly gleamed after a good scouring.

"So, what's Matt doing for Thanksgiving?" Daddy asked as we ate.

"He and his mom are going to a restaurant. They do it every year."

"Oh, maybe we should have invited them to come here," he said.

"It's okay. It's kind of like their tradition, since his dad left."

"Well, traditions are fine, but sometimes it's nice to mix things up a little. Like this." He waved his hand around the kitchen. Pies were cooling on the counter and a huge sack of potatoes sat waiting to be peeled.

"I still don't see why we can't just go to Grandma's," I said.

"Because, she always cooks. And I thought it would be nice if she didn't have to for once." He smiled. "Plus, Treva and I wanted to have everyone together this year. It'll be fun!"

"If you say so."

"Judy, I hope you have a better attitude by tomorrow. I don't want you sulking around being rude to everyone."

I shrugged, not looking at him.

"Seriously, I mean it." His voice was firm. "Treva's family is coming here for the first time, and it's important to me for you to be on your best behavior."

I said nothing.

"Do you understand me?"

"I get it," I said.

"Okay, good." He sounded relieved. "Now, why don't you start peeling those potatoes?"

By the time I trudged upstairs to bed, my whole body ached. Cleaning and cooking was a lot harder than it looked. I wondered how Grandma did it, day after day.

The next morning, Treva arrived at ten, carrying a big casserole dish and a huge bouquet of chrysanthemums.

"What's that?" I asked as she sat the casserole down on the counter.

"Oyster stuffing," she said, raising the lid for me to see.

"Gross!" It looked like cat food and smelled worse.

"It's a family tradition at my house," she said. "You'll love it."

"Yeah, right," I mumbled.

Daddy walked in just then and gave me a hard stare. Then he kissed Treva, saying, "That smells great!"

She laughed and kissed him on both cheeks. "I just hope it's as good as my mom's."

"I'm sure it is," Daddy said.

Treva stuffed the turkey while Daddy poured them both a glass of wine.

"Cheers," he said, raising his glass to hers.

By three o'clock, the house smelled like Thanksgiving, Treva's nasty stuffing notwithstanding. Grandma and Grandpa arrived with a jug of apple cider and two bottles of wine.

"What can I do to help?" Grandma asked as soon as she'd taken off her coat.

"Nothing, Mom." Daddy kissed her. "We've got it all under control."

"Well, I feel useless," she complained.

"Sit down, have a glass of wine, and enjoy yourself," Daddy commanded.

"If you can get her to do that, you're a better man than I am," Grandpa said, laughing.

"Oh, go on, the both of you." Grandma laughed and accepted the glass of wine Daddy handed her.

The doorbell rang again and Treva's parents arrived. I'd met them once before, but it still surprised me how much younger they looked than Daddy's parents. Carl, Treva's dad, was an insurance salesman. He smiled a lot, talked a lot, and was constantly patting people on the back. Rose, his wife, looked just like Treva, except twenty years older. She wore jeans and a sweater and high-heeled boots like a fashion model.

Just before four, Treva's brother, Mike, arrived with his wife, Lorna, and their daughter, Morgan. Morgan was a year old and just beginning to walk. Lorna spent the entire afternoon following her around, her arms outstretched to catch her when she fell. I smiled watching them, remembering when Kamran was that age. What was he doing this Thanksgiving? I wondered.

We sat down at the dining room table and Grandpa rose to pray. Then we ate.

Everyone praised the turkey and stuffing, the potatoes and pies, even the slightly burned rolls. When we had finished eating, Daddy rose and raised his glass.

"I'd like to propose a toast," he said, smiling.

Everyone looked at him expectantly.

"To Treva," he said, "my friend, my love, and soon to be my wife!"

Treva rose then and stood beside him, his arm around her waist.

"Oh my!" Rose said. "When's the date?"

"We're getting married on New Year's Eve," Treva said.

"New Year's Eve? But that's only a month away! That's not time enough to plan a wedding." Rose sounded appalled.

"We're having a small wedding," Daddy said. "Just family and a few friends."

"But . . ." Rose began.

"Mom," Treva said firmly, "this is what Kirk and I want. It's our wedding and we want to keep it small and simple."

"That sounds lovely, Treva." Grandma rose and kissed her cheek. "No need for a big to-do. Where will you have the service?"

"Here," Daddy said.

"Here?" Rose sounded like she might just faint.

"Sure, here." Daddy waved his hand toward the living room.

"Oh, no," Rose said. "Your house is lovely, Kirk, but it's not big enough for a wedding."

"I told you, Mom. It's going to be a small wedding." Treva's frustration was beginning to show.

"Well, at least have it at our house," Rose said. "We have the room. Let me take care of it."

"We'll talk about it later," Treva said.

"Well, congratulations," Mike said, shaking Daddy's hand and kissing Treva's cheek. "I know you'll be happy."

"Yes, congratulations," Grandpa said.

Everyone was on their feet now, kissing cheeks and shaking hands. Only I sat still, watching them.

"Judy?" Daddy turned to me with a smile. "Don't you want to say anything?"

I managed a small, tight smile. "Congratulations," I said.

"Thank you, honey." He kissed my forehead.

"Oh, Judy, it's going to be great!" Treva came and wrapped her arms around me tightly.

I nodded, holding my fake smile firmly in place.

I wanted to scream or cry or maybe just throw up. Instead, I sat smiling and nodding as they all chattered about flowers and invitations and music for the wedding.

That night, I lay in bed staring at the ceiling. Just before eleven, Daddy opened the bedroom door.

"You awake?" he whispered.

"Yeah."

He turned on the light and sat on the bed.

"So, what do you think?" he asked.

"About what?"

"About me and Treva getting married."

I shrugged.

"I'm sorry I didn't tell you before. I was going to, but she really wanted to tell everyone at once," he said.

"Whatever."

"Judy, it's going to be okay. You know that, right?"

"Sure."

He leaned over and kissed my forehead. "You'll see, it's going to be great."

I rolled over and closed my eyes, and after a minute or so, he turned out the light and left.

I lay there just letting the tears drip down my cheeks. I'd known it was coming. It wasn't a big surprise. Hell, Treva practically lived with us already.

But seeing her with her arm around Daddy, everyone toasting them and planning a wedding, it felt like a punch in the stomach, like having the wind knocked out of me, like . . . like when Mama left.

That was silly. I knew it was silly. Daddy wasn't leaving. Daddy would never leave me. He loved me. He was Daddy, for God's sake. And he'd been alone for a long time. In a few years I'd move out, and he needed someone. And Treva was okay. I mean, she wasn't great, but she wasn't awful.

So why did I feel like I'd been sucker-punched?

She'd move in here, sleep in Daddy's room, in Daddy's bed. Or maybe . . . God, what if Treva wanted a new house? Would they move? Would I still go to Howe?

I rose from my bed and padded softly down the hall to the phone. It was eleven, too late to call, but I dialed Matt's number anyway.

"Hello?" His voice was sleepy.

"Hi," I said.

"Are you okay? You sound . . ."

"They're getting married," I said.

"Who? Your dad and Treva?"

"Yeah, on New Year's Eve."

"Wow," he said, "that's soon."

"What am I going to do?" I asked. "What if they want to move?"

"I don't think your dad's going to move just like that," he said, his voice calm and sure. "I think he'd probably talk to you about it before he made any decision like that. Right?"

"Yeah, I guess so. I just . . . Why does he have to get married?"

Matt laughed. "Because he loves her," he said. "And he's been lonely. And she makes him happy. You want him to be happy, right?"

I sighed. "I guess so."

"Look," he said, "In a couple years you'll be getting ready for college. And when you go, he'll be alone. You don't want that, do you?"

"I guess not."

"Besides, you don't hate Treva. I mean, she's okay, right?"

"I guess so."

"It'll be okay, Judy." His voice was warm. "I mean, it will change some things, but not the important stuff. He'll still be your dad. He's not going to leave. I mean, he's not like my dad . . . and he's not like your mom. He loves you."

I sat a minute, just letting that sink in.

"I know," I said finally.

"And, Judy, I love you, too."

"What?"

"I love you."

"I love you, too," I said, my breath catching in my throat.

"Go to bed now," he said. "I'll come over in the morning."

"Okay. Matt? Thank you."

"For what?"

"Just for being . . . you."

I hung up the phone and went back to bed, pulled the covers over my head, and drifted away to sleep. Matt was right, it would be okay. Treva wasn't awful. Daddy loved me. And Matt loved me.

It would be okay, just like Matt said. Life was good.

❧ 41 ❧

"It'll be okay," Matt repeated. "I know you're not excited about it, but Treva is okay, and your dad seems really happy."

"I know." I sighed and leaned my head on his shoulder. We were sitting on the sofa at his house, watching television.

"She's there all the time anyway," he said. "It won't be so different."

"Yeah, right."

"Can I come to the wedding?"

"Sure," I said. "I think so."

"Okay, good."

Having Matt there would help, I thought.

"Do you guys want a soda?" Matt's mom walked into the room.

"No, thank you," I said.

"So, I hear there are going to be some changes at your house." She smiled at me as she sat down.

"Yeah," I said. "I guess so."

"Are you excited?"

"I don't know," I said. "I guess I'm still getting used to the idea."

"I can understand that," she said. "It's a big adjustment, I imagine."

"Yeah."

"I hope it all goes well," she said.

"Thanks."

I liked Matt's mom. She was nice.

"You want to take a walk?" Matt asked.

"Okay."

We put on our jackets and walked outside, wandering aimlessly and holding hands. Before we'd gone far, I heard someone calling my name. Down by the train tracks, Luce Watkins was waving frantically.

We jogged toward her. "What's wrong?" I asked.

"You've got to help!" she yelled. "Mitch has gone crazy."

"Who's Mitch?" Matt asked.

Oh, hell, I thought. *Not now, please not right now.*

"He's got Trent and Sarah at the house and he has a gun," Luce said, grabbing my hand and pulling me toward the abandoned house Lee Ann and I had explored the previous summer.

"Whoa," Matt said, grabbing at my arm. "If someone has a gun, we need to call the cops."

"You can't!" Luce shrieked, staring at him. "Trent will get busted if you do."

"I don't care," Matt said. "We should call the police."

"You have to help them, Judy. Mitch will listen to you."

Matt stared at me in confusion. "Who the hell is Mitch?" he said.

"Wait here," I said.

I ran after Luce toward the house. I wasn't sure what I would do once I got there, but I did not want anyone calling the cops. Trent would rat me out in a heartbeat.

I climbed on the wooden crate someone had put under the broken window and looked inside. I could hear Mitch yelling from another room. I climbed in as quietly as I could and tiptoed toward the kitchen. Mitch stood in the doorway, his back to me. Sarah was crouched in a corner, Trent standing in front of her. Trent was a lot bigger than Mitch, but Mitch was holding a gun, waving it in front of himself and yelling.

"I want my fucking money!" His words were slightly slurred.

"Hey, Mitch," I said, as calmly as I could.

He spun and pointed the gun at me. His eyes were unfocused, like they'd been the night at the park. He stared at me for a long minute, then slowly lowered the gun.

"This prick owes me three hundred bucks," he said, pointing at Trent.

"I don't owe him anything," Trent said, looking past Mitch at me. "I don't know what he's talking about."

Mitch walked toward him, the gun raised again.

"I gave you good stuff and you never paid me for it," he yelled. "I want my money!"

"Hey, Mitch," I crooned, "hey, I was there when you sold us the stuff. We paid you for it. Remember? We were at the park and the car went by. And I gave you the money and we counted it together. You remember that, don't you?"

He turned toward me and froze, his eyes focused on something behind me.

"Who the hell are you?"

I turned and saw Matt, standing in the hallway. He was staring at the gun in Mitch's hand.

"I, uh," he stammered.

"He's my friend," I said, planting myself squarely between them. "He's okay, it's cool."

"It's not cool," Mitch said, glaring at me.

"It's all right," I crooned. "Matt is leaving now."

I looked at Matt. "You're leaving now, right?"

"I'm not leaving without you," he said, his face grim.

"Go!" Mitch shouted. "Both of you just get the hell out of here. I got no problem with you. It's him that's the problem." He turned back to where Trent stood. "And I'm gonna solve it."

"Mitch," I said, "don't do anything stupid."

"I said get the hell out!"

Matt grabbed my hand and started pulling me down the hall toward the bedroom with the broken window. I let myself be dragged along. I didn't know what else to do.

"Stop right there!" a man's voice shouted.

A policeman was standing in the bedroom, his gun leveled at Matt and me. We froze.

"Officer," Matt said, "there's a guy in the kitchen with a gun. He's stoned out of his mind and he's threatening another guy in there."

Another officer had climbed through the window by then.

"Check out the kitchen," the first cop said. "And you two, up against the wall."

He patted us down and made us stand facing the wall, our hands above our heads. From the kitchen we heard the sounds of a scuffle.

"You okay?" the cop with us yelled.

"Got him," the other cop yelled back.

In a minute, he had marshaled Trent and Sarah into the bedroom, along with Mitch, who was wearing handcuffs and yelling obscenities.

"Okay," said the first cop. "We're all going downtown."

They called for more police cars. Then they put Sarah and me into the backseat of one car, and Matt and Trent in another. Mitch rode by himself. Sarah didn't say a word the entire time. She just sat in the car crying.

At the police station, they took Mitch to a holding cell. The rest of us sat on a bench in a crowded room that stank of sweat and urine. I looked around at the other people in the room—most of them drunk or stoned. These were the people my dad represented in court.

And now he'd have to represent me. I gripped the bench tightly and felt like I might throw up.

Matt sat next to me on the bench, but he never spoke. He wouldn't even look at me, just stared straight ahead, his mouth set in a straight, hard line.

After an hour or so, his mom arrived. Her eyes were red and her hands shook as she signed some papers. They left without a word. He never even looked back.

Piper Watkins arrived next. She glared at me as she led Trent out the door.

Finally, Daddy arrived. He scanned the room when he walked in, caught my eye, and shook his head. After he had signed the papers, he walked over to where I sat beside Sarah. She was still crying, her arms curled around herself.

"Hey," Daddy said, touching her shoulder. "Do you want us to stay until your parents come?"

She nodded, running the back of her hand across her eyes.

"Thank you," she whispered.

We sat, not speaking, for another fifteen minutes. Sarah's father arrived then, signed the papers, and took her by the hand. We watched as they left.

"Okay," Daddy said. "Let's go."

I followed him to the car and we drove home in silence.

"I'm sorry, Daddy," I said as we pulled into the driveway.

He said nothing, just parked the car and got out, slamming the door behind him.

I followed him into the house, wondering what he would say when he finally spoke to me.

"What the hell were you doing in an abandoned house with a drug dealer?"

"I . . . That is, we . . ."

"Now, Judy! I want an answer right now!"

"Trent and I were buying pot from Mitch and then reselling it." I said it very softly, not looking at him while I spoke. "I tried to get out of it, but Trent wouldn't let me."

Daddy sat down on the couch and put his head in his hands.

"Honest, Dad, I wanted to stop. But Mitch wouldn't sell to Trent. He'd only sell to me. And Trent said he and Sarah would say I was dealing acid if I didn't help him. And that everyone would believe them because of Mama."

"Why didn't you come to me?" he asked.

"I didn't want you to know."

"So . . . you and Trent were selling pot. And Sarah was part of it. What about Matt?"

"God, no!" I said. "Matt didn't know. He just followed me to the house because he was worried about me. He probably won't ever talk to me again."

Daddy sighed. He looked older than he had just the day before and very tired.

"Well, you'll have to go to court," he said. "I don't think they can charge you with anything except trespassing, but we'll have to wait and see."

"I'm really sorry," I said.

He just nodded.

The police did charge me with trespassing. Matt and Sarah and I all appeared before a judge, apologized, and got a stern lecture about wasting our lives and throwing away chances and disappointing our families. Our parents had to pay fines of two hundred dollars each. I knew it would take a long time to pay my dad back. And probably longer to regain his trust.

Trent got charged with trespassing and drug possession, because he'd been holding when the cops showed up. His parents had to pay a five-hundred-dollar fine and he got kicked off the football team. I'm sure Piper Watkins believed I was the devil incarnate by now.

Mitch was the only one who went to jail. He got convicted of possession with intent to sell, trespassing, resisting arrest, and assault with a deadly weapon.

Matt didn't speak to me at the hearing or even look at me. He didn't wait for me after school or call or acknowledge me in class. It was like I didn't exist anymore. I called him twice after the hearing, but his mother just said he didn't want to talk to me. I felt like the floor had collapsed beneath my feet, like there wasn't enough air in the world to fill my lungs, like I was drowning in pure sadness. And I knew it was my own damned fault. I had spoiled things with Matt. I had spoiled things with my Dad. I had messed up my life, just as surely as Mama had ever messed up her life.

Did that mean I was like her, after all?

❧ 42 ❧

"You missed a spot." Treva was inspecting the dining room, which I had spent the entire morning dusting and mopping and waxing. She pointed to a lower shelf on the hutch that I'd forgotten to dust.

I sighed and sat down on the floor to clean it.

I sighed again as I rose and trudged into the kitchen to start cleaning out the refrigerator. Daddy had left me a long list of chores for the day, and Treva had come to make sure I did them and didn't go anywhere.

The phone rang, but Treva answered before I could.

"Yes, she's here, but she can't talk right now."

I stared at her. I couldn't even talk on the phone?

"Yes, I'll tell her. Bye."

She hung up and said, "Lee Ann wants you to call her back."

"How come I can't just talk to her now?"

"Because you haven't finished your chores."

Treva sat down at the kitchen table with a cup of coffee and a magazine.

"That's not fair," I said, hating the very sight of her.

"Suck it up, buttercup," she said flatly, not raising her eyes from the magazine. "You screwed up big-time, and now you're paying the price."

Tears filled my eyes but I swallowed hard, turned my back to her, and began pulling things out of the fridge and throwing them onto the counter.

"You're going to break something if you're not careful," Treva said.

I didn't answer. Instead, I piled vegetables onto the table and moved the veggie drawer from the fridge to the sink. I scrubbed at it furiously, wishing I could slap Treva and kill Trent and, more than anything, talk to Matt.

He hadn't spoken to me since we got arrested. Lee Ann explained to him how I'd tried to get out of the business, but he wouldn't listen to her.

"She lied to me," he said each time she brought it up. "I can handle a lot of things, but not lying."

Lee Ann was sure he would come around eventually, but I didn't think so. I'd seen his eyes when his mother appeared at the police station to take him home. I didn't think he would ever forgive me for that.

I dumped some old chili down the garbage disposal and started wiping down shelves in the fridge. It actually wasn't in bad shape. Daddy had cleaned it before the big Thanksgiving dinner.

When I had finished cleaning, Treva inspected the refrigerator, then checked it off the list.

"Okay," she said, "bathrooms next."

I sat down at the table and put my head in my hands. I wanted to scream. I wanted to slap Treva's pretty face. I wanted to leave and never come back.

She put her hand on my shoulder and squeezed gently.

"Okay," she said. "Why don't you take a break? Call Lee Ann back. We can do the bathrooms after lunch."

She walked into the living room, taking her magazine with her. I sighed deeply, glad for a moment alone. For the last week, I had done nothing but go to school, stay for drill team practice, come home, study, and do chores. No visits from Lee Ann or anyone else, no walks to the park or Smoots, just school, practice, and home.

I was grateful to still be on the drill team. I'd worried Sarah and I would both get kicked off after we got convicted of trespassing. If we'd been charged with drug possession, we would have been off the squad. But Miss Harrison decided to let us stay, after a long talk with us and our parents. They all agreed it would be better to keep us busy and supervised. So at least I was still a Hornet Honey.

I called Lee Ann, sitting on the floor in the kitchen.

"What are you doing?" she asked.

"Cleaning the house," I said. "Every damned room."

"God," she said, "how much longer are you going to be grounded?"

"I don't know."

"You should ask your dad."

"Maybe." I was afraid to ask, in fact. Daddy had been so angry with me, I was afraid I might just be grounded until I graduated from high school.

"Well, see if I can come over," Lee Ann said. "I'm bored to death and there's nothing to do."

"I still have to clean the bathrooms."

"Maybe I can help."

"I doubt it."

"Well, at least ask." She must have been really bored if she wanted to come clean bathrooms.

"Hey, Treva," I said, walking into the living room. "Lee Ann wants to come over and help me clean. Is that okay?"

She looked at me and I was sure she was going to say no. Instead, she smiled.

"Yeah," she said. "I think that's okay."

"Thanks."

Five minutes later, Lee Ann was at the door. I was so glad to see her, I didn't even mind that she didn't actually help clean the bathrooms. She sat on the toilet while I cleaned the bathtub, then sat on the edge of the tub while I cleaned the toilet and sink. And she talked the entire time.

"Okay, you have to be ungrounded by next weekend," she said.

"Heather Perkins is having a party, and everyone is going. You have to come."

"I don't know if he'll let me," I said, scrubbing the toilet with a brush.

"Just talk to him," she said. "He can't stay mad forever. You have to come to the party. Matt's going and maybe you guys can finally talk."

I stopped scrubbing to consider that. Maybe if I told him how sorry I was and how much I missed him, just maybe he would forgive me.

"I'll ask," I said. "But I don't know if he'll let me."

Lee Ann smiled. "Well, if you think you've got it bad, you should hear what Trent's parents are doing."

I sat on the floor and wiped sweat from my forehead. "What?" I asked.

"They're sending him to military school." She paused to let that sink in.

"No way!" I couldn't believe Piper Watkins would actually believe her son was in the wrong about anything.

"It's true," she said, grinning. "Luce told me that her dad had already called the school."

"Wow," I said. "I can't picture that."

"Speaking of Luce," Lee Ann said, "how come she didn't get arrested with you guys?"

"She was long gone before the cops came," I said. "She never even came in the house. She just made sure I went in."

"Bitch," Lee Ann spat.

I nodded.

"I'll bet she's Piper's favorite now," she said. "Saint Luce, that's probably what they call her at home."

I laughed. "Someday she'll get caught," I said. "She's too stupid not to."

Once I'd cleaned the bathroom upstairs, we moved downstairs. Lee Ann pulled a chair from the kitchen and sat in the hall just outside the bathroom while I cleaned the toilet and sink, then mopped the floor.

"Hey," I said, "I'm kind of surprised your mom let you come over. Doesn't she think I'm a bad influence?"

Lee Ann laughed. "My mom loves you. She says you just need a mother."

"That's because she hasn't met my mom," I said.

"I don't think she means your real mom," she said.

"She thinks I need Treva?" I laughed.

"Actually, yeah," Lee Ann said. "She likes Treva. She thinks Treva will be a good stepmom."

I rolled my eyes. Lee Ann laughed.

When I'd finished cleaning, Treva inspected the bathrooms and pronounced them clean. She checked them off the list.

"What's next?" I asked, sighing again.

"I think that's enough for today," she said, folding the list and putting it in her pocket. "It's three o'clock and you've been working all day. You deserve a break."

"Thanks, Treva," I said, smiling at her. I knew there were more items on the list. I wondered if Daddy would be mad at her for letting me off early.

"See?" Lee Ann said as we turned on the stereo in my room. "She's not so bad."

43

I was grounded for another week, but thankfully, Daddy relented just in time for Heather's party.

"This doesn't mean you can just go anywhere you want," he said, holding my gaze. "I want to know where you are all the time, and who you're with."

"Okay," I said, returning his gaze.

I knew he still didn't trust me, and it made me sad and angry all at once. Sad because I'd disappointed him; angry because he didn't know how hard I had tried to get out of the business. He didn't understand.

On Saturday, Lee Ann arrived at my house in the late afternoon to get ready for Heather's party. She wore a light blue sweater that stretched tight across her chest and skin-tight jeans. I wore the outfit I had bought for my first date with Matt, hoping it might make him remember how much fun we'd had then. I even let Lee Ann mousse my hair and put makeup on me.

"Home by eleven," Daddy said before we left. "And if there is any pot or alcohol at that party, I expect you to come straight home."

"Okay." I nodded.

He kissed my forehead then. "Have fun," he said softly.

"Thanks, Daddy."

Lee Ann drove her dad's big Dodge Lancer, her eyes barely making it over the steering wheel. We parked on the street in front of Heather's house.

"Okay," Lee Ann said. "We need a game plan. I'll find Matt and get him to come out on the front porch. Then you come out like you're looking for me. Okay?"

I nodded. My stomach was doing flip-flops.

"So, you just stay in the living room, near the door, so you can see when we go out. Okay, let's go." She applied one last coat of lip gloss and we walked to the house and rang the doorbell.

"Hey!" Heather smiled as she opened the door. "Come on in!"

Dire Straits's "Money for Nothing" blared from the stereo. Some people were dancing, but most were sprawled across chairs and couches, drinking Cokes and eating chips and salsa. I sat on a couch beside Sarah. She'd been a lot nicer to me since our arrest together. She'd managed to convince her parents that the entire episode was Trent's fault, and she and I were simply in the wrong place at the wrong time. I backed her up. We were friends again.

"Hey," she said, "I think Matt's in the kitchen."

"Oh," I said. "Okay."

"You guys still on the outs?"

"Yeah."

"I'm sorry." She put her arm around my shoulder. "Did you hear about Trent?"

"Military school, yeah, Lee Ann told me. Crazy, right?"

"Yeah," she agreed. "But maybe it'll do him some good."

"Maybe." My eyes scanned the room for Lee Ann. She was nowhere to be found.

I ate some chips and sipped a tepid Coke. The ice bowl was empty, but no one else seemed to mind.

A few minutes later, Lee Ann came into the room. She stood a moment until she spotted me, then came and sat on the arm of the couch beside me.

"I couldn't find him," she said under her breath. She glanced at Sarah, but she had her back to us and was talking to a guy from our geometry class.

"Sarah said he's here," I said.

"Well, I don't know where," she said. "I looked all over."

I breathed in deeply. Maybe he wasn't coming, after all.

Lee Ann and I wandered from the living room to the dining room and kitchen, talking to people we knew. Then we wandered back to the living room, where the stereo now featured Madonna singing "Crazy for You."

"Hey!" Steve, the boy Lee Ann had been dating for three months now, touched her shoulder. "Let's dance."

She glanced at me and I smiled. "Go ahead," I said. "I'm okay."

I watched them merge into the crowd of swaying couples, her arms around his neck. I wondered where Matt could be. I wished so much we could be dancing like that.

"Hey, Judy." Luce Watkins was at my elbow. "Have you seen upstairs?"

I shook my head.

"You should go see it," she said. "Heather's room is really rad."

I shook my head again. I didn't care much for Luce these days.

"Come on," she said, taking my arm and pulling me toward the stairs. "I'll go with you."

"Whatever," I said, letting myself get pulled along. I didn't have anything better to do anyway.

We walked up a hallway to a closed door. Luce turned the knob quietly, then opened the door and turned on the light in one swift, fluid movement.

"Hey!"

My heart dropped into my stomach. Matt's voice was startled. He lay on a bed with Tricia McDaniels, her blouse halfway unbuttoned. He froze when he saw me, then looked away.

"Oh." Tricia giggled. "Hi, Judy."

I turned and ran down the hallway, then back down the stairs and out the front door. I stopped on the porch and leaned against the railing. For one brief moment, I thought I might faint. Then I just felt sick. I gripped the rail tightly, willing my stomach to settle down.

"You okay?"

I turned to see Patrick St. Clair in the doorway.

"I'm fine," I said.

"You don't look fine." He closed the door behind him and came to stand beside me. I didn't know Patrick. He was a senior and on the student council. I had seen him at football games and school assemblies, but I'd never actually talked to him.

"I'm okay," I repeated.

"Okay," he said. But he didn't go back inside. He just stood there beside me.

"I saw you come out here," he said. "You looked kind of . . . upset."

I said nothing. I just wished he would go away and leave me alone.

"Who did you come with?" he asked.

"Lee Ann Dawson," I said.

"I'll go get her."

He walked back into the house. A minute later Lee Ann appeared.

"What happened?" she asked. "Patrick St. Clair said you're out here and you look like you're about to cry."

I leaned into her and began to cry.

"Oh, Judy, it's okay. What happened?"

"I went upstairs," I sobbed. "Luce dragged me up there to see Heather's room. And Matt was in there with Tricia McDaniels."

"What?"

"They were making out."

I cried for a while longer while she patted my shoulder and fumed.

"You know they set that up on purpose," she hissed.

"Matt wouldn't do that," I said.

"Not him," she said. "Luce and Tricia. Why else would she make you go upstairs? Tricia got Matt to go up with her, and then Luce made sure you saw them."

"He didn't have to go with her," I said.

"No," she agreed. "He's acting like a dickhead, if you ask me. I mean, my God . . . Tricia McDaniels is a total skank."

We sat on the front step for a while, until we were both shivering.

"Come on," she said, pulling my hand, "let's go back inside."

I shook my head. I didn't want to see Luce or Tricia or, God forbid, Matt.

"Yeah," she said, "come on. Let's go in and find you someone to dance with."

"I don't want to dance."

"I don't care if you want to or not," she said firmly. "You're gonna dance with someone. You're gonna dance slow with someone. And when Matt sees it, he can eat your shorts!"

We walked into the living room and I looked around quickly, but I didn't see Matt or Luce.

"Here," Lee Ann said, pulling me along, "you should dance with Patrick St. Clair."

"What?" I stopped still. "I don't even know him."

"You do now," she said.

She walked right up to Patrick and said, "Thanks for being so nice to my friend."

"It's okay." He smiled at her and then at me.

"Now, if you really want to help her, you should dance with her."

My cheeks burned and I thought I might sink into the ground from sheer embarrassment.

"Okay," he said. "Why not?"

He walked toward me as the stereo began "Separate Lives."

"Shall we?" He took my hand and pulled me toward him, one arm around my lower back.

I felt awkward and stupid at first, but finally I let myself relax and move to the music. As I leaned into his chest, I saw Lee Ann heading upstairs. *Oh Lord,* I thought, *what the hell is she doing now?*

A minute later, she reappeared on the stairs, followed shortly by Matt. I watched him as he stopped on the stairs and stared at me dancing with Patrick. For a minute he just stood there, watching. I moved closer to Patrick and felt his hand slip from my lower back to my bottom. I tilted my head back and smiled at him. When he leaned in to kiss me, I closed my eyes. When I opened them again and glanced toward the stairs, Matt was gone.

Good, I thought. I hoped I had hurt him as much as he'd hurt me.

"Hey," Patrick said softly in my ear. "You want to get out of here?"

Honestly, I did want to leave. I wanted to go home and cry.

"I can't," I said. "I came with Lee Ann."

"She won't mind," he said. "I'll tell her."

He walked to Lee Ann and said something to her; she smiled and waved at me.

"It's cool," he said. "She said to have fun."

I followed him from the party to his car, a bright red Toyota. It reminded me of Treva's.

"I live on University," I said as he started the ignition.

"Okay," he said. He turned to smile at me. "But you don't want to go home yet, do you? It's still early."

It was only nine o'clock.

"I promised my dad I wouldn't go anywhere except the party and then home."

"He won't know," Patrick said. "Come on, it's early. Let's get something to eat."

"Okay," I said. I don't know why I said it. I didn't even want to go with him. I wasn't hungry. I just wanted to go home. But . . . okay. Matt was probably with Tricia now. Why shouldn't I go out with someone else?

He pulled into the driveway of a big house on the Parkway.

"Come on," he said. "My folks are out."

I followed him into the house and stared at the two-story entry-way.

"Wow," I said. "This is nice."

"It's okay." He shrugged and took my jacket, hanging it in a closet.

"You want something to drink?"

"Okay." I followed him into the kitchen.

He pulled a can of Coke from the fridge and poured it into two glasses. Then he reached into a cabinet and pulled out a bottle of rum. He poured a generous splash into each glass before I could say a word. Finally, he dropped an ice cube into each and handed one to me.

Aside from a taste of champagne on New Year's Eve with Daddy, I'd never had alcohol before. I didn't want to admit that, though. I didn't want to look stupid. I took a small sip. It's wasn't bad.

"Here," he said, taking my hand. "We can watch music videos, if you want."

He turned MTV on and we took off our shoes and sat on the couch, his arm around my shoulder, sipping rum and Coke.

I felt strangely disembodied, like I was watching myself sitting there with a boy I had just met, drinking rum and watching television, as if I did this all the time.

Then he kissed me, so I kissed him back. When he pulled my shirt off, I raised my hands to make it easier. When he kissed my chest, I even arched my back a little, like I'd seen women do in the movies. And the whole time, I was watching myself like a movie, wondering who this girl was sitting in her bra in a senior boy's house.

Patrick took off his shirt and then reached around my back to unclasp my bra.

"Wait," I said.

He stopped and looked at me, smiling.

"I never . . ."

"I know," he said. "I can tell."

He unhooked my bra with one hand, pulling it from my shoulders.

"You're really pretty," he said, kissing my neck and shoulders. Meanwhile, his hands were unbuttoning my jeans.

I let him pull me up to stand, so he could pull my jeans down. I stepped out of them and sat back down to take off my socks.

He took off his pants and socks, and then pulled down his boxer shorts. His erection was huge.

"Oh," I said. That was all. Just, "Oh."

He leaned me back on the couch and pulled my panties off, dropping them to the floor. And then he was over me, lowering himself onto me. I bit my lip and closed my eyes. I didn't want to see his face, his chest, didn't want to know what was happening. I cried out when he entered me; the pain shot through me like an electrical current.

I willed myself not to cry, squeezed my eyes tight, waiting for it to be over. Was Matt doing this with Tricia? Is this how it was supposed to be? Would it ever be over?

And finally, it was over. I opened my eyes as Patrick pulled back, limp and wet, and smiled down at me. I turned my head away, afraid I would throw up.

"Where's the bathroom?" I asked.

"Down the hall," he said, pulling on his boxers.

I grabbed my clothes and ran toward the bathroom, locking the door behind me. I knelt in front of the toilet, waiting to throw up. But eventually my stomach calmed. So I got up to dress and caught sight of myself in the mirror above the sink. Mascara had smudged beneath my eyes, my moussed hair spiked in all directions. Between my legs blood and . . . stuff smeared. I didn't even look like me. I looked like . . . a slut. *Just like my mother,* I thought bitterly. *Just like Mama.*

I dressed and walked back to the room where Patrick was buttoning his shirt.

"Do you want another drink?" he asked.

I shook my head. "I'd better go home."

We didn't talk as he drove me home. He did not walk me to the door, just leaned over in the front seat and kissed me.

"I'll see you," he said.

"Okay."

I was inside before I realized he hadn't even asked for my phone number.

"How was the party?" Treva was sitting on the couch beside Daddy, her hand resting on his knee.

"It was okay."

"Did you have fun?"

"I guess so."

I walked up to my room and got undressed, shoving my panties into the trash can beneath some tissues. Then I put on my pajamas, brushed my teeth, and climbed into bed. After a very long time, I cried myself to sleep.

❧ 44 ❧

"Seriously? You had sex?" Lee Ann stared at me, her mouth agape.

"Yeah," I said. I tried to say it casually, but it came out wobbly, just the same.

"You had sex with Patrick St. Clair," she repeated. "Stop it, Rufus." She swatted at the dog chewing on her toes.

"Yeah, I did." I bent down to scoop Rufus up, scratching his ears and letting him lick my face.

"I can't believe you did it."

"Why not?" I asked. "You and Steve do it."

"Well, yeah," she said. "But we're a couple. I mean, we've been together three months."

"Yeah, but you were doing it almost as soon as you started going out."

I knew this because Lee Ann told me everything.

"Yeah, but we were *dating*." She said this as if it mattered, and I guess to her it did.

I shrugged.

"So, how was it?"

I shrugged again. "It was okay."

"Did you bleed?"

334 • *Sherri Wood Emmons*

"Yeah." In fact, I still felt sore down there. I didn't tell Lee Ann that.

"Was he . . . nice?"

"I guess so."

She simply looked at me for a while, then she took my hand.

"I'm sorry," she said. Her wide blue eyes held mine.

"What for?" I asked.

"It was your first time. It should have been with someone you love. It should have been special."

I shrugged again. "Whatever."

"Oh my God," she said, sitting up straight. "Did he use a rubber?"

I shook my head.

"Jesus Christ, Judy!" She looked at me, aghast. "You didn't use any protection?"

I shook my head again.

"God, what if you're pregnant?"

I hadn't thought of that. I know it sounds crazy, but I hadn't.

"I don't know," I said.

I sat a moment, letting it sink in. What if I was pregnant?

"Your dad would shit a brick!" Lee Ann said. "I mean, seriously, he'd die. First you get arrested, then you get pregnant? What the hell were you thinking?"

I stared at her. What had I been thinking? What the hell had I done?

"Oh, God," I said, collapsing onto the bed. "Oh my God." Rufus yelped as I squeezed him to me.

"Okay, look, you're probably not," Lee Ann said, taking my hand. "I mean, my God, what are the chances? It was your first time. It never happens on your first time."

"Really?"

"Sure," she said. "I don't know anyone who got pregnant their first time. It's like there's some cosmic rule against it."

"That's not what they said in health class." I shuddered, remembering the cheesy movies we'd seen on teen pregnancy and sexually transmitted diseases.

"Yeah, but they're just trying to scare us," she said.

"I hope so." I scratched Rufus behind the ears.

"Me too." Her voice was small.

"The good news is, Matt saw you leave with him," she said.

"Really?" I rolled onto my side to look at her. "Did he say any-thing?"

"No," she said. "He watched you leave and then he got his coat and left. I think he was pretty pissed."

"Good." So the evening hadn't been a complete waste, after all.

We spent the next few days ice skating at the park and shopping for Christmas gifts. I didn't take much time with my shopping. I bought a poinsettia for Grandma and Grandpa, some guitar music for Daddy, and a cheap gold-plated bracelet for Treva. Lee Ann spent days looking at things before deciding on a blue and red tie for her dad and a tiny silver locket for her mom. She put a picture of herself in the locket.

"What do you think?" she asked, handing me the locket.

"It's pretty," I said, my breath catching in my throat.

I held the locket for a minute, wondering if Mama would wear something like that, wishing for . . . I wasn't even sure what. Then I put it back in Lee Ann's hand. "Your mom will love it."

I hadn't heard from Mama since the letter in September. Nothing more had been said about her coming to visit. Probably she had decided not to come. I hoped so, anyway.

On Christmas morning, Grandma, Grandpa, and Treva arrived early. We ate pancakes and sausage and opened presents by the tree.

I got a pretty green sweater from Grandma and Grandpa and a new boom box from Daddy. I handed out my gifts then. Grandma kissed me and said she loved the poinsettia. Daddy liked the sheet music.

Then Treva opened her box and held up the bracelet. "Oh," she said, smiling. "How cute. Thank you, honey."

One box still lay under the tree, a long shallow one in silver paper. Daddy pulled it out and laid it on my lap. It was from Treva.

I tore off the paper and opened the box. Inside was a beautiful bolero-style leather jacket, black and soft with gold trim, kind of like the one Madonna wore in *Desperately Seeking Susan.*

"Wow," I breathed. I pulled the jacket from the tissue paper and held it up. "Wow."

"Do you like it?" Treva asked. "We can exchange it for something else if you want."

"It's great. Thank you!"

She smiled at me, and I was surprised to see tears shining in her eyes.

I felt bad about the cheap bracelet. Seeing her there, sitting by Daddy smiling at me, I felt bad about a lot of things. Treva might be annoying, but she tried. She tried really hard. She'd put up with my sulking and whining when she and Daddy first started dating. She'd put up with my smart mouth when I came back from California that last disastrous trip. She'd put up with everything I'd thrown at her, and she was still here, sitting on the couch crying because I liked the present she'd gotten me.

It hit me then, it hit me hard like a slap, that Treva had been my de facto mother for a long time. She'd been more of a mother to me than Mama ever was. Even when I'd tried to push her away—and I had tried hard—she never left. It took my breath away, seeing her there, loving me.

I rose and walked across the room, bent down, and hugged her. It was the first time I'd ever done that, and I think it surprised her almost as much as it surprised me.

"Thank you," I said over the knot in my throat. "Thank you for everything."

Daddy hugged both of us for a minute, and then I felt weird about what I'd just done. So I retreated back to my chair and began shoving wrapping paper into a trash bag.

"So," Grandpa said, leaning back in the recliner, "one more week till the big day."

"Yep." Daddy grinned. "It's finally going to happen."

"How many folks will be here?" Grandpa asked, looking around the living room.

"About twenty," Treva said. "Just you all and my folks and my brother and his wife and a few friends."

"You gonna leave the Christmas tree up?" Grandpa asked.

"Yes, we're going to get married right there." Treva pointed to the hearth by the tree.

"That will be beautiful," Grandma said. "Do you have everything you need for the wedding and reception?"

Treva nodded. "Everyone is bringing a covered dish," she said. "So it won't be a lot of cooking. And we've ordered the cake."

"Are you sure I can't bring more?" Grandma asked. "I could make a fruit salad or a Jello mold."

"Mom, you're doing enough," Daddy said, hugging her. "Your chicken and noodles will be the hit of the party, I'm sure."

Grandma smiled at him and patted his arm. "I'm just glad you're finally going to be happy."

"Me too," he said, smiling from her to Treva. "It's about time this family had a little bit of happy."

I swallowed hard. My period was two days overdue.

"Judy, why don't you try on that jacket?" Treva said. "Let's see if it fits."

On the morning of New Year's Eve, Lee Ann waited while I peed on a stick. Then we sat staring at it, watching as a tiny blue cross appeared.

I was pregnant.

"Shit," Lee Ann breathed. "Holy shit."

I squeezed my eyes closed for a long minute, then opened them, willing the blue cross to be gone. But it was still there.

"What are you going to do?" Lee Ann asked, putting her hand on mine.

"I don't know."

And truly, I had no idea what to do. I'd never thought about being pregnant. It was never a worry or even a thought, because I'd never had sex. I had watched Lee Ann freak out one time when her period was a couple days late. And a girl in my algebra class had gotten pregnant last year. But I had never had to worry about it.

"It's not fair," Lee Ann said. "Your first time . . . God, it's just not fair."

I lay back on the bed, my arm over my eyes, trying hard not to cry. My stomach churned.

"I can't have a baby," I said. "I'm only sixteen."

"Amy Hodgins had an abortion," Lee Ann offered. Amy was a year older than us.

"I didn't know she got pregnant," I said, uncovering my eyes.

"Like I said, she had an abortion."

"Where?" I asked.

"I'm not sure," she said. "I can ask her, though."

"Okay."

She lay down beside me on the bed and held my hand.

"I know it cost her three hundred dollars," she said.

"Where am I supposed to get three hundred dollars?" Most of the money I had made from the business had gone to pay Daddy back; the rest I'd used for Christmas presents. I was broke.

"I've got seventy," Lee Ann said. "You can have it. And I'll bet if you ask Patrick, he'll give you the rest. His family is loaded."

I shook my head. "I can't ask him for money. I don't even know his number."

"We could look it up," she said.

I just shook my head again.

"Look," Lee Ann said, sitting up. "This is his fault. He took advantage of you while you were upset. Why shouldn't he have to pay for the abortion?"

I stared at the ceiling.

"I can't ask him."

She sighed and lay back down beside me.

"When you talk to Amy, ask if she had to have permission from her parents," I said.

"Okay," she said. "Are you going to tell your dad?"

"I can't," I said, finally letting the tears stream down my cheeks. "I can't tell him right after I got arrested. And he's getting married today. God, Lee Ann, what am I going to do?"

She squeezed my hand. "Do you want to tell my mom?" she asked. "She'd probably help you."

"No," I said. I couldn't imagine telling Mrs. Dawson that I was pregnant. I couldn't bear to see the disappointment in her eyes, after she'd been so good to me.

I couldn't imagine telling anyone. I couldn't imagine it was true at all.

"Maybe you'll have a miscarriage," she said. "Lots of women have miscarriages. My mom had three."

"Maybe," I said. "But I can't count on that, can I?"

"Okay," she said, sitting up and pulling on her boots. "I've got to go home. I promised Mom I'd go shopping with her today. We're buying your dad's wedding gift. But I'll call Amy before we go and ask her that stuff."

"Thanks."

"Judy, it's going to be all right." She smiled at me as she pulled on her jacket. "We'll figure out something."

I tried to smile back, but all I could manage was a small grimace.

After she'd left, I lay on the bed, my mind spinning with doubts and fears. Why had I gone with Patrick in the first place? Why had I let him take me to his house? Why had I kissed him? And why, oh, God, *why* had I had sex with him? He didn't force me. I could have just said no.

"Judy?" Daddy knocked at my door. "You in there?"

"Yeah," I said, wiping my eyes and turning to face the wall.

He opened the door and said, "What are you doing?"

"Taking a nap."

"You feel okay?"

"Yeah, just tired."

"Okay," he said. "Well, Treva and I are going to the mall. We've got a few things to pick up for tonight. Do you want to come?"

"No, thanks."

"You sure you're okay?"

"I'm fine."

He stood a minute longer, then closed the door. I rolled onto my back and stared at nothing. My boyfriend had broken up with me, my dad was getting married, I was sixteen, and I was pregnant. It wasn't fair.

Lee Ann called later that afternoon.

"I talked to Amy," she whispered. "She had it done at a clinic right across from Community Hospital. It cost three hundred dollars, and her mom went with her."

"Okay, thanks."

"You okay?"

"No," I said. "I'm not okay. I'm screwed."

~~45~~

"I, Kirk, take you, Treva, to be my lawfully wedded wife."
Daddy's voice shook a little as he said his vows. He held her
hands and looked straight into her eyes while he spoke. Then she
said hers, looking straight back at him.

After the ceremony, everyone crowded around to hug and kiss
them both. Daddy looked very handsome in his dark blue suit, and
Treva was beautiful in a cream-colored cocktail dress.

Lee Ann and I headed for the kitchen to start putting out the
supper. Crock-Pots and casseroles lined the counters and filled the
table. We had enough food for an army.

"How do you feel?" Lee Ann asked.

"Okay."

"No morning sickness?"

"No." I shook my head. "Just . . . I don't know, kind of pan-
icky."

She nodded. "I'll bet."

Her mom walked into the kitchen carrying Treva's flowers. "I'm
just going to put these in a vase on the table," she said, smiling at
us. "What are you two doing in here?"

"Treva put us in charge of the food," I said, waving my hand at
the array.

"Need any help?" she asked.

"No," we said in unison.

She walked into the dining room with the flowers.

"She probably would help you, if you asked her," Lee Ann said. "She's weird sometimes, but she'd probably help you."

"I know." I sighed. "You're so lucky to have a mom like that."

"Yeah," she said. "I know."

We handed out plates and dished out food and poured drinks for the next hour, then retreated up to my room with our own loaded plates.

"God, I love your grandmother's chicken and noodles," Lee Ann said. "They're so good."

"I like your mom's chicken thing." Mrs. Dawson had made chicken and broccoli in a cream sauce.

"Do you have your stuff packed?" Lee Ann asked.

"Yeah." I pointed to my duffel bag, sitting at the end of the bed. I was staying at Lee Ann's house for a few nights while Dad and Treva took their honeymoon. They were going to stay in a cabin at a state park.

We ate in silence for a few minutes.

"Was that the doorbell?" I asked.

"Sounded like it."

"I wonder who's here?"

I walked down the hall to the top of the stairs, arriving just as Daddy opened the door. Mama stood on the porch, bundled in a big blue parka.

"Hi, Kirk," she said, smiling. "Is this a bad time? It looks like you're having a party."

"Cassie," he said, "why didn't you call first? This is a bad time, actually. I . . . that is, Treva and I, well, we just got married."

"Oh," she said. "Oh, I'm sorry . . . I mean, that's great. Congratulations." She hugged him briefly.

"Oh, hi," she said, looking over Daddy's shoulder. "You must be Treva?"

Treva nodded, looking from Mama to Daddy.

"I'm Cassie," Mama said brightly, before Daddy could say a

word. "Congratulations on your marriage. I hope you'll be very happy."

"Thank you," Treva said, putting her arm through Daddy's. "I think we will be."

"Cassie, like I said, this really isn't a good time. We have people here and . . ."

"Okay," she said. "I'll come back tomorrow. Is that okay?"

"No, actually, it's not," Daddy said. "Treva and I are leaving tonight for our honeymoon and Judy is staying with a friend."

"Well, then, just give me the number for her friend," Mama said. "I'll call her and set something up."

Behind me, Lee Ann coughed. I turned to shush her, but it was too late. Mama looked up the stairs and saw me.

"Judy," she cried, holding open her arms. "Oh, my beautiful girl. Look how much you've grown up."

She started toward the stairs, but Daddy stepped in her way. I ran to my room, Lee Ann just behind me, and slammed the door. From inside, we could hear Mama arguing with Daddy.

"I just want to see her, Kirk. Just for a little while. I need to talk to her. I need to make things right."

We couldn't make out what Daddy said in reply, his voice was low. Then Mama began pleading and Daddy's voice rose. Finally, we heard the front door slam and I exhaled a huge breath.

"Wow," Lee Ann said. "What's she doing here?"

"I don't know." I sat on the bed, shaking all over.

"Poor Treva," Lee Ann said. "And your poor dad. What a psycho, coming to their wedding like that."

I didn't answer.

"Judy?" Daddy knocked at the door. "It's me. Can I come in?"

"Okay."

He opened the door and came to sit beside me on the bed.

"Are you okay?" he asked, pulling me into a hug.

"Yeah, I guess so."

"She's gone now. I told her she'd have to wait until I get back on Sunday, so we can talk. I told her she's not to contact you, that you obviously don't want to see her. And I didn't tell her where you're staying."

"I bet she knows it's with Lee Ann," I said.

Daddy sighed. "Maybe Treva and I shouldn't go," he said.

"No, Daddy." I put my hand on his arm. "It's your wedding and you deserve a honeymoon. I'll be okay at Lee Ann's."

"She'll be okay," Lee Ann chimed in. "My dad won't let Judy's mom get anywhere near her. He's got a gun."

Daddy laughed. "I don't think he's going to need a gun," he said. "Are you sure you'll be okay? You can stay with Grandma and Grandpa, if you want."

"No," I said. "I'll stay with Lee Ann. It'll be all right."

He kissed me and stood.

"Daddy, I'm sorry she ruined your wedding."

He smiled. "She didn't ruin it, honey. She couldn't if she tried."

I smiled back at him. "Is Treva okay?"

"Yeah," he said. "Treva's fine."

He paused at the door. "Thanks, honey."

"For what?"

"For asking about Treva. For caring if she's okay."

I shrugged, but I could see he really was pleased.

Later, I kissed them both good-bye before they climbed into Daddy's car. We had all changed into jeans and sweaters, but Treva still wore a gardenia in her hair. Lee Ann and I stood with her mom in the driveway and waved as they drove away. Then we walked to Lee Ann's house. I carried my duffel bag. Lee Ann's mom carried her nearly empty casserole dish. Lee Ann carried a huge chunk of the wedding cake.

We changed into our pajamas and settled in front of the television with the cake to watch the New Year's countdown. I remembered the first year Treva had joined us for New Year's Eve. It seemed like such a long time ago.

"Is it weird, knowing your mom is here in town?" Lee Ann asked.

I nodded.

"Where do you think she's staying?"

"I don't know. Last time she came she stayed at the Ramada Inn. We swam in the pool."

I remembered the way she looked in her swimsuit, her pregnant belly bulging against the nylon fabric. We had talked that night for the first time, really, about things that mattered.

"I liked her then," I said softly. "She seemed really happy with Navid."

"Do you ever hear from him?"

"Yeah," I said. "He sends me a birthday card every year, and one at Christmas. And he sends pictures of Kamran sometimes."

"That's nice," she said. "Why did your mom leave him? He sounds like a nice guy."

"She leaves," I said. "That's just what she does."

"But . . . I wonder why she's like that," Lee Ann said. "What made her that way?"

I shrugged. I'd wondered that a lot. Her own mother was pretty awful, that was clear. But it wasn't an excuse for her to keep leaving husbands and children.

"Do you think she's going to stay in Indy now?" Lee Ann asked.

"I doubt it," I said. "I hope not."

❧ 46 ❧

Lee Ann dialed the number we'd looked up in the phone book, then handed me the receiver. It was three days after New Year's Eve. I was three weeks pregnant.

"Community Women's Clinic," said a voice.

"Hi," I said. "I, um, that is . . ."

"Okay," the woman's voice was gentle. "Let me give you the information. You have to be between six and twelve weeks pregnant. The cost is three hundred dollars. If you're under eighteen, a parent needs to come with you. Have you had your pregnancy confirmed by a doctor?"

"No," I said. "I did a home pregnancy test."

"Well, you have to see a doctor before I can make an appointment. Do you have a doctor?"

I did have a doctor, the pediatrician I'd seen my entire life.

"No," I said.

"Okay, you can make an appointment with Planned Parenthood. Do you need the number?"

"Uh, yeah." I dug a pen out of my purse and wrote down the number she gave me.

"Once you've had the pregnancy confirmed, call back and we'll send you some information and make your appointment."

"Thank you," I said. I hung up.

"What did they say?" Lee Ann was watching me closely.

"I have to go to a doctor to get a pregnancy test before they can make the appointment."

"Dr. Beyer?"

"God, no! She gave me the number for Planned Parenthood."

"Okay, let's call them," she said. "The sooner you do this, the sooner you can get the whole thing over with."

"She said I have to have a parent come with me."

"Oh." She stopped dialing and hung up the phone. "Oh," she said again.

In three days, Daddy and Treva would be back from their honeymoon. I'd kind of hoped I could just call and get the abortion before they got back.

"What are you going to do?" Lee Ann asked.

I shook my head. "I don't know."

We sat there a few minutes, waiting for a great idea to appear. But, of course, it didn't.

"Let's go feed Rufus," she said, pulling me up from the floor where I was sitting.

We'd been making several trips a day to my house to feed the dog and let him out. He couldn't stay with us at Lee Ann's because Mr. Dawson was allergic to dogs.

The cold air felt good on my cheeks as we walked to the house. It felt like it might snow.

A car was parked in our driveway, one I didn't recognize.

"Whose car is that?" Lee Ann asked.

"I don't know."

We stopped walking.

"Do you think it's your mom?"

"I don't know," I repeated.

"We'd better go home," she said, taking my hand.

"Yeah," I said. As we turned to walk back to Lee Ann's, I heard her familiar voice, calling to me.

"Sweet Judy, hey, stop."

Lee Ann took my hand and pulled me along as she walked faster.

"Judy!" Mama called again. I turned to see her walking toward us.

"Come on," Lee Ann said, pulling my arm now. "What are you doing?"

I had stopped and turned to face Mama. Lee Ann stood beside me, still holding my hand.

"Oh, honey," Mama said as she pulled me into a tight embrace. "Oh, God, I have missed you so much."

I stood rigid, my arms at my sides.

"What do you want?" I asked.

"I just want to see you," she said, still holding me tight. "I had to see you, to talk to you. Oh, baby, you just don't know how much I've missed you."

I pulled away from her and took a step back. She smiled at me and reached her hand out to touch my hair.

"Look how beautiful you've become," she said. "God, you're so pretty."

She was thinner than I remembered. Her cheekbones stood out sharply against her sunken cheeks. Her once beautiful blond hair hung stringy and dull. Maybe she was sick, or even dying, and that's why she wanted to see me.

"Can we just talk?" she asked.

I shook my head. "I don't want to talk to you."

"Please?" she said, reaching for my hand.

"Go to hell!" I shouted, jerking my hand away. I turned and started running as fast as I could down the street toward Lee Ann's house. Lee Ann ran behind me.

"Judy!" Mama called after me. "Please come back."

We didn't stop running until we reached the house. Lee Ann locked the door behind us. I dropped onto the couch, breathing heavily.

"Lee Ann?" Mrs. Dawson called from the kitchen. "Are you back already?"

She walked into the living room and stopped short when she saw me.

"Was your mother there?" she asked.

I nodded.

She sat down on the couch beside me and pulled me into a hug.

"It's okay," she whispered. "You're safe here. Lee Ann, call your father, please, and tell him we need him to come home."

Lee Ann went into the kitchen to make the call. Mrs. Dawson held me and crooned, "It's okay now. You're okay."

"I want my dad," I said.

"Okay, I'll call him when Lee Ann is off the phone."

Daddy had left the number of the lodge at the state park. Mrs. Dawson left a message for him. Half an hour later, he called us back. Mrs. Dawson talked to him for a few minutes, then handed me the phone.

"Are you okay?" he asked.

"Yeah," I said. But my voice shook.

"We're on our way home," he said. "Stay at Lee Ann's house, don't leave the house. We'll be home in a couple hours."

"Okay."

"Judy," he said, "it's going to be all right. I love you."

"I love you, too."

We listened to music on Lee Ann's tape player. Downstairs, Mr. Dawson sat in the living room, watching out the window. I felt better knowing he was there.

"She looked sick, didn't she?" I asked.

"Yeah, she did," Lee Ann said.

"Do you think she's dying or something?"

Her eyes widened. "Maybe that's why she came."

We listened to Tears for Fears singing "Mad World." That's exactly how I felt, like it was a screwed-up, mad world.

When Daddy arrived, I ran downstairs and into his arms and started crying. I cried until I felt like I might throw up. He patted my back and held me until I had stopped.

"Where's Treva?" I asked finally, looking past him.

"She's at the house," he said. "She thought you might need some time."

"I'm sorry I ruined your honeymoon."

He smiled. "It's not your fault, peanut. Are you ready to go home?"

I got my duffel bag from Lee Ann's room while Daddy talked

with Mr. Dawson. When I came downstairs, I saw Mr. Dawson hold a gun out toward Daddy. Daddy smiled and shook his head.

"No," he said. "I don't think she's dangerous. Just . . . messed up."

I hugged Lee Ann and her mother, then Daddy and I walked home.

"Did you talk to her?" he asked.

"I told her to go to hell," I said.

He didn't even remark on my language.

"She looks like she's sick," I said.

"Yeah, I noticed that when she came the other night."

"Do you think she's dying?"

"Oh, I don't think so," he said. "She would have told us before now, don't you think?"

I shrugged.

"She can go ahead and die for all I care," I said.

He took my hand.

"Judy," he said. "I know you're mad at her, and you have every right to be. But I don't think you really want her dead, do you?"

I shrugged again.

Rufus yelped and jumped up on me when we got home. Treva gave me a long hug and kissed my forehead.

"I'm so sorry," she said.

"It's okay. I'm sorry I messed up your honeymoon."

"It's not your fault," she said. "Do you want to help me make dinner?"

I dropped my bag on my bed and went to the kitchen to help with dinner. Upstairs, Daddy was calling Mama at the hotel. When he came downstairs, he gave me a sad smile.

"She says she's not sick," he said.

"Okay."

"She'll be in town for a week. Then she's going to Los Angeles."

"You better call Navid and tell him she's coming," I said.

"I already did."

"Why did she come?" I asked. "Why didn't she just stay in India?"

"She says she wants to apologize to you. She's trying to right some things, I guess."

"She can go to hell."

Daddy smiled and shook his head. "I don't think you really mean that. I think you still love her in a way."

I stared at him.

"If you didn't love her, she couldn't hurt you," he said. "I know, because when I was still in love with her, she hurt me, too. Now . . . well, I'm sad for her, but she can't hurt me anymore . . . unless she hurts you."

"Why is she so . . . Why is she the way she is?" I asked.

He sat down at the kitchen table.

"I'm not sure," he said. "I have some ideas, but the only person who can really answer that for you is your mother."

Treva set a plate of pork chops on the table.

"If you want to see her, one of us can go with you," she said.

"Maybe." I didn't think I wanted to see Mama at all.

"Okay," Treva said, carrying a bowl of macaroni and cheese to the table. "Let's eat."

The next day Daddy went into the office, even though officially he was still on vacation.

"I just want to finish up a little bit of paperwork," he said, kissing Treva good-bye.

She laughed. "Go," she said. "Have fun, and come back early if you can tear yourself away from your desk."

I watched them and smiled. Daddy really did seem happy.

"Mama always said he's a workaholic," I said.

"Your dad loves his work," Treva said. "It's one of the things that makes him so interesting, I think."

We sat at the kitchen table drinking coffee. She drank hers black, but I liked mine loaded with milk and sugar.

"So," she said, "are you ready to go back to school?"

I shrugged. "I guess so."

"Will you have any classes with Matt?" she asked, smiling.

"I don't know."

"I hope you two can work things out," she said. "He's a good guy."

"Yeah, he is."

She rose and took her coffee cup to the sink. I took a deep breath and blurted out, "I'm pregnant."

"What?" She spun to face me, then grinned. "Very funny," she said.

My cheeks reddened and I didn't reply.

"Judy?" She sat down at the table again. "You are joking, right?"

I shook my head.

"You're pregnant?"

I nodded.

"Oh, God, honey . . . how . . . I mean . . . does Matt know?"

"It's not his," I whispered, not meeting her eyes.

She sat quietly for a minute, then asked, "So, who is the father?"

"A guy named Patrick. He's just a guy. I don't even really know him."

"Judy, how did you get pregnant by a guy you don't even know? Were you raped?" She leaned forward and took my hands. "Honey, if you were raped we need to report it right away."

I shook my head. "He didn't rape me," I said, still not looking at her.

She leaned back and said nothing for a minute.

Finally, she said, "You'd better tell me what happened." Her voice was calm and quiet. She didn't yell or cry or anything.

I took another deep breath and began. "I went to that party at Heather's, remember?"

She nodded.

"Matt was there, and he was making out with some girl."

"Oh, honey, I'm sorry."

"I went outside and Patrick came out because he could tell I was upset. And I danced with him to make Matt jealous. And he drove me home, but we went to his house. And . . . we had sex."

"Oh, Judy," she said softly. "Honey, I'm so sorry. Are you sure you're pregnant?"

I nodded. "I took a home pregnancy test on Tuesday."

"Well, those aren't always reliable," she said. "We need to get you to a doctor."

She rose and began pacing the kitchen. "You can't go to your pediatrician. Maybe I can get you in to see my OB-GYN."

"I have the number for Planned Parenthood," I said.

She stopped pacing and looked at me.

"Are you thinking about terminating the pregnancy?"

"An abortion, yeah, I think so."

"You know, you don't have to do that," she said. "I mean, you can, if that's what you decide you want to do. But there are other options. You could have the baby and put it up for adoption."

I shook my head. "I can't have a baby."

"You're sure that's what you want to do?"

"Yeah, I'm sure."

She sighed deeply. "Okay, well, we still need to get you to a doctor. And then we'll make an appointment at the clinic. I'll go with you."

"Thank you." I looked up at her then. "Treva, can we not tell Daddy?"

"No, honey." She shook her head. "We have to tell your dad. I can't keep something like this from him."

I knew she was going to say that, but I had to ask.

"I'll be with you when you tell him," she said. "If you want."

"Will you tell him?"

She looked at me for a long minute.

"Please, Treva?" I begged. "I can't tell him. I just can't."

"Judy," she said very quietly, "you're not a little girl anymore. You're old enough to get pregnant. You're old enough to make choices. And you're old enough to take responsibility for those choices. You need to tell your dad yourself."

"But . . ." I started.

"I'll be with you," she said. "I'll be right there when you tell him. But you have to be the one to tell him." She sounded firm.

"When?" I asked.

"The sooner the better," she said.

She rose and wrapped her arms around me. "I know you're scared, but it's going to be okay. Your dad loves you more than anything. He'll be sad and maybe angry, but he won't ever stop loving you."

I leaned into her and cried.

That night after dinner, Treva told Daddy that I had something to say. We sat in the living room, Treva next to him on the couch, me in the recliner chair.

He sank into the couch when I told him, his hands on his face, and cried. Treva put her arms around him and held him until he stopped. He asked if Matt was the father, and I had to tell the entire story again.

He rose and paced the living room. I'd never seen him so . . . furious.

"We ought to call the police and have him arrested," he yelled. "She's only sixteen, and he's a senior. He ought to be horse-whipped."

I watched him, my eyes wide. Treva came to sit on the arm of the recliner and put her arm around my shoulders.

After a few minutes of yelling, Daddy just kind of crumpled onto the couch. He dropped his head into his hands and sat still for a long time.

Finally, he looked at me and then at Treva and asked, "What should we do?"

"Judy wants to terminate the pregnancy," Treva said, squeezing my shoulder. "I'll make an appointment for her with my doctor to get the pregnancy confirmed, and then we'll go to the clinic."

He said nothing, just stared at her.

"It's a simple procedure," she went on. "Just an outpatient thing with a local anesthesia."

I was grateful she was a nurse and knew about these things. And I was grateful beyond measure that she was here.

Daddy rose then and walked up the stairs to his bedroom. Treva patted my shoulder. "He needs a little time," she said. "It's a lot for him to take in."

She rose. "Do you want some tea?"

I nodded.

"Treva?"

She turned in the doorway.

"Thank you."

"It's okay," she said. "I'm really proud of you for telling him."

47

Three weeks later, Treva and I pulled into the parking lot behind the women's clinic. A large group of people stood at the edge of the parking lot, holding signs that said, "Mother, don't kill your baby!"

"Oh, God," I said, covering my face.

"Just ignore them," Treva said. She turned off the engine and got out of the car. By the time she got to my door, a man had appeared. He wore a blue vest with the word *Escort* printed in white. He carried a big boom box on his shoulder that was blaring music.

I got out of the car and Treva wrapped her arm around me. The man took my elbow and I walked between them to the door and escaped into the quiet of the waiting room. Twenty or so young women looked at me as I entered, then went back to their magazines or conversations.

Treva filled out the papers and wrote a check. Then we sat on a bench to wait.

"Are you okay?" she asked.

I nodded.

"It'll be over soon."

After an hour or so, a nurse called out several names, including mine. Treva hugged me, and I walked with the other girls to another room. The nurse handed out small cups with pills in them and cups of water. I swallowed my pills and waited until it was my turn for an ultrasound. I turned my head away so I wouldn't have to see the image on the screen.

After another long wait, a young nurse came and called my name. I followed her to a small room with a doctor's table. I took off my pants and covered myself with a paper sheet. After a few minutes, the nurse returned with the doctor. He was an older man, with glasses and a stethoscope around his neck.

After he'd examined me, he nodded to the nurse. She leaned in close to me and started talking cheerfully, asking me about school and what movies I liked. She talked so that I almost couldn't hear the vacuum sound coming from beneath the paper sheet . . . almost.

It was over really quickly. The doctor patted my hand and left. I put my sweatpants back on and followed the nurse to the recovery room, where she had me lie down and handed me a glass of orange juice.

"Drink this and eat some cookies," she said. "You're going to be just fine."

I lay there for half an hour, sipping juice and eating cookies and avoiding eye contact with the other women in the room. A couple of them looked even younger than me. I stared out a window and focused on just breathing.

Finally, the nurse reappeared and said I could go.

When I walked into the waiting room, Treva rose and wrapped me in a long hug.

"You okay?" she whispered.

I nodded.

The parking lot was empty when we left, thankfully. We drove home in silence.

"You go rest," she said when we got home. "I'll make us some soup."

As I walked upstairs, I heard her dialing the phone. She was calling Daddy to tell him it was over. I put on pajamas and lay down on the bed. I felt a little spacey. Treva said that was probably from the Valium they had given me before the procedure. We ate chicken noodle soup and crackers. Then she left me alone, telling me to sleep.

I lay with my hand on my stomach, thinking about the tiny life that had been there just a little while before. In my head, I heard the vacuum sound again. Squeezing my eyes shut, I tried to ignore the sound. Finally, I put on the stereo. After a long time, I fell asleep.

When I woke up, it was almost dusk. Daddy stood in the doorway of my room, watching me. We had not talked much since I'd told him I was pregnant, and when we did, it was mostly about school. He'd told Mama that I was not going to see her while she was in town, and I was grateful for that. But he was mostly quiet around me. I knew he was really sad.

"Hey, peanut," he said when he saw I was awake. "How are you?"

"I'm okay."

He walked over and sat on the bed, brushing the hair from my forehead.

"I'm really sorry, Daddy."

"I know," he said. "Me too."

He hugged me and I started to cry. I cried because I'd made him so sad. I cried because I felt like we would never be the same. I cried for the baby that was gone. I cried and cried and cried. When I had finally cried myself out, he kissed me and rose.

"Treva is making spaghetti," he said. "Are you hungry?"

I wasn't hungry, but I nodded anyway.

"Do you want to come down or eat in bed?"

"I'll come down."

"Okay." He smiled at me. "I love you," he said.

"I love you, too."

❧48❧

Life went back to pretty much normal. I had a checkup a couple weeks after the abortion, and the doctor said I was fine. She asked if I wanted to go on birth control pills and I said no. I thought I probably would never have sex again.

No one at school ever knew what had happened, except Lee Ann. She still fumed that I hadn't made Patrick pay for the abortion, but I didn't want him to know. I saw him at school sometimes and he always smiled and said hi. The whole sex/pregnancy/abortion thing started to feel like it was a dream, something that had happened a long time ago.

Matt never spoke to me at all. I passed him in the halls at school and sometimes saw him at the mall or the movies, but he never made eye contact, not even once. After a while, what had been a sharp, excruciating pain dulled to an ache. I still missed him, but I didn't feel like I was going to die of sadness anymore, so that was a start.

In April, I got another letter from Mama. She was still in Los Angeles, spending time with Kamran when Navid allowed it. I wondered what Kamran thought about her. He was too young to remember her at all from before. Who did he think she was, this beautiful, funny, odd woman?

In the letter, Mama said she had been working hard to accept responsibility for the things she had done. Couldn't she please come and talk to me? Wouldn't I let her just apologize for how much she had hurt me?

I crumpled the letter up and threw it in the trash can. Then I pulled it back out and rubbed my hand across it, trying to press out the wrinkles. Finally, I carried it down to the kitchen, where Treva and Daddy were drinking tea.

"She wants to come see me," I said, putting the letter on the table.

Daddy read the letter, then looked at me. "What do you want to do?"

"I don't know," I said. "Part of me wants to tell her to go to hell."

"What about the other part?" Treva asked.

I sighed. "Part of me wants to see her," I said. "I want to ask her some things."

"I think you should," she said.

Daddy looked at her in surprise.

"She's your mother," Treva said. "You have questions and she needs to answer them."

I nodded.

"So, are you going to write back?" he asked.

I nodded again.

"Okay," he said. "If that's what you want to do, then that's what you should do."

I wrote a letter, then rewrote and rewrote again. Finally, I put it in an envelope and mailed it. A week later, Mama called.

"Judy," she said, "my Sweet Judy, I was so glad to get your letter! I'm coming to Indianapolis next week. Is that okay?"

"Okay," I said.

A week later, she pulled into the driveway. Daddy and I stood on the porch, his hand on my shoulder.

"Hi!" she said, walking up the steps and pulling me into a hug. "How are you? Oh my God, I'm so glad to see you!"

I let her hug me.

"Hey, Cassie," Daddy said. "How are you?"

"I'm okay, Kirk. I'm really glad to see you."

She looked a lot healthier than she had in December. She was tanned and had put on a little weight. She looked like Mama again, but older.

We sat on the porch swing and Daddy went inside. I knew he was in the living room. I could see him in the recliner through the open door.

"How are you?" she asked again.

"I'm okay."

"How's school?"

"It's okay. I'm a pom-pom girl."

I watched her face carefully, waiting for a rebuke, I guess.

"Really? A pom-pom girl? That's . . . that's great, I guess." She smiled.

"I'm really good at it," I said.

"I'll bet you are," she said. "You were always good at dancing. Not like me." She laughed. "You must have inherited that from your father."

"I got arrested for selling pot." I said it right out loud, watching her face again.

"What?" She looked startled. "When?"

"In November. My boyfriend broke up with me because of it."

"Oh, honey." She reached to hug me and I backed away.

"Then I got pregnant and had an abortion."

She stared at me, her mouth open.

"Oh my God," she finally managed. "I . . . oh, Judy, I'm so sorry."

I shrugged.

"Oh, Judy, I should have been here. I should have been here for you."

"Treva took me."

I watched that sink in.

"Oh," she said quietly. "Well . . . I'm glad you had someone with you."

She sat quietly for a minute.

"Do you hate me?" She asked it not looking at me.

"Sometimes."

"I don't blame you," she said. "I haven't been much of a mother to you."

"Why?"

"What?" She looked confused.

"Why haven't you been my mother?"

She looked at me, then looked away. After a long minute, she sighed.

"I guess I just thought I didn't deserve it," she said.

"Why not?"

She turned toward me again and took my hands. "It's a long story," she said.

"I want to hear it."

Another long pause. Finally, she dropped my hands and rose, pacing back and forth across the porch.

"When I was sixteen, I was raped. It was at a party I went to with Karen. Some guy drugged me and raped me. I was your age."

I nodded. I'd heard this before.

"And . . . a few weeks later, I found out I was pregnant."

I leaned forward. "You got pregnant when you were sixteen?"

She nodded. "That's why . . . oh, honey, that's why I should have been here for you. I know what that feels like, how scared you were. How alone you must have felt."

I nodded. "I was scared."

"I know," she said. "I was scared, too. I didn't tell anyone at first. I guess I thought if I just ignored it, it might go away."

I nodded again. I'd felt that way, too.

"Finally," she said, "I told Karen. And she . . . well, I guess she thought she was doing the right thing, but she told my mother."

"Oh, God," I said. I couldn't imagine that woman being kind the way Treva had been to me.

"She was furious," Mama said. "She slapped me and called me a whore and said I was a disgrace to the family."

She sat down beside me on the swing and I reached for her hand. I didn't mean to, I just did. I could picture her mother saying that, and I couldn't even imagine how it must have felt to Mama.

"So, she sent me to a home for unwed mothers here in Indianapolis. Abortion wasn't legal in Indiana then, so she just . . . she sent me away like garbage. I lived in a house with a bunch of other girls who were pregnant. It was awful. The woman who ran the house was a bitch, not kind at all. When I went into labor, she drove me to the hospital and just left me there alone."

She stopped and gazed past me.

"I was in labor for twenty-two hours," she said. "I was so scared, I thought I might die. And then, finally, the baby was born."

I stared at her. She had another baby?

"A little girl," she said softly. "I only got to see her once, just for a minute. She was so tiny and pretty. She looked like you."

"What happened to her?"

"A nurse came and took her away and some family adopted her. I never saw her again."

I sat staring at her. I had a sister, an older sister. Mama had another daughter. It made my head ache, just trying to take it all in.

"What did you do then?" I asked finally.

"My father came to get me from the hospital, and he took me home. They all just pretended it never happened."

She rose and began pacing again.

"I stayed another year and then I left. I came back to Indianapolis. I'd kept in touch with one of the other girls from the home, and I lived with her and her boyfriend for a while. And then I met your dad."

She smiled at me.

"He was so great, so gentle and funny and nice. We got married a couple months after we met. God, his parents were so upset. I think they hated me at first. But then I had you, and . . . well, they were nicer after that."

She sat down again and took my hand.

"I've been doing a lot of thinking and a lot of praying and a lot of reading," she said. "And I think I left you and your dad because I felt like I didn't deserve you. I'd let them take my baby, and I wasn't good enough to be your mother. And then I met Navid and I thought I could make it work. I thought it was my second chance to prove I could be a good wife and a good mom. But I messed that up, too.

"I can't tell you how sorry I am, Sweet Judy. I have missed almost your whole life. And Kamran hardly even knows me. I let you both down. I screwed everything up."

She paused, but I didn't say anything.

"I've got an apartment in Los Angeles now," she said. "I'm working in a restaurant and taking classes at night at the community college. I'm trying really hard to make a normal life, so I can be part of Kamran's life again.

"And tomorrow, I'm meeting with an attorney to see if I can get any information about my daughter, the one I gave up. They have a registry now where birth mothers and adopted kids can sign up and find each other. I'd really like to know where she is and . . . just know she's okay."

"Do you think she's here in Indianapolis?" I asked. It seemed so weird that I had an older sister who might be right in the same city.

"Maybe," she said. "I'm betting whoever adopted her lived somewhere in Indiana. Maybe someday we can both meet her. Would you like that?"

I nodded. I would like that.

We sat for a minute, both of us deep in our own thoughts.

"Do you think you can ever forgive me?" she asked quietly.

"I don't know." That was the truth. I didn't know.

"I hope you can," she said. "And not just for my sake, but for yours, too. I'm taking a psychology class now, and what I'm learning is that forgiveness isn't just for the person who needs to be forgiven. It's for the person who's been hurt, too. That's why later this week I'm going to see my mother."

I stared at her. "Why?"

"Because I need to forgive her, too," she said. "Whether she wants it or not, I need to forgive her so I can move on and be sane. And maybe . . . I don't know, maybe she really does need it, too."

She smiled at me. "So, I'm going to be here for a few more days. Can I see you again while I'm here?"

"Okay," I said. I had a lot more questions for her.

"Good." She took a deep breath and seemed to relax. "I'll go now. I expect you've got some thinking to do, and so do I."

We both stood and she took my face in her hands.

"You may not believe it, but I have always loved you. Even when I left, maybe especially when I left, I loved you. And if you can't forgive me, I'll keep on loving you anyway."

She hugged me and kissed my cheek.

"Mama," I said as she turned to go.

She stopped.

"I love you, too."

She hugged me again, crying this time. Then blew her nose, got in her car, and left. I watched her drive away, wondering if this time she really could settle down and be happy. I hoped she could. She deserved that, after all. We all did.

Daddy walked onto the porch and put his arm around me.

"Did she tell you what you needed to know?"

"She told me she had another baby before me," I said. "Did you know that?"

He nodded.

"Why didn't you tell me?"

"It wasn't my secret to tell."

"So, I have a sister," I said. "I have Kamran and now I have a sister, too. That's just . . . weird."

He laughed. "Yes, I guess it's pretty weird."

Treva came onto the porch, carrying a tray with glasses of lemonade.

"You okay?" she asked, kissing my cheek.

"Yeah," I said. "I have a sister out there somewhere."

She smiled at me and then at Daddy. He grinned back at her and nodded.

"What?" I asked. They obviously had a secret joke.

"You're going to have another brother or sister in a few months," Treva said.

"Seriously? You're pregnant?"

"Three months," she said, patting her stomach.

"What do you think about that?" Daddy smiled at me hopefully.

"I think that's . . . I think it's great!" I hugged him and then I hugged Treva.

"I hope it's a girl," I said. "Don't you?"

"I just want it to be healthy and happy," Daddy said. He sat down on the swing and Treva sat beside him, her head on his shoulder.

I sat on the step just watching them smile at each other. They looked like a real family.

And then it occurred to me, *we* looked like a real family. Daddy and Treva and me, we were a real family. And pretty soon, there would be a new baby. I could babysit sometimes, maybe. And I'd be the best big sister ever.

"You okay?" Daddy said. "You're awfully quiet over there."

"I'm just . . . happy," I said.

He smiled at me.

"I've gotta go call Lee Ann!" I said, rising. "She won't believe it!"

I heard Treva laugh as I ran inside, and Daddy's low voice talking to her softly.

Life was good.

**Please turn the page for a very special Q&A
with Sherri Wood Emmons.**

Where did you come up with the idea for The Sometimes Daughter*?*

Several years ago I watched the documentary *Woodstock—3 Days of Peace and Music.* Sometime on the second day, I think, the announcer called over the PA system for a man to come to the medical tent, because his wife was having a baby. And I wondered, what would that be like? What would it mean to be born at Woodstock? And the first line of the story, "I was born at Woodstock," just stuck in my head. So I had to write the story to find out what happened to the baby.

Did you know when you started how the story would end?

No, I don't know what will happen when I start a book. I knew the crux of this story would be the relationship between Sweet Judy and her mother, Cassie, and that Cassie would be both wonderful and terribly flawed. But I didn't know what their journey would be until I wrote it.

Why did you decide to have Cassie get involved with Jim Jones and Peoples Temple?

I used to be the managing editor of a magazine called *DisciplesWorld.* On the thirtieth anniversary of the Jonestown tragedy, we did a special issue on Peoples Temple and I interviewed several Jonestown survivors. I was struck by how smart and sane and *normal* these people were, not at all my preconceived idea of the kind of people who would join a cult. They were idealistic folks who wanted to change the world, and even though it ended in tragedy, their faith and ideals were real.

So it made sense to me that Cassie would be drawn to a group like that, a group of idealists who wanted to create a just and loving society. Cassie needed so much to find a place where she fit in, and the Temple drew a lot of people like her.

Your first book, Prayers and Lies, *was set partially in the Irvington community of Indianapolis, and* The Sometimes Daughter *is set completely there. Is Irvington a real place?*

Yes, Irvington is a lovely old neighborhood on the east side of Indianapolis, and it's where I grew up. It really was an idyllic place when I was a kid, the kind of place where neighbors knew one another and held block parties and ice-cream socials. It's still a beautiful community, and you'll find three and sometimes even four generations of families living in the neighborhood. It feels like home to me.

In both of your books, you write in the first person, from the view of a child. Why?

I guess because it comes more easily to me than other kinds of writing. With *Prayers and Lies* I tried writing from the third-person perspective, but it just didn't work. And with *The Sometimes Daughter*, the first-person narration came naturally from that first line: "I was born at Woodstock." I'm going to try writing in the third person for my next book, just to see if I can do it.

How was writing a second book different from writing the first?

In some ways it was easier, because I had a little more confidence. But in other ways it was a lot harder. I wrote *Prayers and Lies* over the course of several years. Sometimes I put it away for months at a time. I wrote it just for fun, to see if I could do it.

I wrote *The Sometimes Daughter* in just over a year, which forced me to be a lot more disciplined and focused. I had to learn to think of writing as my job. And then there's what some people call "second-book syndrome"—the fear that the second book won't be as good as the first one can be almost paralyzing, and I had to learn to just work through the panic and keep writing. Thank goodness I have a great editor who is very patient and encouraging!

What have you learned in the past year about being an author?

I have been overwhelmed by just how kind people are! From the bookstore managers who set up signings to the people who came to the signings to the folks who've written me e-mails, visited my Web site, blogged about the book, and "liked" my Facebook page, I've been amazed and humbled by the kindness. It reaffirms my faith in the basic goodness of people, and that's been wonderful.

A READING GROUP GUIDE

THE SOMETIMES DAUGHTER

Sherri Wood Emmons

ABOUT THIS GUIDE

The suggested questions are included to enhance
your group's reading of Sherri Wood Emmons's
The Sometimes Daughter.

DISCUSSION QUESTIONS

1. When Kirk decides to go to law school, Cassie accuses him of selling out his ideals for money. Is that an accurate assessment?

2. What role does Derrick play in the story? Does he bear any responsibility for the breakup of Cassie and Kirk's marriage?

3. What responsibility, if any, does Cassie's mother bear for her daughter's choices?

4. Is Kirk irresponsible for allowing Cassie to live with him when she returns from California?

5. After the Jonestown tragedy, Cassie continues to believe in Peoples Temple and Jim Jones. How can she hold on to those beliefs in the face of the mass suicides in Jonestown?

6. Why is Judy so angry with Cassie after their visit to Malibu? Is her behavior toward Cassie at Disneyland appropriate?

7. In Cassie's absence, Judy is mothered by three women—her grandmother, Lee Ann's mother, and Treva. Were there extra "mothers" in your life? What role did they play in making you who you are?

8. Is Matt's reaction to Judy after their arrest reasonable? Why can't he forgive Judy?

9. Why does Judy have sex with Patrick? Does this constitute rape?

10. Does Cassie's final revelation to Judy about her own teen pregnancy explain her behavior toward Judy and Kamran? Does it excuse her behavior?